3

# A GODDESS NAMED GOLD

# A GODDESS
# NAMED GOLD

*By* BHABANI BHATTACHARYA

CROWN PUBLISHERS, INC. • NEW YORK

For
Arjun, Ujjaini, and Indrani

# A GODDESS NAMED GOLD

## Some Unusual Pronunciations

| | |
|---|---|
| Nago | Nahgo |
| Sohagi | Sohahgi |
| Munni | Moonni |
| Kato | Kahtoh |
| vaid | vahyid |
| Bai | Bahyee |
| Sona Mai | Sonah Mahyee |
| Chamundi | Chahmoondi |
| Halwai | Halwahyee |

CHAPTER

1

"Hei-ee! Hold your fretful feet away from the well—" Lakshmi peered out of the cowhouse door, calling to her son, Nago, as he flew a red-and-green kite and his three-foot figure hopped past in the sunlit yard, the reel gripped in his small hands, eyes fixed skyward.

"Kato-o-oh!" came the shrill challenge of his voice. "Cut that yellow-tailed fellow. Kato-o-oh!"

She smiled to herself, though half in disapproval, and pulled the sad gravity back to her face before she wheeled round to meet again the hot assaulting tongues of her visitors, five young women of the village seated on the floor mat in a rigid wrathful group. Her troubled eyes ranged all that glumness, needing understanding, seeking sympathy.

"What can a woman do? What strength has she against her household king? Tell me, dear sisters."

No one pitied her. No face softened.

"Add the juice of bitter leaves to the kneaded flour of his bread," an edged suggestion came.

"Salt in his bowl of milk," another quickly followed.

"Let your household king go foodless one whole day—and again."

"Think out a hundred ways to make his life a misery, let him cry panting to the Mother of Mercy."

The youngest of the battle group, Meera, said, "Drop powdered chilli into his bath oil. He will rub his limbs with oil and how his skin will smart—wah! The oil will get into his eyes—wah!" She clapped her hands, and dark-blue glass bangles on the slim but rounded wrists tinkled responsively.

A hush fell. The image of the hefty man, his eyes streaming as he grunted and groaned like a tortured bear, held the women's fancy. But Lakshmi, as she shared in the vision, summoned a cry of protest.

"Dear sisters, let me tell you then. Her son's begetter hungry and wretched, a woman's life is not worth two cowdung pellets. Meera, unmarried, cannot have such a feeling. Not so the rest of you. Did I not stand by you all in the year of the big struggle? Did I fail you at the time? Search in the pits of your minds, search twice, then speak."

The hush continued. The women hung their heads. Lakshmi pushed her advantage.

"Those days—Sohagi, remember? Gandhi-ji touched our spirit as it slept. Wakened, we became the equals of our menfolk. Proud, chins up, we marched in a column of our own, across the meadow to Pipli, onward to Kanhan. 'Quit India!' we shouted to the Engrez aliens in one big voice."

"We were all afire," Sohagi said, leaning back against the earthen wall, a three-month-old baby boy naked save for a *taveez*—amulet—on its arm fast asleep in her lap. "Wherever we went, women came flocking out of field, barn and kitchen to cry with us, 'Quit!'"

"That thunderclap made the aliens in Hindusthan tremble in their coat-and-pantaloon!" Bimla's mouth, red with the spiced betel Lakshmi had just given her, curved with mild irony. A newcomer to the village, she had had no part in the struggle of those earlier days.

"I marched with Nago in my womb," continued Lakshmi, husky with recollection of her pregnant figure. Too modest to claim all her due credit, she broke short and bent over the sheaf of moistened *pan* leaves, smoothing one, applying lime with a twig brush.

"Your seventh month, Lakshmi-sister!"

"Seventh month." There went the heavy-bellied mother-to-be with short quick steps, breathless in her effort not to be left behind.

"Your first bearing."

"First and last." With a sigh she returned to the betel, sprinkling it with sliced nuts, cardamom and cinnamon, all neatly assorted in the cubicles of a round, high-polished brass case.

"Cut the yellow-tailed fellow!" The excited challenge rang in the yard.

"Lakshmi marching with Nago in her womb." Champa nodded her grave homage. "That is why he is so warlike."

"This little monkey on my lap is sure to take after his kite-flying brother," Sohagi squeezed his cheeks with one hand while she reached out the other for the betel, folded, a clove stuck through it like a pin to keep the triangular shape.

"The man in my household flies kites as happily as Nago," said Munni, a tenderness in her voice, and her eyes snapped to Champa. "Do not forget to say, 'you stupid!'"

Champa retorted, "It is for your good that I pull you up, Munni."

"Kato-o-oh!" Nago flashed by, hounding his victim on the skyway, his brown legs bare to the knees, his shaven head tilted back.

Meera said, "The big struggle should have come a few years later. Today!"

The women laughed.

"Meera, why were you not born four or five years earlier?"

"Meera, to give you a chance to fight, the Engrez people should stay on for a while. They have ruled this country for two hundred years; where is the hurry to quit?"

"Ho! A hundred days left until we are free—free!"

"Think of it and the breath stops in each nostril, then blows fast—faster."

Meera was wrapped in a moody silence. Lakshmi gave her a broad smile. "Hei-ee, Meera!" soothingly. "Though you were only ten-eleven at the time, you did have your share in the big struggle. How help it, with such a grandma? She mocked her age-old gout, marching with us in hard sun and heavy downpour. She made us forget the fear we had in our bones and we faced lorryloads of Red Turbans as if they were mere goats."

"Do I not remember?" Meera made a face. "Grandma locked me up in the kitchen before she went with the tricolor flag. 'This game is not for a small squirrel to play,' she said."

"The small squirrel climbed to the roof thatch, pulled off straw in armfuls, crawled out through the hole. Down Main Road she came running—"

"Thin as a squirrel she was, truly, at that age," broke in Munni, wagging a big callused finger by way of illustration.

"And then?" Bimla demanded. "The goats in the lorry bleated baa baa in fear?"

"Straw on hair and clothes—what a picture. The women stood squeezed in one police van, the menfolk in four others. How the child yelled 'Quit India!' lest she miss the ride to town and to prison! Grandma saw her captured and muttered angrily, but the glow of pride in her face!" Lakshmi smiled with reminiscence. "All that seems to have happened yesterday."

Champa said, "Do you know, Bimla, that before the big struggle Lakshmi had been aloof from the village? Rich man's wife. In prison she became our true friend and sister."

13

Yes, Lakshmi agreed in her mind, it was in those four weeks that she fitted herself into her rightful place in life. On the very first day in prison she had yielded to the spell of Meera's Grandma. Then she took to her cell-mates, Champa and Munni, peasant wives, and Sohagi, wife of the cartman who carried field produce to the market.

She winced with an unhappy thought. She had gone to prison with two hundred others, both men and women, but her husband? On the crucial day set for saluting the national flag, an act against the Englishman's law, he had managed to disappear. He was said to be away on a business trip to town, but the people of Sonamitti felt sure that he was in hiding, he would show himself when the storm had passed. A stigma had clung to him since then.

Could it be that Meera was thinking on the same line? "Lakshmi *Bai*," she spoke abruptly, using the address of aloof respect. "Hold your spine erect, as you did five years back."

"*Bai?*" Lakshmi was startled. "*Bai*, Meera?" Not for a long time had she been given that appendage. She was Lakshmi to her friends.

The chord of sympathy had snapped and the tension was back. "Lakshmi Bai, hold your spine erect."

"Listen, dear sisters—"

"The fight, once more, is yours as much as ours," Meera flung, "even though you do not have to wear tatters."

"Even so," the stern chorus affirmed.

Lakshmi had no tongue to answer this. The clothes the women of Sonamitti wore—saris patched over and over, jackets cut from cast-off gunny sack—that was why the price of old bags was going up. At night, to save their saris further wear, some of the women slept almost naked. This, in a village of rich black earth yielding a hundred bales of good-fiber cotton every season, enough to clothe the whole district.

It was all due to her husband, Lakshmi knew. The Seth, great merchant, as he was named, the respectful *ji* affixed to the epithet, owned the sole clothshop in Sonamitti and the six villages around. Making use of the countrywide sari shortage, he had cornered the supply and pushed up prices. Not millcloth alone. He had bought up in advance the full output of the village weaver, Dhannu, who had been forced to tie down his loom to the 'Belly-that-ate-all,' so he could get the cash he needed for his father's funeral. For the Seth was not only a cloth merchant; he loaned money. The village was neck-deep in debt to him and tethered to his stiff rate of interest.

14

Lakshmi had gathered courage and pleaded with him. "All they ask is one sari for each person, to last for a year or longer."

"Have I manacled their wrists?" he had asked. "Or have I stolen their money bags? Or have I hidden the bundles of cloth in the fat pouch of my stomach?"

"The price. It is five times more."

"My fault that the price has gone up? Han! I am expected to make a gift of all I have? The hussies are not ashamed to complain to you, and you, mother of my only son, have both your ears ready for the venomous talk."

"The fair rate—" she ventured still, her voice small.

"If they think I am a robber, why don't they go to the law courts? We have the district courts, the High Court, the Federal Court in Delhi, and on top of all the great Privy Council across the black waters in London city. Who stops the hussies from going to the Privy Council?"

Twisting his luxuriant black mustache over a thick lip, he glared hard at his tiny wife and the resistance went out of her. Even after eight years of her marriage, Lakshmi was as afraid of her man as when she was a young bride. More so, perhaps, since her father, a farmer in a village six hours away by railroad, had been forced to mortgage half his holdings to his son-in-law against a loan, last winter. His lot would be sad if in a blaze of wrath the son-in-law decided to foreclose.

He lost no chance to remind her about the humbler status of her parents and their heavy indebtedness. He had married her because of a rare star-conjunction in her horoscope, he said. "Also because of your fairness of face," he conceded in a sentimental mood, fondling her with his plump hand and then adding quickly lest her woman's head be turned, "Mainly it was the stars. Your horoscope agreed so well with mine, it was plain that you were made for me. Jupiter crossed the ellipsis of Saturn at the moment you were born and the deep shadow of Mars..."

Yes, back from prison, she was one at heart with those village women. Her home was their meeting-place for an hour or two at midday, a respite from toil, except at seed-time and harvest when they must bend their backs to the fields from early dawn to sunset. But then, what if the Seth came back from his clothshop at an unexpected hour and saw the group of visitors at the veranda's western wing? The hard words his angry tongue would be sure to drop!

The cowhouse settled that question. The Seth's milch-cow died and he would not replace it; the jug of milk needed could come from the milk-woman by way of interest on the loan she had taken after her husband's sudden death by snake-bite. Between the house and the shed was a patch of land where stout orange trees hung their leaves and ripening fruit. At a sign of danger the thatch door could be shut and the women would then be as safe as in a citadel.

It was because of the shed that they gave themselves the name Cowhouse Five. Five, though there were six of them including Lakshmi. But Lakshmi had said, "I am a part of you all. I do not have to be counted separately. Cowhouse Five sounds better, anyway."

Was that excuse plausible? Or could it be that Lakshmi had accepted the Cowhouse Five with mental reservations and somewhere in her mind she was still unconnected with her friends, well apart?

Stretched on the dung-washed earth were mats of colored reed and at the room's corner stood two brass pitchers of cool water to drink. The dark-brown walls of mud were decorated with shiny pictures pasted on them row on row; colorful prints of goddesses, heroes from history, landscape. The prints were trademarks of cloth mills and had been peeled off saris and dhotis in the Seth's stock—the assistant at the store, Bulaki Rao, had given these to Lakshmi at her bidding. A faint aura of cow smell lingered in the shed, a minor inconvenience.

But all through the days of the past fortnight tension had been growing in the air. The women of the village, denied cloth, were ready at last to fight for it. They who had stood their ground before the muskets of Red Turbans and flung their battle cry at fury-creased faces, could no longer be overawed by the trader. But the Cowhouse Five must lead.

What precisely was to be done? They had racked their heads. One scheme had held their fancy and then another.

"He goes to the temple once every month, he gives the Devi blossoms and incense," Sohagi had spoken thoughtfully.

"So what?" Eager necks had craned toward her.

"The Devi could bid him sell cloth to us."

Faces fell, a moment's quick hope was lost.

"The Devi is at our beck and call, so you think. She will leave her abode, go running to Seth-ji and plead on our behalf."

"Why not?"

"Sohagi, hold your tongue. We are in no mood for fun."

"We have a life-and-death problem before us."

"Let me speak." She had her baby boy on her lap as usual and bent for a moment to touch his face with her lips. "Could you imagine—" She paused, rocking the boy, her crossed legs moving up and down gently.

"What is it?"

"Deep in the night. Through Lakshmi's bedroom window moonlight creeps in. The Seth is fast asleep, snoring. Awakened by a strange voice he rubs his eyes, and then gapes at the figure in the doorway. The figure is garbed in red, face streaked with votive vermilion, neck hung with strings of marigold."

Bimla cried, "Why, Sohagi, the Devi—only she—"

"Yes. He hears the strange voice again, flute-shaming in its sweetness. 'I am moved by thy devotion,' the voice says. 'I shall bless thee. But I have a bidding. Sell cloth to the women at a fair price. Or else my fury will smite thee like a thunderbolt.'"

Munni broke into a giggle. Sohagi scowled at her. "You do not understand, Munni. One of us will impersonate the Devi. Lakshmi will keep the house door unlocked at night. As soon as the Devi is gone she will draw the bolt. Her husband will lose his doubt when, at daybreak, he sees the barred door."

The women looked at one another. "Meera, what do you say?" Adding quickly, "You will make a wonderful Devi, Meera!"

"Of course. I have a flute-shaming voice." And her voice was a harsh croak.

Lakshmi, who had been silent, now shook her head saying, "Dear sisters, you do not know my husband. He is no fool. Tough as he is, he will surely jump out of bed for a close view of the Devi before she could vanish."

The women considered the prospect of the Seth's scrutiny and their hearts sank. Sohagi made one more attempt to save her plan.

"The Devi will bid him sternly not to move out of bed."

But Lakshmi shook her head again. "Dear sisters, you do not know my husband."

An idea came from Meera two days later. A hundred women would line up on Main Road and march behind a banner of rags held aloft between two tall bamboo poles, march west-east, south-north, finally

17

sweeping into Tamarind Alley, which led to the raised stone portico of the Seth's clothshop. They would stamp their feet in unison while crying in one big voice, "We demand cloth to wear, cloth."

Old means used for a new end. The Seth would understand, for he was aware of the spirit of the times. He could not defy the combined will of the people, he would have to submit.

But if he did not? What then? Meera had taken that point into account.

"A desperate remedy will then be called for. We shall make a threat to strip ourselves bare. 'Take the rags off our bodies, add them all to your hoarded shame.' That will shake him to the roots of his hair and he will see sense."

"That's the talk!" the women had approved, even if dazed by the boldness of the plan. The winds had changed and no woman could now afford to be timid.

"Do we really have to be naked?" Munni had asked, her eyes wide.

"Munni, you stupid!" Champa had cried with relish.

They would take Lakshmi with them, they had decided. Lakshmi did not have to suffer from her husband's greed; all the more reason why she must take part in the fight. It was a cause of the people. In its way it was a cause of the whole country.

So, today, Lakshmi was in a tight corner. She must have her part in the struggle against the tyrant, even though he was her son's begetter. She must join the procession to start within an hour. Or else all her marching in the past would prove to have been in vain.

The women were relentless. "Lakshmi Bai, we put this to you in plain words. Will you come with us? Yes or no?"

"Yes or no?" Sohagi slapped her baby boy on the buttocks by way of emphasis. He woke up, blinked surprised eyes and started screaming. "Yes or no?" Sohagi pushed up her bodice to give him her breast. It was a red bodice tight at the neck, broadening to the hips.

There was silence except for the boy feeding audibly. But he jerked his lips away in a minute, his face twisted in a scream.

"Stop, Govind."

The thin voice grew louder.

"Owl!" One more slap on the bare buttocks and Sohagi scrambled to her feet. "Owl!" she stamped out through the door. Let him breathe some fresh air.

"Look at that new batch of pictures." An accusing finger pointed to the row of color prints freshly stuck to the mud wall. "Yesterday we did not see them there."

"New cloth has come."

A week before, the women would have been happy about the acquisition on the wall. They would have studied the prints with keen interest. Munni was well up in ancient lore though she could not read and write; she would have explained the themes which were based on myth. Today none of them cared for such talk. Their eyes were fixed beyond the prints: The newly arrived stock of cloth—not one sari was to be sold fairly.

Lakshmi felt wretched. Under her husband's implacable will she was a lump of clay. The habit of submission was her ages-old inheritance. A woman had to obey her husband and household king. Yet the obligation to one's friends—how let them down?

"Listen," she begged, trying to ease the tension. "As you know, dear sisters, I sit and stand, I laugh and weep with you all. That has no meaning, no value?"

Meera blurted out with her girlish impatience. "The time for words is gone. Now it is time for action. Lakshmi Bai, will you be with us? Just say yes or no."

"Why, Meera-sister—" She drew a deep breath, still unprepared to commit herself. "In all fairness, I have to say that—"

The words were lost in an alarmed shriek from the yard. Hearing it the women jumped to their feet in a blast of panic. As they moved quickly to the door they saw Sohagi come hurtling across the yard, the child plastered to her breast.

"Nago!" she panted. "Nago has fallen in the well!" Her anguished voice trailed off in a burst of weeping.

The women with horror-struck faces took up the cry in an instant. "Nago has fallen in the well.... Nago-o-oh!"

2

Lakshmi stood rigid. Dark circles spun before her and the life-sap oozed out her limbs as cold sweat, while within her was an echo, a re-echo: "Hold your fretful feet away from the well. Hold your fretful feet..."

She wrenched herself from stupor and whirled forward, eyes enormous with madness, casting her voice to the lamentation: "Na-go-o-oh!"

The women kept pace with her, seizing her at the well's edge lest she follow her son over the crumbled rim of the foot-high parapet. While she struggled in Champa's arms, Munni and Bimla scurried like terrified hens, crying for help. There was not a soul within earshot. A thousand-tree orchard lay between the Seth's red-tiled brick house and a shabby huddle of mud huts a furlong away, and the peasants who lived in the huts had gone as usual to their fields of cotton and millet.

Stunned eyes turned to Meera with hope against hope, for she alone had not rushed about or screamed. Her face showed a raptness, of thought or feeling or both. The desperate women watched her intently, knowing that look in her face, and saw her hitch her sari well above her knees, the loose folds gathered at the waist in a beltlike loop. In a moment she was leaning over the well and between her hands was the iron bucket attached by a thick dangling rope to a pulley on its wooden stand. The women broke into a gasp.

"Pull me up as soon as I tug twice."

They waited in a daze of silence while Meera sat down, settling her feet in the bucket and holding on to the rope, "Ready?" Prodded out of inaction the women in a line picked up the rope's free end: Munni and Champa, hefty, with ample hips; Sohagi, lean and tall; Bimla, short and delicate, like Lakshmi. Each woman took three deep breaths, then tightened her stomach.

"Meera, think well before you descend. Meera-sister—" The warning was close to Sohagi's lips but a quick glance at the grieving mother made her silent. At this moment Munni reached for her coiled-up hair in which several twigs, two inches long, lay tucked. She plucked one and, mumbling mysterious words, cast it into the air. It was a charm that countered evil. Munni had inherited fifty of those twigs from her mother-in-law, who had obtained them from a holy man passing through the village. Half the number was already used up.

Cool as ice apparently, Meera now stood in the bucket, clinging a moment to the pulley's crossbar for balance. "I hope the woodwork can bear my weight," she murmured and took hold of the rope. "Let go!"

The bucket moved slowly, swinging a little before it steadied, plunging into the dark depths.

Champa, at the forefront, saw fear leap into the girl's eye as her face tilted forlornly. With a sharp command Champa tugged hard at the rope so that the bucket paused. But the voice from the well rang, "Let go.... Fast."

The bucket moved on. Pulses pounded. A plop and the pull eased. Meera was knee-deep in water, waist-deep; presently the water buried her and the weight dropped.

All were silent except the distraught mother wailing intermittently, "Na-go-o-oh!"

"Save the boy, Mother of Mercy!" Each woman, poor as they all were, vowed the Devi five pice worth of libation—deep-red hibiscus, sugar-loaf and vermilion.

Eternity was dragging by.

Would the signal never come? What was there at the well's bottom? Deep slime? Water snakes? And with that fearful thought time slipped back to a day last summer, an hour of fading light, and recalled the slim whipcord of the snake.

The toilers in the fields were wiping the day's sweat off their faces when the snake struck. Ganeshi felt the stab on his leg, a little above the knee, and with a howl of pain he grabbed the evil thing by the tail before it could sneak away. A big black cobra with its fangful of venom. Ganeshi whirled it overhead and dashed it to the earth, smashing it up. Now his voice rose in a different howl. "Ho-oh, I am bitten." People came rushing from the fields and cast one glance at the snake and shuddered. An old man produced a knife from his waistcloth and made a gash to let the blood flow out. The poisoned blood, however, needed to be sucked off. The people looked askance at each other.

21

None had the spunk to suck off venom. There was no time to seek help. The peasant lad lay at death's door.

A voice, soft, abashed yet firm, said, "I shall try." Startled eyes turned to the girl who had come running from her cotton field a few strips away, black earth on her hands and hair and face.

How let the maiden press her lips to a man's body? The people looked again at each other, unable to say Yes or to say No, but either way it would not have mattered. For she, not waiting for an answer, knelt, put her mouth to the wound. She sucked hard and spat out blood, sucked again and spat. The silence held as she went on, blood reddening her mouth, dripping to her chin. At last the old man who had made a gash with his knife nodded saying, "It is enough."

Could it be that in that same awesome minute her thoughts were full of her father who, too, had been bitten by a snake and had died— even before she was born?

Out of the group of people set like pieces of sculpture, a figure moved off and brought her a bowl of water to rinse her mouth and another, a woman, stepped up and with her sari she wiped blood from the stained chin and throat and said in a murmur, "May the goddess give you every bliss, my daughter." There was a united hum of assent. "May the goddess give you every bliss, my daughter."

This was the bliss? To get buried in a well?

Munni, clutching the rope, could not bear the agony. "I will jump in," she raved and Champa said, "Munni, you stupid!"

The signal—there was the signal from the well's bottom, the pulley-rope quivering with urgency. Feet firmly planted, the women took deep breaths and pulled. The mother's eyes were now alive with an inner flame, a crazy strength in her arms. As the pulley spun slow, hearts shrank with a new dread: What if Meera came up with her hands empty? The mother alone was calm. Her body was clenched, purposive, with a single aim.

Champa hated to be at the forefront. First to see Meera emerge, she must communicate what she saw. But the gasping cry she uttered could be one of great joy or utter dismay. Hands grew limp and the bucket could have plunged back, but Champa was now pulling with all her strength. The others took heart. The weight grew. "Pull, drag! ...Pull, drag!" Sweat ran into eyes or coursed down to join the smears on stiff lips. Inch by inch the bucket moved up.

There—on Meera's shoulder a figure lay flung sackwise. Lakshmi, darting with a moan, took the boy in her arms as he drew level with the well's rim.

His heart was beating, he had been gone barely five minutes. The women wept in their relief. Only Champa held herself in check while she gave first-aid. Her strong peasant hands damp with exertion whirled the inert figure to make the stomach turn. Then she laid the boy on the ground and worked his arms to restore his breathing while the mother, all exhausted, gazed down at the pallid face and cried softly, "Nago . . . Nago, boy!"

Meera, stretched on her back, panted with her eyes closed, arms and feet covered with slush, gold-brown thigh visible through a new rip in her threadbare garb. Her long hair had got unbound in the water and lay spread in thick masses.

Champa's heavy breasts under the gunny-sack jacket leaned over the boy, the muscles ached in her arms, but she worked on with hardly one pause.

"Nago! . . . Nago, boy!" The voice sank to a muffled wail.

"Mother of Mercy! Mother Parvati, Siva's spouse, healer of the hundred woes!"

Only Munni did not join the prayer. Her fingers, reaching again for her hair, plucked another twig.

Meera sat up. "Champa, let me try." "Lie down," cried Champa sharply, pins and needles in her arms. Then the moment came when all faces tensed again, as if controlled by a single nerve. "I feel his breath." Bimla had her forefinger at Nago's nostrils. With a fear lest it was her fancy she centered all of herself at her fingertips. "I feel it," she affirmed. Other hands reached forward in mechanical unison.

Nago stirred, his eyes blinked open. But there was no cry of joyous response. Bow-strings drawn too hard had snapped and the women sat rigid, lifeless.

A minute later Lakshmi with Nago in her arms staggered off toward the house. Sohagi called after her, "Give him a bowl of hot milk sweetened with honey."

Lakshmi turned round to say, "Do not run away, any of you. Wait for me." The words caught in her throat under a heavy backwash of emotion.

"Govind, little monkey!" Sohagi was free at last to turn to her treasure lying neglected on the ground. The child was busy collecting earth in his tiny fists and stuffing it into his mouth. The young mother

23

picked him up, scooped out the mess with her finger. "Were you an earthworm in your past life?" she asked him, whispering, and squeezed him against her body. Her eyes moved to the well and with a shudder she squeezed him hard. Then her face glowed with the thought that the little one had saved his brother's life! It was because he howled so stubbornly that she had to go out to the yard in the nick of time to see Nago fall—infants did have a sixth sense!

"Each and every kite in my house I will pull to pieces, every thread-reel must go into the kitchen fire," cried Champa darkly, her mind on the pranks of her five-year-old ruffian.

"What can I do with the man in my household?" Munni asked. "He flies kites with the gusto of an infant."

Sohagi said, "This little monkey will take a few more years to reach the danger age." Soothed by that thought, she squeezed him again.

A quarter-hour passed before Lakshmi returned to the scene. Meera was still flat on her back, the others bending over her, massaging her body under the wet clinging clothes, deaf to her cries of protest.

"Save me, Lakshmi," Meera moaned, trying in vain to sit up. But the spentness in her face could not hide the secret ecstasy. She had done the incredible!

"Keep quiet." The women kneaded with vigor. "Wait until the breath has eased in your chest. You do not seem to know how you have strained yourself."

"Your bones and blood will feel soothed when we have done our work."

"Let her change her wet clothes." Lakshmi had a lovely blue sari and a jacket in her hands.

But the habitual smack of her lips conveyed a firm No. "I will get dry in the sun, Lakshmi," she added in explanation.

"Meera—"

The smack of her lips again. To wear new clothes, and her friends in tatters?

Lakshmi gazed down, arm still outstretched, and in her eyes a mist of tenderness grew. You who saved my son's life. Such an image of grace, and not one strip of bright metal anywhere on her, no silver, not to speak of gold. Even the pierced earlobes were bare. Six bangles of glass, thin blue ones, on each arm—no, only three on the right arm, the rest seemed to have been lost in the well. One day Lakshmi had tried to slip a silver bangle of her own on to Meera's wrist. Meera had pushed it away, hot in the face, crying, "No, Lakshmi." And now, stubborn as ever, she rejected the sari and jacket.

She had started giggling! "No!" She wriggled and writhed as she tried to break away from a hand kneading her body under the wet clothes.

"She is ticklish!" The women were fascinated by the discovery. And Meera grew convulsed until her breathless "No!" was a mere whisper.

"Ticklish? Is she, truly?" As if this was to be confirmed, they tested her on armpits, knee-pits, waist, ribs. Champa tried the soles of her feet and the space between toes. Bimla blew into her ear.

"Such a brave girl and look at her!"

Meera screamed, reacting to something else besides the fingers: She had done the incredible!

The women shook with merriment. The overwhelming impact of relief hard to bear, they seized this outlet with full abandon.

"We did not know she is ticklish!"

"On her wedding night we will pass the word to the groom. He will bless us."

"No, Bimla. That will give him a power over her."

"Ho! She climbs a tree like a monkey; but—diving frogwise!"

"One more minute in the well," Champa spoke archly, "and some-one would have been there by her side, sharing her fate."

Munni was not shamed by this arch allusion. "I would have jumped in for sure," she agreed. She beamed at Meera protectively and clutched the glistening hair in big fistfuls.

There was a last round of activity which made Meera groan "I die!" and amid the gales of mirth, Lakshmi, anxious but unable to shield the girl, pleaded for the tenth time, "Do not torture her, I beg of you. She is all spent, do you not see? She must get up, rinse water out of her hair and change her clothes."

The women paused at last and Meera seized the chance to roll over to her stomach, so that the sensitive areas of her body were beyond attack. Lakshmi, shaking her head in pity, passed the clothes to Champa. "I must return to my son."

"Do not leave his bedside. Let him not feel fear."

"Tell him a fairy-story to keep his mind occupied."

"Have you lemons in the house? Press one, let the juice pour on a thick paste of crushed pumpkin seeds, and—"

Lakshmi said, "Will one of you go to the *vaid*? In case the boy needs a drug or sleeping potion."

Champa held the clothes in one hand, offering them to Meera, while the fingers of her other hand made a threat. Meera yielded abruptly, crying "Ogress!" and sitting up. She snatched at the sari and jacket, sprang to her feet and walked off behind a screening tree trunk.

"Like a king's daughter she looks!" Munni was rapturous at sight of Meera in the blue garb.

In a minute the Cowhouse Five were walking away and as they passed the orchard Sohagi spoke in a sad murmur. "So our great demonstration ends, before it started."

"What do you mean?" Meera cried snapping.

"We are limbless without you, Meera. You know that."

"Am I dead and gone?"

Sohagi gave a stern answer. "Go straight to bed and sleep."

"Shall I ask Gran'ma to tell me a fairy-story?"

"Dear friend, pray listen. You have shown your mettle, and not for the first time. We join our humble palms to you and cry, 'Jai Meera!' Don't we, Bimla, Munni, Champa?"

"Jai Meera!" Each woman held up her folded palms as if mock-seriously, yet each in her heart paid silent homage to the girl of sixteen, bowing to her strength of spirit.

Her voice was a command. "The procession will start exactly as planned."

So, at midday, a hundred women assembled in the shade of the aged banyan tree, under the eyes of a minor goddess on a foot-high mud pedestal. No one made worship to this Devi except a few young women and one of them, smearing the stone feet fondly with vermilion, had said, "You are like a poor relative of the proud, flower-clad Devi in the temple—not even a cloth canopy on your head to protect you from the sun. For this, Mother, we love you all the more." The hundred women, one by one, touched their fingertips to the vermilion and marked their foreheads with it before they lined up three abreast. A tattered sari stretched between two poles for their banner, they set out toward Main Road and their voices came in unison, "We demand cloth to wear, cloth." People who saw the strange procession shook their heads saying, "Words will melt a ripe coconut, but not the Seth's heart in its cast-iron shell!"

"He will get a bellyful of good laugh."

"He will spit at the demand."

"Go back, women, to your household work and leave it to the menfolk to fight with Seth-ji."

Deaf to all advice the procession went its way. "We demand cloth to wear, cloth." As they passed the weaver's hut in a lane off Main Road, they saw the man, bare except for a loincloth, plying the loom in his front yard. A sari of green and yellow was nearly ready. Eyes smarted, hearts felt heavy as lead.

"He sits inside the python's stomach and toils day and night."

"He wears off in the digestive stomach juice; the python fattens."

There was an interruption at the lane's other end. The village constable, Hoosiar Singh, barred the way with his arms lifted in challenge. "Have you a permit for the procession?" His pock-marked face was stiff with authority.

"What permit?" the women retorted hotly. "It is a crime to walk the village road? We must fly in the air like birds or crawl in the fields like lizards? This is your father-in-law's property, this road and the others?"

"The old tale is to be retold!" The constable, small and shriveled by age, gave a slow nod of comprehension. "The British Lion is to be tickled again. When you feel his wrath, women, you will shiver. You will drop down on your knees and lick dust. Halt. Go back."

Loud laughter met this challenge.

"The Lion? Tail between his legs he is about to leap across the oceans to his homeland. Our freedom is only a hundred days ahead. Where do you live? Do you hear nothing?"

Hoosiar Singh grunted scornfully. "Women! Swallowing whatever they hear. The Lion will roar over India as long as the sun rises and the moon sets and even one star twinkles."

The women tittered. "*Hai Ram*! Such talk is still to be heard!" The potter's wife pressed her hand to her puffy cheek in honest wonder.

"Uncle Red Turban, let the Lion put his tail around you and leap across the black waters."

"Stop!" Grim with official anger Hoosiar Singh banged the brass-studded end of his bamboo stave on the road. Then Sohagi tried to appease him. "Old Uncle, pray listen. Our banner is not raised against your alien masters. This is a fight with one of our own skin and sweat. Seth-ji. You know how he has denied us."

27

A clamor of voices added affirmation. "We demand cloth to wear, cloth."

Hoosiar Singh reflected for a minute. The ragged banner on the bamboo poles was not the familiar tricolor of the Nationalist rebels. He passed his eyes over the serried ranks. What clothes! The combined effect of the tatters! The women now resumed their marching and as the middle of the procession passed the old man, his eyes peered hard. That one, walking stiffly with her face veiled and averted —did she not look like Bimla, his daughter-in-law? No, that was impossible.

Why, it was she!

Staggered, dumb for a minute, he managed to say, "Bimla, it is not you?"

There was no answer, but the woman's back as she marched on seemed to stiffen more.

"You have shamed our proud family tree, you have made us noseless," croaked the old man, keeping step with the procession. "And whatever for? The Seth is mindful of the needs of my house, as if he were our mother and father. My second son's spouse, you have no reason to wear what you have on your body. The Seth has asked me to give a glance to his new cloth stock which has just come. And now, I cannot even stand straight in his presence."

Bimla still gave no answer, but a fat woman at the rear turned her face with a flash of her brass nose-stud. "Unity. You do not know what that means. Unity."

It would do no good to annoy Bimla overmuch. Her husband worked in town as an office peon and sent home a quarter of his wages. If Bimla went away to him in anger, the remittance would surely stop. That would not do.

The procession pushed on, making a round of the village, while Hoosiar Singh took a short cut to the clothshop to give the Seth a timely warning. After all, the danger to peace was not as serious as he had feared. The real trouble-merchant, Meera's Grandma, was not among these marchers. That terror of a Grandma. A freak, for she could read and write!

Meera, banner in hand, was quiet amid the commotion, reliving her moments of fear. Cold fear had seized her halfway down the well, with her imagination at fever heat. The bottom of the bucket breaks under her weight.... The rope snaps, she is hurling down.... The

28

boy, having fallen face up, lies with his head buried in slime. Like a yawning monster the dark-green water meets her and swallows her—to the knees, to the hips, throat, face, all of herself.

She gripped the banner hard, veins showing in the back of her hand, and with the sickness welling up, she clenched her lips together. *We demand cloth to wear, cloth.* Four or five times had the cry rung in front of the Seth's clothshop before the door swung open. The Seth came out on the portico, a sneer on his round, full-cheeked face. "Why tire your throats? Let one of you step into my room for a talk."

Taken aback, the women looked at each other and with one common thought they looked at Meera, who alone was the Seth's match.

"I—" Meera began, but her eyes dropped under the compulsion of trustful glances and she took hold of herself. She did not speak a word, did not even look back at her friends. Up the stone steps of the portico and into the room. The door closed behind her. She was in dark depths. Would she make it once more?

The minutes dragged on until the door burst open and Meera came out, her breast heaving hard. It was a minute or two before she could speak. The Seth, she said, had not been rude or even angry. He had already heard about his son's rescue. He called her the pride of the village. He would write a letter to the newspaper in town, he said, so that the world would know about Sonamitti's Meera Bai. But as soon as she came to the subject of cloth his manner changed. He shook his head firmly. Business was business, he said; it had no place for soft sentiments. She pleaded with him still. No use. Then she used her weapon. A hundred women would strip themselves bare and throw their rags on his hoarded shame.

She paused in her recital, taking breath, resuming in a minute. The Seth had cried "What!" as if he could not believe his ears. When she had repeated her threat he dropped into a long silence, thinking. She felt hopeful. Then he leaned forward over the desk. "I am waiting," he said. "What for?" "I am waiting for you to strip yourself—and be followed by the ninety-nine others, one by one."

The women walked back through the alley, sore-throated from their shouting, deeply dismayed. On Main Road they saw Lakshmi hurrying toward them. Her clothes were stained with the well mud from her son's body. She asked no questions for the story was written on every face.

"The *vaid* has seen the boy. There is nothing to fear, he said. Nago sleeps peacefully."

"Why have you left him alone? He may wake up and get a fright."

Lakshmi said, "Do you want to leave me out? Have I ever failed to be with you all?" Before they could answer her, she added quickly, "We won't be beaten. Come."

"No!" Meera declined vehemently.

"Give me a chance."

"You, Lakshmi?"

"Yes, give me a chance."

So the procession turned round, though with no zeal, no real hope. *We demand cloth to wear, cloth.* The voices were hollow, with no fire, no life at all.

"Back again?" The Seth's melonlike face beamed at them. "Come. One of you."

Lakshmi walked up. At sight of her, he cried in a rush, "Why, Lakshmi, I was about to go home. You did not have to come—the *vaid* was here and he told me everything. Now rush back and send a libation to the Devi"—a break in his voice revealed his feeling—"it was she who willed that our frogling's life be saved."

"It was Meera who—" began Lakshmi, but the Seth chimed in, "Look, give me ten minutes. There is a small business to be settled with that howling crowd there."

"I am in the same small business!"

"What!"

She stiffened. "We demand cloth to wear."

"You don't say you came marching with the hundred sisters of vixen? You?"

"So I did."

He let her pass through the door and slammed it behind him. His face was now thoughtful. "I know, Lakshmi, how you feel." His voice was gentle and soothing. "Meera has placed us both in her debt. Happily, she has been paid back; she wears a twenty-rupee sari of yours, the best she has ever had. The four other women must also be rewarded with good millcloth, seven-rupee ones. I shall give you the pieces to distribute. Then all our debts will be canceled. Wait, there is the debt to the Devi, above all." His folded palms rose prayerfully to his brow. "Add a coconut to the usual offer of vermilion, sugar wafer and red hibiscus."

"We make a demand for everyone."

"Don't plead for the women. Don't sing the same song. It will do no good."

"Plead? We have done that long enough. We demand."

He gave her a close, speculative look, then sat down on the reed mat spread behind his low desk. Beside the desk stood a tall brass-bowled hookah with two yards of flexible pipe. He picked up the pipe, drew smoke, and as the hookah was bubbling in response, he resumed.

"Do you wear tatters, Lakshmi? What ails you?"

Her answer amazed him. "Unity." She stood with her head erect, her eyes ashine. This was not Lakshmi, the humble cow. This was an alien woman! What had happened seemed plain. The wily vixen at the well had worked on the mother's heart just after she had borne great agony. Those vixen should get a sari apiece, the fair price of their help, and also a feast by way of a happy celebration. But here was their big chance to make trouble. A street procession, banner and all, and the brazen claim of a hundred saris. Fantastic!

"Go back, wife," he ordered sternly. "How could you leave Nago alone at home? Have you no sense, no feeling?"

Lakshmi gathered herself for the perilous plunge. "Mark my words." She gazed straight into the accusing eyes. "Unless you sell the cloth fairly, a hundred saris, I will take off what I wear. I will, on behalf of all, throw my clothes on your heap of hoarded shame."

He was even more astounded than when Meera had made her threat. But he pulled himself up in a minute. He threw back his close-cropped head and broke into a chuckle. And the women outside, crowded on the portico, heard the chuckle and knew that the fight was over.

"Meera made the same threat," he said, his eyes now fixed on Lakshmi in a steady gaze. "She fled fast. All the others saw that the bluff could not work. Yet you, Nago's mother—"

The fury of the united voices cut him short: "We want cloth to wear, cloth." That desperate challenge acted on Lakshmi like a stimulant. She met the Seth's gaze with smoldering eyes.

"This is no bluff. I will strip, for certain. Even though I may be the only one."

"What! You, Lakshmi, my lawful spouse?"

"I, your lawful spouse."

"You, the proud mother of that pig, my son and heir!"

"I, proud mother of your pig."

She saw the menace as his face turned grim, the hundred torments to come. But she saw also beyond the menace: she saw Meera rise dripping from the well, one arm on the pulley rope, the other thrown about the inert form across her shoulder. With that vision before her she clutched the upper part of her sari and swept it aside.

Was that brother of a bug, his assistant in the back room, peering through the crack in the bottom panel of the communicating door? His face twisted with anxiety, the Seth moved along to place his bulk against the door, blocking the crack, and cried with a sudden switch to emotion, "Wifeling!"

She shook her head firmly. "Don't plead. It will do no good." Her fingers grasped a button of her white jacket.

"Enough!" he lashed out. "Strip, if you must. After that grand performance pick up your clothes, put them on and go home like a hussy who has had her fun."

"Fun!" Her lips hardened. "Naked I will leave this room. Naked I will walk on Main Road. All Sonamitti will see a woman, a mother, put to disgrace." The jacket flew open across her bosom.

"Where is your honor?" he cried hoarsely. "Even to think such thoughts is to be unclean."

"Your spouse, your partner in virtue—how think of honor?"

His angry eyes were rolling in their sockets. "Think twice before you give way to sheer madness."

He was tough. He would not yield. Nothing could stand in the way of his business gains. She would have to do it. She would have to be true to her promise. Strain enlarged her eyeballs but she did not pause until her unbuttoned jacket lay discarded at her feet.

He gaped, gaped at his half-naked wife as she started to untie her sari's waist knot.

Her vision filled with fog. As the waist knot loosened, her head felt awhirl. One instant, one turn of her fingers, and the sari would drop off; she would be naked. She had never stood naked before her husband even in the darkness of night. She shrank and closed her eyes and there was the girl descending the well, a man-height of cruel water, two man-heights.

"Give us cloth to wear, cloth," the chorus rang once more and a voice that was surely Meera's added its high shrill, "Or else, take even our tatters!"

This was the only way to repay her debts; it was all she could give and was so little. You who saved my son's life. . . .

The Seth twisted his thick mustache, watching the new strange woman, troubled by her exposed body. She had a birth mark at the root of one breast and in lamplight it was such a mark of beauty, but now it was piteously plain.

"Stop, Lakshmi!" he wanted to say and in this crisis of their relations a longing seized him that she understand his dilemma, his utter helplessness. He did not enjoy the sight of ragged women, far from it. But how, otherwise, could he get more value for his limited cloth stock? This trick of cornering the market was not his invention. He had learned it by watching his betters during the rice famine in Bengal four years before. At that time three million men and women had to die so that there could be thirty new millionaires, and none condemned the profiteers. His present role, set beside theirs, was a child's prank.

Would that Lakshmi knew how things were. He had chosen his vocation in life and must fulfill its demands. He, a trader, with his duties and loyalties and a time-honored code of conduct, could not afford to be soft. Once he yielded ground, there was no knowing how far he would have to retreat. A lamb of a trader was an anomaly. A tiger living on grass was poetic fancy!

All the same, he heard himself say, "Be it so, Lakshmi." His hand was lifted in a gesture of pleading. "Let the saris go." He saw her open her eyes as if startled and unsure that she had heard him aright and he added in a sharper tone, "Your bread-giver will gasp in poverty, remember that. The child of your womb will turn one day into a whining beggar boy." He watched her for a minute, hoping to see repentant tears, but her eyes gave him a bright, happy glance. Resigned, he jerked his shoulders. "Bulaki Rao!" he shouted for his assistant.

The answering voice sounded only a few inches away.

"Let the new cloth go on sale. Each and every word of mine you have heard with one ear stuck to the crack in the door, so there is no need to explain. Give away all that I have. Let my throat be slit."

"*Jai!*" The women on the portico, listening raptly, were first astounded and speechless, and then their excited response came in a burst of great jubilation. "Victory in unity. *Jai! Jai!*"

33

CHAPTER

3

Later in the day, as the Seth sat at his desk with his short thick legs crossed, his spirit was sunk in gloom, his body tattooed with defeat. A small fortune was gone; sugar had dissolved in water. The hundred wolves in the procession had not been the only ones to buy cloth; the scent of gain had drawn others, pack after pack. Of the three bolts of saris meant for slow, judicious sale over an area of fifty miles, not one piece was left. Mean coppers, shabby savings of peasantfolk, filled a green cashbox up to the lid, a baleful reminder of it all.

To have been so gullible, and panicky beyond reason. The hand on the sari's waist knot had hesitated visibly. But even if Lakshmi had carried out her first threat—what then? It was no sin or shame for a woman to bare herself before her son's begetter. To have taken her other threat seriously, that she would go out to the street naked, was stupid. Easy to see what would have happened. Standing stiffly with her head bowed, she would have burst into tears, cried as never before in her life. After five minutes he would have spoken to her soothingly. "Enough, Lakshmi. Now put on your clothes and go home. All's well between us, Nago's Mother."

That would have been the tale's end. Lakshmi would have learnt a lesson and kept it always in mind. A stern lesson not to lift rebel eyes ever again to her husband.

That was not to be. The ass of a husband, befooled, brayed humbly and ate grass.

He straightened his neck and propped his elbows on the desk top beside the red-bound ledgers. Why cry for the milk which the cat had lapped up? Better think out how to cover the loss. The extortion could be made to look as a willing gift. He had seen the women in rags, felt unhappy, and out of kindness given the cloth away. To lose a thousand rupees in three hours. Who but he could make such a donation—in Sonamitti, in all the Seven Villages, in the whole district and even beyond? Here was material that should pass into legend!

Not that he cared to be a legend. Silver in his hand had more meaning than a halo about his head. Yet there were times when glory was real value, a solid investment.

Such a time was, indeed, not far ahead. An election, the first of a series, was to take place soon after freedom. District boards. The board for this area would have members sent by a hundred villages, grouped in units of five or six, but Sonamitti, large, a thousand voters on its list, would be a unit by itself. Sonamitti would exclusively elect a member. Twenty such members would sit together as brothers and friends and impose taxes for all to pay and spend the money on paved roads, culverts and bridges, wells. But the twenty men could not all be equal in girth. One or two would outweigh the others. One or two must take up leadership.

Glory, no hollow word. Glory's shrine was set in a courtyard strewn with good cash. But the path to that shrine was full of pitfalls. You needed preparedness before you started to pick your way, or else you would get lost.

The saris were part of the preparedness, the first item in his election accounts on the debit side. For, among the women in rags were many whose husband or son would have a vote. What if they let their civic sense be foiled by a private pique?

That problem lay solved unexpectedly. The bone of contention was buried. Sonamitti's top man had revealed his true metal. What benevolence, what self-sacrifice! Such guts for what was simply charity in disguise.

The Seth could now be at ease and look months ahead to his accounts on both sides of the deal.

The figures he saw did not have to be in his ledgers, yet they were clear, specific. He had trained himself to cast up accounts as a sort of mental picture, the credit and debit columns neatly entered, the balance worked out, and no paper wasted, no telltale records kept. This capacity had guided his progress in the dim alleyways of the black market. Even big dealers paid him respect for this gift, even the sharp-toothed city sharks called him a brother and an equal.

He narrowed his eyes as though for a sharper view. The debit side came first, the initial investment. The hundred sisters of vixen had given him an idea! Squads of youngsters from the village school to go around crying a slogan in one voice. This could be arranged at once through Master-ji; the learned vulture, up to his beak in debt, would happily lend his services. The piglings would get enthused by a weekly feast, fried bread and flour-and-sugar *laddoo*, at four annas per mouth. The united frog-cry day on day, month on month, and the effect piling up!

So to the credit side. First, the wooden bridge to be built across the stream. The board must sanction a fat "two pice" for the project, the new people's Government at the State capital adding a liberal grant. Sonamitti's member would work with right contacts and good instruments of pressure. The project had to be in his care; none else among the wise crows on the board could handle accounts better. Sonamitti would bless its member for this gift of a bridge and nothing for anyone to lose if he claimed a flat ten per cent from the contractor, the shark of sharks who would anyhow make his bagful of profit.

Then, again, the village would benefit when the clothshop quota was raised by right manipulation—he knew where to pull strings and how. When the clothshop doubled its profit, the new quota having been sold at the so-called black rate, there would be more cash on its counter and the bliss of extra loans for all the village owls to take.

Absorbed in his bright vision, he broke into a hoot of laughter because of an incongruous thought. What if he disclosed his mind to Nago's mother, inflated as she was with her one victory? What if he showed her his ideas, plans, calculations? She had gone to prison for freedom, with no objection on his part, and had a special claim to its first fruits. Those would come to her, appropriately, through her husband. But she would misunderstand him because of her notions of what was wrong and right. Tall talk. She might as well ask her bread-giver to turn into a mendicant, with nothing in the world except *lota-kambal*, a blanket and a water-bowl. She would, if she knew what was in the offing, clasp her husband's feet and beg of him not to become a member of the board and, in course of time, its president!

"You called me, Seth-ji?" Bulaki Rao peered through the inner door standing ajar.

"I only laughed. Do I have to say, 'May I?'"

The assistant withdrew his head quickly and closed the door. But the sight of him had reminded the Seth of an urgent task. The cinema show. It would be the first show of this kind in Sonamitti. He had arranged the preliminaries, but much else remained to be done.

"Ho, brother of a cockroach!" he called.

The face peered again. "Ji?"

"You have prepared the cinema list? Where is it?"

Bulaki Rao shuffled in, three long sheets of paper in his hand. The Seth took them and went over the names heavily scrawled with a reed pen. Halfway through, he looked up speculatively. This ass might bray to the village about the scene he had just witnessed.

"*Han!* The potter fellow sits tight on your list. That jackal, maybe, gives you mud vessels free of charge. Is that it?" His eyes with pinpoints of light prodded hard. Will you bray? Will you?

Bulaki Rao scratched his chin and having heard the unspoken question along with the one spoken, he answered both in silence, wagging his head from side to side.

"Use your precious tongue." His master was unappeased.

"The potter fellow with his mudwheel—"

The Seth cut him short.

"What was my instruction? That you will make a list of the people to be asked to the picture play, the very first picture play in Sonamitti. Why is it that the Peerless Products Company will send us a mobile film unit and give this free show, Friday next? Is it because there is no cinema house within a circle of seventy miles, the people are denied, and the Company's tender guts have melted with pity? Or is it because the Company wants to advertise Peerless with a film specially made for them, so that people will eat the tinned vegetable *ghee* in preference to local butter-oil? Search in the wooden case of your head and tell me what you think."

"That rogue of a potter eats butter-oil, I have made sure," Bulaki Rao explained. "We can sell him a small Peerless tin every month. He will—"

"As Peerless agents, it is not our task to look for every mouse and lizard who can eat our product. The first man on this list should be the *Halwai*, who can buy more of this stuff for his fried breads and sweet laddoos than anyone else, including myself. He may well use a Peerless tin every other day and more on festive days. Yet"—the Seth's angry hand slapped the sheets—"your list does not hold that pig."

"Seth-ji!" The assistant bent over the desk and his forefinger darted. "There!" But his master grunted in disgust. "Far down on the list. What sense of priority!" He smote the man again with his stern glance. "How many names in all?"

"About a hundred. These men are sure to bring their wives and children. The place will get too crowded. Maybe we could add a few more cubits of space to the canvas hall. If Seth-ji takes a stroll to the meadow and sees for himself—"

The Seth grunted again, propped his hands on the desk top and clambered to his feet. He had a yellow turban on his head and his stocky figure was oddly draped in a bathrobe of blue-and-mauve toweling, ankle-length. The unusual garb gave him an air of sophistication. Awe-struck eyes would gape at the large, blue buttons and the silken tassel with its smart loop. The Seth was known to possess a half-dozen costumes of this kind in different colors, all purchased, it was said, at an English store in Bombay, the great city five hundred miles away, where the Seth had gone twice on business trips.

A parasol stood in a corner. Bulaki Rao touched it with deference, having first wiped his hand on his dhoti. "May I open the head-protector, sir?"

The Seth snatched at it. "What! The sun is still strong, you cannot see?" He glared at the other's face, not missing the suppressed smirk.

The parasol, small and delicate, also had come from Bombay. Its yellow silk had wide green bands and the small squat handle was highly polished. The people of Sonamitti had seen no other umbrella of this kind; like the bathgown it was an item of dignity in the Seth's outfit, an insignia of prestige.

He had to be careful about its use, however. The delicate silk could not be exposed to sun and rain and wind. And here was this ass itching to open the parasol to the hard glare. Nitwit! Would he keep his word not to bray about Nago's mother?

The meadow lay all along the north side of Sonamitti, a stretch of pasturage reaching to the fields of Pipli village. The Seth trudged off in that direction, squinting in the glare and shielding his eyes with his palm. The road passed through fields of mustard, carpets of golden bloom somewhat shabby with the driven dust. Every field was an entry in the Seth's ledgers—mustard or millet or maize or cotton—set against the figure of a loan and made valid by a peasant's thumb-mark. The Seth felt his heart swell with pride and in that instant he saw the young peddler who had walked into the village one day at the turn of the century. A cloth bundle lay heavy on his back and barefoot he took his wares from door to door. He had to compete with the local weavers and made a meager living.

The Machine Age helped him out. Millcloth became cheaper than handloom products. The hard-working vendor could at last set up a store. It was a mere hovel. The white ants ate his cloths and had to be held at bay. Next, he bought a piece of land and built a house, a mud hut with straw thatching. Here his three sons were born.

His business prospered. The mud hut was replaced by a yellow-washed brick house, first one floor, then a second floor and an orange orchard around. Meanwhile his sons were growing up. They were sent to school in town. Two of them took up service and drifted to other cities. Only the youngest echoed his father's zest for trade, tied himself to the old man's ledgers, and became his prop and solace.

"Here in Sonamitti your true sources lie." Those were almost the last words the old man spoke before he died.

So the young Seth came into his own. Bowing to his father's will, he stuck to his roots in the village even after his business had vastly expanded. He had several shops in the countryside but his crowning achievement was Gay Peacock House in town. Further, he followed the old man's practice of lending money. (Never let money sleep, the old man used to say. Let it work, let it breed, so it may increase tenfold.) In rural living money was in poor supply. Even a small cash loan would often take people over a crisis—a marriage ceremony, a birth, a funeral. The benefits were shared equally by the hand that supplied the cash and the hand that received it. Was there in Sonamitti a single brother of a mule who had never taken a loan? Was there one fox or owl who wished the loans to stop? Even Meera's Grandma, so inflated with pride because of her power over the people, had borrowed with both her hands. She had thumb-marked away almost all her holdings to meet her hunger for cash.

In a clearing of the fields stood a shack, a raised porch under an overhang of thatch, and three cement steps flush with the roadside. This was the sweetmeat shop. The lean Halwai, uncle of a scarecrow, sat on his buttocks behind the wooden counter. Dark-blue glasses covered his eyes as if they were too tender to be exposed to the sun. The Seth smiled knowingly. The glasses were mere ornament! The strange foible of people, the itch to make a show of oneself!

He passed the shop, then turned back with a thought. Sweat was pouring down his face. He would rest for a minute in the shade and at the same time do some business.

"What poison brews in your cauldron?" He bent his body to the protection of the thatch.

39

The cauldron was set on a portable oven of baked mud, with a slow fire, and contained three fingers' width of *ghee* bubbling and hissing around a batch of floury convolutions.

"*Jilebi*, Seth-ji. Pray taste a morsel." The Halwai turned to the trader, ignoring the other customers waiting to be served with *laddoo* piled on a large brass tray. He picked up a treacly sweet with his fingers. "See how it drips with thick syrup."

"Let it cool and it will be a hardship for human teeth."

"Seth-ji!"

"The ghee causes the stiffening."

"I use the best ghee in the Seven Villages. Melted on fire, its aroma flies up the road, far and farther, and people sniff it with delight and say, 'The Halwai sends his emissaries to tickle our palate and pick at our purse strings.'"

"The ghee causes the stiffening." The Seth held his ground. "When you have used Peerless you will see the difference."

"Peerless? What peerless?"

"Wait, friend, until you sit at the picture play. Then you will—"

There was an interruption, one of the other customers, an old gnome who ran the grocery, exclaiming, "Picture play? Why, the mother of my grandsons is all agog about that. No other thought lies in her head. Lost in her fancy she lets the bread turn black on the fire."

"The same tale with my daughter!" observed his tall companion. "She raves about the cinema even in her sleep."

"The women know all about the coming show and we do not," the grocer complained. "Seth-ji, will the menfolk be left out—what? We also have eyes ready for fun."

The Seth's ears filled anew with the cry: we demand cloth to wear, cloth. And the great idea struck him all at once. It made him speechless for a while.

"Indeed!" His voice carried a throb of mystery.

"Indeed what?"

"The women know all about the cinema show. They are agog for the show." The throb of mystery quickened.

"So they are," the Halwai affirmed. "I have no women in my household, but a good few come to my counter and there is one word on every tongue. The queries I have to answer—" That was because he was a repository of news. He collected gossip and ladled it out along with his sweetmeat.

The Seth was twisting the loop of his girdle, playing with it. The wonder of his ever-resourceful mind! His face looked unusually smug as he released his shaft:

"Women will not be admitted."

"What!" Three voices joined their bewilderment.

"No women." Adding after a dramatic pause, "None will see the picture play."

"Only Nago's mother?"

"No, not even she." He imagined her dismay and was happy. How eagerly in the past five or seven days she had sounded him for details of the show, passing her knowledge to her friends!

Silence, and the old grocer shook his gray head disapprovingly. "Seth-ji, the women are sleepless with expectation. You cannot deny them. Since there is not enough room, let the men stay out."

"Or else the poor creatures will drop dead with misery," his companion added.

The Seth untied his girdle and with slow deliberation he tied it back in a neat loop before he spoke again. "Listen to the henpecked ones." He pointed with his fat, scornful finger. "Maybe you missed the street show the peace-loving doves gave a few hours before. Maybe you did not have your eye-fill."

"And your ear-fill," the Halwai added jeering. "Unity among womenfolk—ho! The old saying goes, 'A thousand mustaches can live together in amity but not four breasts!' "

The Seth ignored the interruption. "I ask you, what has happened to their modesty, a woman's most precious possession?" he went on. "I was hot with shame and frozen with sadness when I heard their barefaced threat. I gave them what they asked for, not because I was scared out of my wits. Far from it! Have you ever seen me eat mud when challenged? Had they acted on their word, they would have blackened their own faces, not mine."

"True, true"—but the voices lacked conviction. While it could not be denied that the women had been altogether brazen, the unexpected result had made almost everyone in the village happy.

"Loosen the reins of restraint and the women will get out of hand. The times are bad. We cannot be too careful. Do you agree?"

Heads nodded in assent. The times were bad.

"Children and women are alike in a way. Spare them and they get spoilt. It is for their own good that, now and again, they should be

41

taught a hard lesson. Here is one. The women are crazy about the cinema show and I therefore announce: Women will not be admitted. None. Not even Nago's mother. I do not make false distinctions."

"This picture play is their chance of a lifetime," the old grocer pleaded again. "Missing it they will be wretched forever."

"To lure thirsty tongues with cool water and keep it just out of reach!"

The Seth's forefinger stabbed the air with disdain. "We are not afraid to give punishment where it is due."

"Such harsh denial to the mothers and sisters of our sons!"

"We are no nincompoops," the Seth's voice was a growl. "We are lions."

"We are lions," the Halwai echoed, his lean chest thrusting out, and he glared at the two diffident men who were now reduced to silence.

4

The anger of the Cowhouse Five was mixed with despondence. "Better for us to have been born as cattle," Meera cried. Her body was damp from toil in the sun-baked field.

"Such tyranny!"

"Freedom, four steps ahead. Not for us, women. We live to press our masters' legs."

"Let ten women go to the show, any ten in the village, and we shall have no grouse. This ban against all womenfolk!"

"We have shouted in anger at the alien coat-and-pantaloons. Our dhoti-clad fellows are ten times worse."

"We shout at them also, 'Quit!' "

Amid this gloom, someone struck a hopeful note. "It is the Seth's joke, nothing else. He is laughing at our expense."

But Lakshmi shook her head mournfully. "You do not know that man. He is a monster."

The day before, back home after the disaster at his clothshop, the Seth had fondled his little boy and made him promise not to touch a kite ever again. Lakshmi, awkward and shrinking, had awaited his outburst of anger. She would take it in meek silence. But his face was quiet, as if he had no hidden soreness. After a time, she felt reassured. Grateful, she tried to redeem herself.

"I have prepared a milk relish for you with pistachio. You will like it."

"Prodigal as usual," he answered with a heavy nod. "Pistachio!"

She mused for a minute and tried again. "I, too, gave a loan," she told him. "A rupee saved from the daily expenses, a pice or two at a time. Here is a month's interest." A half-anna bit lay upon her palm.

"That rupee has flown away for ever." His hand rested on Nago's shaven head, feeling the bristly scalp.

Too late she saw her error. Mentioning money she had reminded him of his loss at the clothshop. She should give him a token of

43

submission. Acting on a strong impulse she had defied him as never before and got away with it. Time to slip back under her accustomed yoke.

"Will you not give me a new sari to wear on Friday?" Her mouth made a girlish pout.

"Friday?"

"The picture play." Her eyes were soft with admiration. To bring a picture play to the village—none but he could do the magic feat.

His placid look did not change as he answered, "Women will not be admitted."

"What!"

"No women."

She stared at him. "What kind of a joke is this?"

"No joke."

She gestured with her arm. "As if I am dying for a new sari! One day Nago will give his mother all she wants. Won't you, Nago, boy?"

The boy was fretting to be rid of his father's hand. "A blue sari, Ma-ji?" brightly; "I'll rush and bring one from the shop."

"You can have all the saris you need," the Seth assured his son's mother. "Even though you tear them in no time because of sharp knives on your buttocks."

"On the night of the picture play—"

"No women."

"What!"

"Not even you."

Her heart felt faint, for the meaning was now plain. Could she ever again lift her eyes to her friends?

To plead, beg, cajole—she knew it would all be useless. Still she made an attempt ending up with, "You are a brute. To hurt those who gave your son a second life. You are a monster."

The serenity in his face survived this fierce assault.

"You do not understand, Lakshmi. No one can save a life. Everything is worked out by fate. Nago could not die before his time. The star-conjunctions give him a fairly long life. Those women were the tools of fate. Not unlike the pulley and rope so conveniently at hand. Tell me: What could they have done without the pulley and rope?"

But Lakshmi answered this profound wisdom with, "Ingrate!"

"Anyhow, your friends will be paid for their five minutes' work,

44

as I have told you. Figure out the rate." He paused as if to give her time for the arithmetic. "Would that I were a brute, as you say. Then there would be a really big patrimony for this boy, our only son and heir. I have too much softness in my bones. Or else, this afternoon—" He broke off with an expressive shrug of disgust.

Lakshmi, stupefied, could not answer such logic.

Her husband had regained his villain's mantle: he could not be without it! No escape for her from the wretchedness of split feelings, her daily fare and her lot for a whole lifetime.

"Even though he is a monster, let us not lose heart," she cried to her friends in the cowshed. "I am with you all in this fight. There must be some way."

"Bid me and I will eat fire." Munni lifted her hand expressively to her mouth.

Sohagi clasped Meera's hand. "Sister, there is still time. Think hard. Think until the stomach begins to ache."

"Yes, yes." She smiled wanly in answer.

Champa had a suggestion. "Eat fishhead. Then your thinking will be cool and bright. I shall make a dish for you well seasoned with mustard."

So Meera racked her head as she walked homeward. A second demonstration would do no good. What if they rushed into the canvas hall, all in a body? The show would stop. That would be no good, either.

There stood the gray sagging mudhouse, half screened by an old fig tree on the roadside. The lush pumpkin vine on the straw thatch looked like streaks of green paint. There was no Grandma on the veranda, dim eyes astrain for the young toiler's return. Gout had kept Grandma away from the field for two or three days.

The kitchen was dusky, a barred hole on one wall serving for window. Grandma lay on the bare earth. Waiting, maybe plying awhile the spinning-wheel by her side, she had fallen asleep. Thin and wispy, the white bun of her hair a cotton ball caught in firelight. Two platters of food lay near the oven, protected from flies with pieces of banana leaf.

Meera stood looking down a moment, then dropped to her knees, bent over, and with one finger she traced a deep line across Grandma's forehead. That was the line she had chosen in a whole network as one she herself had made. Toil, gout, Grandpapa; the faltering rains, the Seth's red ledgers, the heart's warmth—all had made lines in that forehead, but the one line her finger traced was she herself.

Grandma woke with a start, blinked her eyes like a child shaken out of sleep, then abruptly she raised her voice in complaint: "You do not have to eat, you can live on air and sunlight."

Meera said, "Gran'ma, what are we going to do?"

"A half-day in the field makes you lose all appetite. I, at your age, worked hard enough. That did not fill my stomach though! Why, at reaping time, the millet all heavy and drooping—"

Once she was set on the familiar theme of her feats of harvest in the long-ago days, Granda would not be pushed from it; so Meera hastened to say, "Bad news, Gran'ma."

"I, at your age, with your father just born—" She could turn her eyes to a day fifty years back and see it as clear and sharp as yesterday. But the tale stayed on her tongue and her voice changed its tone. "You said bad news?"

"The picture play. We cannot see it."

"Hai!" Grandma saddened. "It is not coming, after all."

"The picture play will come. But we cannot see it."

Grandma drew a happy breath. "We will see it for sure."

"Women will not be admitted. None. Not even Lakshmi."

All the wrinkles in Grandma's face quivered with her merry laugh. "Nothing will hold us back from our fun."

"The door will be open to none but menfolk." And she explained how the vengeful Seth was going to hit back.

Grandma lay quiet, eye sockets deep, cheekbones high, a shadow of down on her upper lip. After a minute's silence she spoke slowly, moodily.

"Picture plays, they are a real wonder, so people say. A railway engine goes by, sound and all, and even the smoke is real!" Grandma felt the smoke of the engine in her nostrils and eyes. "There stands a goddess, singing, and your heart cries out, 'Mother of Mercy!'" Grandma saw the shadow goddess and lifted her hands to her brow, devoutly.

The girl's mouth, however, curved with mockery. "A mere city woman. Let me paint my face with the stuff from a jar and I shall be just like her."

Grandma shook her head with a smile.

"It is the power, girl, not the face. The power to move us into a

46

feeling. We make a Devi with clay, stone, wood, and the image gives us a feeling and so it becomes more than its material, it becomes a goddess. We worship what is thus created, not the wood or clay. The same is true for the woman who is a Devi for one hour. She may be a slut in her real life."

"Even so?"

"Years back, when you were unborn, a folk-play came to this village. The young fellow who played the godlike Ram Chunder, his name was Sambhu, I remember, took our hearts in his fist every night. On the last night of the show people went up to the dais and touched Sambhu's bare feet, crying, 'Jai Ram Chunder. Jai!'" Grandma saw it all in a clear vision. Her voice lowered. "Yet everyone knew that Sambhu at daytime prowled about looking for a chance to make eyes at a comely maid. Whenever he could, he crossed the meadow to Pipli which has a toddy shop. He sat with the louts of three villages bunched together, drank pailfuls of the potion and sang dirty lines that befoul the tongue."

"Yet those people touched his feet!"

"They touched the feet of Ram Chunder. They had nothing to do with the wicked lad."

Meera said, "Gran'ma, how would you like to see a foreign picture play? Men and women of a far-off land. You will see how they live, how they—" She stopped. In the cowshed, one day, Bimla had spoken of foreign pictures; city-born, she had seen many of them. They showed men and women in love, cuddling lip to lip. "Sh!" Lakshmi had breathed a warning and Bimla had answered, "It will not be long before our Meera is given to a man. Let her learn something about life."

Grandma said, "I will give you in marriage to a boy from town. Then you will see a hundred picture plays."

"Stop, Gran'ma."

"The matchmaker in our village, the old barber, goes to town once in a while. He will keep his eyes open."

Marriage! Meera turned her lip. She drew Grandma back to the problem in hand. "Here goes your big chance and there is nothing we can do."

Grandma, baffled, shook her head and was silent.

"Next time I will go away with Grandpapa. He roams over the world, he sees everything. And I?"

47

Grandma sat up. "Meera——" She fumbled excitedly under her pillow.

"Stick to this mud-hole, if you must. I am going away."

"Big news!" Grandma's hand flourished a postcard.

"Grandpapa?"

"Thursday!" Grandma yelled.

Meera snatched at the letter. Grandpapa coming home! Thursday, the twenty-third of the month.

Grandma said, "Thursday, yes, but which Thursday? The twenty-third—when is that? Go to the Halwai, Meera, and ask him. He has an almanac. He has to know the festive days which always bring extra business."

"Yes, Gran'ma."

"Wait. First eat your bread. Hei-ee, beti——" But she was gone!

She felt overwhelmed as she was walking again in the hard mid-summer sun. Grandpapa coming home. Her mind went back to his last visit, three years before. Despite his long white beard he was young enough. For ten years he had been a minstrel, wearing a yellow garb, a tunic almost ankle length. A one-string lyre in his hand, he sang to fellow passengers on the railway coach as he traveled, and thus earned his fare. The throats of listeners grew thick with feeling when his theme was tragic; but when he made mock of bigwigs in doggerel he had composed, there was much laughter.

If only she could go wandering with Grandpapa, Meera sighed. Nothing better to ask for. But here was Grandma tied to the home earth because of her gout. Grandpapa would have happily taken her along, but she had said, "No, I can only be a drag on you. Stay well and send me a card once in three months, so I may know that I still have wifehood's bliss. Come back whenever you wish to see us."

Meera was tethered to Grandma. Given the choice, would she really leave home? Had she not had Grandma alone in all her past years? Father, dying of snake-bite, left a widow with a child soon to be born; and before the child had learnt to sit up, the mother died of her broken heart. Grandma had reared the infant girl. Today Grandma was her all.

Grandpapa coming home. Grandma was like a young woman whose "fellow" was about to return after years of absence. Soon would she get busy preparing the rice-powder with which to paint auspicious symbols on the veranda floor: seven elephants and a lotus. Then she would tend to the hammock, cushioning it with a new strip of mattress.

48

The hammock hung from a rafter at the veranda's corner. Grand-papa had a fancy for hammock beds and his wife made much of it. No one was allowed to touch his hammock. Once, three years back, Meera had acted on a stupid impulse. Grandpapa had just departed; the hammock, used for a brief while, was vacant again. Meera climbed up in it and swung.

Grandma happened to come to the veranda and stood dumfounded, as if she could not believe what she saw. Then, "Meera!"

"Why not?"

Grandma spoke gently. "It is the only thing in this house he calls his own. Everything else he has given away to us."

"I am not eating this up."

"Meera, get down."

There was a rebel in her. Maybe it really meant that she was angry with Grandpapa who was gone so soon. Or maybe she was challenging her own strong feelings for him.

"No."

"Pay heed to my bidding." Grandma's face had a look both implor-ing and stern. "And do not sit in that hammock ever again."

The smack of her lips was her answer.

Grandma took three quick strides and slapped her, first on one cheek, then on the other.

She was stunned, more with surprise than hurt. Grandma beating her! She stared at the angry face and saw it crumple; the mouth began to work; tears glistened deep in the eyes; Grandma sank to the floor and began to cry quietly.

Amazement turning to shame, Meera left the hammock and dropped down beside Grandma, burying her remorseful face in the aged bosom. Taken by the ache of parting from a beloved one, they drew solace from each other in a silent communion.

That scene came back to her mind as she walked down the road. "Twenty-third day," she said to herself lest she forget.

A sudden cry of many boyish voices: "Vote!" From Schoolhouse Lane a score of youngsters came trooping down, books and slates slung to their shoulders. They had formed up in a line. "Vote for Sam-sundar-ji, vote!" they yelled.

They were mimicking the women's procession, thought Meera, amused. But—the slogan? When the boys drew near, she asked, "Children, what game is this?"

"Vote for Samsundar-ji, vote!" the stern chorus answered.

"Kishen," Meera addressed a tall boy, "you can tell me."

"At school today our Sir asked us to go shouting in this way at tiffin time."

"What for?"

"We have to go yelling like devils, 'Vote for Samsundar-ji, vote!' so that we can have a feast on Sunday."

"Big feast," a happy voice contributed. "Laddoo. Jilebi. Poori."

"Yes. We will eat like elephants."

Meera was surprised. "Who pays for the feast? Not your master-ji?"

"Samsundar-ji. He pays."

"Who is this Samsundar?" Her brows knit.

There was silence for a while and then a small boy chirped, "He is our Nago's father, don't you know?"

The Seth, of course. No one ever called him by his name. He was Seth-ji to everyone. Why had he turned prodigal? The vote—what was that?

"We are lion cubs," one youngster cried.

Lion cubs! Meera felt baffled. The explanation came. "We will have an earthen lion to carry before us. The potter is making the lion."

That was the idea. The Seth was the lion. These boys were his cubs. The Seth was playing a mysterious game.

The Halwai had just risen from a nap at the back of his counter and was stretching his long thin limbs, cracking his finger-joints, in readiness to open his shop and exhibit the brass platters filled to the brim with a variety of attractive wares. At sight of the girl he broke into a grin of welcome. "Meera Bai!" He turned to the platters. "Boondia? Or something sweet-sour?"

"No. I only—"

"Fried bread with bean curry on top?"

"I have some other business."

"O-ho!" with a grimace of expectation. But when she had told him what she had come for, he grunted, looked sad. His answer had a heavy ring.

"Almanac? Do I have to pry into the almanac for a date?"

"Then tell me."

"What makes you breathless? Is that the day of your betrothal? Your Old Mother has strange notions. Such a big girl, ungiven. Maybe she has changed her mind?" He swallowed, his adam's apple wobbling in his scraggy throat as he watched the girl's face and the grace of her shape contained in an old jacket that had become too tight. For a better view he removed the dark-blue glasses from his eyes and laid them on the counter.

Abashed by his hard stare, she looked down, murmuring, "Tell me."

His eyes stuck to her as wasps to a honeypot. "A teen-age maid forced to do a man's work on the furrows. Has that Grandma no sense left?"

She answered him hotly. "Grandma? Have you seen her work-worn hands? Even today, stiff with gout, she comes to the fields to help me when I need her."

"There is a fellow ready to help you—to raise more than cotton."

"What fellow?" she asked. "What help?"

Such innocence! Pleased, the Halwai went on, "A half-year has passed since the day when the mother of my two girls, Tuti and Kuti, quit her abode of clay."

She nodded to him with a becoming sympathy. Tuti-Kuti married and gone, the old man was lonely. Each daughter deigned to return to the parental home only for the delivery of her child and the old miser had to bear all expenses of the birth and the eighth-day ceremony.

"The sadness that our castes disagree, mine and thine." With sudden familiarity he had passed on to *thou*. "Otherwise, lass, I could take thee for my second spouse."

What! A marriage proposal—from Tuti-Kuti's old father! He was now leaning forward and his voice was almost a whisper. "Still there is a way. Money has heat! Money will buy even the milk of a tigress!"

Her shock eased off and her eyes began to shine with a merry light. It was hard not to burst into laughter.

"The Five Elders will overlook our caste difference if I pay a fine."

She broke into a giggle and he, taking this for her approval, joined his laughter to hers, *hen-hen-hen!*

Suddenly they stopped as if with one accord and their faces became grave.

"The barber will take the proposal to thine Grandma in due time," he assured her. "Now tell me, wife-to-be, what will you eat?"

A mischievous imp looked out of her eye. "A sweetshop spouse sits tight and eats, eats all day." Her face seemed to fill with joyous anticipation. "Laddoo! Sour curds! Salt nimkin! Wah!"

"Han?" the Halwai was somewhat confused by her zeal.

51

"No payments to make, no questions to answer."

His romantic mood could not stand such materialism.

"The mother of Tuti-Kuti was ever mindful of the good of her bread-giver. In a full twelvemonth, only on the night of Festive Lights would she put a laddoo into her mouth. Just one, by way of celebration."

"Maybe she ate a palmful of boondia on the sly," Meera suggested. "You may watch the big laddoos like a goatman keeping count of his flock, but the boondia is a heap of beads that you will not miss from the platter if cunningly pilfered." Then she grew troubled. How dared she malign the dead one who still resided in this house! The Halwai had omitted to perform the ritual that would release a spirit from earthly bonds and send it heavenward. He claimed to have acted according to her wish, for this house was dearer to her than heaven. People said, however, that his motive was simply to avoid the expense of the ritual.

His eyes clung to her, intent. "Thou art clever, wife-to-be! Easy to see whose belly delivered the trick: Naked shall we walk the street." And his eyes were hard and gloating as they stripped her naked.

"We won, did we not?"

"You will be paid back. No woman will see the picture play."

Her lower lip stuck out in scorn. "Do we care?"

"You do!"

"With Grandpapa coming back home?"

"What!"

"He, back home on Thursday."

The Halwai had to make sure. "The minstrel? Really? Which Thursday?"

"Twenty-third day. When is that?"

"Tomorrow."

"Tomorrow?" There was a glow in her face.

The Halwai was impressed by the news. "Three years have passed since his last home-coming, but his songs of devotion still live in our ears, as if we heard them yesterday. He, Atmaram—"

She felt overwhelmed. "Atmaram. You know?"

"Ask the wild parrots. Even they know the tale."

She knew the tale like everyone else, but hung on its recital.

"A thousand miles northward the minstrel went, as far as the railroad could take him, then started to walk. He climbed the Himalayan

52

peaks and higher and higher he went. At last there was the land of snow, all white as milk. As he plodded on toward Kailas, earth-abode of the great god Shiva, he heard a voice call, 'Ho, Atmaram.' A yogi was stepping down a slope, but where was Atmaram? The yogi drew close, a very old man, his beard reaching to his ankle. 'Atmaram, three score years I have waited for thee. Now follow me, dear son.' The minstrel, as if in a trance, fell in step with the stranger until they entered a cave. Something lay at the back, a pile of moldering clothes. 'Look, Atmaram.' He looked and the wonder happened." The recital came to a climax. "Yes, brother, the wonder happened."

Meera shared the tenseness of the moment. "The minstrel went back to his past life," she supplied quickly. "In that life he had been named Atmaram."

"Atmaram," the Halwai affirmed gravely.

"And then?" Meera demanded. She loved to hear every echo of her own inmost faith.

"Atmaram had lived in that cave as the yogi's disciple. Dying young he had been reborn in a village, our own Sonamitti. Nothing much happened in his life until he was sixty, an old peasant content with his lot. Then a strange restlessness took hold of him. It forced him to leave home in a minstrel's yellow garb. It led him to the Himalayas, as I have said. So here he was, back to his *guru*, still in mortal existence, though long past his hundredth year. The old peasant's training had to start over again. He had to reach the state of bliss when you leave your earth-body for a time as you sit in the lotus posture of meditation and move about in your spirit-body which is like a beam of light."

Her eyes opened wide. "He can do that? Grandpapa?"

The Halwai reflected for a minute. "Not yet," he decided. "One day he will win his guru's full favor. Then he will be a yogi himself."

"Yogis can do great miracles, so people say. Who knows what is true and what is fanciful talk?" Not that she doubted this Himalayan yogi—or Atmaram!

The Halwai said, "Remember this: When there is smoke, there must be fire; when there is blood, there must be a body."

Smoke, fire, blood, body—she tried to see through the riddle, but he hastened to make his meaning clear. "On the Himalayan top they have knowledge of great secrets. For a hundred thousand years the yogis have guarded the knowledge." His face was wistful. "If you can find out something of what the minstrel has seen and heard!"

She warmed to the man because of his belief in Grandpapa. In contrast, Grandma had said one day, "He goes to the cities and nowhere else. Mountain heights? He hates cold! The lore around his name? He built it up! Over seventy and still a barrel of mischief! He threw bits of a fable here and there; people picked them up and put them together the way he wanted. He must be choking with laughter, that minstrel fellow."

"Gran'ma!" Meera had been shocked by such irreverence. Sharp words had come to her tongue but she had only said, "You have no belief in him!"

"Belief, child? As if he is a deity!"

"So he is."

Grandma had smiled, her eyes tender. "He has all my belief. Yet maybe what I think of him is my fancy and he is a real yogi, after all, a dull old man chilled to the bones by mountain snow."

Smoke, fire, blood, body! "Maybe," she cried to the Halwai playfully, "maybe Grandpapa will do a miracle for you, he will turn your laddoo and jilebi into silver."

His eyes moved from the young beaming face to the platters of sweet and then back to the face. "Silver jilebi, nice hangings for thine ears. Laddoos on a string, a girdle to go round thine waist." He recaptured the naked figure now adorned with silver ornaments, then interrupting the pleasant vision he picked up a palm-leaf fan to keep a swarm of flies away from the trays.

"Shoo! Shoo!" he tried to swat the flies with his fan.

"Shoo!" She waved a hand to help him and he returned to her youthful form well outlined under the jacket. She read the meaning in his pointed look and her eyes bent to her rising breasts a quick instant; and abruptly she turned on her heels.

"Wait," his voice was hoarse; "eat a nice peanut cake." He would catch hold of her arm as she reached for the leaf plate. But she was walking along.

Miracles. She was frowning thoughtfully. The *bhajan* itself was a miracle! No picture play could compare with it, as the Seth would have to admit. Then, in a flash, an idea came upon her, a whisper of an idea, and she stopped.

"Eat," the Halwai begged again, hopefully.

She was walking back. Han!—He nodded grinning to the peanut cake. But she did not reach out for his leaf-cup. She said in a murmur, "He will sing to the village but some of the people will not hear him, that is the sadness."

"Why not? . . . Shoo! Greedy bellies, shoo!"

"That is the sadness." A tiny movement of her nostrils, a sure sign of inspiration.

"He will build a canvas hall?" A sly smirk in the face. "He will admit none but his friends!"

"No." Her nostrils gave the sure sign again, even more confidently.

"Then what? The minstrel will sing under the stars. Every one will come and sit on meadow grass and have a good rare treat."

"As rare as the picture play? As good?"

"As rare, as good," he affirmed. "We will have both the treats." He leaned forward to be closer to her breath and a drop of perspiration moving down the bony slope of his nose fell into a pile of sweetmeats.

"No, Old Uncle." She shook her head quietly. He winced and drew back. Old Uncle!

"You menfolk will have to make your choice, Old Uncle. This or that; not both."

"Why?"

"The picture play will come day after tomorrow. Will it not?"

So it would, he agreed.

"That is the bhajan night. The picture play will start soon after darkfall, will it not?"

So it would. He felt his mouth go dry.

"That is the bhajan hour. Soon after darkfall."

55

5

He was no taller than his granddaughter and lean, wiry, his broad face tapering off in the lime-washed mop of beard in the thick of which the mouth exposed its unfailing irony with quick soft laughter. His old man's eyes under the gray streaks of brows could deny the hand of time by an echo of their early sparkle. So it had been when he was home three years before and so it was today.

He entered the village in the twilight of early dawn, borne as though on a chariot of song, and he did not make for home but wandered around, turning out of Main Road to a lane here, an alley-way there, his voice beating on every housedoor. Meera, waking, felt for a moment she was asleep and in a dream. She breathed, "Gran'ma!"

"It is he."

She sprang out of bed. But Grandma restrained her with grave words.

"No. When he sings in the street, he belongs to the people. When he is under this roof, he is ours."

While they waited at the window, the singing voice drew closer and at last there he was with the Five Elders and many others paying eager homage.

"We have grown in age, minstrel-brother, we are deadwood in the current. You alone have defeated the current."

"*Maharaj*, great one, this time we will not let the chance go. We will follow you all the way to the great heights."

He asked in surprise, "Great heights?"

"The Himalayan summit where the gods and sages dwell. We will touch the yogi's feet and cry, 'Give us your blessings, Father.' "

"Yogi?"

Grandma nudged Meera with her elbow. "You see? What did I tell you? He made up the fable of Atmaram. He has forgotten what he said years back!"

Meera, all eyes as she gazed at him, could have said in answer, "He does not want his secret exposed." But before she could speak, Grandma called out through the window, "Why did you not choose some other hour to come home? Why do you have to wake up the village as if with the beat of a drum?" She was shielding the harassed man from his ardent admirers who now looked at the window and said, "Minstrel-brother, you hear that gay music? We must move off before things begin to be hurled at us thick and threefold."

"Come, Gran'ma," Meera pulled her by the arm to take her to the door. But Grandma stood rigid, like wood.

"What now?"

"Meera, maybe he has set up a home somewhere with a young hussy."

"Stop!"

Grandma seemed to become more and more troubled. "Maybe he will find out that we have thumb-marked his fields to the Seth."

"We could not help it. When he knows that we needed the loans badly, and not one pice for our own use—"

"Maybe he has become hardhearted. He will not see why poor people like us have to help other poor people."

Meera was getting angry. "To think you have lived fifty years with Grandpapa. You know him much less than I do, I who have not seen him for even fifty days."

His voice rang from the threshold. "Meera, *beta*!" He had always called her beta, son, not *beti*, daughter.

In an instant she was out of the room and beside the old man who was now alone. He peered at her closely.

"This is not our Meera. A young woman in the house—who is she?"

Meera hung her head, awkward, hating to be a young woman, hating the shape of her body.

"Yet the same fair face with its complexion of ripe maize, and eyes that the Devi in the temple could envy! Beta, open your mouth."

Her lips parted, startled.

"The same broken tooth."

Then she had to laugh. In her childhood she had fallen from a guava tree and broken a tooth slightly at the tip.

"Do you have to make a hymn to her beauty and turn her head?" Grandma stood at the doorway, her hands on her hips. "Is that why you have come back home after ten years?"

"Three years," Meera said.

"Ten or three, it is all the same. He has no thought, no feeling, for his kinfolk. He only wants to enjoy himself. What does he care if we die of snake-bite or a panther takes us? A man-eater came this way not long ago and the rag-woman's husband lies in his belly." Grandma paused for a bit but resumed before the minstrel had a chance to open his mouth. "Would he have cared," she dropped her voice but deepened the accent on each word, "if Meera had stayed in the Seth's well? Just two days—"

Meera cried angrily, "Stop, Gran'ma."

The minstrel looked at both. "The Seth's well?"

"Grandpapa, come and wash your feet, then take a look at Soondri. You remember Soondri? You saw her as a calf. Her mother—"

"Young Nago went toppling into that well. The Seth's only son. Flying a kite, eyes skyward and feet stepping back in a hurry, he stumbled over the broken parapet."

Meera said, "Yes. People came rushing and rescued the little boy. Now, Grandpapa—"

Grandma held her ground. "They call themselves Cowhouse Five, this young woman and the other ladies who meet in a cowshed. One of the five stood in a bucket and let it plunge into water, all the way to the bottom, others with waistcloths tight hanging on to the pulley-rope. Something could have happened to the bucket-borne beauty."

"Grandpapa, will you come with us or stand listening to this *khit-khit*?" She stiffened, seeing herself at the well's bottom, and drew her breath with a slight gasp.

"Who was the bucket-borne beauty?" The minstrel was gazing hard at Meera.

His wife nodded. "Ask that young woman. Ask our Meera Bai."

"Gran'ma would have done the same thing," Meera retorted. "Old as she is and gouty, she would have gone into the well to save the little boy." She whirled round with accusing eyes. "Yes or no? Gran'ma?"

Grandma was cornered.

"If only you had a bit of sense, Meera." The white bun on her head shook morosely. "A man is drooping with fatigue and needs rest and quiet and you feed him with wild talk. Be it so. Pray continue. I will milk the cow. I will light the kitchen fire. I will boil the tea leaves. Be it so." She spun round and was gone.

The minstrel's ringing laughter filled the house.

58

"Listen, Meera's Grandma—"

Meera did not follow him as he moved off. She stood still for a minute, smiling to herself. Poor Grandma. How she had gushed with talk simply to conceal her fluster. Let them be alone for a while and she would recover herself. In an hour or so the house would get crowded with people eager to see the small old man, one like many others in Sonamitti yet far apart. Owning nothing, he had the dignity of a king. He had more power than a king, for he could take the hearts of people in his fist, he could make them laugh and cry at his will.

Presently she sat on her heels, milking the cow, the frothy stream ringing against the pail. A curious thought came to her mind. She would ask Grandpapa a question: what is Gran'ma's name? No one seemed to know it! She was Meera's Grandma and that was all. She had once said with a laugh, "Why, Meera, Grandmas do not have any other name. Just Grandma." But there was a time when she was not a Grandma. She had a name then?

Bemused, she heard the sound of sniveling and as she looked up in alarm a spurt of milk missed the pail.

"Gran'ma!"

"Only three days," Grandma moaned.

"Three days?"

"No more. That is all we deserve. We mean nothing to him. Nothing."

Meera said, "He must sing to the village tomorrow, the same hour as the picture play.... Be quiet, Soondri. You know who is going to taste your milk. Pour out all you can."

"It is as I told you. He has a young hussy in town. Maybe she has borne him children."

"For shame, Gran'ma. Such wild fancy at your age! What young hussy would marry Grandpapa?"

Grandma bridled. "What is wrong with him, pray?"

"The young hussy will have to call him Grandpapa—he has no other name. As for children—" She hid her wrinkling face behind the udder of the cow.

Grandma felt reassured. "All the same, in three days he will be gone."

Meera sprang to her feet. "He knows nothing about the picture play. Hold the pail for a minute, Gran'ma."

The minstrel listened to her while he scrubbed his teeth with a *neem* twig that yielded its bitter juice.

"So you see why it has to be tomorrow."

"No, beta."

"You do not understand?"

"Meera," his voice was gentle, persuasive. "You cannot right one wrong with another. You cannot fight malice with malice."

She began in protest, "But, then, Grandpapa—"

"Listen, child. Let the Seth have his way. Let him deny the women and in his heart he will suffer. True victory will be yours."

She had not expected this. For a minute she was silent. Then: "With what pride I told everyone that the two events will take place in the same hour." Her eyelids began to flutter. "How everyone will laugh at me!"

"No, beta, no. People will admire you all the more. Those who mock at goodness mock themselves; for, there is a secret goodness in them also."

She implored, "Grandpapa, do not let me down."

But the old man could be stern. "Beta, do not let me be disappointed in you."

Those words stung. They had more power than arguments. She closed her eyes tightly to keep back tears.

There was to be no rest for the minstrel. Barely had he eaten four pieces of flat wheaten bread with some pickles—Grandma made the best pickles in the Seven Villages—when the house front, right up to the fig tree, became crowded with people. Grandma resented the intrusion. Those men would keep the minstrel engaged in talk for hours. It did not really matter, however, since she herself would have to be busy all that while in the kitchen, preparing several relishes. No young city hussy could beat her in that one art.

"He has let me down," Meera complained in a sore voice.

Grandma stared into space and her eyeballs were like black pebbles faded by long exposure to sun and rain.

"Look at it this way," she seemed to be speaking to herself. "He cannot let the people be split in two waves, one moving toward him, the other away from him toward the picture play."

"They are free to come to the bhajan—"

"He has to be above our petty battles. A song-maker must not live only for himself or his kith and kin. He has to carry a flame in his hand, passing it from age to age. Let him stumble and the flame will falter. Let him fail and there will be the chillness as of death."

Meera was astonished. Grandma had no belief in Atmaram, yet such faith in the minstrel!

So had all Sonamitti. Men were not content to sit with him under the fig tree, listening to his flow of talk. He would have to visit them, house by house. "Do not deny us, minstrel-brother. There is sanctity in the dust of your feet."

"I am a mere vagabond," he said, shaking his head. But he yielded to the people's insistence. After food he went on a round. It was well past sunset when he came back.

"One full day gone," sighed Grandma.

He said, "I will sing day after tomorrow. It has been fixed up."

Meera was surprised at herself—she was reconciled to defeat. It might not be defeat, though. She had, anyway, no right or power to draw him away from his set path. He belonged not to her, not to Grandma, but to all the people; or else he would not be a true minstrel. The Grandpapa was lost in the song-maker. Looking at him with worship in her eyes, she could almost see the flame held aloft in his hand, the flame handed to him from other song-makers, who reached far back through time, through the spaces of hundred-years, to a dim past when words were not written on paper or palm-leaf or tree bark, they had to be passed from mouth to mouth, memory to memory.

That night, however, he was theirs alone.

Three wanderers traveled a thousand miles, by train, bus, ox-cart and ferry-boat and often on foot, and they saw the monuments of old: great sculptured temples, images of Devas and Devis, ruined fortresses. They saw also the modern achievements: the fast-wheeled traffic in splendid cities, the festive illumination on towering structures, the glamour behind shop windows. They heard many strange tongues unlike their own and saw costumes of many kinds. They ate well one day and starved the next. They slept on string cots at Inns of Piety or on street pavements. Men and women befriended them but there were some who shouted at them with scorn. Each day was novel because it was uncertain. What fun would it bring, or what pain?

"You have denied me much too long," Grandma spoke at last and her tone was sharp. They were squatting on a reed mat, their backs against the earthen wall, faces shadowed in the light of burning bean-oil. Meera was doing up her hair for the night; the wooden comb in her hand came to a pause as she heard Grandma's complaint.

His answer was strange. "Sometimes I begin to think that I have more to get from the village than from all the world."

Grandma's retort was equally strange. "Are you tiring out? Are you getting old?"

Meera said, "Grandpapa, do not leave us."

But he seemed to contradict himself in the next breath; or was that his answer to Grandma? "The fair at Hathras has started. I shall miss it unless I rush off."

"Grandpapa, come back after the fair. Then we will be together for all time." Her voice was burdened with prayer.

"For all time?" He broke into a laugh. "Beta, you have to go to a home of your own. How long can you remain with us? It is time already that—"

"Time already that we sleep." She stopped him with a shrill yawn and stretched her legs and lay down, her arm under her head.

She slept fretfully and every time she woke she heard a low murmur of voices. Those two had so much to tell each other. "Will you not sleep, Grandpapa?" she said, trying to see him in the dark, and heard his clear, answering laugh.

CHAPTER

 6

Somewhere in the fig tree a woodpecker was busy, like a carpenter on his job. The minstrel stood listening to the steady beak-blows while he waited for the girl, and he smiled at sight of her, the new-washed hair enveloping her shoulders and throat and her face happy in the dawn twilight. "To the fields, beta," he nodded.

A skirting path led through a barren tract with limestone outcrops and ended at the edge of plowland. Then began the narrow, foot-high ridges between strips of cultivation, here cotton, there maize. Reaching the field where he had toiled for fifty years, he touched the sun-lustrous cotton plants with vein-corded hands and it was a caress. He walked at a slow pace between the thick rows, stopping, peering hard, and Meera prayed that he find thorn weed to pluck.

He straightened up, holding the tough plant, a deadly pest, and flicked earth off the white gnarled roots. He looked pleased. "One day I was as good a farmer as my granddaughter today," he said to her with a smile.

"Better," she assured him. "I missed that weed. So did Champa-Munni. Weed eating up the earth's richness—"

"Champa-Munni? Who is she?"

Meera laughed. "They are two, Grandpapa, two hefty peasant wives —you don't remember them? They come and help me whenever they have time."

"The wonderful Cowhouse ladies! What conspiracy do they hatch in the shed?"

She answered gravely, "Unity." Adding after a pause, "The Cowhouse want your advice. There are things that we do not understand—"

"What is this unity for?"

"It gives us strength to face the tyrant. We marched in a procession with scores of others, we marched to the clothshop—"

His voice sharpened. "The tyrant made indecent fun of you. Good reward for saving his son's life."

63

She felt hot in the face. He knew everything. That treacherous Gran'ma!

"You went to the well's bottom to save his boy, risking your life—" The alarmed admonition was mixed with proud approval.

Her lips smacked in denial. "It was easy."

"Easy?"

"A pulley-borne bucket under my feet. Five pairs of hands to pull me up."

The minstrel turned to see the girl's face. The child of yesterday was now a heroic figure. She had led the women of the village against the tyrant—an hour after she had rescued his son.

"Lakshmi made full recompense for her husband's lack of heart. It was she who brought us victory."

"It must have been hard for her," he cried. "Very hard."

"She is with us in part, away from us in part. She is two in one!"

"Poor Lakshmi. Better far to have been a peasant's wife. The man she has to live with—"

Meera saddened. "He will eject Old Father one day. So people say."

"Our neighbor next door? Gopinath?"

"Yes, Grandpapa."

"He told me nothing when I was in his house."

She nodded. "A man of pride," softly.

But several other peasants had spoken of the Seth in bitter anger, he recalled. A loan standing in the Seth's ledger doubled itself in a twelvemonth. When he paid out twenty rupees, the figure he entered in his book was forty—a year's interest charged in advance as soon as the loan was given. The debtor could whine or howl but had no option. If you dislike my terms, go elsewhere. Go to the big moneylender in town. Or else go to the Imperial Bank of India. That was how the Seth talked. So the debtor swallowed his saliva and put his thumb-mark on the bond and went his way. When he returned to the clothshop after harvest the money he paid lessened the balance but the remainder doubled itself with the new year's advance interest added. So it went on, year after year.

Gopinath's pride would not even let him complain against the Seth's tyranny. "He is close to his eightieth year," the minstrel resumed in a murmur. "Three generations under the same roof. Not a yard of land ever added to his holdings. How could he help falling under the Seth's power?" His eyes under the thick white brows narrowed.

"Now I remember. Gopinath's second grandson was about to say something to me when the old man cried snapping, 'Hush, boy!' And the boy, Roghuvir is his name, I think, gave me a peculiar look, a helpless and pleading look, before he moved away."

Meera felt her eyelids grow heavy with the tears behind them. Roghuvir, her childhood companion. Only three years older than she. Always quiet and reserved, in the past six months he had become altogether glum. Grandma had asked him one day, "Boy, why do I never hear you laugh? You are as owlish as an old man!" He had said in answer, "I feel as old as Old Father." Only with his childhood companion he could relax and be happy. Three days back, when he came to her field to give her a hand, he told her a joke and they laughed together. His thin face would crumple up like an infant's when he laughed!

The minstrel spoke stiffly. "What chance has he, Gopinath?"

She tried to clear the huskiness from her voice. "No one has a chance against the Seth." She saw his eyes turn to her in alarm and his apprehension was clear to read. But he must not know the truth. He must not know that the field he saw, black and yieldful, was not theirs any more; the Seth could attach it at his pleasure. It was the same with the other fields where maize grew. If Grandpapa knew, he would lose his peace of mind. He would never again wander with his heart easy.

Gazing around he swung his arm in a broad gesture. "This fruit-giving earth. Enough earth for all if shared fairly. So much belongs to so few. The same tale everywhere. One man owns half a village; the tillers have the rest in five hundred morsels."

"Grandpapa," she broke in tactfully, "look at that blue bird— there. To see the blue bird is to have a wish come true. Have you a prayer in your heart?" She had to draw him to safer ground lest he ask an awkward question.

He saw the tiny bird perched on a date-palm, a bright spot on the scaly bark. Watching, he broke into melody:

"Who painted thy wings, stranger, who gave thee sky-blue?
Who gave thee lily-blue?
Sky-blue! Lily-blue!"

His powerful voice was tender, as if coaxing the bird, begging for some response. Meera smiled with proud satisfaction—he was singing

65

only for her ears! Presently they were walking again. This was the time to explain her position, she thought. Grandpapa had accused her of malice.

"You see how the Seth has insulted us. You cannot hold us to blame if we want his picture play to fail. We have scores to settle and we are no forgiving saints!"

He spoke soothingly. What good was he against the mighty Seth, he asked. If it came to a choice, no one would give up the city attraction only to hear an old minstrel sing.

Her answer was firm. "You do not know yourself. A picture play cannot stand between you and the people. Take that from me, Grandpapa."

He chuckled. "Your Grandma raves about the show. She asked me, 'Have they picture plays in the Other World?' I said, 'How do I know? Wait until I get to the Other World, then I will send you a message.'"

"That Gran'ma!" Meera pulled a face. "All the good things in heaven are not enough, she must have picture plays also." Her voice grew amused. "Huh! She has no belief in Atmaram, that Gran'ma!"

"And you, beta?"

"Do you have to ask?"

The quiet intensity in her face worried him. He shook his head slightly and became thoughtful. Then he turned to the girl, beaming, as if an exciting idea had come to his mind. "Maybe you can have a defense—in Atmaram."

"Defense? What for?"

"Defense against the Seth. Against his power over you."

Her face turned pale. He knew about the land in the Seth's grasp! The people, maybe one of the Five Elders, had told him and the mischief was done. She watched him as he sank again in meditative silence. Not one more word he spoke until they were on Main Road. He woke up at the sound of voices: "Vote for Samsundar-ji, vote!" The schoolboys were marching again and they had their clay lion, tail poised aloft in a proud curve.

"Beta?"

She explained. The Seth was anxious to sit on a "board-moard." He would have to be chosen by the people. To impress the people and set up his claim he was making use of the schoolboys. He was the lion; they were his cubs.

"District board?"

66

"Yes, district board. We know nothing about this vote business."

"You have to know." A frown sank in his forehead. "Will you send the tyrant to the district board to speak and act for you?"

She asked, "What is this vote-mote?"

He explained. Since India was to be free, the wheels of life would run henceforth under the power of the people's vote. Wheels of many kinds, big and small. . . .

She nodded, crying, "I understand. No, no, the Seth cannot be our voice. Does he know our heart?"

They were now close to the fig tree. A man was seen standing on the veranda—it was the Seth himself. "We will not let him go to the board-moard, Grandpapa," Meera said in a whisper.

"You must not."

The Seth came forward with a greeting. "Ram-Ram, minstrel-brother!" He was the only person whose house the minstrel had not visited, but he had not taken offense, apparently. His sturdy arms held the frail old man in a friendly embrace. "What joy is this!" he gushed.

The minstrel said quietly, "Let all be well with you, Seth-ji." They sat down on a reed mat.

"You will not leave us again? You will bless us with your presence, for ever?"

"Two more days."

"Two days?" The relief in his face broke through the fake sadness. He turned to Meera saying, "Nago's mother has come with us. She is in the kitchen with your Grandma. Han, that Grandma!" He shook his head from side to side, in admiration. "What wonder? Our minstrel-brother's spouse!"

Meera would not move away. She squatted on the doorsill. The Seth had plainly come with a motive. Grandpapa would have to be protected from his wiles. When the man said, "Minstrel-brother, I have a favor to ask," she became doubly alert.

"Bid me, Seth-ji."

"Will you hold your session of song in my orange orchard? It is as good a place as any other."

"Why not?"

"When?"

He answered as if casually, "Tonight."

Startled, Meera stared at him. He had changed his mind. He was taking up the Seth's challenge. Bhajan against picture play. No, no, she wanted to cry out to him, you cannot let the people be divided, Grandpapa. And the fear was there: what if his friends, the Five Elders and others, went to the picture play? That would hurt him. No, no, Grandpapa.

How would the Seth take it? She watched him, unaware that he was ready to make a tactful retreat. Whatever the Seth lacked, it was not a sense of proportion. What he had to gain from the minstrel outweighed a petty revenge and much else.

"There will be a cinema show this evening, fit only for men's eyes. However, if you bid me—" An arch glance at the girl who would not take a hint and sat tight, listening. How reverse his proclaimed will? It had to be a grand gesture of appeasement which would leave his face untarred.

The minstrel said, "Do not worry. The hours will not clash. The song will follow later in the night. Some time after the cinema show. We have the whole night before us."

Meera felt relief. Grandpapa was following a middle course. A treat, tonight, for every man and woman in the village. But the Seth was astounded. What, the minstrel had let down his own kin! The womenfolk, daughters of vixen, boasted of their unity. There could be unity in the other camp, too! Meera's wicked design was foiled. The Seth could have gleefully slapped his thigh. He resumed his talk— this was the right moment to divulge the second purpose of his visit.

"Minstrel-brother, I have a deep urge of the spirit. It is, as it were, a live coal inside my heart. The urge to see the great yogi on the Himalayan peak and sit at his feet, seeking the light of wisdom."

"Indeed! Seth-ji will become a mendicant? He will walk with a begging-bowl?"

"Ho, minstrel, if only you knew! I care as little as you for worldly goods. People do not understand me. They do not see that I collect money for their benefit. It goes to them as loans without which the newborn will not hear the priestly chant, the marriage music will ring hollow, the dead will be denied the last ritual. Life itself will stop."

"The woe. The calamity."

"The demand for loans gets stronger every day. People are hungry for cash and more cash. How keep them supplied on my limited means—that is the problem."

"Seth-ji, yours is a dedicated life."

68

He nodded in happy acknowledgment and his manner became confidential. "All Sonamitti watches to see who gets a taveez."

The minstrel said, "Ji?"

The Seth explained. "Two of those you gave away when you were here the last time. Each has done good to its recipient. Will there be more lucky people? Hope whispers in every ear. . . ." He touched his own, as if absently.

Han! thought Meera. The Seth's greedy look was accounted for—he wanted an amulet. The minstrel, she noted, was watching the man, intent.

"You want a taveez for yourself?"

Excitement made the Seth stutter. "I? What am I that I may have such luck? The bloated son of a pig!" Then his voice begged, cringed. "All the same, maybe you think I am not unworthy—"

"It will be yours."

Amazed by his all-too-easy victory, he heard the minstrel add, "You will get it for a payment."

The contraction of one eye—his shrewdness was fully at work. He studied the grave, quiet, aged face and felt reassured. "For a payment," he nodded and it was half question, half pledge.

"In due time."

"Tell me at least this much," the Seth was all on edge. "How long?"

But the answer was brief, indecisive. "Not too long."

When the minstrel was alone, Meera stepped up, her face puzzled. "What is this riddle?"

"Maybe there will be protection for you, for the village, against the all-grabbing hand."

"What!"

"Maybe you can make the tyrant come to terms—for a while."

"Grandpapa," she cried, "my head reels!"

He laughed. "Beta, send Lakshmi to me." He was moving away toward the fig tree.

Wondering, Meera went to the kitchen. Lakshmi stood up. "Has the Seth left?"

"Yes. Grandpapa wants to see you." She turned to Grandma who was kneading millet flour for bread. "Han! Your stomach will not feel heavy any more, rid as it is of the tale."

"What tale, Meera?"

"My heroic deeds. Deeds for the whole world to know and admire."

69

Grandma's toothless mouth opened wide. "What ails you, girl?"

No need to parry with her. "Come, Lakshmi."

Grandpapa sat cross-legged under the fig tree, his face stooping, eyes intent on an object in his palm. A taveez—it must not be given to the Seth.

"Lakshmi!" the minstrel looked up.

She came to his side. He was absorbed in thought, his hand clutching his beard. Presently he spoke. "Lakshmi," he said, "what a sari you have given to your friend. To think that she will wear such fine apparel!"

"Grandpapa, do not make me feel awkward. Could I ever pay back a thousandth part of what I owe Meera? My son's life. Also my own life; if Nago had not been saved, I would have thrown myself into the well."

He nodded beaming toward Meera. "You hear? You have saved two lives, not one."

Lakshmi continued, "I have longed to see her wear an ornament. Once I tried to slip a bangle on to her arm. She snarled at me in anger."

Meera said, "A gold bangle, Grandpapa. How could I take that?"

"You could not take it from your sister?"

"No, not gold."

Grandpapa said, "Lakshmi, there is no gift as precious as your love. Ornaments? What is wrong with Meera's glass bangles? Or, the ring on her finger?"

Meera held up her hand. "This is copper, Grandpapa. With a gold wash it looks good enough. Hard to understand why people hanker for pure gold or at least silver."

"A dig at Lakshmi!" Grandpapa turned his glance to the bangles and rings she wore.

"No, no! Lakshmi-sister stands apart from everyone else."

A brief silence, and then Grandpapa spoke with a sudden switch to gravity.

"An old man whose voice has filled this country for thirty years has a curious wish in his heart. It is to wipe every tear from every eye."

Meera savored the words. "To wipe every tear from every eye," she repeated softly and her mouth curved with pleasure. "Who has such a wish?"

"The Father of the nation."

"Gandhi-ji."

70

The minstrel said, "Every one of us could wipe a few tears from eyes of misery, if we tried." His glance came to rest on Meera's face. "Do not be afraid," he went on. "Do not step back, whatever happens."

"No, Grandpapa." She had taken the loans, each one of them, with that purpose, had she not? And Grandpapa approved!

He rose slowly to his feet. Reaching out, he patted the girl on the shoulder. "That is it." He turned to Lakshmi. "Daughter, if you are going home, I will take a stroll with you."

"Come, Grandpapa."

Meera, happy beyond measure, stood motionless, watching the two figures cross to the road. Her thumb-marked bonds had lost their menace. Grandpapa approved!

CHAPTER

7

"A monkey fellow has come," Nago announced to the cowshed, peering through the door. "Up there in the tamarind tree, munching the sour fruit."

"Go, play with him," said his mother absently and caught herself up. "What! A monkey! Leave him alone."

Twilight lay lightly in the air but it was deep gloom for the Cow-house Five. This was the hour.

"The minstrel has let us down."

"He spoke well of us. 'Five faces of one crystal piece,' he said. And yet—"

"Why does he not take Grandma to the show? Even if one woman was admitted, the ban would be broken."

Meera was silent. How tell her angry friends that Grandpapa's wisdom was never to be doubted? And however much Grandma yearned for the picture play she would not care to see it without Meera.

"Why did we not set fire to the cloth hall at night? Then there would have been no picture play."

"The sun-soaked cloth would have burned brightly. Wah! What a spectacle!"

"If only our heads had worked in time. Now it is too late."

"Too late." The sighs were of regret and relief in equal measure. Who would have undertaken the task? Meera felt sure that the choice would have fallen on her. "Too late," and she clicked her tongue for emphasis.

"Hai!" breathed Lakshmi. "All my life I must bear the yoke of a monster." Having spoken the hard words she repented at once, lest harm befall her husband, and closed her eyes in a furtive prayer: Let all be well with him, Mother of Mercy, Parvati, spouse of Siva, healer of the hundred woes.

Nago was making faces at the monkey and coaxing him to do like-

72

wise. He feigned to hold food in his hand as a prize. "Just once, beta!" he pleaded. The animal sat heedless and stubborn, dangling its tail. Nago lost his temper and threw brickbats. The monkey rose languidly and climbed higher in the tree. "Hop off!" the boy shouted. "Monkey fellow who cannot pull faces!" And in the wake of a brickbat his outburst came, "Vote for Samsundar-ji, vote!"

"You hear that?" said Sohagi darkly.

Lakshmi sprang to her feet. "Nago!" she called aloud. As the boy came sauntering to the shed she snapped at him, "Do not let us hear that cry ever again."

"Vote for—" Nago began at once and Lakshmi, pouncing upon him, became incoherent. "Five more minutes in the well and you would have been dead, do you hear? Dead, and reborn as a mean thing, a frog."

"Frog?" Nago's interest was roused. "Why was I dragged out?" he complained.

"Idiot."

"A frog has plenty of fun." Full of challenge, he resumed the interrupted cry: "Vote for Samsundar-ji, vote!"

"Go," said his mother. "Keep away from my sight lest you get two tight slaps."

Meera had been silent, gazing intently at the tamarind tree. Following her eyes, Sohagi asked, "Will you also bid the monkey make faces?"

"I am thinking."

There was an instant hush. The women turned hopefully to watch Meera's expression. Let her nostrils twitch, they prayed and pledged the Devi under the banyan tree a platter of bright-yellow marigold.

Meera clapped her hands excitedly. "Done!"

"Tell us," her friends begged.

"It may not do any good. We can only take a chance."

"Tell us."

"Listen." While she spoke, she kept on looking at the monkey in the tree and all the others followed her glance. Finally, she ended with a shake of her head. "I have been carried away by a foolish fancy."

"Wait," said Sohagi, thoughtful in her turn.

"I can speak for the Seth," Lakshmi said. "One cloth piece has more value for him than ten picture plays. If only he is taken in by our word—"

Zeal grew and a crisis became a plan. Then came feverish activity. Lakshmi rushed into the house and returned with a jar of treacled rice and big bunches of bananas in a basket. "What waste!" sighed Champa and Lakshmi answered, "The monkey will deserve the feast in case the plan goes well."

"Now he must hurry and ask the women to come. All those who were with us in the procession on Monday."

"Do not forget to ask Grandpapa. He may wish to see the fun. Of course he cannot be told what we are going to do."

"What if we fail?"

"We lose nothing."

The canvas hall had been set up in a flat area of the meadow, about ten minutes' walk from Main Road. A motor truck stood at the rear, fitted with a dynamo to make current. Two hundred men filled the hall, sitting on the grass, row pressed on row, knee against knee. The Seth, wearing a splendid purple bathrobe and a half-smile of content, had a fat pillow at his back, his brass-bowled hookah bubbling to the pull of his mouth. Ahead the silver screen hung, a magic carpet, about to carry the expectant audience into enchantment.

As the screen lit up, a figure came out of the dark meadow and drew close to the canvas door where a peasant boy stood guard. He watched the figure and cried, "Meera Bai herself!" adding with gay mockery, "Go home, sister. Women will not be admitted."

"Who cares?"

"Then why hang around, sniffing? The picture play does not scent the air."

"What nincompoops! They squat like a bunch of Seths filling their bellies with fun while all they have at home gets pilfered."

"Mad talk. Go home, sister. Sleep off your bile."

"The homes the fun-crazy ones will return to. Piles of foodgrains scattered in the dust, clothes torn to pieces, lumps of cotton from mattresses cast about."

The peasant lad looked perplexed. "Robbers?"

"Monkeys!" Fear seemed to pinch her face. "Big, red-faced beasts!"

"No!" The lad grew anxious. "Where could they have come from? Hordes of red-faced beasts dropping from the sky!"

In a minute Meera was walking away. The dark night enveloped her.

"What goes on here?" The Seth peered out the door.

74

"Monkeys have invaded the village," the peasant lad cried in a voice of horror.

"What!"

"Hundreds of the red-faced animals. No maize or millet to be left for us to eat. Every cotton piece in twenty strips—"

"Fool! How will they get in, the hundreds of monkeys, even if they have come? Our doors are not kept open invitingly." His thoughts went to the bales of new cloth received that day, to replace those which had been lost. Some bundles had been sent to the shop, some lay stored in the house.

The young peasant rose to the drama of the moment.

"What do they care for bars? They climb to the roof. With claws and teeth they strip off straw. Thousand on thousand of red-faced fellows."

"Hai Ram!" the Seth wailed. His main house had a tiled roof, but the cloth was kept in an outbuilding with straw thatch. To lose that cloth on top of what was given away—that would mean the end of his business. Panic forced him to stride off at once in the dark, not waiting to light the kerosene lantern, the bathgown flapping, catching at his thick legs, and the parasol squeezed in his armpit. The peasant lad, noting his master's reaction, raised an excited yell, "Take heed, all. Monkeys have come, monkey folk. Ho-o-oh!" Men scrambled out asking, "What has happened?" Hearing the news they too wailed "Hai Ram!" and slipped off, rushing homeward. In two minutes the hall was empty except for a score or so of carefree men determined to enjoy the show. Then, like ghosts out of deep shadows, a hundred women in brand-new saris stepped up quietly, walking through the unguarded door, Grandma at their forefront.

Hoosiar Singh, the village constable, had kept away from the stream of people and made himself invisible. Men were shouting his name in the dark but he gave no answer. Sadly he shook his head to himself. What could he do against a whole troop of monkeys? It would have been a different tale if he were given a posse of constables to lead, muskets on their shoulders, heavy leather boots on their feet. He could then show his grit and win the coveted police medal. But in the present circumstance it would be wise to sneak back home. His son's mother would hold the fort against people who persisted in looking for him and demanding help. She would open the window a crack

75

and say, "The constable is out fighting the monkeys. What else do you expect?"

The Seth, speeding on his stocky legs, was also parted from the mass of people. As he found himself all alone in the pitch-dark meadow, a word ran icily through his blood. The *bhootni*! In his rush he had taken the pathway skirting a neem tree which the bhootni haunted. An owl screeched, adding to his dread. Four men in Sonamitti had seen the apparition, the female of the species, dangling skeleton legs from its roost. One of them, attacked by her, had gone mad and had to be treated by an *ojha,* an exorcist, brought from Bhimtek twenty miles away. Nothing could have induced the Seth to pass the haunted tree at night and yet here he was, a stone's throw from the danger spot. No use veering off the tree; on either side of the track the meadow was all puddles and potholes and he would sprain an ankle and then, all the more, he would be at the bhootni's mercy.

The owl screeched again in the pitch-black branches. . . . Would he turn round, rush back the way he had come? The bhootni was sure to follow him, her bony fingers reaching for his throat, or else she would make his body her abode.

He wanted to scream but his teeth chattered and he could only gurgle. His knees shook, his stomach quivered. What would happen to Nago if his father became ghost-possessed? Bulaki Rao would usurp the cloth business. And Lakshmi would scrap the ledgers and bonds, releasing every yard of the pledged land.

The stark injustice. Was it for such an end that he had built up his house of riches, brick by brick? A fierce cry tore at his throat. Be careful, Nago's mother, stupid, easy-going woman. Do not let our son lose his patrimony. Beware, Bulaki Rao, brother of a bug. When I am dead I will haunt you and sit on your chest while you sleep. I will drive you crazy. He felt his breath blow in labored gasps and his heart hammered against his ribs.

Surprise broke slowly through his anguish. Where was the neem tree? As the truth became clear, his body relaxed. In the grip of excitement he had been walking very fast and the haunted tree was left well behind.

A speck of light was twinkling ahead. That was the rag-woman's hut at the meadow's edge. He was safe! O-ho, it was hard to believe. But the bhootni might still be at his heels.

"Ram-Ram!" Men spoke the sacred name to greet each other and

76

to express several emotions, but used it also to hold evil spirits at bay. "Ram-Ram!" the Seth breathed as he sped on. The rag-woman's mangy dog started barking. For once the Seth loved that cry, though the mongrel was hurling abuse—he had hit it one day with a stone. "Daku! Tchu . . . Tchu!" he called, grateful for that impact of life on the eery atmosphere. "Daku! Tchu . . . Tchu!"

At last he was on Main Road and his fighting spirit was back. The bhootni had been foiled. Next, it was the monkeys' turn. In the elation of his escape he felt equal to them all. . . . Where was Nago's mother? Chill with fear, hiding herself in a room upstairs!

He saw the lone beast crouching near the front door, munching slowly, as if surfeited by a feast; the darkness enlarged its figure and gave it a menacing air. He stood still a moment, then rushed to the housedoor. It was shut, hung with a padlock. He hurried to the back door and that also was locked. Lakshmi could not be in the house.

The peasant lad had now appeared, carrying his master's lantern. "Hundreds and hundreds and all like that monkey fellow," he moaned, gazing at the animal. "Not one *pau* of maize or millet left for us to eat, as Meera Bai said—"

Meera Bai!

"What! She brought the news?" the Seth asked in a shout.

"None else. Hai, not one cotton piece left whole to cover our shame—"

The Seth was thoughtful for a minute, summing up what he had seen and heard. "Where are the hundreds?" he demanded of the lad still lost in lamentation, then whirled round and waved his parasol at the monkey. "Go," he yelled, "hop off." And he dashed forward.

The peasant lad, now emboldened, joined his voice gruffly to his master's. "Go, beast. Hop off." Then he was screaming with laughter. The Seth lay sprawled on his back—he had trodden a banana peel!

Five minutes later the Seth was walking back the way he had come. On Main Road a group of men who saw him cried, bewildered, "Where are they?"

"Here," Seth-ji answered with a sweep of his hand. "They are here. You and I and many others. Two hundred monkey fellows."

Why blame those fools? Had not he himself been as gullible as any offspring of ass?

All the deceived people were soon back in the meadow, walking fast. As they filed in through the canvas door, faces glum, the women

77

were laughing hilariously at the antics of a fat clown on the screen. The men slunk in quietly, like sheep. The women had their fun twice over; the picture play, now halfway through, started afresh for the men's sake.

When the lights were turned on and the people were ready to leave, there at the flap door stood the minstrel, a curious smile on his face. He seemed to have enjoyed the women's triumph. As Meera came out with Grandma, he said, "Beta, you are pleased with yourself?"

"Yes, Grandpapa."

He gave a big shout of laughter and instantly it found echoes, both from the women and the men, from the victor and the vanquished alike, so that anger was blown away and even the Seth regained some of his poise.

"Beta." The minstrel's voice had changed quickly for Meera and his face was grave. "I have a wonderful gift for you. It will bring you great power. In a world where gold has the last word—" He shoved his hand in a slit of his yellow robe while she waited in astonishment. Then he paused, hesitated. He changed his mind and the hand came back empty.

"No. Wait. The moment is not yet. Let *bhajan* be done."

"Yes, Grandpapa."


A late moon appeared in the sky and the hundred lanterns in the orchard were trimmed low. The men filled one arc of a half-circle and the women completed it. The minstrel was seated at the center, occupying an expensive rug which the Seth had brought out for the great occasion. Bare, rustic feet staining the gold-and-blue rug—that was a sight for the gods, and so was the thick garland of white blossoms which the Seth placed on the old peasant's neck. "Jai to the minstrel," the spontaneous cry came in unison from five hundred throats. Then the Seth, for some reason, lifted his voice in another cry, "Jai Atmaram!" and the people, not slow to catch the allusion, gave response, "Jai Atmaram!"

It was a marvel that the minstrel could compose poems of great length and remember each and every word. The first one he sang on this occasion was based on an episode from the ancient epic, *Ramayana*. The listeners were lost in an age-old enchantment, but they were active participants, too.

78

"The ten-headed Ravan, all iron and rock, had wickedness tenfold" —and the minstrel's voice was strengthened by a hundred others: "had wickedness tenfold."

> "And yet a little clay
> Beside the iron and rock
> A little softness as of clay..."

That was the central theme. The wicked king of demons stole Princess Sita from her exiled husband and bore her away in his winged chariot to his far domain. He held her imprisoned in a bower. But a streak of decency in his evil heart prevented the use of force. Mad for her, he craved only her willing love. He was as helpless and wretched as his fair captive. He guarded her honor from himself— until his doom.

"Sing, brethren. A little clay, ho, a little clay baffled the massive iron-rock!"

This, Meera felt, was meant especially for her ear. An elaboration of what Grandpapa had said to her before; there was a secret goodness even in a wicked demon—and even in Seth-ji! He was now singing with all the others....

The minstrel, after a pause, turned to another theme and then another. Finally, an hour after midnight, he rested for a bit and drank a bowl of water before he resumed with new energy.

"Listen, brethren, to the touchstone tale."

That tale out of another ancient epic, *Mahabharata*, was part of the country's legendary lore. But the minstrel gave it a new dramatic force. Jambuban, the cruel and greedy bear, king of all the bears, had acquired a touchstone, having killed its owner, and hung it on his neck, a crystal of power and pride. The demi-god Krishna, born on earth to punish sin, went to the bear kingdom and demanded the stone. A furious combat followed; the world had never before seen its like. The minstrel's voice throbbed with passion. One minute he was the Bear-king, fierce, grunting, fuming fire; the next minute he was Krishna, cool and poised and all tempered steel, or fate itself. At last the monster fell panting and lay on its back and whined for mercy. Krishna spared its life.

Sweat poured down the minstrel's face and his aged body sagged exhaustedly; but his long white beard touched by moonlight had an added silver sheen.

"Jai Atmaram!" There on the Himalayan peak the minstrel stood in glory for all to behold!

He called Meera's name. When she was by his side he rested his eyes on her for a minute, in silence, then cleared his throat and spoke.

"This is the moment I have waited for." Out of his *kurta* his hand emerged with an amulet! He took the girl's right arm and pushed back the jacket sleeve.

"A taveez, as you see, but not like any other of its kind." Slowly he tied the red string to her upper arm, then fell again into silence, the old man no taller than his granddaughter, and in the light of the lantern as she lifted it breast-high he seemed to be looking deep into her and beyond her.

"This taveez holds a stone. The stone has power. It is a touchstone."

She stared at him. Was he still afar, fighting the king of the bears?

"Wearing it on your person you will do an act of kindness. Real kindness. Then all copper on your body will turn to gold." No response from her, and he went on, a sudden sharpness in his tone, "Remember, all copper touching your body will become gold. Gold with which to do good—"

She dropped her eyes to the taveez, wanting to loosen the string drawn tight in the flesh. Then the idea came upon her to play up to the curious game, whatever it meant. "Let no thieves hear you, Grandpapa, or else the touchstone will go from my arm in no time!"

"Parted from your arm, the touchstone will be dead, a worthless pebble."

She watched the alien gravity in his face, the detached sternness, and behind it apparently no concealed laughter. He meant all that he had said!

"An act of real kindness—that is the key, remember."

"Yes, Grandpapa"—not knowing how else to answer him.

People who heard the minstrel were dumb awhile. Then the slow murmurs grew. A touchstone? No, brother, it cannot be, not in these sinful times. Such things are of the past. Created life is a cycle of four ages, each a period of a milliard years. First the illumined age of truth, then the sunset age, then the age of twilight and finally here is the age of darkness to end in life's total annihilation. To think of a miracle happening in these evil times!

There was Atmaram striding the Himalayan peak, striding out of an age that was gone. That image was no less real than the minstrel's.

The murmurs became edged with excitement. A touchstone, he said? Truly, brother? That was what he said? A touchstone!

"You understand?" the minstrel's voice was hard, compelling.

"Yes, Grandpapa."

The Seth, who had stepped forward so that he could catch every word, felt a lump of pain in his throat. The taveez pledged to him, as good as given—the bargain had been struck—there it was on Meera's arm. *You will get what you want, for a price.* He had been ready to pay. *In due time.* The time was gone! A taveez not like any other given before. What! A touchstone! Fantastic. Incredible.

Angry and puzzled, eyes glaring, he watched the minstrel walk through the shadowed grove and pass into a stream of moonlight.

CHAPTER

 8

A fortnight had to pass before the minstrel's amulet made any kind of impact. For, with his departure, the glitter of his promise seemed to fade. The Five Elders had come to him, anxious to know what the strange taveez meant, and though the Seth had kept away because of his hurt feelings, he had sent an emissary. The minstrel had answered them all with stubborn silence. Once he had taken Meera's arm and touched the amulet saying, "Maybe this will force the greedy man to make terms." Watching her perplexed look, he had smiled mysteriously, but had nothing more to say.

Grandma was down with gout and moaned faintly, lips parched and drawn. Meera, by her side, rubbed the knots of pain in the leg with a medicated oil. "If only we could get a jar of tiger fat," she said to herself yearningly.

"Tiger fat?"

She explained. There was this notice in the weekly paper the postman delivered at Lakshmi's house: "Tiger fat. Sure cure for rheumatic ailments. Result guaranteed or else money refunded. Post Box No. 2214, Bombay." She had taken down the words on the back of a used envelope.

"One jar—" Grandma seemed hopeful.

"Fifty rupees!" said Meera under her breath.

"Fifty?" Grandma's heart sank. No chance to get a fraction of it. Yesterday Meera went to the Seth for a loan of ten rupees to be given to the Old Father. The Seth paid the money but added grimly, "This is the last time."

"What can we do, Grandma?"

She tried to ease the girl's despair. "Wait, until the gold comes."

"What gold?"

"Wait until the touchstone has worked."

"Touchstone?"

The aged eyes prodded Meera's arm under the white jacket. "Where is your faith in Atmaram? He gave you a touchstone, did he not? It is supposed to work as soon as an act of kindness is done. Are you not capable of such an act?" Even in her pain Grandma could speak light-heartedly.

The enigma of the amulet. Meera sighed, her fingers dipping into the oil contained in a shallow earthen bowl. What else but a strange man's whim? Yet she wore it on her arm. Gran'ma laughed at her, knowing the depth of her trust in Grandpapa.

"You cannot be sure one way or the other," Grandma went on, mock-serious. "Maybe Atmaram is more than a fable. Who knows?"

As the women were busy rinsing clothes at the stream in the usual hour, Meera spoke impulsively about her great need of tiger fat. So unlike the proud girl who kept her private worries concealed. Then she tried to cover up her embarrassment in Grandma's manner. "Wait until the touchstone has worked!"

"Touchstone, Meera?" All eyes turned to the taveez—Meera's jacket sleeve was pulled back to her armpit.

Bimla said, smiling, "Let me get drowned in the stream, then Meera will have her chance for an act of kindness."

Sohagi looked thoughtful. "What if we sell the taveez to the Seth for a jar of tiger fat? He had gone to the minstrel begging for a taveez—"

There was a brief silence.

"Will he be taken in?"

"After his two good lessons he will be wary."

Lakshmi was there, washing clothes like any other peasant woman. She gave her support to Sohagi's idea. "The Seth is sore about the taveez," she confided. "It was as good as given to him, but it went to Meera instead. Why should he care unless the thing meant a great deal to him? Touchstone or no touchstone—"

This was Munni's chance to serve out legend. "The touchstone that Krishna snatched away from the Bear-king—" But Champa pulled her up: "Even a newborn calf has heard that story. Why waste your breath?"

"There was another touchstone," Munni persisted. "It so happened that—"

"Everyone knows everything about every touchstone in our ancient lore." A gesture of Champa's plump hand clinched the point. They must not be distracted from the main issue.

Sohagi said, "The Seth is a simple-hearted man. The Chamundi bridge—remember?"

"That bridge!" Munni started giggling and Champa pulled her up again. "Munni, you stupid. Must you make Lakshmi-sister feel bad?"

"I think he will gulp the bait," said Lakshmi. "Here is his chance of great gain, even if a gambling chance. Gold!"

A cloud of uncertainty came, but was dispelled in a minute. They needed tiger fat. The Seth was their only hope. He could not fail them.

Away from her friends, Lakshmi began to lose hope. Attuned to their zeal, she had underrated her husband. Evening fell, the Seth was back home, and by this time Lakshmi was in a sweat of desperation. She hovered, mute, watching him as he worked at his desk in lamplight. Her sad eyes rested on the pawned goods displayed on the desk top for the periodic check-up. There was the silver hairpin, the only silver ornament Meera had owned. You who saved my son's life. The little trinket would remain in the black steel box amongst a hundred other emblems of distress. Were the emblems to break into speech (Lakshmi had the odd fancy) so that story-tellers' voices came from the box, what tales they would make! There were, for instance, the tiny ankle bells of Rupa's baby girl. The baby had died, the mother was forced to pawn the bells for the funeral and no longer heard the sweet jingle which could make her live with her lost child.

At bedtime, finally, Lakshmi summoned up courage.

"Sonamitti is all agog about the touchstone," she made a direct assault.

The Seth had no ears for idle chatter.

"Meera's touchstone."

"Han?" he looked up casually.

"The minstrel should have given it to you. He almost made a pledge, did he not? The touchstone will bring no good to Meera. Her gold, her riches will tempt every robber in the Seven Villages and her life will be in danger." Gold, riches—those were words that made music in the Seth's ear, she knew.

"Touchstone?" His brows shot up in apparent surprise.

"The taveez on Meera's arm. Tied with a red string and holding a touchstone. It will not be long before—"

His grunt stopped her. "Women!" But she saw the contraction of his eye and took heart.

"Meera could be coaxed into a deal. She needs tiger fat. Fifty rupees per jar. Her only chance is to pawn her taveez, so to say. It has to be on her arm, but she will sign a bond. Whatever riches come—"

"Touchstone!" His voice was scornful. "What next? Lakshmi, do not let your wily friend make an ass of you again—she has done that twice. Now run along and put Nago to bed. I have work in hand and no time for gossip." His quill pen, poised on the ledger, ticked off an item he had just checked. Three nose-rings. Correct.

"Let the gold come and it will be too late for you," Lakshmi cried warningly but there was no response from her husband. She waited for a minute more, with dwindling hope, then turned away with a sigh.

The night grew, the Seth worked on. But his thoughts strayed from the book, his eyes went far beyond the columns of figures. There he was, Atmaram, striding the cliff-side. There, also, was the Master, a hundred years old and ageless. "Sing, Atmaram, son." Wild animals padded close to hear the voice of incantation. Ahead was the slope dipping down to the Holy Lake, the vast blue expanse of water on top of the world. Beyond it rose the steep mass of Mount Kailas, where the god Siva dwelt. No feet, human or animal (apart from the hoofs of the god's mount, the Bull) had trodden this snowclad region. "Sing, Atmaram, so the god may hear you. Sing until the skies tremble."

A pair of anklets, two tiny bells in one and five in the other missing. Correct.

Atmaram sang in his minstrel's voice and the feeling he roused made the air warm so that the hard white crust of ice began to melt. He sang, heedless of the threatening deluge, his voice growing in power, until the Master with a gesture of command made him stop. And smilingly gravely, the Master held out a pebble, a tiny black one, the size of a pea.

Seventeen toe-ornaments of silver. Correct.

"Atmaram, you and I have no use for a touchstone. When you go back to the land of sacred rivers, give this plaything to anyone you like. Deluded people have a hankering for gold."

You will get what you want—for a price. Even when Atmaram gave this pledge, he had the touchstone in his *kurta*. It will be yours—in due time.

For a price. A price paid to the girl—that could have been his meaning!

One waist-chain of medium girth. Correct.

85

A jar of tiger fat. That much for a touchstone!

What! You have forgotten Chamundi bridge? The price you had to pay?

The bridge was earthen in those days and the rain-fed stream wrenched it away every year so that it had to be rebuilt. Five years back, after it had been rebuilt as usual, word spread that the new earth of the bridge had a magical power to cure serious ailments. The Seth listened and acted with great speed. He went rushing in a bus to Chamundi village, fifty miles away, met the authorities and offered them a stone bridge. A memorial for his dead mother, he told them, lest he draw suspicion. A deed was signed and the old bridge became the Seth's own. Meanwhile, word spread on and people cried, "A gift from heaven!" Those who lived farthest from Chamundi were the first to react. They came flocking to the scene, scratched at the bridge and took the earth in handfuls. Then greed grew and the handfuls of earth began to be sackloads. Soon there were hundreds of men and women jostling for a share. The Seth woke to the peril when it was too late. How hold back a tide? His men were swept aside. Determined hands tore at the bridge, day after day, until nothing of it was left.

That was the end of the red cardboard boxes, to be printed with the inscription *Magic Chamundi Earth* and a slip of paper in each box listing the ten virtues of that earth and prescribing a brief ritual to go with the treatment.

The story did not end there. The Seth, tied to the deed he had signed, was compelled to build the stone bridge. It cost him a pile of money. He added one more blunder to the others. While he should have kept his lips sealed, he bewailed his misfortune. He fell ill and raved about his evil destiny. Everyone came to know what had happened. That was five years back. The story was revived off and on and the village laughed.

An infant reaches out toward fire and, burnt, never repeats the gesture. But the wise Seth of Sonamitti let his fingers be burnt a second time. Three years had passed after the bridge episode when the news flashed in the press that a village lad in Orissa State had acquired a miraculous healing power. The Seth once more flung himself into action. He traveled to the Orissa village, two hundred miles away, and took the peasant lad under his wing. He worked out a scheme. People would soon come flocking to that village and they would ask to be housed and fed. Seth-ji set up scores of tents and five cookshops. He did it almost overnight, no mean feat. He made the news of healing run fast and far. The press carried excited reports. The cavalcade began, as expected. The tents filled up, the kitchens made good business. Then, as luck would have it, cholera broke out at the end of the second week. Hundreds of people died. The cavalcade reversed itself. The tents stood empty. Food lay rotting in the kitchens.

He placed his hand on the desk top and surveyed his fingers reminiscently as if he looked for scars.

"Atmaram, son, give this plaything to anyone you like."

Nothing to lose but the price of tiger fat. Nothing to lose—not face?

If only one could be reasonably sure. One would then buy a live tiger and tie it up at the old woman's door; let her draw from the beast all the fat she needed!

"Atmaram, son, deluded people have a hankering for gold."

Touchstone? What next? A flying carpet. An ointment to turn you invisible. A *dano*, spirit-being, toiling in your service like a bond-slave....

Fifty rupees for a jar. Here is the money, Lakshmi. Give it to your friend and ask her to sign this agreement....

Burn your fingers again, the old sores still unhealed. Burn your wretched nose.

Miracles had happened in the past. That could not be denied.

What if the old misery is repeated?

There can be no gain without risk. To be a man of business and yet to fear risk! Then let the touchstone go to a more daring pig. The Halwai will not sit tight, scratching his arse. That son of a wasp . . .

The ledgers lay neglected on the desk. The quill pen stayed balanced on the ear. Seth-ji twisted his mustache fretfully in his agony of indecision.

9

Later in the evening, when it was nearly bedtime, the Seth took the quill pen off his ear and wiped its point dry with a piece of rag. He snapped the ledger shut, trimmed down the lantern's wick and shouted for his wife, "Ho, Lakshmi." When she appeared at the door, he hunched over the desk and spoke without looking up.

"Go to the temple at dawn and offer five quarter-rupees' worth of *puja*. Just before sunrise—that is the right hour."

"Five annas' worth?" she corrected his apparent slip of tongue. That was the set figure. He made it a point to win the Devi's good will before launching on a new business deal. But more than five annas on that count was unthinkable.

"Five quarter-rupees," he affirmed. "This is a special occasion. To-morrow I will get my *phut-phutti*."

She nodded happily. At last he would permit himself a luxury. A motorcycle! But he hastened to add, as if his act of extravagance had to be explained, "It is cheap. Second-hand. I have got it repainted, a brick-red color."

"*Parnam* to the goddess that you will not travel by bus any more. The terrible accident a month back. The bus to Bhimtek loaded with passengers went toppling into a river."

His face showed a self-satisfied grin. All Sonamitti, every ass and owl and monkey, would have something to talk about when they saw the dart of red lightning on Main Road. Then they would know whom to vote for!

"It is not for business trips only that the phut-phutti is needed." He seemed to be in a communicative mood. "A district board member has his touring duty. After the election, about three months hence—"

"I know," she said in a peculiar tone. Other words came to her tongue, but remained unspoken.

He was amazed. "You know? It is no business of yours to know these things."

"Why not?"

"Women! Hai Ram! You may as well ask to be members of the board itself!"

"Why not?"

She could not tell him that the Cowhouse Five had been worried about the election since the minstrel had explained the issues involved.

"Women!" He snapped his fingers in disdain. "Long hair, short wits, the saying goes. Twice have you bitten into nuts not meant for your teeth. This time, beware!" He took a lungful of breath to make his chest bulge. "Here is something big. So the puja must be five quarter-rupees. Make sure that the marigold blossoms you give are the only ones to be hung on the divine neck the whole day. Pay the Brahmin *pujari* an extra four-anna as recompense; it will not be money wasted."

She mumbled a half-answer and left the room, the Seth watching her and nodding to himself. Poor Lakshmi! Prompted by her friends, the wily vixen, she had set a trap for him. Touchstone! He had almost let himself be caught. Touchstone, indeed!

Meera's Grandma was behind it all. It was her brain that had hatched every evil. In the past four-five years she had put her thumb-mark on bond after bond, as if it meant nothing to her. Meera, too, was unconcerned and once she had said, "Gran'ma can write—why not let her sign the paper?" As though, in the thousand years gone by, each and every peasant had not thumb-marked a bond. A Grandma who could write. A knowledge of the letters did not make a woman more sensible. Or else this Grandma would have seen the red scorpion lengthening under her name on the ledger page!

Early the next day, he set out to catch the first bus passing westward on the highroad. Near the bus stop a tree uprooted by storm lay conveniently sprawled at the roadside, leafless and turning into firewood. As he composed himself on the thick trunk, legs tucked up, something caught his eye. Across the tall dried-up grass at his feet a patch of spider net lay tossed like a dark-gray rag of the finest silk. Nets, each about a cubit square, lay spread over a wide area in some sort of pattern.

He left his perch and took a leisurely stroll, eyes prowling for a sight of the spider. But it was as he had thought. A creature commanding such a network of business would not be open to vulgar inspection! Invisible in its sanctum, it would watch all and bide its time. There—a large red ant sauntered into a patch of net. Would it stop?

Could a mere strip of carpet hold up a proud red ant? The Seth watched and saw it press ahead. The net caught at its feet. The stubborn ant dragged on. Two or three inches away it became flurried. Torn strands of netting clung to its body like soot.

"Now!" the Seth's eyes narrowed to white slits.

The ant paused. With energy renewed, with violence, it struck off to a new path. More soot covered its body. It was a moving blob of soot.

"Red ant!" the Seth growled his encouragement.

The ant became quiet. It could not move this way or that. There was nothing for it but to wait for the spider. The Seth picked up a twig to help it out, but changed his mind. Why deny the hard-working spider its well-earned meal? Here was an instance of the way nature worked its ruthless principle. The slow-witted were meant to be the prey of their betters. The weak had to feed the strong with their flesh. The fittest alone were fit to survive.

He lighted a match, tossed it down to a patch of net and saw it shrivel. He struck a second match. As he was ready with one more he heard the approaching rattle of the bus. "Your house of business is now safe from my attack," he told the invisible spider. "Carry on. Trap the fools. Fatten on their meat."

There was destructive work for him to do—on a different plane. To set a match-flame on other well-laid nets, those of his business rivals. Here, also, nature's stern principle was involved. None but the fittest. . . . Then, the election ahead—that might require several match-flames! Who could say that there would be no other contestant? The Halwai was a sly jackal. The Five Elders with gray mustaches were all sly jackals. And the five hundred brothers of crows who had taken loan after loan with beak wide open—what if they repaid their benefactor with votes cast for his rival?

The bus drew up and a voice hailed brightly from an open window, "Ram-Ram, Seth-ji!" It was Bajoria, a tradesman who had several toddy shops in the countryside. Toddy was not sold in Sonamitti but there was a booth in Pipli just across the meadow. The licensed trade was under rules and regulations and a district board member could make no end of trouble! The Seth knew each and every possibility. He could make the viper, Bajoria, wriggle under his thumb. Was there any good reason why the viper should not share his spoils with a brother and friend?

"Sit here by my side," Bajoria, having read the Seth's thoughts, cooed ingratiatingly. He made room at the middle of the three-seated wooden bench which he and a second passenger occupied. "Brother, what luck that I share this trip with you."

The Seth spread out the commanding bulk of his thighs so that they squeezed Bajoria at his left and the scraggy peasant at his right. Having made himself cozy he invoked the lord of creation, "Jai Narayan," and withdrew into himself.

"Strange talk flies from your village." Bajoria came to the point after a minute's calculated pause.

"Tails must wag and tongues chatter," the Seth answered with a shrug but his curiosity was roused. "What talk?" he demanded.

"Taveez."

The Seth withdrew again. He had nothing to say. A creature of deep water! Bajoria would not give up, though.

"Touchstone."

The Seth grunted, as if amused. "What! You do not believe in fairy-tales?"

"You, Seth-ji?"

Many ears were astrain to catch his answer, the Seth knew. People were perplexed about the "miracle" and his noncommittal attitude toward it. With cool contempt he could destroy the great promise which, in his mind, he had already rejected. But the quick thought came upon him that here was a chance to let Meera fall into disgrace. Let her be the center of great expectations which were sure to be unfulfilled, and then the scorn of the deceived people!

So the Seth abruptly reversed his position. "Who am I to say this or that? The talk goes that Atmaram knew a yogi on some Himalayan peak, a holy man of great power. Why, brother, even common people perform miracles, these days. Electric current—is that not a miracle? Mere workmen produce it. What wonder, then, that a yogi on the snow-draped heights—"

"One is science," Bajoria pointed out; "the other is belief."

"Belief is the mother of science," the Seth answered. "Belief in things unbelievable. Fifty years before, when a man of science declared that he would fly in the air, the world laughed at him. Now tell me: Is the touchstone more of a miracle than the airplane? In the reckoning, say, of villagers who have seen neither?" and having made his point he dropped into silence and Bajoria could not revive the talk. All the same, the Seth was apparently in a happy mood, for the pressure of his thighs on either side became stronger; the thin peasant cornered against the wood wall felt his legs go to sleep, while Bajoria was forced to resist lest he topple off the seat's edge.

A month-old baby had been crying intermittently in the lap of its young mother. She tried to soothe it with a lullaby, but the little one kept up its yell.

"Conductor-ji," called an old woman who sat beside the girl, "will you stop the bus for a minute so that my third son's wife can get down to the fields and feed her child at her breast?"

"Ma-ji!" The young mother threw a bashful glance of protest.

"Old Mother," said the conductor, "we are close to the teashop. There will be a break of journey for a half-hour."

"Will you not stop even if we have to attend a call of nature?" An old man cried thickly. "Have we paid for our trip or not?"

"We are a mile or two from the teashop. Let the call of nature wait for a few minutes."

"Will they give us *cha*? Is it included in the heavy bus fare?" the old man asked hopefully.

"Aged father, do not be content with *cha*." The conductor's face was merry. "Ask for hot fried bread with curried cauliflower."

"Huh?" The old man gaped. "Is that the truth?" he said, eager to believe. The conductor's talk made him feel hungry.

The bus slowed, turned to a clearing at the roadside and stopped in front of a shack with a sign: *H. Singh's Paradise.*

"A half cup of tea?" the Seth offered generously but Bajoria shook his head saying, "No, friend, let me pay." Half cup! You saved two copper bits. No wonder that the Seth of Sonamitti had earned his unique reputation: speak his name in the kitchen, and the rice pot on the oven would crack into halves, your midday meal would be lost!

"What will you have with your tea? Let us get into H. Singh's Paradise and see what it can give us."

So a good half-hour followed, the Seth enjoying himself at the viper's expense. When they got back into the bus it appeared that the lean peasant had moved to another seat. The happy Seth now let his head drop to the viper's well-padded shoulder and fell asleep.

Asleep, he caught the swish of pouring water and there in the Paradise a life-size idol stood on a table, people scrambling up on iron chairs to reach the idol's head with bowls in their hands. But it was not water poured in devotion, it was tea! Under the streams of hot tea the idol began to melt—not wood, not brass, it was only clay! A big clay goddess, the painted face now bloated, shapeless in the evening twilight. As the tea flowed on, H. Singh dropped to his knees, his long black beard brushing the idol's lumpy feet, and he let the tea collect in a bucket so it could be sold again to his clients.... All at once the scores of hands deadened. Eyes bulged in shocked surprise. H. Singh looked up and began to gasp and groan. The idol was shapely again and ashine, metallic! A covering of clay had been washed off and the inner body lay exposed. It was gold! Brother, it was an image of gold!

"Gold goddess!" The prayer of many voices came in unison. "Gold goddess!" That strange cry broke the Seth's peaceful sleep. He lifted his head in surprise and Bajoria, rubbing a stiff shoulder, smiled wryly. "Feel happy, friend?"

All through that day, as the Seth stooped over his desk at Gay Peacock House, checking up accounts, the dream occupied his mind. Did it have a meaning? Could it be that the image he saw was an emblem of his hidden belief which he would not admit even to himself?

Late in the afternoon he went to the automobile dealer further down the street. The phut-phutti shone with red paint, handsome and proud. The Seth climbed into the side-car for a trial run. "Go three times along Srinivas Street, the whole length," he instructed the driver, a tall young man in khaki dress.

"Three times, Seth-ji?"

"Three times. Up and down. Slow, fast, then very fast. That is the way."

When the drive was completed, he went to another busy street lined with shops and teahouses.

"Repeat," he said. "Up and down, the same way. Three times. Slow, fast, very fast."

Then it was the turn of five other crowded streets. At last he was satisfied. All his business friends (enemies for that matter; smiling masks hid daggers) must have seen him drive by and how they must have smarted!

He turned to the driver with a look of survey. "Your name—and alias, if any."

"Name, Sohanlal. Alias, none."

"Age? Married or single? Any family to support? Ever got sacked from a job?"

"Twenty-three. Single. None. Never."

The motor dealer handed him a paper to sign. "Buying it for a friend?"

"It is for my sole and exclusive use."

"Your driving license is in order?"

The Seth's face turned livid. "What! You bid me drive the phut-phutti?"

"Well, then?" The dealer was taken aback.

The Seth cried, "What is that brother of a hawk for?"

"What hawk?"

"I will buy the machine on one condition." The voice was stern. "Your driver fellow will work for me. Same pay. Free food and lodging. Is that fair enough?"

"Sohanlal? He will drive the motorcycle! And you?"

"The side-car—what is it for? It cost me so much extra money."

The dealer turned aside, fighting with his face, and leaning forward over his desk he fussed over some files.

"Is it settled?" the Seth demanded. "Or shall I walk out?"

"Settled," said the dealer, "provided that Sohanlal agrees." He paused for a bit, then added, "You see, he was in Military Transport for five years, he sat at the wheel of huge trucks. And here is such a different proposition!"

CHAPTER

# 10

"Times are bad," the postman said. "You stop at the Paradise with your mail bag and ask for a half-cup of cha to freshen your spirits and H. Singh puts up a fat paw demanding an anna. "I have a letter for you, H. Singh-ji," I tell him pointedly but he shakes his beard and puts up both his paws, one for the letter, one for the price of tea. That is how the wind blows." The postman turned his glance to the Halwai and under the shadow of his turban his eyes had a stern glint.

The Halwai, behind the counter, caught the meaning. "Do not pay for the whey," he mumbled in a sad voice. "It is good thick one-anna whey, is it not?"

"A little more sweetened it would have tasted well." The postman lifted his bowl to his lips with qualified approval, then turning to his audience of several customers he picked up the thread of his interrupted talk.

"H. Singh holds out both his paws and in disgust I drop an anna onto the table. 'The letter?' he says, one paw down, one still extended, and I tell him gruffly, 'Wait. There is no time limit for a letter's delivery. Wait.' In my own time I open the mail bag. 'Three annas to pay—' I reach out a paw in my turn and the grin goes from H. Singh's face. The envelope bears no postage; it is collect, which means the postage is doubled."

"Good businessmen should be like dear brothers ever willing to press each other's feet," the Halwai said. "H. Singh acted stupidly. The bird he drew out of your purse cost him two of his own. Why did he not make a deal?"

"What deal?" The customers craned their necks with interest.

The Halwai winked at the postman. "It is so simple. H. Singh could have borrowed the letter for five minutes, gone to an inner room. He could have opened the envelope with the flap moistened, read the message, sealed back the cover and returned it to our postman-brother with refusal to pay collect fee."

95

The men were impressed. They watched the postman hopefully. Would he do them a like favor when the occasion came? The letters they received or mailed were always collect—that made the delivery certain.

The Halwai winked again. "Do not be in a hurry to open your bag, brother. Take your time. How do you like your new circuit, the Seven Villages?" The ooze of brotherhood lay on his face as sticky sweat.

"One village is like another." The postman shrugged. He kicked at the mail bag lying on the floor. "Who is this new fellow, Sohanlal? Staying with the Seth. A visitor, I reckon."

"No, he is the Seth's hired hand driving the phut-phutti. Ten, twelve days he has been here. Why?"

"Two newspaper packets to deliver at the same place, one for the Seth, one for Sohanlal."

The Halwai snorted. "Strange! If this fellow must read a newspaper, he can surely borrow his master's copy."

The postman waved a disparaging hand. "Choh! The Seth's paper comes from our district town; that is not good enough for this Mister Sohanlal. He has to get a paper from Delhi, seven hundred miles away. I looked at the postmark."

"Think of the postage," said one listener. "A paper coming all that way."

The postman laughed. "The rate is the same for mail going from anywhere to anywhere in India. Seven miles or seven hundred, no matter."

The three men looked doubtful. "Letters do not fly on wings. They have to be carried in bags all the way by railroad or bus or both. Then how can the rate be the same for one and all?"

"We may hear next that it costs no more to travel to far-off Delhi than to our district town."

Such goats, the postman thought, wiping his whey-stained mouth with the back of his hand. He stooped over his bag, picked out an envelope. "Halwai-ji!"

The Halwai grabbed the envelope and the glow of brotherhood left his face instantly. The envelope carried postage stamps, one blue, one green. His bowl of whey given free was wasted.

The postman suppressed a grin, stretched his limbs and hitched himself to his feet. "Just that paper for the Seth's man. All else in the

96

bag goes across the meadow. Nine letters for Pipli. So many in one day; is there a wedding, or a child's name-giving ceremony?"

"Who knows?" The Halwai had been quick to swallow his pique. "In Sonamitti, however—"

"Yes?"

"A wedding! Your bag will bulge like a pregnant belly."

Eager voices cried, "Who will marry whom, Halwai-ji? We have heard no word about a wedding to come."

The Halwai in silence fixed his gaze far into the meadow, but in the sudden wobbling of his adam's apple the postman seemed to read a wordless answer. "It must be your cookfire, then; unlit much too long by a woman's hand."

"Who knows?" the Halwai spoke evasively but his adam's apple moved again as if in prompt affirmation.

The postman was amused. "Truly! The messages of greeting in my bag will be collect, for sure. Maybe you will then want to make a deal, my friend."

"Who knows?" The imperturbable man had nothing more to add.

When the postman had delivered the mail at the clothshop and left, the Seth summoned his hired hand and addressed him with a lofty air. "You do not have to buy a paper with your hard-earned money. You can borrow mine when it is a week old."

"This is not the same paper as yours, Seth-ji."

"No matter."

Sohanlal smiled. "Seth-ji," he said, "tastes vary."

Eyes screwed up, the Seth took stock of the tall erect figure with its military bearing. "I understand," he nodded. "It is the kind of paper with photos of naked foreign beauties."

"No, Seth-ji. This paper, called *New Vision*—"

"You do not have to explain. I understand, I am not blaming you. All I ask is this. When you drive the machine, keep your eyes free from foreign beauties. For I do value my life and limb."

"This paper—"

The Seth turned to his ledger. "Now, go to Kanhan with four bundles of cloth. That is all your work today."

"Ji."

Bulaki Rao helped him load the side-car. "Let me take just one look at the foreign beauties in your paper," he begged. "Are they bare only in this part," his hands made a demonstration, "or—or—"

97

"For shame, Bulaki Rao. Man with a wife and five children!"

"Friend, just one brief look—"

Sohanlal, without answer, started the engine, waved the sheets of paper on the expectant face and sped off in a cloud of dust. In a minute he was on the highroad. He enjoyed the solo rides on errands to the Seth's chain of clothshops around the countryside. Not so when the Seth, glum cargo, occupied the side-car. Eyes on the instrument panel, he would say in a slow heavy croak, "Twenty-five. That is fast enough. That is the limit, for two good reasons. One, I travel in safety. Two, I get the best value from the petrol. Never pass that limit. I gain nothing if I save ten minutes or fifteen, I only risk my life and limb and make a needless dip into my purse."

Such contradictions in him, Sohanlal thought. Absorbed in making money which he did not want to use. He lived almost like a peasant, yet he had bought a motorcycle. He was barefooted at home and wore a shabby pair of slippers when out on the street, but he had to exhibit a colorful bathrobe to prop up his prestige!

Sohanlal had jumped at the Seth's offer even though he would have to drive a motorcycle with its owner in the side-car. His Army friends would have a good laugh if they saw him today. What a change from the trucks loaded with troops or ammunition!

His mind went back to the past. The sandswept roads in the Middle East. The forest-clad desolation of Burma. See-saw battles—four steps forward, three steps back; ten steps back, twelve steps forward. One day there was a road block, the enemy strongly entrenched, and retreat cut off. The men took sackloads of flour and sugar and tins of ghee from a dump and the cook was asked to prepare jilebi, enough jilebi for the whole unit; it was like a marriage feast! They ate merrily, the road ahead blocked by a 25-pounder and enemy troops approaching fast from the rear.

One day, near Rangoon, the truck in front of him hit a land mine and blew up and the man who had been Nihal Singh was five gory pieces of flesh, but the bearded head, lying severed, still carried its turban intact!

The Seth's offer had meant the promise of new experience. Born and bred in town, he had traveled much and seen much, but the villages of his own homeland were beyond his field of knowledge. The National Movement had swept the countryside while he was away at war, the Movement that was about to bring freedom.

An ox-cart coming his way. It was piled high with straw. Better slow down, lest the animals get scared by the din. A woman was perched on top of the straw, a baby in her arms. Slow, slower. Alas, the precaution was of no use. The animals, as the motorcycle passed them, veered madly. A scream rang out and Sohanlal pressed the brake, turned on his seat. The oxen with the yoke had gone down the yard-high bank to the grassland below. The cart hung precariously at the road's edge. The carter had jumped to his feet in time and was struggling to hold back the vehicle, while the young woman on the straw pile, now tilted precariously, screamed hard in helpless terror.

"Jump!" Sohanlal shouted to her. Goaded out of inaction she slipped down fast, the child squeezed against her bosom—not a moment too soon. The cart-wheels slid and one was ripped off its axle.

Sohanlal came running and in the stiff silence that greeted him he surveyed the accident he had caused. "I tried—" he began, but the woman cut him short.

"City swank!" Her eyes snapped in anger. "This is your private road, you think. It is a good joke to frighten the oxen, you think. You—" Words failed her.

But her husband seemed to take it placidly. He released the cart-pair from their yoke, his rueful head wagging at them: "You have done it, gentlemen!"

"Tell me, brother," Sohanlal said guiltily. "Anything I can do?"

"Do! Do what?" The woman had regained her voice. "Will you carry the straw load in your phut-phutti? Just let us know."

Sohanlal had an idea. "The cart-wheel has to be repaired. I will rush off and bring a carpenter." He turned to the angry woman for her approval. Her face seemed familiar. Yes, he had seen her in the street with a few other women who had all called him "City swank"—in merriment, not in anger.

The cartman and his spouse looked at each other. "The Drunk," he said and she nodded assent.

"The Drunk? What Drunk?"

"He made the wheels. He can set them right."

The Drunk, yes, that was the carpenter's nickname, his real name unused and forgotten. He had one day come to the clothshop for a loan, Sohanlal recalled. Bulaki Rao had gleefully recounted the story of the luckless man.

The carter's wife, now appeased, smiled at the stranger. "Brother, you will pass through Pipli on your way back from Kanhan. There is a toddy shop, the Drunk's usual haunt at this hour."

He saw what she meant. "Yes, sister. I will find the Drunk and bring him here."

She was now ashamed of her burst of temper. The accident was not his fault. He had to pass the cart-oxen and had gone as slowly as he could, so that the din would be least.

"You understand our plight?" her voice pleaded. "This cart is our cornfield and the oxen our plow-pair. Without them, there will be no bread for us to eat."

He rushed off. Kanhan was seven miles away. The bundles of cloth delivered at the store, he drove back the way he had come until he reached an untarred byroad leading to Pipli.

Bulaki Rao had a word to say about Pipli too. *The Bad Woman of Pipli.* Of all the seven villages Pipli alone had one of that kind, so Bulaki Rao, dirty pig, had said, his voice thick and insinuating. "Bad Woman? She has no other name?" he had asked, and Bulaki Rao had said in answer, "What else but her trade name counts? It is such a good label." "What label have you under 'Bulaki Rao'?"—with unconcealed scorn. The man had not taken offense, however; he had simply sniggered.

There, on Pipli's Main Road, was the toddy booth. Yes, the Drunk was there, huddled on a bench. "Take him away," the toddy-seller gestured with his hand. "A bucketful of water poured on his head will make him fit for work."

No carpenter like him in the Seven Villages, Bulaki Rao had said. Every good house had products of his craft—doors, bedstead, carved thrones for house-gods. An orphan boy, self-taught, he had taken to his ancestral calling—a duck must swim and a rat steal grain. He had married, settled to a busy life and all had been well. Then his wife died at childbirth. The infant followed the mother. Out of that shock the Drunk was born.

"The wretch tried to drown his grief in toddy and himself got lost," Bulaki Rao had said. "Toddy took hold of him. He neglected his work. Needing money, he sold off his ancestral holdings one by one. And here he is again in the clothshop, parting with some of his last clods of earth."

Sohanlal stared at the broken man with pity and some disgust.

Three years had sufficed for the man to lose his identity altogether and become the Drunk of Sonamitti—in his twenty-fifth year.

When he had completed his mission, the cartman's wife cried jestingly to him, "Brother, do not try to knock Meera down as you go!"

Meera! Sohanlal smiled to himself as he drove off. Meera!

He had seen her the first time on Main Road, returning from work with a group of women. Trim of figure and a great coil of hair at the back of her head. The women had stepped aside, but the girl, unafraid, kept to the middle of the road. For fun he sidled close, just behind, and went at a crawling pace. "Meera! Look out!" her companions shrieked. She did not care. She walked with easy strides. The side-car drew abreast, almost grazing her. Still she did not care. "Wah! Wah!" he cried, half mocking, half admiring. As he passed on, he heard the women call at his back, "City swank! You could not frighten our Meera." And he heard them yell, "Hei-ee, Phut-phutti-ji! Hei-ee!" ending with peals of laughter.

That was Meera. Her massive coil of hair was somewhat awry, as if the thick black mass would be undone at any moment and pour down her back, reaching well beyond her hips.

Later, he had seen Meera's Grandma and she was all by herself, limping with a stick in her hand. He had drawn close, stopped. "Have a ride, Grandma." He had indicated the empty side-car. All the village called her Grandma, he knew. Meera's Grandma.

Her face had been first amazed, then radiant. "You really ask me?" A good while she had stood gazing at the machine and before she climbed in, she wiped her bare feet carefully with a corner of her sari lest the carpet get stained. As the machine started to move, she clapped her hands with delight like a young girl. She leaned over and her hand crept to the handlebar, close to his fingers. "You do not feel fear, going arrow-fast?" Excitement in her eyes, she touched the machine here and there, the white lines of metal, the red leather, the thick green carpet underfoot, and said in a low conspirator's voice, "We will race the fire-engine one day. Han, beta? For miles the road and the iron track run alongside." At the ride's end, when he had helped her alight at her housedoor, she reached for his head with an uplifted hand. "May you be happy, my son." He stooped to touch her feet in salutation, but she shrank back, her voice husky as she said once more, "May you be happy, my son."

Meera was a girl from story-books, both real and unreal!

For the village, or a good part of it, awaited a miracle from her, the fulfillment of a promise made by a man of mystery, and it was said that Meera herself nursed a secret expectation. Her belief came plainly from a wish every young girl has, that some wonder happen to her and her life be changed. But—this fantasy!

The Seth was helping to build the illusion. He had said no word about the miracle itself. But he had spoken of a report he had read in his paper from the city. An old minstrel was singing in a railway coach when a checker turned up, demanded his ticket. The minstrel had no ticket and the checker threatened to hand him over to the police at the next stop. The train pulled up. The minstrel had vanished. Yet his singing voice came as before, the voice of an invisible man! In two minutes the train moved again and there on the wooden bench the minstrel sat with his lyre. Sobbing with fear and remorse the checker clasped the holy man's feet. "Who art thou, Father?" All the passengers asked the same question as they jostled to touch his feet, and he smiled and said, "Atmaram."

Sonamitti had thrilled to the story. No one had doubted the Seth's word. Its bearing on Meera's taveez was obvious. Beside the miracle of the invisible man a touchstone was a child's toy!

Why did he have to build Atmaram? What did he hope to gain?

The miracle was a dim rainbow in the village sky. To make it luminous, the Seth must read one or two more reports about Atmaram!

A girl from story-books—her heroic deeds were folklore!

Meera. Since his first glimpse of her he had waited twice on Main Road to see her pass. Her companions were now more friendly. "You look well, brother," they had greeted him; "it is good that our village air agrees with you." Meera had been silent; it was not seemly for a maiden to speak to a stranger. She was named after the great poetess of olden times, Meera Bai, whose bhajan songs, so tender and intense, everyone in India knew. Named, apparently, by her Grandpapa, the minstrel. She did have a poet's fancy. The touchstone!

On one side of the road was a broad stretch of plowland where scores of peasants, men and women, were picking maize. In one field, somewhere, was Meera with her Grandma. Why not see them at work? He stopped the motorcycle and sat thinking for a minute. Then he set off, walking over the foot-high ridges between strips of fields. Voices hailed him, "Ho-oh, Phut-phutti-brother!" A woman called, "Come and lend me a hand with the crop if you have nothing better to do." Her man, twenty plant-rows away, turned his face with a mock scowl. "Ho-oh, woman, I am not out of hearing. Do not let a city Phut-phutti eat your stupid head. Leave him to his queer beauties."

He walked on, puzzling, "Queer beauties?" In a while he stopped to ask an old peasant, "Meera's Grandma—where's her field?" The peasant pointed toward the left. There, Meera and the old woman were busy filling their baskets and emptying them. The girl's face, oiled with perspiration, glistened in the hard sun like metal.

"Grandma!"

She looked up, amazed. "You? It is good to see you standing on our poor earth."

He stepped up, his dhoti drawn to his knees. "Let me help. How is your gout?"

"What gout?" Grandma asked as if she had not heard of that ailment.

"Let me have your basket. This is no work for one loaded with age."

"What age?" she growled.

Meera said, "I have begged of her: Gran'ma, don't. There isn't much work left. Tomorrow Roghuvir-brother will come and help. If you have to do something, Gran'ma, sit on the ridge and watch—" She stopped. Her eyes rested on him with a kind of questioning frown, then withdrew.

This was the first time she spoke to him and neither words nor glance faltered, though the frown was hard to make out. Watching her he felt a new strange happiness. The smudges of black earth on her forehead and chin—she had wiped sweat with her hand—seemed becoming!

"Work never killed a peasant woman," Grandma answered the girl. "Not that I am what I used to be. After your father was born—I had been away from the fields almost a month, expecting him—one day I had more maize on my stack than your Grandpapa. At the day's end he peered with wonder at the stack I had built—in those days he wore no white beard—and he said—"

"Grandma," Meera interrupted in a whisper, "the paper from Delhi." Her face was very grave.

"Han!" Grandma hesitated before she spoke. "Beta?"

"Yes, Grandma?"

"It is not true?"

"What is it?"

She paused for a bit. "Pictures," she said.

"Pictures?"

"The village talks."

He cried, surprised, "I do not understand—" and caught Meera's look as the black pupils of her eyes swerved toward his coat pocket in which *New Vision* lay folded, visible at the top. Now he understood. Queer beauties—the meaning was clear.

"You want to see the pictures in my paper, Grandma?" Turning, he gave Meera an amused glance. The village maid was shocked!

Grandma was silent. Meera hung her head. Laughing within himself Sohanlal prolonged the moments of strain before he pulled *New Vision* out. "Foreign beauties." He nodded. "See for yourself, Grandma."

Her fingers were unwilling as they fumbled with the sheets. Meera turned on her heels, looking away, a hardening in her face. A minute later Grandma cried perplexed, "Where are they?"

"You cannot find them? Look well."

She fumbled again through the pages and cried at last, "Have I gone blind?"

"No. You have good eyes."

She stared hard at him. Then Sohanlal shrugged his shoulder and said, grinning, "To find them you need other eyes. The Seth's fanciful eyes."

Grandma cried sharply, "Is that it?"

"But it must have been Bulaki Rao who cast the story about. I refused to show him the 'foreign beauties' and he was piqued. He has worked fast with his tongue."

"Meera—" The two looked at each other, knit in a common relief, happy. But all at once Grandma's face crumpled as if she was about to break into tears. "Beta, my aged head is bent with shame. Meera knew better, for she said, 'Maybe it is a lie.' I said, 'We cannot trust city folk.' I have learned a good lesson. Never again shall I think ill of you, never. Hey, Meera?"

And Meera, silent, shook her head firmly in affirmation.

"Then Bulaki Rao has done me a good turn, indeed."

Grandma cried, "Beware of that evil one." Maybe she had something more to say but she gave Meera a glance and held her tongue. And a thought struck Sohanlal: The Bad Woman of Pipli?

Could it be that Meera, too, knew? For, she moved off and resumed her work, plucking maize. Sohanlal watched the rhythmic swing of her arm, dark-blue glass bangles tight.

"Do you use the white manure?" This was a chance to show his knowledge about new ways of cultivation.

"White?" Grandma's eyes twinkled. "Hey Meera, white cowdung!"

"Not cowdung, Grandma," Sohanlal smiled. "I am not such a big fool! It is a stuff made in factories. By its use the earth becomes three times more productive." He recalled words he had read somewhere and went on, "Cowdung is outdated. The starveling earth shares the same denial as the tiller: everything taken from them; nothing much given in return."

"We have seen no such white stuff."

He cried happily, "Then I will get you a bagful from the city. We will experiment." A city fellow could well be the farmer's worthy partner!

"No," Grandma decided. "That stuff may hurt the soil and nothing will grow on it ever again. Or it may poison the crop and bring about a calamity."

Sohanlal said, "Wait till freedom comes and bagfuls of the new manure will be rushed to every field. Then the very face of India will change."

"As if the big masters would care! Whether the people live or die—"

"The people are going to be the masters. It is they who will own everything. The land, the rivers, the railways—"

Grandma spoke excitedly. "Railways? Then we will travel and pay no fares. We will be free to go anywhere, just for a wish and a sneeze."

"My Gran'ma will ride an airplane," said Meera. "She will rush from sky to sky."

"Meera, is that true? Not making a goat of me, the two of you?"

The girl paused in her work and threw back her head, laughing. Sohanlal lost himself in that upturned face, lips parted, eyeballs bright between half-closed lids. But she seeemed to have felt his glance, for she stopped abruptly and turned away.

He pulled himself up and resumed, "A new dawn is about to break after many hundreds of years—"

Meera spun round. "I know. The vote-mote!"

"How much do you know? Do you—" He stopped, hearing a snivel.

"Gran'ma!" Meera cried. She drew close and gave her a supporting arm.

Sohanlal felt awkward. "Is it something that I have said—"

"The song," Grandma mumbled.

"What song?"

"The same words! A new dawn is about to break after hundreds of years—" Her face took on a rapt look. "I can hear the voice. That night, in the Seth's thousand-tree orchard—"

Sohanlal stared in bewilderment but Meera understood and her face grew sad.

"He gave you the taveez that night, Meera, after his last song. Three hours of sleep still remained but he hardly closed his eyes for one moment. I had never before seen him so restless. Some secret worry. He would not tell me what it was."

Meera nodded. Their thumb-marked bonds. Grandpapa had to be unhappy.

"Next day he was calm as usual. Then he went away."

"Why did he leave? He cared so little for us?"

"If only you knew how much he cared!"

"Yet—"

The hundred wrinkles in Grandma's face seemed to deepen.

"What could he do? We are not enough for him, Meera. He has to be true to himself. He has to be just what he is—a homeless, ever-wandering minstrel."

Two or three men from this village had gone to war and none had returned. Their wives and children were perpetual reminders of war's evil impact. Once an illumined shape had been seen in the night sky, moving fast, and the Seth had said that it was an airplane bristling with guns and carrying fireballs, one of which could destroy this village in the space of five breaths. However, an Elder had shaken his head saying, "It is only a pilgrim star flying from space to space to reach the Creator's feet," and people had admitted the truth of this word and lifted their joined palms in a *pernam* to the star.

The face of war had been seen once when a great convoy of vehicles, painted a dull gray, had gone along the highroad in an endless line. Some of them had no wheels, yet they had trundled fast. You could hear bones crunch in the bodies turning to pulp as those steel monsters went to attack.

Sohanlal was a man from that strange cavalcade! No less than five peasants had seen him at the wheel of a passing vehicle. "The medals across your chest—wah!" He had not driven a truck on this road, Sohanlal had said, and he had not won medals. But his denial was taken to be plain modesty.

It was the Seth's pride that a military fellow ate his salt. Pity, though, that the fellow did not hold his chin up. He was too close to the peasant folk. He called them "brother" or "uncle," and ate bread at their houses. He joined in their games and gave a good account of himself.

For the village, however, one fact outweighed all else: he had given Meera's Grandma a ride. That, in a way, was a treat for everyone. It was as if, in the person of Meera's Grandma, the whole village had ridden in the phut-phutti!

No one in Sonamitti apart from Meera and her Grandma knew of his life before he became a soldier. None except those two saw his roots stuck deep in poverty and privation.

After sunset, almost every day, those three sat together, Grandma with her rosary of a hundred and eight beads and Meera with the spinning-wheel, and that was the time when he opened his heart readily.

His father, too, had been a motor-driver. He went with his employer to a place in Bihar on tour, and the great earthquake struck. Buildings toppled, streets cracked open, fire gushed out the earth and towns and whole districts lay devastated.

The widowed mother had to earn a living for herself and her son. She worked in a tobacco factory. She went from house to house scrubbing kitchen utensils. It was a hard struggle to feed two mouths and keep the boy at school. The years went by, joyless, dark. The boy took to his father's calling as soon as he attained the age, and looked for employment. But the times were bad and there was hardly any job for a newly licensed driver.

The war gave him his chance. He enlisted in secret and left a note for his mother. "You have borne enough hardship. Live well for a time."

It was after he went away that he understood his mother's feeling. The violence of nature had taken the father and now it would be violence again—of man.

She bowed to the inevitable. Day on day, month on month, she waited for the postman to bring the terrible news about her son. The perpetual fear wore her out. Life and spirit were drained off her body, disease struck her, and death came as a release. When the son was back home on leave from the Middle East, it was too late. Off to war again, facing days of peril, but there was comfort in the fact that mother was gone, she was not waiting to get the evil message which now seemed inevitable.

Grandma, having heard the story, made an unexpected remark. "Strange that Meera's father and yours suffered a like fate from accidents," she said. "And so it was, in a way, with the mothers, for both died of heartbreak."

"Why talk about it and make him feel bad?" Meera said, a hint of tears in her voice.

"He wants no easy escape," Grandma answered with surprising conviction.

True, Sohanlal agreed at heart, recalling how he had often lived in his past. That was why he had been lonely even among a thousand men. He had become used to it. But sometimes it had hurt. Sometimes he had longed for relief, for a flight from himself.

It was easy to talk to Grandma and a load moved off his chest. Grandma did not blame him for leaving home. He had to go; even his grief-ridden mother knew that and was secretly happy, so Grandma said. Dying of forlornness, the mother had still been happy.

"A mother cannot live only in herself; she lives in her son, in his fight to improve his lot, in his needs, wishes, feelings."

Grandma soothed his ache of self-accusation. He had done what had to be done. All mothers knew these things by instinct; or else they would not be 'mother.' So Grandma said.

And as the darkness grew and Grandma could no longer put off telling her beads, the young people moved away a few paces to the fig tree. Grandma's lips would now make the words in silence over each bead:

> "Harey Rama, Harey Rama,
> Rama Rama, Harey Harey,
> Harey Krishna, Harey Krishna,
> Krishna Krishna, Harey Harey."

So would she repeat the words a hundred and eight times, chanting them rhythmically within herself. But the young people would be absorbed in their own talk. One inevitable theme was Grandpapa.

"If only he were here with us and you could see him," Meera spoke longingly.

He gazed into her face alight with belief. The man of mystery had created a strange problem. Maybe he knew what he was doing. Maybe he thought that a girl of Meera's temperament needed to live a fairy-story; that, having lived it, she would grow up in her mind. If that happened to Meera, all would be well. One day she would look searchingly for the gold in life, truer than mere metal.

"There is so much in common between you two—" Meera said.

He laughed. A half-century stood between him and that strange old man. Meera went on, "The election is soon to come. He warned us against the Seth."

"Why did he not stay back and fight?"

"How could he?" Her face showed honest surprise. "He is a minstrel. He lives beyond such battles. It is for us to fight them."

Sohanlal could not argue the point and make her feel awkward. How she worshipped her Grandpapa! She resumed in a moment, "These were his words: 'Freedom is the beginning of the road where there was no road. But the new road swarms with robbers.' Are they not true words?"

The theme was after his heart and he had an eager listener, so he let himself go. Yes, there were the robbers, Seths of many kinds. The cities had a greater variety and profusion of them than the countryside. There was the money-Seth, of course, to whom freedom meant a chance to seize fields of trade vacated by the aliens. Then the Seth of politics, ready to dupe the people with the power of his glib tongue. The official Seth, a man of arrogance ready to change masters without a change of mentality, human chattel open to the best offer. The Seth of religion with gods for sale. The Seth with a Gandhi cap on his head and the cap itself a deceit. And several others on the list....

"Yes, Meera Bai." He seemed both angry and amused. "I have seen the masks—and the real faces."

Meera asked, "Have you not seen true men? Men like my Grandpapa?"

"It will be no surprise if the true men are forgotten on freedom day when it is celebrated two months hence," he spoke slowly, moodily. "I can see the flag salutation at our Curzon Park. The police have cordoned off the space for men of privilege. They sit in comfort with their backs to the rope barrier watching India step into independence. Those men were the prison guards of yesterday's slavery. They are to be the guardians of tomorrow's freedom."

Meera said, "Let them watch the show. It is the men beyond the rope barrier who will count finally."

That pleased him. "Yes, Meera," he said beaming. For the first time he called her Meera, the formal Bai dropped! The longing came upon her instantly that he call her again and her prayer was answered. "Meera," he said, "you have such understanding—it is wonderful!" And the tone of his voice made her heart miss a beat.

Not that she was content to hear him talk about freedom. She had to share his memories, his battle experience.

One day in Arakan, during a retreat, there was heavy bombardment and the men of his unit had to leave their vehicles and take cover in slit trenches. He slipped into one but it was already occupied. A soldier lay stretched on his back, dead. There was no time to move elsewhere, and as a bomb whined in the air he laid himself flat upon the dead man. Then he saw the little wooden doll clasped against the bosom under a stiffened hand, the kind of doll sold for a few pice in every village fair. The painted wood was stained with blood.

In the dying hour of that soldier the little doll of his baby daughter had been his solace.

That was one face of war hard to forget. Then there was the sheer horror. The look in the eyes of the wounded—it was something far deeper than pain.

He could not see himself when he carried the familiar look of the doomed.

His voice had a weary intensity; but several days had to pass before Meera knew what he meant. The dark nights yielded to the new moon and presently the moon was three-quarters full, when he went back to the theme, speaking without reserve.

His wounded leg was to be amputated.

She gasped, her hand flying to her mouth. He smiled at her, but his face was tight with recollection as he dwelt on the terrible night in Tripoli. He was in the stream of trucks crossing the desert. No lights on. There was peace—a desert on a dark night and a great forest were one. A whine grew in the air. It became a roar of fury. The sands lit up with flares dropped from the sky.

The bombs came.

The line of trucks were one great sheet of flame, a half-mile in length, but he was unhurt. Stunned, he managed to jump out of the driving seat. He heard a groan. His mind cleared. He rushed into the blaze, pulled out a man, dragged him to safety. In a minute the planes were back. More bombs came. He felt his body explode in pain and there was darkness.

When he regained his senses in the field hospital, he saw the state of his leg and heard a murmured voice and knew what was to come. "No!" he screamed with all his strength. "Not that." He would let his flesh rot, he would die, but not that.

His scream fell flat on ears all too used to such desperate protest.

III

Meera, at one with the doomed man, felt her heart pound. He paused for a little, basking in her compassion, before he resumed.

There was talk in the hospital of a wonder drug just discovered. Penicillin it was called. A supply was expected a week later. But that was too late, the nurse told him. The doctor could not wait so long lest there be gangrene.

A week—an eternity.

Then he fought his toughest battle. He induced the busy doctor to listen to his story—how his mother had toiled hard, strained herself to the breaking point on his account. Back home, legless, he would be a burden on her hard to bear and she was old beyond her age and ailing. It was t.b.—

"Even so, she would be happy to have you back—" the doctor said. "A crippled son is better than one who is dead."

But her own days were numbered. Who would feed the cripple when she was gone? His small pension would be too inadequate.

The doctor said, "Do you suggest that, as an act of mercy, we should kill all our wounded, or most of them anyway?"

He could not answer that. The fight was over. All he could add was, "I speak only for myself. Give me a week, sir. Let my fate be decided in that week. It is not quite sure that in a week the leg will rot."

"Not quite sure," he agreed, hesitatingly.

He lay on a bed of nails until, two hours after, the nurse came. She was going to take him to the operation table? But the nurse smiled reassuringly. "The C.O. has just sent a signal to London asking for a quick despatch of penicillin."

The wonder drug came on the fifth day and it saved his leg!

Penicillin, said Meera softly and her mouth loved the name. She would like to see that doctor in soldier's garb, she would touch his feet in gratitude.

She would like to see the deep scar left by the wound. Her eyes rested on his thigh propped up in the circle of his arms. She would like to touch the scar and trace the lines of pain with her fingertip.

The strange thought startled her and brought the blood heaving into her face. All the same, the thought came back later and over and again. How she wanted to see the battle scar in his body and touch it lightly! Does it hurt you still?

And a second thought, no less strange, followed: she would let no

112

harm befall him ever again. She laughed with lips set in a line, mocking her decision. As if she had any power over his happiness!

She did have this power! Amazed by the answer, shame renewed in her face, she looked around quickly as if the wind might have caught her unspoken word and borne it away for everyone to hear.

CHAPTER

## 12

The network of lines in Grandma's face showed a new, deep emblem of worry.

Here in Sonamitti, soon, Free India would be put to a test. But it was clear that the Seth would ride to the board on the people's vote. That was not to be his journey's end, though. "How would you like to serve a Deputy Minister?" he had asked Sohanlal meaningfully. He had gone on to state that the exalted position would be within his reach one day.

"Grandma," Sohanlal had said, "Free India will die a hundred deaths. Beware, lest one such death takes place at the polling booth of this village."

"*Nehi, nehi,*" she had cried agitatedly. Sohanlal had given her a long steady look. "What will you do about it, Grandma?"

"I?" The voice was weak.

"You who are of the people, their trusted Old Mother. Remember the *Quit India* days? *You* cannot quit!" And as he spoke, the sad thought came upon him that freedom's new battle would be more difficult in a way than the battle that had been won. For the great tide of feeling that had carried the people onward had receded. The drama had ended.

His words were not lost on Grandma.

At this juncture the Seth threw his bait to the village, an offer of relief on the loans he had given. A three-months' remission of interest, to take effect on the day he was elected to the board.

Grandma limped down the street to an Elder's house. In what ways could a board member use his position for personal gain, she asked him, and he pointed out one or two ways; but many others were sure to occur to a shrewd black-market brain, he said.

"What will you do about it?" Grandma asked peremptorily.

"I?"

"You demanded freedom. You went to prison."

He smiled. "The goal has been reached. Let there be peace."

114

"Peace, brother?" Her voice was grave. "Freedom cannot be given. It is to be built by our own hands—" She fumbled in her mind for other telling words that Sohanlal had used, then ended up bruskly, "What! Must we be ruled by robbers?"

The Elder said, "What do you want of me, Meera's Grandma?"

"Your voice must be heard. You cannot keep silent as if you approve."

"There are bonds bearing my thumb-mark. You know?"

"Bonds!" she scoffed. "To speak of bonds at this time! No, brother. The people must be told what to do."

"Landless, shall I feed seven ever-hungry mouths with the meadow air?" But the look he gave Grandma carried admiration and love.

In a black mood she went to another Elder and stormed, "A tiger watches your flock, ready to spring. Will you lock yourself up in the kitchen and peer from the window?"

"If I have no weapon against the animal—"

"There is always a weapon."

"It may not be good enough. Go home, Meera's Grandma, and set your thoughts on the Hereafter. Give all your time and breath to repeating the holy names on your prayer beads." He paused, hesitating, then added softly, "Sonamitti cannot bear to lose you, Meera's Grandma."

Grandma gave herself to brooding. For long hours at night she sat on the veranda, frowning into the darkness where the crickets crackled. A word spoken to amuse her, and she answered, "Hush!" and returned to her gloom. So it went on until there was an unexpected turn.

The schoolboys had been feasting on laddoo and marching and shouting with great zeal, "Vote for Samsundar-ji, vote!" But half the youngsters in Sonamitti could not afford to go to school. They had to make a living. They took the cattle to the meadow or did odd jobs of various kinds. One day, acting on an impulse, these boys formed a squad of their own and came out on the road with the counter-cry, "Don't vote for Samsundar-ji, don't!"

The rival squads converged as they came from two directions and when twenty yards apart their voices blended in a confused clamor, "Vote for Samsundar-ji, vote!"..."Don't vote for Samsundar-ji, don't!" Halting, they stood in stiff silence, face to face, eye upon eye. Then each side advanced a few paces, alert, measuring the strength of the other side. Shouts of challenge crossed like bludgeons. Ten paces apart, they stopped again.

"Vote . . . !" one set of voices yelled.

"Don't vote . . . !" the other set answered.

With each repetition the voices grew in fury. Forgotten enmities revived. Each boy in one group found vent for his wrath in a boy of the other group. The youngest of them stuck out their tongues and made awful faces. Then, as if catapulted by the earth under their feet, the two groups clashed.

The chances were almost even. The schoolboys, better fed and self-assured, seemed the stronger fighting force, but their thin, scraggy adversaries had work-roughened hands and were reckless. Here, one youngster sat on the chest of his fallen foe and punched his face. There, two grappling figures went rolling into a ditch. The air filled with shrieks. But the fight ended abruptly. A schoolboy was seen in headlong flight. That was a signal for his party. As they fled, the cry of victory hit them in the spine, "Don't vote!"

Grandma reacted curiously to this incident. Strengthened as though by some tonic, she pulled herself out of stupor.

"Mere youngsters have shown us what to do," she spoke to the Cowhouse Five. "We also must build up our *Don't Votes*. We must go marching on the street."

Meera clapped her hands excitedly. "That's it. Don't vote . . . !"

The words rang hollow. Grandma shook her head and spoke thoughtfully, "It is not good enough to say don't vote for somebody. People have been given a power. They must use the power."

That was true.

"We must have our own man on the board," Grandma went on. "We must fight for his election."

Meera had an instant inspiration. Her eyes lit up. "Vote for Gran'ma!" the cry came shrilling from her throat.

"Do not be frivolous, girl. This is no laughing matter."

"I am dead serious, Gran'ma. You will be our choice against the Seth. Vote for Gran'ma, vote!"

"No!" Grandma screamed.

"Yes!" Meera yelled.

"Have you gone mad?"

"Grandma, leave it to us. Give us a chance. We must rush off at once and tell everyone. A real fight at last!"

"No, Meera."

"Yes, Gran'ma."

Her voice trembled. "I am a woman."

"So what?"

She gave an anguished groan. "Meera, you will be the death of me. There is a terrible sickening in my stomach. Be kind—"

"Gran'ma, you are scared stiff! Take heart. Hold your spine erect. Vote for Gran'ma, vote!" She sprinted off to the road and was gone before she could be stopped, while the others rushed after their friend.

"What if they all agree? What if they give way to this madness?" moaned Grandma, left alone under the fig tree.

And, sure enough, the village women were quick to catch Meera's fire. Vote for Grandma. This was something positive, something to fight for.

There were twice as many women in the new procession as in the one that had demanded cloth. The drummer's wife gave it a theatrical touch: she had borrowed the drum from her husband and each united shout of "Vote for Grandma, vote!" was followed by *doog-doog-doog* for effect. It so happened that the schoolboys had gathered courage again and on this Sunday morning they too were out on the road, marshalled by Master-ji himself. The two columns surveyed each other, the boys alarmed and the women scornful, and then an odd thing happened. Master-ji spun round, facing the youngsters. "Dismiss!"— and he was in swift flight.

"You saw?" Master-ji's hefty wife beamed at the procession, her arms on her hips.

"Because of you he fled?" asked Sohagi in surprise.

"What else?"

"Sister," Sohagi was wistful, "all husbands should be just as brave as yours." And she turned to Lakshmi as if to say, "You will agree."

So the tension reached a higher pitch. How would the Seth answer this menace to his chances?

He was unruffled. It was for the people to decide who should be their voice, he said. The district board had to make better villages and its members must have knowledge, acumen, initiative, energy. If Meera's Grandma was thought to be the right choice...

But the truth was that Grandma's fields were not free and the Seth could foreclose at will. Landless, she could not be a candidate. Holding this trump card he could well afford to be placid. He could even ignore the fact that Lakshmi had joined the procession, crying "Vote for Grandma, vote!" Grandma's role of glory would be her undoing.

He had no option in this matter. The old woman had thrown him a challenge and he had to act in self-defense. If she must play with fire, let her not squeal when badly burnt. After all, her motive was plain malice. There was nothing for her to gain from the district board—no ten per cent on contracts, not even one!

Lakshmi was unaware of his decision. She had waited for his hard words but he had been silent. She now tried to provoke him so that his anger would break to the surface and spend itself.

"All Sonamitti has gone crazy about Meera's Grandma."

"You, too." His voice was casual, without rancour.

That was her chance for an open assault. "Why not? Is there a Grandma like her anywhere in the Seven Villages? Is there—"

"None like her in all Hindusthan." He smiled at her encouragingly. Then, in a flash of understanding, she saw his mind. But she could not believe what she saw. It could not be. He was no brute...

He was watching her and enjoying himself. As he took note of her horror, he let the mask slip off his face. His eyeballs were stern.

"When an ant grows wings and starts flying in the air, it is not far from its doom."

Lakshmi cried angrily, "The people love her. They will not let her be harmed. Beware!"

"What!" His voice came like the blow of a cudgel. "That old woman has no self-respect, then? She pledged away her land for cash and cash and more cash. All I seek is a repayment. I stand by my rights, that is all. There is so much talk these days about justice and fair play and yet, when a pig asks for his dues he is warned, Beware! Tell me. Will this wonder of a Grandma disown her thumb-mark?"

An overwhelming fear possessed Lakshmi. She was helpless against this man. Grandma would not shirk her obligations to the people and back out. In peril she would not take help either. There was one path for her. Arm in arm, she and Meera would walk out of the village, two homeless destitutes.

Lakshmi was in agony. She fell at her husband's feet, wailing, "Do not let them perish. Take pity, I beg of you." The Seth listened and seemed to soften. "For shame, Nago's mother." He leaned over, patting her on the head, and as she wept piteously and her tears fell warm on his feet, he repeated, "For shame! You have no reason to grieve. Listen, then—"

She looked up in a flurry of expectation. He had relented! For the first time in his life he had submitted to his wife's pleading. A turning point in their relationship. At last she would find happiness.

He wiped the wet off her face with his palm. "There, there!" And how grateful she was! Never again would she have to be split between her two devotions. She would belong to her husband, ever, with nothing to push her apart.

Watching her, he spoke gently. "I take it, Lakshmi, that you wish me well. Then you must understand that I have no option in this matter. Meera's Grandma is too strong a rival. People are crazy about her, as you have rightly said. With so much at stake, I cannot take chances. Meera's Grandma must be disqualified; there is only one good way."

Her illusion had to be all too brief. Cornered, she made a desperate stand. "If you do harm to Grandma, no one will vote for you."

He agreed with her. "You are right, Lakshmi—almost. Not quite, though. People in general will keep away from the voting booth. But a few sons of vixen will come—out of a good incentive. All the bad people, drunks and the like, will vote for me. That will do, with no second ballot box."

Neither pity nor prayer nor threats nor tears could draw him from his objective, Lakshmi knew. Stretched on the floor, she broke into renewed sobbing, hating the man who had brought this misery on her, speaking broken bitter words. He, silent, gazed at her, disheveled and limp, and an image from the past occupied his mind. Lakshmi in the clothshop, stripping herself bare. Naked I will leave this room. Naked I will walk on Main Road. Her jacket was off her body and she was fumbling with her sari's waist knot....

The rebel woman who had bent him under her stubborn will and forced him into abject loss of face lay crushed at his feet.

Masterful and proud, he reached out toward her, "Enough of this, Lakshmi, enough." She winced as she felt the weight of his arm on her bosom and tried to edge away, but he caught hold of her breast under the jacket. She wriggled, but his fingers clutched tightly. His caress grew imperative in its demand while she shook her head from side to side but even while she shrank from his touch, she was yielding to his need, and in a while she closed her eyes with a deep sigh and lay still.

In the moments of intimacy the decision came upon her that she would somehow carry out the minstrel's bidding—she had put it off too long. That seemed to be the only way Meera could be saved—for a time.

She would let down her man, as twice before. But she could not bear to watch him stepping into the trap. She would leave the village. She would leave in five or six days, or even earlier if her work was done.

# 13

The Seth had a solid basis for his decision that he could not afford to take chances.

Twice before, a golden harvest he was about to reap had turned into dust. The earthen bridge. The magic healing. Behind those two, however, imponderable forces had acted. This time it was something tangible. It was the wily brain of an aged woman.

Strange that she had such power over the people. *Meera's Grandma. Meera's Grandma.* As though there were not fifty other Grandmas in Sonamitti. As though the village had no other name to cry. As though there was no Seth dwelling in this jungle of his own free choice. Scour the countryside and find another man with so many possessions. Find a man who had a phut-phutti, driver and all. Sonamitti did not care. Sonamitti was unimpressed. Sonamitti would rather cast its votes for a peasant woman—and truly it deserved no better.

Here in the red-bound ledgers was the life-story of those ingrate people. Each loan had to be the peg for a biographical note, amended and added to as time moved. For, a loan could not be given haphazard. You had to know the receiver's antecedents. His character, his ways of life and thought; his ability to repay; and his willingness to repay, the effort he was likely to make. Each loan needed to be watched with care like a growing plant in an orchard. Some sprouts dried up when inch-high—the loans were paid back. They left barren beds in the ledgers. Others grew to the height of saplings before they canceled out. Still others became full-bodied trees and each of them needed frequent study. How long would it draw sap, bear fruit? When should it be felled for firewood?

Two or three had to go every year. That was when a loan, doubling itself in a twelvemonth, exceeded in course of time the borrower's total assets. First went the trinkets of his wife and daughters. Then the kitchen utensils and knickknacks, which Bulaki Rao traded at the used-goods market in town. Lastly, the land. Bite by bite the land was reduced. The fattening loan could devour with the zest of a pig! The time came when the mortgage had to be foreclosed. What happened to the dispossessed man? He drifted away to town for a new living. That was no concern of the ledgers. The tree became firewood and there the biographical note had to end.

Who would complain that the Seth had acted harshly, without human feeling? Every man who migrated in distress received a cash gift from him. Five rupees, ten rupees, or even fifteen, depending on the acreage he had lost. There were no real grounds for such a gift. You bought wheat and ate it, you bought cloth and used it up—the dealer would not make a free replacement of even one grain or one strand of thread. But the Seth of Sonamitti was too soft in his dealings. That was his trouble. He had good need to watch himself and hold his softness subdued lest it overpower him, lest it hurt his son and heir. For one added to one's property so it could be passed on as a worthy inheritance. That was the inward meaning of property. Your parent left you richer than he had been himself. You would have to leave your sons better off than you were. They would continue the process. The progeny to follow must do likewise. So would riches grow. So would the story of life be made. So would the world shape its destiny and the pages of history carry the shining glory. Inheritance, the key motif in the social pattern. It gave you a bedrock of principle on which to stand. Man had never struck on a sounder thought, a truer philosophy of life. Inheritance.

Meera's Grandma would be here in a minute. The time was ripe for a reckoning. She who had puffed herself up like the frog in the tale would share the lot of that conceited creature.

She had written her fate with her own hand. The minstrel had left her six broad fields, half of them black cotton earth. Only two mouths to feed. Two depending on the land could have all they needed. But then, they had to gain popularity. They had to go out of their way to give help. Even he, the Seth, kept clear of such mental luxury, knowing that he could not afford it. Later he would have to give in charity so that he could earn merit for the Hereafter, but it would be done with well-calculated purpose. To give unto a Brahmin was more meritful than to give to any other man. It was even better to give unto a priest. Best of all, to give unto a Deva or Devi.... Toward the end of his life he would build a new temple, an impressive structure with the polished top bright in the sun, the image in the sanctum pure marble and its eyes black gems.

The reckoning for Meera's Grandma had to come. The tree depicted in the ledgers was full grown, shorn of sap, fit only to be firewood. But she would have been safe behind the protection of the minstrel's name. If only she had not exceeded all limits. Vote for Grandma, vote!

Ho, she did have one good reason to be pleased! Her last loan, ten rupees, was meant for the man next door, the Old Father, as Meera had admitted. That aged owl, so close to his doom, was now safe. His place on the list was to go to Meera's Grandma!

Good that Lakshmi was away. She would have made trouble. Her stupid tears gone to waste, she had decided to leave the village for a time, visiting with her parents. That fitted in with his plans. "Go, Lakshmi. The cartman will take you to the railway station. Remember, the train stops here only for a minute." "My son?" "Take him. You may stay with your people for a month." A month should be long enough for the excited feelings in the village to quiet down. He had then given her a palliative because of the misery in her face: "Tell your father that I will cancel his debts to me on the momentous day. The day I go to the board."

And the hour set for the final reckoning was at hand!

Elbows propped on the desk, he held his eyes expectantly on the outer door left open for fresh air. He looked far into the alley. There! But Meera was alone. The old woman had lost her courage, apparently.

"Seth-ji." Her joined palms touched her brow while he was deep in the ledger. A minute passed before he looked up.

"You?"

"Your summons, Seth-ji."

"Han! Pray be seated." His finger pointed to the bare cement floor. "Grandma could not come. Gout."

His glance sharpened. She was trying to touch the softness in him. Too late. Retribution was at hand. And he turned back to the ledger, flipping the thick pages, muttering some names. "Here it is, your Grandma's account." While he was absorbed in the figures Meera watched him and felt her heart flutter. Never before had she known such fear. She recalled the premonition of evil that had struck her early this day in the plowed field now ready for millet. She had burst into tears and, dropping down, laid her wet face on the dear furrowed earth in the way she snuggled to the bosom of Grandma. Was that premonition about to come true?

He looked up. "Bad. Unspeakably bad."

Eyes big, she met his glance. The ledger held her trapped. There could be no escape.

"Bad," she echoed faintly, tonelessly, and in that instant she was down in the greenish depths of well water. The blood was pounding hard in her ears and her chest was bursting with breath. One moment more...

With desperate effort she shook off her trance of fear. But other visions from the past filled her fancy. A woeful group, old and young, walking out of the village. Every hand had something to carry. The women had earthen pots. The grandmother had a framed Devi, the glass cracked. A tottering child clasped her shabby rag doll against her naked belly. All in the group hung close together and walked in silence with downcast faces. Beside them walked Grandma. When they reached the highroad Grandma stopped and everyone stopped. Grandma touched the head of each, man and woman and child. "Bide well," she said. "You are not alone or helpless, for the gods walk with you. Bide well."

What kind of a picture would Grandma herself make, walking out of Sonamitti? Knee joints stiff, she would go limping, when her great need would be to walk straight and proud. Better to slip away under cover of night, no one to bid farewell. But where would they go along the dark road so lone and frightening? Grandma had been happy in Sonamitti. And what would she, Meera, do? All she was good for was to work in plowed earth. She could also be a minstrel, wandering with a lyre in hand. But she was afraid. If only Grandpapa were here to take them away. Would they ever see him again?

She had been happy in this village. Everything one could wish for had been hers. What could be more fulfilling than the love of her friends? Those friends, to be lost to her for all time. Sohagi, dear sister, your Meera would be as remote from you as if dead and gone.

There was the other ache even harder to bear. An ache for a mere stranger. A month before he had not existed in her life. That could not be—she had known him in lives past. Or else, how meet a person once, twice, thrice, and he took hold of you, and the very thought of parting made your breath catch in the throat?

Not to see him ever again after her departure. Tears weighed down her eyelids. Such punishment. Would that he had never crossed her path. Why did he have to be so kind, making her lot harder?

She would quit without a word to him lest he go out of his way to offer help. She would vanish and leave no trace.

"Move closer." The Seth's voice was gruff. "Check up these figures. Make sure. Or else you will bear me a grudge."

Sweat came out on the palms of her hands as she held the ledger. She bent over the page but all she saw was a face. She had known him in other lives....

The Seth said, "If only that Grandma of yours had sense in her head. She has squandered all she owned. She, so very reckless—"

Those words steadied her. "Let it pass," she cried without looking up. But he went on, "All very well to indulge in charity. It is a question of rupees, though. Even I cannot afford such charity, I who may claim to have some means. You have to pay for your Grandma's folly. Or is it her conceit?"

Goaded into challenge she cried sharply, "Let it pass."

The old-woman stupidity applied to board funds, he reflected. A disaster for the people. But they were going to be protected.

"You cannot deny that you are paying for your Old Mother's action. If she had not—"

"I will not hear such words." Strength flamed in her and the tears dried.

"Indeed?" he scowled. She had to spit at his sympathy, rush head-long to her doom. Be it so. He gathered anger in him and summoned the deadly words to his tongue. Her face looked curiously withdrawn, as if she felt no fear, but her hand on the ledger was restless, clenching and unclenching. Odd, how her hand spoke while her face was mute. One beringed finger—

"What! A gold ring?" Amazed, he reached out quickly for her hand. But she drew it away.

"A gold ring?" he was looking intently.

She snatched the ring off her finger and tossed it to the desk. He picked it up. Out of his desk came a smooth black stone on which he rubbed the ring and studied the yellow mark it left. There was apprehension in his face as he spoke again. "Now, Meera, don't get it into your head that the gold ring will make any difference to you. The sum total of your loans—" Empty words! That ring could release a fair-sized field, so that her Grandma would not get disqualified.

Her voice was strained. "Enough!"

She knew the ring's value, she knew that her Grandma would sit on the board. He felt the ground slide from under his feet. All his great expectations gone! As he gaped, speechless, he heard her say, "The ring is worth a rupee. That is all I paid."

She seemed to mean what she said—her face was without guile. He must get to the bottom of this mystery.

"It is a gold ring," he stressed each word. "I knew at the very first glance."

"Of course!"

"Of course what?"

"Just that."

His professional pride was hurt. "I have tested the metal. I have made sure. You question my knowledge of gold!"

A shadow of hesitation in her face. She looked at the ring. Gold? It did have a peculiar shine.

"A rupee was all I paid," she repeated under her breath. Gold?

"Stolen and sold to you for a pittance. Who was it?"

"The old bangle-seller."

"He is no thief."

She shook her head. "He sold that ring to me along with ten glass bangles. That was five-six months back. He made a mistake. Copper with a gold wash, he said."

"It is not the same ring."

"The same. I did not buy any other."

"Where could he get a gold ring? If he had one, he would not treat it as copper. He would take good care of it."

"Copper with a gold wash, he said."

"Copper has turned to gold on your finger!"

She nodded, faintly ironic. "Unheard-of magic!"

His voice rose to a shout. "Magic? It is a miracle!"

She smiled. "The miracle had to happen to me—I do need one! Copper has turned to gold—" She broke short, scowling with some sudden thought, and bent her eyes to her jacket sleeve. With slow deliberation she rolled her sleeve back on her arm, revealing the taveez.

"What now?" He had caught the flash of expression in her face and followed her eyes. He watched her with mounting interest.

126

"I must ask Sohagi." In a low murmur. "She also bought a ring from the bangleman."

"Do not bother. Gold rings are not sold a rupee apiece."

Her breath was fast, her head awhirl. The Seth's voice seemed to travel from a distance. "That is the taveez we have heard about?"

"Yes."

"The taveez the minstrel gave you?"

"Yes."

They lifted their eyes to each other, caught in the violence of shock. He pulled himself out of it quickly. "The touchstone will turn copper into gold, so the minstrel said?"

"Yes, Seth-ji."

"What else did he say?"

"Only under certain conditions the touchstone will work. Only when I have done an act of kindness. Real kindness."

"Real kindness?"

"So he said."

"What could he have meant? What is real kindness?"

Bewildered pupils dilated in her eyes. "I do not know. Grandpapa did not explain." And while he gazed at the amulet as if trying to penetrate its deep secret, she was afar, listening, ears filled with song. *The ten-headed Ravan, all iron and rock, had wickedness tenfold.*

The moonlit orchard athrob with the great voice. . . . The terrible fight for the touchstone, the defeat of the Bear-king. Atmaram or not, he did create magic. . . . The unaccountable gravity in his face as he tied the taveez to her arm and she was gazing at him, her lantern lifted breast-high . . .

The enormous scope of his promise, the full force of its meaning, burst upon her like a shaft of blinding light. Scared, she bit her lip and flung her first challenge to Grandpapa. "No, it cannot be."

The Seth grew troubled. "You bought a copper ring and here it is, a thing of gold." With a swift movement he leaned over and held the amulet between his fingers. His fingers grew possessive, his face set hard. This had been pledged to him and as good as given.

"Seth-ji—"

He drew a deep breath and pulled himself together. "Meera," his voice carried a pleading, "Go home. See me later in the afternoon."

"The loans—" Her hand touched the menace on the desk top and her heart beat with both fear and hope.

With a slap he swept the ledger aside. "Give me time to think, to see the truth."

"Yes, Seth-ji."

"Not a word to anyone. You understand?"

"I hide nothing from Gran'ma."

"Only for a time. Until I see the truth."

When she was gone, the Seth sat rigid a long while, the ring clasped in his hand. There stood the clay idol, streams of tea pouring on its head. The face was first bloated and then it was a new face, bright gold! The Gold goddess. Could a dream foreshadow the things to come? Could it be that man, in rare moments, rose above the limits imposed by knowledge and realized the unknowable in an inward flash?

There was, too, the writing in his horoscope—it had puzzled him often. His stars made "gold-mine luck," so the horoscope said. The period indicated on the yard-long sheet of handmade paper was his forty-fifth year. That was still two years ahead. But the time schedules in a horoscope were often a little amiss due to slips in calculation. "Gold-mine luck." What could it mean? What chance was there that Sonamitti had gold ore in its bowels and the treasure would be revealed to him one day?

Here was the answer! Gold ore, vein after vein, but no long and painful digging, no complicated processing. Just transmutation. Was that it?

An awful excitement filled his blood with fever. Would the stars make retribution, at last, for Chamundi Bridge? A hundred bridges, bottled and sold, could not equal this!

He had no scruples about the ownership of the mine, the extraction of the precious ore. Ownership was the fair reward of discovery. That was the story the world over. He could not stand by and let the treasure lie unexploited; or be pilfered by greedy hyenas. Look, there was Bulaki Rao gliding toward the door, his stomach ready to burst with the secret like an overfull paper bag!

"Bulaki Rao!"

The hyena spun round with a start.

"You heard all?"

"What is it, Seth-ji? What did you want me to hear? Pray tell me."

"Keep this engraved on your breastbone, Bulaki Rao: you heard nothing."

Bulaki Rao, a quarter-hour later, was leaning over the sweetshop counter, speaking in a thick undertone:

"Halwai, friend, do not pass one word of this even to a goat or cow. The minstrel's taveez does contain a touchstone. The copper ring on Meera's finger has turned into gold. Listen. . . ."

# 14

The Seth could make a quick decision. That was the secret of his success in business. He was ready with his result while his rivals still calculated. The decision reached, he would not look back or falter, he would be headlong in action.

He had reflected well. His first rush of excitement spent, he had reflected logically. The amulet's power was beyond dispute. There was no other way the gold ring could be accounted for. It was no bluff, the girl's surprise at its discovery was genuine. Believe it or not, transmutation had taken place. That was fact number one. But the amulet had no power by itself. The person who wore it had to do an act of real kindness. Nothing else could make the touchstone work. It was like light applied to a wick. The wick was dead without the light. The light had no existence apart from the wick. Here was fact number two. The wick—fact number three—was inseparable from its holder, that is, Meera. Take the touchstone off her arm and it was a petty pebble.... Finally, copper and no other metal would be affected, copper, the sacred metal. Copper in contact with Meera's person in a special circumstance....

His neat mind sorted out these facts and the design they made conformed with ancient lore: the touchstone of olden times had also to be wakened—by prescribed ritual. Here, however, the ritual was a deed, not words. The mutual dependence of wick, light and holder had one great merit. The secret would be safe. It could never get stolen. He was thankful to the stars that he had not spoken the deadly words to the girl and alienated her. His attitude had been one of detached sympathy. In a minute it would have changed. He would have become immune to pity, rocklike with his sense of duty. Happily, he had seen the ring in the nick of time. Else, the girl would have fled from him in tears. That was how everyone in like plight had behaved. No one had shown honest understanding. But that was human nature. The Seth had no quarrel with human nature. Go your way, friend, and

I shall go mine. Do what you must, brother, and I shall do likewise. Everyone has to water his own plants. Each for himself. The immutable law of living. The iron will of the Law-giver. Who could challenge the will? Who could touch the sky with an uplifted arm or blow off a mountain with a breath?

One fact lacked precision: the act of real kindness. The act that had made the touchstone work, the key to the great mystery. That key had to be found and used with care. Planned approach. Cautious calculation. Wary step after wary step.

Look at it this way. Meera had no belief in the taveez. She expected nothing from it. But she did an act of kindness. The touchstone came to life. She was unaware of what had taken place. She had to be told. Otherwise she would have gone on wearing the gold ring, taking it to be copper.

When had the transmutation come about? She would have to recall the act so that it could be repeated. The astounding turn in her fortune, just when she was going to lose all! Of copper there was enough on earth to turn to gold. Only a hand was wanting, a hand to apply light to the wick.

The Seth looked down at his hand, plump and smooth, black hair on the knuckles. It had happily filled the pages of ledgers. Presently it would be the hand of a miner! A miner who dug deep in the bowels of kindness for golden ore!

Left to fend for herself, what would Meera do? Sharks would come darting around her. The village thief, Sadhu, would surely steal the amulet, missing the fact that, parted from its owner the touchstone had no worth. On realizing the truth that son of a crab might offer to give the amulet back on one condition: She would be his spouse. Meera wed to a professional thief who had served three terms in prison.

The helpless girl would have to be protected. That was the great need.

Fate was gracious to her in more than one way. It was not enough for her to have the touchstone. She could not do without a business partner, the right kind, honest down to his toenail. The partner would benefit equally with her. Give and take—the bedrock principle of trade. Would Meera understand? Look at it this way. You made an invention and owned its patent. You took it to a manufacturer—your own means for the purpose of production was slender. Then you must go shares with the other fellow. It was to be gainful for both. It was the right way to do business.

Would Meera have the sense to accept his plan, to be offered to her in a minute?

The helping hand was stretched toward her already! She would not have to walk to the clothshop. The phut-phutti had gone to fetch her. She would come riding through the hot noon. You who saved the life of that ass, Nago—the Seth felt a grateful moistening in his eyes. Then he gave a start. *That* was the act of kindness!

The exultation went in a moment. There had been no touchstone at the time of the well episode.

No need to worry. The hidden key would be found in a while. The act of kindness would not escape his scrutiny. Experiments were called for....

He looked up as feet shuffled. A servant-boy came in, holding an aluminum container.

"What royal dishes has your master sent me today, young monkey?"

Lakshmi gone, his daily meals had to come from the sweetshop. Unleavened bread with a little curry to dip it in—that was all his order. Luckily, Nago had gone with his mother. He would have turned up his nose at the plain fare. No, that son of an ass must learn the value of money; or else he would blow away his inheritance with two puffs from his mouth: phooh! phooh!

A new thought struck him, a regret. If only Nago were older, a grown-up lad, and Meera could be wed to him. To have her for his son's wife. The sadness that Nago was born so very late. His mother came late into this household and then took full three years to conceive.

Hardly was the meal over when the phut-phutti came roaring into the alley. The Seth reached for the earthen jug of water, tilting it over his open mouth, not touching the rim. "Remove the feast," he shouted to the young monkey squatting on his heels at the door. "Tell your master not to be stingy with spices. One more pinch of it in the curry would not have hurt him."

A second regret came. He should have asked Meera to eat with him. He could have ordered a bowl of lentils to go with the bread, and even some curds. Meera would have enjoyed the meal. Too late.

She walked in, her face strained and pallid. "Beti!" he greeted her, oozingly tender. I sent for you so that time may not be lost. Be seated." He pointed to the expensive blue-and-gold rug which he used only on

132

ceremonial occasions. "You enjoyed the ride? You were not frightened?"

"Seth-ji, word has gone flying. How fast!"

"Your phut-phutti ride? Who has the spunk to malign you? Tell me the porcupine's name and I shall sit on his chest."

"No, no." The color washed up to her ears. "We were passing the sweetshop when the Halwai called from his counter, 'Stop for two eye-flicks. A word about the touchstone—' "

He saddened. "Who could have informed that jackal? Beti, you had a talk with him?" Relieved by the shake of her head he shouted, "Bulaki Rao!" and as the inner door opened, "So! Walls have ears— and tongues."

"Walls, Seth-ji?"

"Go away," he exploded. "Take a lone walk in the meadow."

"The heat!" Bulaki Rao moaned. "Even the meadow grass is scorched, not one green blade left."

"Indeed! Then what will you eat?"

"Ji?"

"Move off. Stay away for an hour."

The touchstone—Meera was smiling to herself. The Halwai knew what had happened but Sohanlal did not, and he had turned to her a bewildered glance. "Touchstone?"

She had answered him playfully. "That is the name of a new kind of sweetmeat the Halwai has invented."

"Strange name for a sweetmeat."

"Han! Eat the relish and you will turn into gold."

"Wah! Wah!" But it was a false gaiety. The worry was plain in his face, worry on her account. She could take away the worry by revealing her secret. But, promise-bound, she could only speak in a riddle.

"Tell me. A heap of gold has fallen upon your lap. What will you do with it?" she had said, and...

The Seth was speaking again. "Meera, listen with care. Listen with your head as well as ears." Perhaps he had seen her absent look, for he asked somewhat sharply, "Are you ready?"

"Yes, Seth-ji."

His voice was purposive. The gold was real, a miracle had happened, that was an undeniable fact. Now the point was: Could the miracle be repeated? Once, twice, over and over, at will?

133

"As if you have a magic wand." She seemed to be dreaming again. "There is a fairy-tale—"

"This is no fairy-tale."

"No fairy-tale," her voice tensed in an effort at self-conviction, but her questioning eyes bent to her upper arm for the hundredth time.

He lifted a finger by way of warning. "To possess this wonder is not enough. It will act only under certain conditions. You realize that? Two things are needed. First, the raw material. Second, a power-source. The raw material is copper; the power-source is an act of kindness. Each has its problem. Take the copper first. Dealers in the metal will seize every chance to slit your throat. Even household utensils will melt off in the air. Cornering is a great art." Apparently he would have loved to divulge some secrets of that art, vaunting his inside knowledge, but restrained himself. "Copper will become so high priced," he went on, "that it will not be worth while turning it to gold. You see the hitch?"

Yes, she saw the hitch.

"Next, take the act of kindness. It means money. Maybe a great deal of money. You see the hitch again?"

Yes, she did.

"You need a partner who has both business acumen and funds. Only a partner of that kind can make you cross every hurdle. Am I right or not?"

She answered him with an uncertain gurgle of laughter in her throat. He took this for affirmation.

"Your partner will bear every risk in the venture," he went on happily. "As for the net profits—" Pause. "Now, you must not take me amiss when I suggest a fifty-fifty basis. With the right kind of management the profits will get doubled, so you will lose nothing, you will get your cent per cent. You follow the arithmetic?"

"Cent per cent." She nodded promptly.

"You have no objection to fifty-fifty?"

He waited for her to dispute that sharing and was ready to concede first an extra five per cent, then ten and even more, though at that level he must contest every inch of the ground. He was all but disappointed when she simply nodded assent. "This gold, this lunacy about a metal—" she cried, troubled, half shocked by the sudden awareness that she was responding to the lunacy, echoing it within herself. All her fields freed from the ledgers! Not hers alone. Hei-ee, Champa,

134

hei-ee, Munni, you do not owe the Seth even one piece and the earth under your plowshares is all yours!

He sensed the ache of her unwilling surrender. "Beti, this is the way of the world," he soothed. "This is how the life-river flows. We have to sail with the current. Those who dare sail against it—" His hands made an expressive gesture.

Hei-ee, Sohagi, maybe you saw the blue bird? Your wish is fulfilled. You have land, good cotton earth. Your man will have other animals to coax beside his cart pair to whom he cries, "Run hard, gentlemen, run hard!"

A sudden shadow came to the Seth's face. Fifty per cent—he need not have rushed to make that offer. Forty would have been fair enough. Too late. The regret grew oppressive. Honest money thrown away. Fool! No match for a peasant girl. His breath became labored, his head drooped.

"You are not ill, Seth-ji?"

He pulled himself together. "A whiff of air under the scalp." He shook his head vigorously to release the trapped air. Turning aside he picked up the water jug and tilted it over his mouth. With his throat moistened he felt relieved. Why cry for milk which the cat had lapped up?

"Then it is agreed—finally?"

"Yes, Seth-ji."

His smile of happiness was a grimace. After all, she also had thrown away ten per cent or more. She could have asked even for seventy and got it! One squabbled every day with hyenas wanting to eat your blood. Good to do business, for once, with a newborn lamb.

"Here is a draft agreement." Out of the heaped papers on his desk he produced two scribbled sheets. "Read it with good care. Clause one. You, hereafter called the proprietor, grant and assign to the sponsor, that is myself, the sole and exclusive license to produce gold out of you by every legitimate means and to collect, deposit and vend the product. The proprietor is agreeable to giving the sponsor all cooperation asked for and acting as directed, within the limits valid by law and equity. Is that clear?"

"Ji." Confusedly.

"The proprietor guarantees that she undertakes to indemnify the sponsor against any loss, injury or damage (including legal costs or

135

expenses properly incurred) occasioned to the sponsor in consequence of any breach of this agreement. Do you follow?"

"Yes, Seth-ji."

"Move on to Clause four which says that the expenses will be wholly borne by the sponsor, the proprietor sharing only the profits."

"No, Seth-ji."

"No?" He was aghast.

"Costs and expenses—those also I must share. Take my gold ring into the account."

"Beti!" The feeling was thick in his throat. "You must not say that again. Had Lakshmi, your friend and well-wisher, come to grace my household a few years earlier, we might have been blessed with a daughter of your age. Or if that son of an ass, Nago, had been born some years before you—" He cut short with a low chuckle. "Let that pass. Nago is your dear brother. You saved his life. And you saved *me*."

"I saved you?"

"I had fallen into a pit of perfidy, no less fatal than the well. The cinema show, remember? I tried to deny the women. Routing and humbling this son of a rogue, you saved him."

"We outwitted you." She hesitated a little. "We had to do it. Equal rights for men and women, that was the song. We had to fight for that song."

"Indeed!" A growl came into his voice but he caught himself up instantly. He broke into a forced fit of coughing with which to mask his anger and regain poise. "Listen," he changed the subject. "Grandma's gout. Have you got the name of the Bombay ass? The one who sells tiger fat?"

"The price—"

"Leave that to me. Only let me have the name." The quill pen alighted from his ear. "And now for your signature, beti, right at the bottom of this page." Adding with proud approval, "You do not have to thumb-mark an agreement."

*Pernam* to the Devi that the good work was completed. On to the next stage.

"Have you given thought to the missing key?"

"We have no keys. Nothing in the house to lock up." The gold ring lay on the desk. Shall I slip it back to my finger? she thought.

He smiled. The newborn lamb! "Beti, it will not be long before you will have plenty to keep under lock and key. But it is not that kind of key I have in mind. The secret of the touchstone. Through what precise act of kindness the miracle came about."

"Kindness, Seth-ji?" She shook her head quickly, as if this was her chance to tear up his arguments and even the agreement itself. "I have not done any act of kindness. I am tough!"

"It was done unawares. So it happens often with most of us who are good-hearted people. If you ask me, I could cite several such acts of kindness I have done of late. It is in my nature—and yours." He did not see her amused mouth and added, "As for the load of copper—"

"Load?"

"Rings, bangles, amulets, anklets, neck-chain. Yes, waist-chain. A copper nugget under the clothes, next to the skin. Each piece must be solid, heavy."

"I have to stay in bed?"

"The Devi forbid!"

"How shall I work in the fields?"

He gave a hoot of laughter. "You will not."

"Even to walk with all that load. Children on the streets will follow me, yelling, 'Madwoman!'"

He tapped his head with his thick knuckles. "You think I have no sense? The ornaments will have a bright gold wash. You will love to wear them." He paused, saddened by the thought of the needless extravagance. The foolish vanity of women!

"When the ornaments become gold, how am I to know?" That prospect, now specific, resolved in terms of images, filled her with apprehension.

"What you wear under the clothes will not be gilded. The waist-chain and the nugget. One glance at them, and you will know."

"Ji." She was about to reach for the gold ring when she saw him pick it up as if casually and thrust it in the drawer. Her offer to share costs was accepted?

"To experiment and to observe, then deduce—that is the scientific way." His voice was solemn. "That is our way."

The driver fellow must ride off immediately to town and place urgent orders with every available smith. They must work day and night and get the ornaments ready in twenty-four hours' time. Even so, the interim was long enough for Meera to slip into an act of kindness. That act would go to waste.

The problem solved itself in a minute. He turned aside to open a cashbox full to the brim with copper coins.

"Your real work will begin tomorrow. Meanwhile, hold these coins tied up in your waist cloth. Just in case—Meera, do you follow?" He pointed to the inner room vacated by his assistant. "Step in there and get this done, beti."

"Now?"

"Why not? The coins have to touch your bare skin, remember."

"So many?"

He was gazing hard at the shabby brown pile he hated, the token of a big business loss. Loss into gain! Pice into *mohar*! The irony of fate. The Wheel going round and round with unforeseen effects. The all-seeing Devi in her sanctum laughing heartily at the turns and twists of the curious human comedy!

## 15

There was no motorcycle waiting to take Meera back. The Seth had given Sohanlal a list of gilded ornaments and rushed him off to town. "Don't gape at us. Nothing much to see in my face, or hers. Hurry, man, hurry."

Overwhelmed, walking slowly homeward, she went over the crazy happenings of the past hour, trying to make sense out of them. The summons from Seth-ji. Grandma, down with gout, had murmured, "Meera, go and see him on my behalf. Whatever he says, do not feel fear, do not feel shame. We have done nothing that is unworthy." Yet, in the clothshop, fear had chilled her. Not ten minutes had passed before an altogether different feeling chilled her equally. Copper into gold. A touchstone. A fantastic promise come true!

The immediate peril on her head was gone, so it seemed. Back home, she had met Grandma's anxious glance with, "He asked me to come later in the day." The second summons, and this time she was to go riding in the motorcycle. She was grateful to the Seth that he had sent her the person she wanted to see most. He had driven at a slow pace, prolonging the few minutes. "Touchstone? That is the name of a new sweetmeat the Halwai has invented." And then: "Tell me. A heap of gold has fallen upon your lap. What will you do with it?"

"How much?"

She had pondered this while the motorcycle went along and half the way to the clothshop was covered.

"Big heap," uncertainly.

"A thousand rupees' worth?"

"More. Much more."

"Ten thousand."

She nodded, approving. "How will you spend the fortune?"

"I?" And with a whimsical air, "Buy a motorcycle. Ride off to Bombay. That will be a wish fulfilled."

"Bombay? What for?" But he burst into laughter and asked in his turn, "You? What will you do with your ten thousand rupees?"

"Pay off all our debts. Also Champa's, Munni's and the Old Father's. You know the Old Father, our neighbor? His second grandson, Roghuvir—"

"Yes. What else?"

"Buy good plowland for Sohagi. She needs it badly. You helped her once, remember? The cart had broken down and you fetched the carpenter called Drunk—"

"That is all?"

"Ride the green bus. All the Cowhouse on the bus. We will stop at H. Singh's Paradise, eat eggfruit stuffed with mincemeat."

"Nine-tenths of the money is still unspent."

She was baffled. "So much money! There is no way to spend it then."

"You want nothing for yourself?" he cried. "Clothes. Jewelry." And she answered, "When the land is ours again and we keep all that we produce, all the cotton and millet and maize, there is nothing else to ask for."

"A rich husband—"

The smack of her lips conveyed her answer.

"A husband to suit your high status."

"Look at my pair of wings!" Mockful arms flapping up and down.

"Fairy wings," he went on gravely. "Fairy girl—" He turned his eyes to her an instant. "Is it possible that you—you and I—" He was fumbling for words but had to stop. They were passing the tamarind.

She gave herself to the recollection as she walked homeward and her lips smiled quizzically. What had he wanted to say? Why had he hesitated?

The sadness, that he was gone on an errand not knowing what it implied, and his heart heavy on her account. If only he would turn back from the highroad and pull up at her side! She would not, at first, tell him about the miracle. She would wear a look of abject misery, and he would think that the worst was to be her lot. He would flare up against the Seth. That would be the time for her to ask: A poor tiller is forced to borrow from the Seth and put his neck in the noose. The noose tightens. What has your paper from Delhi to say on this problem? He would, maybe, answer that the new rulers whom the people elect would root out the tyranny. But then, by the time it happened, where would the Old Father be? Where would Gran'ma be? And she, Meera?

No, she would not make him unhappy even for a moment.

We are saved, she would tell him. The touchstone has acted. Ask the Seth to show you the gold ring. Look twice at it, both you and Grandma, and then speak.

Truly, it was not easy to believe in a touchstone. But the Seth was no ass; he would not make a business deal with fancy as its basis. The stress of excitement in his face and its deep throb in his voice!

Such madness about gold! A mystic value was set on the yellow metal, so that there could be a game for men to play. Whoever gained the metal, more and yet more, came up on top and all bowed to him with palms folded, "*Maharaj*, great one!" A man's worth was best stated in terms of his gold. A race apart from humbler folk; super-beings; golden gods!

Strange for a peasant girl to be drawn into that charmed circle. The minstrel who cared nothing for riches had brought this upon her —playfully?

Under the fig tree sat Grandma, waiting tensely for bad news. "Meera."

"Hei-ee Gran'ma! Tiger fat coming from Bombay!"

Grandma gaped. "One more loan? He is willing?"

"Just a gift."

"No!"

"True, Gran'ma."

She was scowling hard. "He sent for you simply to talk about tiger fat?"

"What else?" But the look in her face betrayed her.

"Such a change of heart," Grandma began, her voice sarcastic, but she broke short, startled. Following the eyes intent on her body Meera tried to smooth the sari folds over the bulge of copper coins.

"Meera!" Grandma croaked, while the girl's hands flattened under her clothes, pressing, displaying more fully the telltale curve. Horror came upon Grandma. She rubbed her eyes as if she could not believe what she saw.

"You look scared, Gran'ma!"

No, no, it could not be. . . . But it was unmistakable. . . : To have missed this for months, to have gone blind!

In her seventeenth year and yet ungiven. Every other village girl of her age a mother. Grandma on her haunches turned to stone.

A year before, it had happened to Kasthuri, a young childless widow, the youngest daughter  of one of the Five Elders. Such a quiet girl—who would have thought this possible? She was taken to the barber's wife who had drugs and devices.

There was a mother of four whose husband had gone to war. Away three years, perhaps dead, and his spouse started to grow into that shape. The barber-woman had charge of her, too, and the tortured one, a mother of four though she was, rent the air with frantic wailing.

Grandma breathed as if she had been running fast.

"Gran'ma, have I turned into a ghost?"

She braced herself. "Tell me—" the crucial query was on her tongue. She must make sure. She cleared her throat before she forced herself to ask the question and waiting for answer she could feel her heart flutter.

"Why, Gran'ma?" But the puzzled frown cleared in a moment and she was gazing happily toward the road. Sohagi, hurry! Hei-ee Champa-Munni!

"Tell me."

But it was too late. Grandma's mouth stayed open in cold suspense while the women came rushing along.

"Meera! You have befooled the Seth—again!"

"The village is all excited."

"Tell us what has happened. Tell us everything."

Grandma shivered. She could see the gaunt barber-woman with witch talons at work, the devices and drugs. Drugs and devices, hour after hour. Feet trampled the prostrate body, squeezed the womb-flower. Grandma, seeing, hearing, let her hand fly to her throat lest she scream. No, not that . . .

She veered in desperate challenge. Her agony grew solid, making a shield in her hand. A shield for the girl, to hold her from the witch-woman. Whatever happened, Meera had to be defended against the drugs, devices. . . .

Grandma hitched herself to her feet.

"You have no shame in slandering her, though you call her a dear friend. Han, Sohagi? Han, Champa? No matter. We will be off in two-three days. We will give Sonamitti three good kicks and walk away." She lifted a foot heavily, wincing because of the stiffness, and kicked the mudfloor thrice. She gave a gasp, the wrinkles in her face deep as scars.

The women were bewildered.

"What has come upon you, Grandma?"

"We have only asked for the plain facts."

"One day Lakshmi tried to sell the taveez to the Seth. He was about to say yes when he changed his mind."

"It is yes, this time. Han, Meera?"

She shook her head gravely. "It is not what you think. Listen." She paused, recapturing the scene, and started from the point where the ledger had revealed her doom. She had felt her head spin . . . first with fear, than surprise.

"A ring of pure gold! And when this big heap of copper coins under my waist cloth turns into gold likewise—" She patted the bulge dreamily.

Grandma's face had now cleared, but her hand as she fumbled with Meera's jacket sleeve was still unsteady. "Touchstone!" she mocked, gazing at the taveez tied with red string. The shame was rankling in her that she had had such ugly thoughts about Meera. But the big bulge did look just like *that*!

"Gran'ma," retorted Meera, "I do not have to tell you what the Seth's ledger held. Had there been no gold ring on my finger—" She surveyed the stunned faces of her friends. "Sohagi, where is your tongue?"

"Meera, I am voiceless because of great joy."

"Your land is safe; we are rid of a terrible worry."

"We shall make offerings to the Devi under the banyan tree."

"May I touch the taveez, Meera?"

She held up her arm, amused by the thought that her friends had no glimmering of the plans in her mind. She would keep them in the dark. Deeds, not words. When the gold came—

"Sohanlal knows?" Grandma asked abruptly.

"Not yet. The Seth has sent him to town. He will be back tomorrow with the ornaments." The fun that he did not know who was to wear the ornaments he bought!

"Good, anyway, that you will at last decorate yourself," said Grandma. "I, at your age—"

"Bangles and neck-chains and anklets and much else," Meera continued. "The Seth made a long list of the jewelry."

That seemed to add a touch of reality to what was still part fantasy. The stingy Seth would not spend his heart's blood to buy a rainbow! Even so, the women had misgivings.

"Did you take a good look at his face when he said it was a gold ring?" Bimla asked. "He has a kind of half-smile, a sure sign of duplicity."

Munni said, "He must have been wearing his best robe, the blue-and-gold one, which tells he is bent on mischief. With that robe on, he cried to Meera, 'Strip, strip if you must.' And he—"

"Stop, Munni," Meera made an impatient gesture. "The Seth could not have known in advance that we were coming to the clothshop to make the stupid threat."

Champa was more positive. "The ornaments are nothing but advertising," she announced.

"What!"

"The Seth has a fad for advertising. Lakshmi showed me a page in a newspaper; it had the picture of a woman draped in lovely clothes, and the lettering went, 'Sale! Grand sale at Gay Peacock House. Stocks cleared at half rates.' That had cost him fifty rupees."

"So what?"

"Then there was the picture play. It was meant to tell people why they must buy the vegetable ghee, Peerless. The clothshop is going to deal with a new line: gilded ornaments."

"So what?"

"Still you do not understand?" Champa beamed. "The Seth has built up a situation in which Meera has to wear a bodyful of jewelry. She is not like us, she does not care for ornaments, so this device is to be used. Sonamitti women will be fascinated by the gilded display on her body. The new business line at the clothshop will get a wonderful start."

Meera snapped, "How clever you are, Champa-sister. But the Seth need not have taken so much trouble. He could simply have sent for you. Happily would you wear a load of gilded ornaments!"

Champa shook her head. "I? People will laugh at me. Worn by you, the ornaments will be ten times more attractive."

"A hundred times," Munni gushed. "To think that we have such a beauty in Sonamitti!" She took Meera's hand in her protective clasp.

"Beauty, indeed!" Meera turned up her lip. "Take a bus ride to town and there you will see beauty. Han, Bimla?" She gave her city-bred friend an anxious look, fearing affirmation.

Bimla said, "Meera, you do not have to be so very modest. I can tell you this much: Walk the city street and every young fellow will stop to look at you."

"We do not want every young city fellow to look at her," retorted Grandma. "One is enough. Just one."

"Just one," the women nudged each other and Munni broke into her habitual giggle. Then Grandma rushed to Meera's rescue. "Have you, Cowhouse women, come hotfoot only to discuss a face? Have you forgotten the touchstone?"

At this point Meera passed her hand into the neck of her jacket and pulled out a sheet of paper. "There!" gravely. It was a copy of the Seth's agreement. Bimla took it from the outstretched hand and read aloud.

Everyone became serious. Here, again, was the impact of reality. The Seth would not sign an agreement frivolously. He had even used his seal; with its engraving of the lotus-eyed goddess of wealth, it was used only on deeds of great value. And the words heavy with legal flavor—Bimla's face lowered to the right tone of respect as she read: "... grant and assign to the sponsor the sole and exclusive license to produce gold out of you by every legitimate means and to collect, deposit and vend the product. . . ."

There was a minute's silence before Champa spoke. "Some people say this, some say that, but all ask, 'What next?'" She shook her head, conveying the common bewilderment.

Meera shared the bewilderment and breathed, "What next?" She stood leaning against the wall and in the hush that fell again, she found her question answered in her mind. There was the right person on whom to rely—the luck that he had come to Sonamitti! *Nine-tenths of the money is still unspent.* Let it be his headache as well. Why, she must look well beyond the needs of the Cowhouse. Almost every one in the village was heavily in debt. What if she could release every piece of land from its stranglehold? Even to think of such a big thing was to feel dizzy! But *he*, with his knowledge and under-standing . . .

She would repay him for his help with the gift of a motorcycle. It

145

would be a mere token of her gratefulness, but his wish to go riding to Bombay would be fulfilled.

Bombay was five hundred miles away.

No, no, she would not buy him a motorcycle. The swift decision felt like a shock. She hung her head in shame but the decision remained. Bombay was five hundred miles away. . . .

# 16

In the next hour the village was all astir. The Cow-house women had added their contribution to the news first handed out by the sweetshop. The jewelry to come from town. The agreement with its sacred seal. The touchstone did look real!

Touchstone! The utmost surprise on record so far in the memory of aged people was the talking goat, and that dated back forty, fifty years or more. A village Elder had purchased the goat for its meat on the occasion of a marriage feast. When about to be slaughtered, the goat had spoken in a human voice: "Friend, spare my life." The knife had dropped from a trembling hand. A rash youth, scornful of such wild fancy, had picked up the knife, but as he was about to use it the words came once more from the goat's mouth, "Friend, spare my life." The youth had broken down in remorse and touched the animal's hoofs reverentially, praying to be forgiven. Plainly, a human soul resided in the goat's body; maybe it was a yogi engaged in an act of penance. The goat attained sanctity. Fed on votive offerings, it grew to old age and, dying, it became a legend.

That great wonder was to be surpassed. Touchstone!

Not all misgivings were gone, however, and sceptical voices could be heard. Men and women, pulled between opposite viewpoints, came hurrying to Meera's place to find some clue to the truth. But Meera was in the kitchen and Grandma guarding the housedoor. The string of prayer beads in her hand created an inviolable sanctuary.

"Good folk," she broke her silence between two beads, "mind your own business. What is it to you whether Meera's touchstone is real or not?"

In the fading light of dusk the people hung around the fig tree, discussing the touchstone, hating to go back while the puzzle remained unsolved and their minds divided and restless.

Look, friend. The Seth plays a game, to be sure. First he tells us about his dream. The Gold goddess, the bright image under an outer skin of mud. Then, the man with the lyre who can make himself invisible. Both are devices by which the wily Seth shows his faith in Atmaram. Yet he summons Meera to his clothshop and threatens her with the red ledger—as if her touchstone is a figment of fancy. You see the contrariness?

No contrariness, brother. It is only that the Seth had his doubts and gave way to them. We all had our doubts, some more, some less.

You speak the right words, friend. It is the ring that has settled the question for everyone, the copper ring turning into pure gold.

It may still be a game of deceit. Maybe we fail to see the Seth's inner motive. That sly one—

What! A game costing a heap of jewelry, costing his heart's blood!

Listen to the minstrel's voice. *This taveez holds a stone. The stone has power. It is a touchstone.* We cannot distrust that voice.

It may well be something else that he meant. Not a real touchstone. He meant, maybe—

Copper has turned into gold, all the same.

So the Seth tells us. We have not seen the ring.

As if we peasant folk can tell gold from gilded metal!

We can never trust the Seth's word, that is the bare truth.

In this one instance he has nothing to gain by deceit.

Who knows? That fish of deep water—

Even fish of deep water may turn out honest for once.

Time will tell us.

Yes, yes, we have only to wait and watch.

Grandma sat leaning against the wall, telling her beads, but her ears were attuned to the hum of talk. Wait and watch, she echoed under her breath. That was the only way. For, she was as full of doubt as some of those bewildered people. One miracle had happened, though; at the point of striking at his victims the Seth had changed his mind. It was as if the minstrel, so far away, had reached out to them with a protective arm. Grandma felt an ache of yearning for her man and heaved a sigh. Why did he still have to be a minstrel? He was not young any more; his face had a tired look and the soles of his bare feet were all cracked with endless tramping. Maybe, sometimes, he could get no shelter for the night and had to sleep on the roadside with a blanket spread in the dust for his bedding. Maybe, sometimes, no one gave him food and he went hungry. He had a liking for lemon pickles and here at home he could have a portion with every meal—the lemon tree in the kitchen yard was laden with fruit. She could not eat pickles, and not Meera either, thinking of the man far from home, and they prepared the jarfuls only to give them to friends.

How close they had been to ruin! What torments Meera had suffered. Supposing the Seth had not noticed the ring? Fate had hung on the slender thread of a chance.

There was a stir near the fig tree and Grandma woke from her musings. The Five Elders were coming. "May we have a word or two with you, if the beads are done?"

"Come to the kitchen."

When they were all seated on a floor mat with legs crossed, one Elder spoke.

"The village has a new fear," he began. "We have seen you, Meera's Grandma, challenge the Seth and start a vote-mote battle. He had no chance against you, whom all the people love, but we did not expect to see everything go smoothly. The Seth was not the man to sit quiet, cracking his finger-joints, waiting to be beaten. We were worried on your account."

She nodded. "You had to be, brother."

"The Seth would fight back with every weapon. He would fight with every means, fair or foul. We were quite helpless—"

"What could you do?"

"The metal in you is of a harder kind than what we have in us. We bow at your feet, Meera's Grandma. As for Meera—"

Grandma shook her head. "I am nothing. Meera is less than nothing. A village Elder speaking fanciful words!"

A minute's pause. Meera and Grandma looked at each other. The Elders, it seemed, had not yet revealed their minds.

"Speak," Grandma urged. "Let there be no walls between folks of the same blood and bone."

Yet the pause continued. The Elders bent their heads. Then Grandma said, "There is something that troubles you."

"That is true, Grandma." The answer came from Rajaram.

"Tell me. Let your hearts be at ease."

Meera added, "Do not worry about us. The Seth has signed a deed. He will not take our land."

"Beti, it is the deed that troubles us."

"The deed is safe enough." If only she could tell them about the other partner she would have, who would guard her against all likely traps.

"Let them look into the deed," suggested Grandma and Meera pulled it out of its niche under her jacket.

The document passed from hand to hand and when all the five had read it, Rajaram shook his head dejectedly. "This partnership is solid and secure, as we expected. So we have this question to ask: What next?"

"What next in the vote-mote?" Another Elder made the point clear. "Two partners cannot be ranged against each other. The two who sit on the same bough of a tree cannot hack off the bough."

Meera said frowning, "What bough?"

"You cannot work with a person and work against that person at the same time. You cannot be half here, half there."

"No half and half," she answered. "With all of myself I will work with the Seth in one field where our motives meet. With all of myself I will work against him in another field where our motives are in conflict."

Rajaram said, "Meera, beti, look at it from another angle. Grandma will lose her fields unless the Seth grants her a favor and does not use his right to foreclose. Will she accept this gift from his hand and then try to bite the hand?"

Grandma saw the problem. "No," she cried, "I cannot take the Seth's gift. I—"

"The gift has been taken. Meera read the story in the ledger and saw how it must move on to its end. But the story, close to its end, took a new beginning. You know how that happened. The facts are clear, Meera's Grandma."

Stiff silence. Meera held her anxious glance on Grandma as if waiting to see yet another wrinkle sink into the aged face. The dilemma could be solved only in one way. And she heard Grandma speak in sad affirmation.

"In the excitement of our escape from the ledgers I did not see the whole truth. As things are, I cannot oppose the Seth at the vote-mote. I have no place in it."

"Then the Seth will go to the board riding a gay chariot." Meera swept her accusing glance over the five faces.

The answer came from one Elder. "We have learnt our lesson from Grandma. If she permits me, I will be the fellow for the vote-mote."

Grandma stared hard. "You spoke to me one day about seven ever-hungry mouths. All your fields pledged to the Seth—"

"Yours, too. That did not tie up your hands. I need some of your strength, Grandma, to face the tyrant."

"No, no," cried another man. "Let me be the fellow for the board-moard. For I have not much to lose. I have no big household—"

Other voices followed in a clamor.

"I have even less to lose than you. I have—"

"Brother, first look at my claim. It is better than anyone else's."

"No, mine is the best." Rajaram rose to his feet. "Pray listen. Give me a chance. My sons are big and strong. Landless, they will not starve. No unmarried daughter in my house, no dependent widow—"

At this point a voice was heard calling from the yard, "Meera's Grandma!" Everyone in the kitchen turned his surprised face door-ward. The Seth came striding up. Watching the group on the floor mat, he cried, "Do not let me interrupt your talk. I will wait awhile in the yard." But he belied himself as he turned to Meera saying, "Beti, there is little time to spare. We must try hard to find out what the act of kindness was. You will need my help to stir your recollection. Let us start with the day the taveez was given to you, then work slowly through the hours and minutes of each day that has followed."

The Elders took this plain hint. "Our talk is over, Seth-ji, we are ready to leave."

As they stepped out to the yard, he called, "Will one of you do me a favor? As you pass the Devi's temple, will you give the Brahmin a message on my behalf? Tomorrow, toward the day's end, we will make a *puja* offering to the goddess, Meera and I."

"Five annas' worth?"

He hesitated but only for an instant. "Five quarter-rupees," his voice was firm. Then he hastened to add: "It is not the money value of an offering that counts. It is the feeling in the heart. The depth of devotion in two hearts." He pointed a finger to his heart and made a gesture toward Meera's.

Why the quarter-rupees either, since devotion is enough?—Meera was about to ask, but she saw Grandma's eyes blink merrily and kept quiet.

## 17

A reed screen, once dyed blue, hung faded at the back of the sweetshop counter, parting it from the inner living quarters. The Halwai stood behind the screen, close to a two-foot window letting in daylight, a slice of frameless glass in his hand. Watching his lean face contained in the glass he saw his Adam's apple grow fretful in the habitual way under the stress of his feelings.

The collyrium with which he had touched his eyelids had belonged to his wife and lain unused in her wooden box all the years since she was gone. That beauty aid had escaped the grabbing hands of his daughters, Tuti and Kuti, who paid him an occasional visit with their husbands, and the main object of man and wife, each pair, was to stuff themselves with unpaid-for sweetmeat. No village people, not even women, wore *surma* to make their eyes bright and deep, but the mother of those girls had been city-born. In the city even men were known to use *surma*, with one good reason. The Halwai, today, had that reason.

The face in the mirror was without its usual stubble and the inky mustache was well clipped. The hair had a new look, cut uneven, city-style. For, the Halwai had not depended on the village barber's circumscribed art; only a craftsman in town could produce the required sleekness. Not that the Halwai liked it. Better to have an even clip, the short hair proclaiming the right shape of the head, but who was to scorn "fashion"?

The haircut had been expensive. You had to add to the city barber's fee the two-way bus fares and tea at H. Singh's Paradise. The occasion called for such extravagance. More of it was about to follow. There stood on the counter a small brass tray with an exquisite almond-pistachio cream fit for a king's palate. The path to a woman's heart lay across the length of her tongue. Coaxing her tongue you trapped her inner being. The greedy vixen! Meera deserved the treat anyhow. A long rope—it would haul gold!

He made faces at himself as he looked in the frameless glass. He could seldom look for long in a mirror without being tempted into grimaces. The skin folded up, bunching at the cheekbones; the mouth widened ear to ear, snapped to a beaky pout and stretched again, repeating the process back and forth with variations. But while his face amused itself his mind worked without interruption.

The strange march of events in the past few weeks. One day Meera came to the sweetshop with a query and received a marriage proposal. Eyes becomingly dropped, she spoke of laddoo and jilebi. She did not have to be told what it meant to be a sweetshop spouse—she was good enough at calculation! She looked forward to eat the best relishes, no payments demanded, no questions asked.

His thoughts lingered on that scene. *Old Uncle.* He had resented the title but later its meaning stood clear. A word with two tongues! A hint, a veiled reproach, for she wanted him *not* to look an Old Uncle. She was artful for a peasant girl. Her abashed face had betrayed her, though. Ho, beloved!

He nodded to the slice of glass, sniffing and asking a question. Was the attar he had touched to his mustache heavy-scented enough? That attar, drawn out of musk, was no mean expense. Han, brother, no Old Uncle had ever before worn attar!

Truly, his marriage proposal had nothing to do with the touchstone, that was apparent from the time factor. Well before the touchstone came, he had conveyed his wish to the Five Elders assembled under the banyan tree, and they had exchanged glances with each other and said, "Wait, Halwai-brother. We will think it over." It suited him to wait, busy as he was with his new shop in Pipli. The new shop meant extra work and a headache, but it also meant extra money! Leave out the Seth, and none but he in the Seven Villages could claim to have "two pice." Everyone knew that fact and surely Meera; that belly of hers, a gold-brown strip visible under the short jacket and inviting a man's eyes and cuddling touch, was not empty of knowledge.

He also had a sort of windfall once. Word had dropped as if from the sky that on the day of the next solar eclipse the rain-swollen Kanhan would be hungry for sweetmeats. Mothers who made offerings to the river goddess, one *pau* per child, would win bliss for their darlings and safety from future mishaps. Hundreds of them came rushing to his shop and he had to engage five assistants who toiled madly with rice-flour and ghee and sugar, toiled all day and all night, not stopping to eat or to sleep with their wives. From early dawn platter after platter of sweets was emptied, basket after basket. The mothers were not content to buy just one *pau*, for the more they gave unto the river the more bliss their children would gain.

There was a mishap at the day's end, when the mothers had gone away. Brats had been diving in the water, recovering dumped sweets. One, a girl, failed to come back to the surface. Her body was found later a mile downstream. The girl's mother, poor as she was, had not been able to give unto the river and retribution had come all too swiftly.

Today, again, he was having a windfall, even if a minor one, and it was a gift from Tuti-Kuti's mother-to-be!

The act of kindness, the key to the miracle. Seth-ji had lost no time since the gold ring came to light yesterday afternoon. He had spent the evening trying to make Meera recall her act of kindness. On his way back home, he had stopped at the sweetshop. "Five basketfuls of jilebi for tomorrow," he had ordered. "Make them crisp and good to eat. Do not slit my throat, however."

"Seth-ji, how can I slit your throat and lose my best customer?"

He was in a rare communicative mood. "Jilebi unto gold," he had said, and happy as he was, explained what he meant. Meera had recalled one act of kindness, just one. That act was to be repeated—on a magnified scale.

Strangely, that one act had been done in the sweetshop's shadow. The Halwai could have cited every detail to the Seth but had wisely held his tongue.

It happened a few days after the minstrel had left. The rag-woman's Buddhu, a cross-eyed brat, was crouching near the sweetshop in mid-day sun, licking an empty leaf-cup that a customer had thrown away. He wiped the smears of syrup with his tongue, like a dog. Brats of his kind had to be kicked off lest they cast an evil eye on the trays of sweets and upset the customer's bile. "Shoo . . . shoo!" he had cried out. That son of a near-destitute did not care. His mother collected old scraps from door to door and sold them at the market for a few pieces of copper, and here was the young son sitting proud and heedless like a Seth! At this point Meera came down the road, returning from her work in the fields. She stopped, watched Buddhu a minute, then walked up to the shop. "Jilebi—" She dropped a half-anna on the counter.

He would treat her to a bowl of whey to make her feel cool—there was sweat on her face and all over her body. He would like to wipe the sweat off her body with a corner of his dhoti! He had also to tell her that "Old Uncle" was not sucking his thumb, he had just spoken to the Five Elders and the commuting fine would soon be settled. But first of all he would give her jilebi. "This is enough for a half-anna?" he said, and it was a full anna-worth that he held out across the counter. His fingers touched hers and ho, brother, how his body tingled! He tried to clutch her arm, but she slipped off beyond reach. Back to the beggar's brat. Lo, the leaf-cup passed to the grimy hand.

"So very unfair," he chaffed her gently.

She turned her face and there was a strange look in it, a feeling all bare. As he gazed in surprise, she turned away and with her sari she wiped the brat's running nose. In a moment she was walking away.

He was very angry. Why must he lose the extra half-anna-worth? He would snatch the leaf-cup from Buddhu's hand, pull him by the ear and give him two good kicks on the arse. But the cross-eyed rogue-number-one was too quick for him. Smelling danger, he bounced like a rubber ball and sprinted away.

That stupidity of hers was supposed to have turned a copper ring into gold. It was "real kindness" and had made her touchstone act. Kindness at the expense of another person—Seth-ji had failed to see that point. He would let the folly be repeated. All the Buddhus in the village would line up near the sweetshop, have their leaf cups filled from Meera's hand with fried *puri* bread and jilebi, and eat happily. That would be an act of kindness a hundred times over!

Seth-ji, shrewd and calculating, had made a bad slip. The expense of this folly would bring no return. There was no virtue in feeding brats with sweetmeat, you only gave them a craving for what they could not get ever again. Meera would have to think hard once more. What other act of kindness could she have done?

The windfall for the sweetshop was the starting point for the good things to follow. The shock for the Seth in store. The unwritten agreement that he would be compelled to make. The district board was not to be graced by his presence. The place on which his greedy eye was fixed would be taken by the sweetshop!

"Seth-ji," the sweetshop would make this offer, "you have a contract with my spouse and she must honor it. But she must honor also the bidding of her household king. Let there be an understanding

156

between us, as between friends and brothers. I do not ask for a share of your gold to come. What my woman will get as her portion will satisfy me. Now, listen well. Drop out of the vote-mote. Leave it to me. You understand?"

Eyes popping, the Seth would cry heatedly, "You have nothing to gain from the district board. You do not know its business. You—"

The sweetshop would stop this outburst with, "Seth-ji, I am not such a goat as you think. The contractor fellow may just as well deal with me. I know what low-grade cement he has earmarked for the bridge, he bought it from a dump of the Military Disposal. Let him supply it. What do I care, so long as I get my ten per cent?"

"What ten per cent?" The Seth had the innocent look of a newborn infant. "I have never heard of such dealings. Why, it is theft and even worse. Think of an ox-cart crossing the bridge and the structure toppling into the river. The contractor, son of a crocodile, will be skinned alive."

The sweetshop would laugh in the Seth's face. "No, brother. The crocodile will not lose his skin. He will simply have to part once more with some of his gains. Let us talk business. The bridge is just one item among many others, each giving its ten per cent. All that will be the sweetshop's belly-ache. You see what I mean?"

"What nonsense!" And at that stupid remark the sweetshop would have to get tough.

"Look, friend. Just follow my bidding. Keep well away from the vote-mote. I have made up my mind to be a board member. It will be as good a milch-cow for me as for you. Say 'No,' and your agreement with my household woman will become a good joke. She will make the touchstone work under my sole guidance and you will not even know what has happened. Figure out the fortune you will lose. What! The ten per cent means more to you than a half-share of the touchstone gold? Then you are not in your senses. A man who is not in his senses cannot sit on the board-moard. You have lost the vote fight. Will you lose the gold, too? Think twice and then twice over. Come and speak to me when you have seen what is what. Ram-Ram, Seth-ji!"

The Halwai, satisfied with his sharp rejoinder to the Seth, turned again to the mirror, grinning and watching himself. He felt the heady perfume of musk sweep through him in waves of delight. But he pricked up his ears a minute later. A clamor on the road. The brats were coming. He replaced the mirror on the shelf, face back, for a sparrow nesting on the eaves pecked at the glass, fighting the other sparrow it saw. He moved off to the reed screen and drew it aside. Yes, the roadside was crowded—well ahead of the appointed hour. The Seth had consulted the almanac and found a propitious time, the hundred moments of the duration of sunset. In those hundred moments Meera would do her act of kindness and the gilded copper she wore in profusion would get transmuted. Not all the load of copper was gilded, though. Not, for instance, the nugget. It was meant to be hung from her neck, always touching her bare bosom, under the jacket. How could that be done? The red jacket, stretching tight, could hardly cope with her rising breasts! Yet the Seth had demanded of her in the temple sanctum, "You have the nugget strung to your neck chain?" "No, Seth-ji." "You have it on your person?" "Ji." The stupid man, not content yet, had gone on, "Where?" "Somewhere." "It has to touch your body." "I know." "Then you are quite sure—" She had turned her face in disgust and kept quiet.

Where could she have worn it? Intrigued by the Seth's question the Halwai had stripped her naked. But he had failed in his search. He would make another attempt when she arrived in an hour. Meanwhile the brats were squatting in a line on the faded grass and there were people coming down from both directions. All Sonamitti would be here soon, a beating drum in every heart, all crazy about the miracle.

18 The hundred moments had gone by, slow-footed yet swift, and there was no telling whether the miracle had happened. The gilded metal seemed unchanged in sheen but a shade of difference would not be apparent to peasant eyes. The Seth's face betrayed nothing while his hands were busy with the cord of his gown, tying and untying the knot.

At the line's end Meera had dropped the basket onto the grass and walked off, stiff as a puppet, yet fast. Away from the mass of people transfixed and waiting for a sign, she would give a glance to the nugget or waist-chain. But even when she had walked a hundred steps she did not look under her clothes. The heaviness of breath made her press her hands to her breast, but her pace did not slacken.

A minute before, a boy in the hunger line had devised a way to vent his gratefulness. The leaf-cup lifted in his hands, he had yelled, "Vote for Meera Bai, vote!" In the next instant a hundred boys were shrilling that cry with mouths full. Then the angry Seth had bellowed, "Stop. Hold your tongue, one and all."

"Vote for Meera Bai, vote!"—the cry lay in her ears, but her heart was empty. Where was the feeling with which she had given a palmful of jilebi to one little boy?

It was a fake gesture. It was no real act of kindness in which the spirit was involved.

"Meera!" There was Sohanlal standing on the roadside.

He had left the crowd of people and cut across the fields with rapid strides. If only he could have had a word with Meera before the fantastic jilebi test. No chance—the Seth had not left her alone for a moment in the past few hours, since the time the gilded ornaments came.

The bejeweled girl passing through the temple yard, her face absorbed and aflush. The Seth walking by her side, proud and possessive. She was to be his new field of business, his new ledger, the most productive of all!

Sohanlal recalled the strange question she had asked the day before on their way to the clothshop. A big heap of gold has fallen on your lap—what will you do with it? He had not known what she really meant; he had not heard the whisper of her secret excitement—her fantasy was to become reality! And now that the test was over and the delusion had to go . . .

"Meera!"

Her stooping face was marked with exhaustion. Gazing at her as she came along, he recalled a strange verse he had heard at a *mushaira* in town, a traditional gathering in which poets read out their compositions to the audience who loudly and frequently expressed their approbation of every heart-warming line:

> She's painted o'er with a brush dipped in twilight
> she's all bathed in the sad grace of twilight
> it has soaked into her
> it is in her flesh
> it is in her eyes
> it is in her breath
> it is in her spirit
> she's all twilight, the maid of Mithila.

She is all twilight, the maid of Sonamitti, he said to himself with a nod, she with her lost fairy-tale. He reached out on a sudden urge and took her hand. She stopped, surprised, the color mounting to her face, and pulled her hand away.

"I am going home," she said.

"Come."

They walked slowly, in step. Barely had they gone twenty paces when he burst out laughing. She hung her head, without response, stiff-lipped, looking down.

"You do not care to know what amuses me?"

"I do not have to ask."

He said, "No, Meera, it isn't that. I am laughing at myself. No motorcycle on which to ride off to Bombay!"

"There is still the railroad."

"It is not the same."

160

Her voice hardened. "Bombay will not change, whichever way you get there."

He shrugged. "Why should I go to Bombay? I am happy here in Sonamitti. In all my life I have never been so happy."

"Han!" She curled her lip. "What have you found in this mud hole?"

"The image of twilight."

She gave him a quick glance. "Twilight?"

He smiled faintly. A hard-headed driver of military trucks yielding to a poetic fancy. He was talking like a cinema hero! It was the wrong moment anyway. The touchstone had failed. Meera was rid of her obsession. She needed to be consoled.

"Your big worry is gone," he began. "How to spend such a fortune. There is no headache as bad as money!" That was the best approach. Let not Meera feel awkward. Let the miracle be reduced to a jest and blow off like wood smoke.

"The worry remains."

He nodded. "I know. The Seth's ledgers. The touchstone gone, so many basketfuls of puri and jilebi wasted, Seth-ji will be in a mood to blow up the village! I am pleased on one account, Meera. The *Don't Votes* ate well at their enemy's expense. The little boy who was behind it all ate little, though." He paused, recapturing that scene. "I had my eyes on Buddhu. He nibbled at his puri while the others ate as fast as they could. Was he ill? Then I heard someone murmur, 'Look at Buddhu-beta. He saves up his portion of food for his mother. The rag-woman may well be proud of such a boy.' At that moment I saw in my mind another image of you. You stood near the sweet-shop, gazing at the boy as he licked a discarded leaf-cup. The tenderness in your face! An anna-worth of sweet—the touchstone worked at once! No wonder."

"That was the time, you think? Then—"

"The touchstone in your heart—that worked. May it work over and again, endlessly. May your bare touch turn everything into gold."

She felt his eyes caress her and hung her head, walking on, fearing that he would hold her hand again and then she would not be able to pull it away. But he made no move and she sighed, as if denied. She was confused within her, not knowing what she wanted.

"There is no need for any other touchstone," she heard him resume, and cried startled, "Have you no faith in the taveez the minstrel gave me? He had a deeper purpose than you think. How badly we need the touchstone gold! What if one test has failed? This is the beginning—" She paused. How to make a proposal for his partnership?

"Meera," he answered quietly, "you must not misunderstand me, ever."

It is you who have to understand me, she wanted to tell him. Gold in itself has no value. Gold is a strip of field released from bonds. Gold is a new straw thatch on the walls of a mudhut. It is the rag-woman's escape from hunger and the Old Father's wish for a pilgrimage to Holy Benares.

She found her voice, speaking impulsively. He must think with her and feel with her and take part in the adventure to come. Let him disbelieve the touchstone, but let him also be ready to help in case the miracle happened.

He listened with mounting alarm. The touchstone was far from gone! And it had gained new values since yesterday. At first she had wanted to be a good fairy to a few—the friends whom she loved. But many other people were now drawn into her plan, all who needed help.

He searched for a way to make her see reason.

"Let us for a moment believe the unbelievable," he began, haltingly. "Then what? Sonamitti must not live on charity; not even on charity from your hands. We must demand what should be ours, the right to live as human beings."

"Charity? No—no." She shook her head firmly. "The gold will not be mine. I have to pass it on. That is what Grandpapa meant. That is why he gave me the amulet." Recalling in her heart: To wipe every tear from every eye.

At that point he broke into strong, unexpected words. Money poured on a people, unearned money. It poured like rain! It would do no good in the long run.

She could not make that out. "Money is money, is it not? Just because you do not earn it by your sweat, it is not tainted."

"All the people must earn it by their own effort, not one individual on behalf of the community. Or else the benefits will not be real."

She made an imploring gesture with her hand. "Here is a wonderful chance. Do not let me be disheartened."

He was silent for a minute, struggling against an emotion that could carry him away in its tide. He had to be relentless—for her sake.

"Meera, I fear lest this become your escape from the Seth behind a cloud of good thoughts."

"Escape?"

"You may clutch at the touchstone as a drowning person reaches for a twig in the current." Hard words had to be used. "By itself the touchstone twig will do no harm. But when you offer it to a hundred other drowning persons—"

"The Seth—must he clutch at a twig?" She lifted her eyes to his face with bright challenge and meeting her glance, he felt his arguments go to pieces.

"Gran'ma!" he heard her cry.

There she stood under the fig tree, waiting, one of a few in Sonamitti who had not gone to see the miracle. Gout had held her back, but was it gout alone? The surprise that she gave Meera a bare glance and asked no question.

"Beta, you enjoyed yourself in town? I was worried lest you do not come back to the village."

"Grandma, I cannot bear to stay away from you." He was looking at Meera, broodingly. Would that she knew the truth.

"To see the big town." Grandma shook her head wistfully.

She could get enough from life without a touchstone. Did she believe in it? "Let the gold come, and Meera will take you to the big town, Grandma. She will have a house there in the Civil Lines, as if she was a Seth, and then, Grandma, such great fun for you!"

"As if she was a Seth!" Meera hissed her protest.

Grandma looked at one face and at the other and her eyes blinked with mischief. "To think that I shall be a Seth's Grandma! You will have to be a good-hearted Seth, beti. Not like the monster we have."

Sohanlal suppressed a smile. "I have one regret," he said. "Had I known the purpose of the ornaments, I would have added one at my own expense. To be turned to gold and handed back to me."

"Alas, the chance is gone."

"If only—" He stopped as he saw once more the challenge in Meera's eyes. "Grandma," he said, "will you give me something to eat? The day's excitements have made me very hungry."

"Come to the kitchen."

His face was grave as he took bread and pickles from Grandma. "This new trouble," he murmured.

"The Seth has learned a good lesson," Grandma said. "Maybe he will now leave it to chance; he will be content to let the touchstone work in its own time."

He had his doubts. The Seth was full of initiative. He would surely try again to force the hand of destiny.

"What will he do next?" Grandma wondered.

"We would have enjoyed this story if Meera had no part in it—"

"She has a strong will. Nothing can shake her out of her will. She is like her Grandpapa that way."

Sohanlal frowned thoughtfully. "One question baffles me. What was the minstrel's true purpose?"

Perplexity came upon her face, but only for an instant. She smiled mysteriously. "Beta, if only you knew that minstrel!"

"Tell me."

She smiled on and the enigma seemed to sink into the lines of her face, her eyelids drooping as though with the pull of a secret not to be disclosed, and her tone suggestively muted.

"Beta, if only you knew that minstrel!"

CHAPTER

19

Sonamitti caught the fever overnight. The test had failed, yet the word hung in the air in fiery letters: the touchstone is real!

Look, brother. Far from losing heart, the Seth has given Meera a hundred rupee-notes with which to do good deeds.

Not ten, not twenty, but a hundred rupees. Ho, dear uncle!

The shrewd jackal would not part even with one pice except for the best of reasons.

That settles the question. There is no room left for doubt.

A peasant girl is to be the Seth's equal in riches!

The breath-taking thought—the Seth's equal. That was the real surprise. Had the Seth acquired a touchstone, it would be understandable. Fortune always favoured the rich and made them richer. But here was a new tale challenging belief. Hers was a true miracle.

To think that she is our own Meera, our dearest daughter.

Her glory is ours no less. We hold up our heads in pride for all the world to look at us.

The Pipli folks will itch all over with envy. Especially their Five Elders. Remember the time we met those five at the annual fair in Kanhan? Remember the man named Narayan? He preened about with a medal hung on his chest. His grandson had won it in war. The old man gave himself airs, as if it were he who had fought and got the award.

Han! If only the young warrior's spouse had not disappeared from home during his absence and never returned.

We, Sonamitti people, do not have to wear medals on our chests.

The taveez on our dear daughter's arm speaks for all of us.

Go anywhere on earth and see if you can find a touchstone.

There is one sadness. The Seth will have a half share in the gold. He tricked Meera into signing an agreement.

The swine. Have you ever heard of such a deal? Our Meera is at fault, too. She has been hasty. She could have come to us for advice. Now it is too late.

Too late.

You have missed one point, brother. Meera must have a good supply of the metal which is to be turned into gold. The Seth can get her all she needs.

Have we no copper? Utensils in the kitchen. Bowls to hold flowers for the house-gods.

You expect Meera to carry utensils on her body? Think of her ornaments, so prettily gilded. Wearing them she looks like a king's daughter.

Han! That is true enough.

So the menfolk debated the great wonder and felt more and more overwhelmed. But the women reacted differently. They hurried off to Meera's house and squatted in the fig-tree shade.

"King's daughter!" They, too, used the epithet, adding hopefully, "Our own Meera, all the same." And they made no secret of their needs and wishes.

There stood the young woman, broken down on account of her husband, the sole breadwinner in the household. An ailment had twisted his spine so that he could not stand erect; he was bent double. No doctor had seen him yet, for the nearest one lived twenty miles away and to bring him to this village was no mean expense. She had pawned everything she owned and now she could only be resigned to her fate. But if she could get just enough money for the doctor's fee . . .

There was the aged mother whose sons had sold off their plow oxen in a crisis and were now forced to hire a pair from the Seth at a punitive rate. The dues, as they mounted, would eat up their fields. If only they could buy a plow-pair . . .

Spectacles for misty eyes going blind . . . A dowry for a maid, well past her marriage age; she had no good looks, but a match could be arranged for eighty rupees . . . A toddy tapper who had fallen from the tall tree and become a cripple; he would starve unless given some other means of living.

"Good people," Grandma cried to the suppliants, "you have gone mad, one and all. This is the minstrel's joke! He never thought his little leech would become a serpent!" She looked round for support. "Sohagi!"

The Cowhouse women were standing at a corner, bewildered and

166

silent. Munni, unaccountably, plucked a charm off her hair and broke it in the prescribed way. Champa gave her an approving nod, but Bimla shook her head, mumbling, "What use? This gay music is sure to grow louder."

The crowd of suppliants was silent for a time, wanting to tell Grandma, "There is the gold ring and that is enough for us. The gold ring is not a joke, not a fancy." Out of politeness they withheld those words. The potter's wife touched Grandma on the arm and said, "We have our belief. We do not question the minstrel's great power. We do not doubt that our Meera is going to be a king's daughter. But she remains our own Meera still. We ask only for crumbs out of her abundance."

Meera said, "Grandma has no belief in the minstrel. One day she said to me—"

"Stop!" Grandma snapped at the girl, and whirling to the others she continued in that angry tone, "You seem to think that our house is already stacked with gold up to the roof. Better walk in and see with your own eyes and make sure."

They tried to quieten her, "Be patient, Grandma. It is only a matter of time. Meera has to do an act of kindness. Maybe *we* are fallow earth where a seed cast from her hand will bear golden fruit."

One woman, not much older than Meera, withdrew from the group and walked into the kitchen for a bowl of water to drink. In a minute she was heard calling, "Meera-sister!" When Meera appeared in the kitchen the young woman seized her hand quickly and thrust a copper coin into her fist. "My prayer to you," she said humbly. "Wear the copper pice on my account." Adding in a rush of anxiety, "In every procession I have marched just behind you, remember?"

It was some time before Meera understood. The coin was to be turned into gold and given back! The abject pleading in Subhadri's face—

"Yes," uncertainly.

Grateful and overjoyed, Subhadri yearned, "Will the touchstone act soon?" And as they walked to the yard she said, "Take heed that the coin touches your bare skin, Meera-sister. Or else—" The prospect of failure was too terrible to contemplate.

Meera in her turn gave a warning. "Do not let it be known that I am wearing your coin. This must remain a secret between us."

When they were back at the fig-tree, all eyes turned to Subhadri's face. She had really wanted a bowl of water to drink? Or it was a ruse to be alone with Meera and touch her sympathy? Why, even if they could not all use the same trick, there were several other ways...

Ten minutes later the chattering ceased as if squeezed by an iron hand. There, walking down the road, was the Seth in his pink gown and Bulaki Rao at his heels, bearing the hookah with its five yards of pipe. The group started to melt away. The Seth did not speak a word: he sat stiffly in the veranda, hookah pipe to his mouth, drawing smoke, until all the visitors were gone.

"Those vixen will not give you a moment's rest. Something has to be done."

"No no, Seth-ji." And she was looking at him with amazed eyes. He who had held her life itself in his monstrous fist now seemed quite human and, somehow, a pathetic figure!

He hurried to the work in hand. "The act of kindness must be your whole-hearted concern, remember. With each breath you must chant kindness, kindness, kindness, like a deity's name."

"Will that help?"

"Let not your mind get distracted. Think hard. Think hard until the stomach begins to ache."

She was startled by his words, for she had heard them before—on a different occasion. At that time she had been fighting the Seth. Today his aim and hers were one. Only up to a point . . .

"You did not part with your ornaments at night?"

She nodded. "I could not do an act of kindness in my sleep!"

"Who can tell?" he spoke mysteriously. "Yes, I know you are not a sleep-walker."

His voice was thick, eyes greedy. There he sat on the mud floor, drawing on his pipe and urging her to look back into her past weeks. She must search in a wheat-field for one lost grain! One act of kindness which she had recalled quickly and spontaneously had failed at the test. Her memory seemed to have nothing more to disclose. Was it all a mistake?

"Mistake?" The Seth's voice was hard. "You think I cannot tell gold from copper? Since you have your doubt, come to town with me tomorrow. Let the ring be shown to a goldsmith."

"Seth-ji," she cried in a troubled voice, "it is not that." And filling her eyes were the scores of faces in which the darkness of misery was illumined by a new burst of sunshine. She could not afford to fail—

Bespelled by his faith, she did all she could to remember. One deed here, one there, so petty, so obviously empty, that they could not be repeated. Then the thought came to her: Kindness did not have to be an actual deed, it could be a mere feeling in the heart. Even if nothing was achieved—

There had been her night with Soondri, the milch-cow. Soondri was calfing. The pains had struck her after dusk. Something had gone wrong. Soondri lay on her side, a thread of saliva dripping from her mouth. In the dim light of burning bean-oil, her eyes showed stark suffering.

Meera had been helpless. Even Grandma was not there; it was one of her bad nights. Crouching beside the cow, Meera passed her hand gently over the big, heaving body. The nostrils, always wet and pleasing to the touch, were now dry stiff leather. The panting breath was much too warm. Time dragged on.

Soondri felt soothed by the caress, her eyes showed that, too; they seemed to plead as soon as the hand paused, "Help me with your touch. Your touch is all I ask."

She had wept bitterly, but her hands had been tireless. They had ached at the joints, but she had not let them stop. They ceased to be her hands, not needing her propulsion. Soondri, hearing her cry, seemed to forget her own pain and it was as though she yearned to help—you could see that in the way the eyes softened despite the glaze.

Dawn was streaking into the cowshed when Soondri became quiet. Two tiny calf's feet came out of her body and hung limp. Soondri was dead.

That was all.

The Seth was unimpressed by her story. "So what? You could not save the cow. If you had gone out and found someone wise in these matters—"

The cow had died, that alone counted. The feeling was of no use. It had taken the cow's life. How remove the hand Soondri needed, how leave her alone and go to seek help—that very feeling had decided Soondri's fate.

"Kindness has no value unless it is expressed in a deed," the Seth told her out of his wisdom. "The clouds in the sky—what use are they until they turn into rain? So with the clouds in you, called feelings."

However, she could not rid herself of the thought that kindness

169

could simply take the form of an inner communion. And it was the Seth's task to hold her back from such barren speculation. Combing out her yesterdays in which the deed lay hidden—that was the only way. "Think hard, Meera. Think hard until the stomach begins to ache."

20 This was a busy day at Gay Peacock. Piles of material mounted the length of the glass-top counter behind which four assistants employed their tongues and tape measures with the extra incentive provided by the master's presence. Seated near the entrance door, quill pen in one hand and hookah pipe in the other, he was deep in the accounts, but his eyes prowled without cease and his ears were alert.

He was not happy, though. As the hours went by, he felt sure that he was going to be defrauded. His calculations were wrong. The touchstone story, he had figured, had gone hurtling to town. A brickbat had crashed into a beehive. Excited people would come swarming to Gay Peacock, one query on every tongue: "Is it all true?"

His answer was to be a superior smile and a counter-question: "What is truth? What is untruth?"

"The ring. Has it really been transmuted?"

"Brother, the ways of illusion are strange. Which is the mask and which the face? How many of us know what is what?"

But the inquirers would say, "Seth-ji, all we ask for is a plain word."

"Which is the gold and which the glitter? Are they apart?" His plain word was ready, too.

The questions and answers must stay in his fancy. No brickbat had hit a beehive. Even the press, the four-page sheet named *India Speaks*, had carried no news about the touchstone; all it had printed on this topic was a letter signed "Mystified." That letter related the strange happening in Sonamitti village and added some comments. Yesterday's great surprise was today's trifle, it said. One example of this was X ray, which could pass into solid objects. Who, today, would call X ray a miracle? The atom bomb that had of late ended the world war was still a mystery, but time would reduce it to the level of nitroglycerin. The touchstone was not even a new idea. The old legends were full of it and not in India only; the West had its philosopher's stone. But the miracle in Sonamitti had one special feature. The touchstone on the girl's arm could work only under a certain condition, which meant the impact of the spirit upon matter. Out of that impact gold would come. That idea was fascinating in itself. Moral values acting as a spark to transmute a baser element. Would the improbable happen and a peasant girl become the instrument of basic revelation?

An editorial note said, "We print this letter for what it is worth. We have no comments." Could it be that the editor had suppressed other correspondence of which there might well have been a spate? But the paper readily came out with a letter signed by Gay Peacock. The Seth had sweated over the unaccustomed task of preparing a piece of literary work, an eye-witness account—how, at the crucial moment when the peasant girl with her taveez was about to become a pauper, the ring on her finger revealed itself as gold. The facts were undisputable.

Here was the letter in print for every eye to read. Signed Gay Peacock, and that name blazoned with a yard-long splash on the shop's board—how could the clear link be missed? *Gay Peacock*. Gold. Yet there stood the customers chatting as usual, haggling over cloth, with no thought of the touchstone. No curiosity, not even ridicule. A conspiracy of silence. That was all.

Once or twice in the course of the day he had looked up hopefully from the accounts.

One woman in a 45-rupee Mysore crepe had kept a salesman on his toes for half an hour. Her escort sat with *India Speaks* which he had picked up from the counter, the issue that carried Gay Peacock's word. "Make up your mind, Sushama," he appealed to Mysore-crepe and she answered him brusquely, "Go to the bookshop." He stuck to the chair. He was now at page three. The Seth was sitting on thorns. A letter signed by Gay Peacock.

Mysore-crepe studied the heap of material, tissue fabric from Benares, art silk from Surat, muslin from Bengal. One piece of sari caught her fancy. No, the borders were too narrow. Another. No, it was too expensive—Mukhichand sold the same kind at ten rupees less. "Let me see gold borders for a Georgette sari," she demanded presently.

Gold! It rang a bell in the Seth's head and he called from his counter, "Baburam, show the lady the beauties we have received from Indore. Gay Peacock has no dearth of gold." He turned quickly to look at the man who had now done with page three. He must have read each and every line.

The dolt's donkey had nothing to say! He turned to the next page. Mysore-crepe busied herself with the gold borders and ended up with the purchase of three yards of cheap poplin.

Customers came and went and nothing happened. The Seth was in an explosive mood. His hopes revived at sight of 30-rupee Bombay-nylon who looked clever and as though she understood news. While she ordered knitting wool, her little daughter drew imaginary lines on the floor, playing a game; every child in town had played that game on the clothshop floor.

"Have a cold drink, child," he said to the tadpole. "What would you like? One colored yellow, like gold? Gay Peacock will get you a drink of gold color. There is a soda shop next door." Bombay-nylon could not have missed the touchstone story; her memory would click.

"Red," said the tadpole, busy with her game.

"Not gold? But Gay Peacock—" His eyes hung on the mother's face. Yes, she did look intelligent and alert—

"Red," the tadpole was firm.

"Coca-Cola." The mother looked up briefly from the wool. "Give her Coca-Cola."

He was dismayed. Coca-Cola, indeed! Five annas dropped into a ditch. The wool carried a price tag, or else...

Bombay-nylon announced, "I will sign for the wool." She opened her bag and produced a pen.

The assistant, Baburam, looked at his master for guidance, and he, having lost his temper, jerked his head toward a glass-framed lettering hung on the wall, "Terms cash."

"We sell for cash only," Baburam communicated the message.

"My husband is an officer," Bombay-nylon answered solemnly, as if that had to be the end of the matter.

"Then he will enjoy this wool," the Seth nodded amicably; "and I, his good cash."

The surprised assistant stared at his master while the woman spun round in anger. "Roma," she cried to the tadpole, "don't touch the drink. Come, we are going to Mukhichand's."

An evil day in every sense. Would that he had not come to town when there was so much to be done at Sonamitti. Why had he bothered about city gnats? The touchstone would gain nothing from them, or lose.

And there lay the Coca-Cola on the counter—five annas thrown away.

Soon after sunset a tall foreigner walked in and asked for ivory. Gay Peacock sold curios as a side line. With hope renewed—no foreigner could have missed such news out of Mysterious India—the Seth cried happily to his assistant, "Let our American guest see gold. No place in town like our Gay Peacock for gold."

"Ivory," said the foreign camel. "There—" he pointed to a shelf. "Seven elephants in a row."

The Seth saddened. This camel cared nothing about the gold reserves in his country. The threat to the dollar. All he had in mind was seven elephants in a row.

Night fell, the shop must soon be closed. Then a tall thin man appeared at the doorway, watched the Seth intently for a minute, then came straight to his desk. "A word, between us."

When the assistants had melted off at their master's bidding, the visitor started to speak in a half-whisper. "The touchstone, Seth-ji." And the Seth's happiness was like a sudden heavy blow on the chest. At last!

It was not questions, not mere curiosity that had brought this fox to Gay Peacock—so it appeared in a minute. He tried to keep his motive hidden, feeling his way with caution. Hundred to one, the touchstone was false, he said.

"That is not what you really think, brother." The Seth shook his head knowingly.

"Gambling—is it not?"

"Life itself is nothing else. One must take some risk at every step."

"A man of business takes every risk but also insures himself against risk. If one could exchange half the uncertainty for good cash paid in advance—"

The excited Seth pulled at his mustache till it hurt. His best expectations were surpassed! Here was a kindred soul, afire like his own.

The kindred soul had plenty in his bag! What would happen to gold if it became as abundant as copper? Planned production was needed and that was too big a problem for one man to tackle. Listening in silence, the Seth cupped his hand on his lap as if ready to take a concrete suggestion, and it came at last.

174

"Five thousand rupees for a half-share in the touchstone. That is my firm offer."

"Indeed?" The Seth eyed the other possessively.

"Nothing for you to lose. You see that?"

The laughter in the Seth's belly exploded on his face as he slapped his thigh.

"Nothing for me to lose—that is a good joke! Nothing to lose except half of a fortune."

The thin man looked hurt. "Friend, this is no pittance, and it is to be paid in advance."

"A matter of opinion. Even ten rupees is real wealth for a pigling." The laughter had eased off in his face, but his belly was shaking still.

"Friend, I do not want you to feel swindled. Six thousand. There— let us close the deal and speak the holy name thrice, Vishnu! Vishnu! Vishnu!"

Then the Seth felt pity in his heart. Such small fry. A baby snake wanting to eat a python. The big fellow could afford to let himself be held in the petty mouth, for fun, until the stretched baby jaw cracked and split.

So the Seth continued the game. "What a shock for America!" he pointed to a different aspect of the problem. "Half the world's gold lies stored in that country."

The baby snake cried, "This touchstone of ours is going to be a big international headache."

The Seth saw the world of finance lose its uniform spin and totter, slow, like a spent top—it was his hand that could make the top resume its spin or deaden. And he nodded to the baby snake with approval—he had real understanding.

"What is your business in town? Why, brother, I do not even know your name!"

"I live in Bombay. I am Janardan Jain," and he hurried on, "We must do nothing in a rush. Planned action. Each lot of gold on the girl's body—" The happy anticipation made him grin. "Even the harvest from fields needs calculated marketing." A meaningful pause and then, "We can do it, for sure."

*We*, it had to be we every time. Let the baby snake's jaw tire, ache hard, before it broke.

"We must join hands for some other business. Do you understand cloth?"

175

"I deal in bullion."

"Han! That explains your love for the touchstone."

The jaw was weakening already. "Let it be six thousand and five hundred." Janardan Jain banged the Seth's desk with his fist. "I have ideas. They will do good to both of us. You will see."

"Ideas, yes. I have a few of them stored in this box," the Seth tapped his head gently.

"Two heads are bigger than one."

"No. One may be equal to both together."

Janardan Jain smiled. "An error, my friend. The part and the whole—"

"One plus X makes one—"

"No!"

"X being zero."

Janardan Jain fell into a brief silence, but he was still undefeated. "Even if nothing good comes from this so-called touchstone," he resumed, "you will be richer by six thousand five hundred rupees. And I? I shall sit back and suck my thumb."

The Seth said, "When an ass laments the loss of a cow, his guts will not pine for five drops of milk."

Janardan Jain made his last desperate stand. "Give me a quarter-share. That means my offer is doubled. Yes, doubled at one stroke! Do not spit at five drops of milk. Hundred to one, there is no cow to lose. Miracles no longer happen."

"You should know the reason. Do I have to tell you? The men of power keep themselves away from the world which is so rotten with unbelief. They are beyond our reach. Had not Atmaram gone to the Himalayan peak—. Let that pass. Do you really doubt these facts, Jain-ji? Tell me."

"Let me make some investment in the venture. That is my last request."

The Seth's voice roughened. "Why shall I share profits when I can have them all?"

"Friend, you do need a partner. This is too big an enterprise for one pair of hands."

"I am not the father of a pauper. Besides, when the miracle has taken place, the banks will give me whatever advance I ask for—a million, or ten million. You are not talking sense, brother, because of your excitement. I can see your state of mind. Now, look. Pray drink a

Coca-Cola since you have graced my mud hut with your presence. Here is a bottle, already opened—"

Janardan Jain was dripping bitter anger as he strode away.

So the day with all its annoyance ended surprisingly well. The pact of silence was torn up, but that was not all. A kindred spirit blazing with strong belief had revealed itself, making up for the indifference of all the people.

Back, then, to the problem. Success might be delayed, but the quest had its thrill. Even the suspense was worthwhile. Failures would give a knife-edge to resolve. Back to Sonamitti, back to the terrific business.

21   The great excitement had hardly waned a little when the new cry was first heard on Main Road: Vote for Rajaram-brother, vote! The Seth pricked up his ears in surprise. Meera's Grandma eliminated, there would be no other contestant, he had been certain; Bulaki Rao had rallied the scum of the village, whose votes were to be the only ones polled. But—here was the scorpion, Rajaram!

The Seth met the new situation with his accustomed energy. He sent at once for the village constable. "Hoosiar," he said, "you know how a bagful of the Engrez folk have ruled the vast Indian land for two hundred years?"

"They are mighty in battle. They have fire-throwing guns and long spears."

"More than guns and long spears, they have *you.*"

"Me?" The old man was taken aback.

"The likes of you." The Seth tapped him on the chest with his knuckles. "Have you not heard the ancient saying, 'Divide and rule and divide again?'" The constable still seemed perplexed and the Seth went on, "Take the *Don't votes.* They are a swarm of piglings misled by a few wolf cubs. Let the piglings be coaxed away with a quarter-rupee apiece while the wolf cubs feel the strength of our iron fist." He studied his clenched fist, three fingers beringed. "That is the way."

"That is the way," Hoosiar approved.

Their expectations came true so that the school fellows were the only force left on the field. To their rations of sweetmeat Master-ji had added tales of heroism from history and legend; and nourished in body and mind, they let the few stones hurled furtively at them in shadowed lanes touch their heads but not their spirits.

The women's procession was a far more serious problem, Seth-ji had to acknowledge. Those sari-clad soldiers with nose-rings and bangles! Divide and rule must work on them as well, though in a more subtle way. Meera could not escape the pull of her new partner-ship. Besides, she could hardly march in step with her load of heavy copper. The nugget would graze her skin at every footfall, the waist chain would make every movement awkward.

His calculations proved again to be right. On the first occasion Meera had hardly gone two hundred paces when she had to stop, out of breath. She handed the banner to Sohagi and dropped out of the ranks. This happened three times and then she gave it up. She sent word that she could not come and the women had to march with Sohagi at their forefront. Without Meera their steps felt weighed down as if they, too, wore heavy anklets.

Meera, in her seclusion, was reasoning with herself. District Board? It was meant to provide the people with certain amenities. Better roads where the ox-cart wheels would not sink into dust or mud. Wells for public use. A free dispensary based at Sonamitti, serving the Seven Villages. All these benefits could be attained equally, or better, with gold. The touchstone could, indeed, do far more good than the board. The board, after all, could not wipe out the peril of the thumb-marked bonds. Gold could. The Seth himself was moving unawares toward that objective. To add more and more to the people's slavery was his avowed purpose; yet, in effect, he was working to remove their chains.

Here was her inherent clash of purpose with the Seth. He wanted the new wealth out of a habit, the habit of getting rich, richer. Making money was his duty as it were. That alone gave his life its meaning and value. Money, an end in itself. For her, however, this end was to be the point of a new beginning. She had to make Sonamitti a bright jewel.

She had opened her heart to Sohagi, but there had been no response. Sohagi was all for the board. It was plain that she had listened to Sohanlal and accepted his view. So had the rest of the Cowhouse. Meera must go her way all by herself.

Even so, after several days' absence, when she heard the cry *Vote for Rajaram-brother, vote!* she had an overwhelming urge to be close to the procession, to see it march along. She went hurriedly to Main Road.

At sight of her, there was silence. Then Sohagi handed the banner to Champa and stepped out of the ranks. "Move on," she gestured to the column. When it had passed, she turned to Meera and took her hand in hers. "Do you have to keep away from us, sister?" she cried in misery.

"Sohagi, you must understand."

"Understand that the election fight is useless and we should give it up?"

Meera stared at her. "No, Sohagi, you must carry on. But do not be impatient with me if I try to attain the same end by some other means."

"After you have destroyed the thing that you worked so hard to build up—"

Meera smiled. "I am of no worth. There are the hundred others ready to march. One more, one less, cannot matter. But time will show which of these has more power—the taveez on my arm or the district board."

Sohagi gave her a look of pity. "It means nothing to you that we have gained a new right, that the people—." She cut short and turned round. "Let all be well with you, Meera-sister; may your wish soon be fulfilled." She ran toward the marching column.

Meera felt an impulse to follow her friend. She saw herself holding the banner again and adding her voice to the cry, "Vote for Rajaram-brother, vote!" But as she took one quick step the waist-chain clanged protest, the anklets became fetters. She stopped, her eyes still on the column. Then she noticed the thinness of the ranks—they had shrunk to half their strength or even less.

And as she walked back the *Vote Fors* were on the road, twice as many of them as before, and at sight of her they cried a new slogan they had learnt: "Jai Meera Bai, jai Sona Mai!" The Gold Mother with Meera and the Seth made the new trinity. "Jai Sona Mai," she whispered the slogan to herself and touched her taveez lovingly. "Yes, Grandpapa," she added, as if she had just heard him speak: We must all have a share in the wish—to wipe every tear from every eye.

Would that one person in particular understood her mind. He came that evening, just after sunset, and they sat under the fig tree, as usual, Grandma in the veranda absorbed in her beads. In the light of dusk his face was very grave.

"Do you not know your own power, Meera?" he began. "Do you not know that you can build or pull down with equal ease?"

She answered him obliquely. "Is it such a big thing, this board-moard?"

"This is more than the board. This is a test. If we fail, we stand as unfit for freedom."

Fascinated, she watched him turn meditative. I cannot bear that taut look on his face, she brooded; it makes me feel his sufferings. A minute went by before he resumed. "The pice game is in full swing."

Pice game! Subhadri, unable to keep back the story of her wonderful luck, had given away the secret. Copper coins were now being pressed on Meera in ever increasing numbers. "Wear this for me. Meera, daughter of mercy.". . ."Do not deny a creature of woe, my sister." Was it due to this pice game that the vote-mote procession had thinned away?

" 'Each for all' has changed into 'each for himself.' Do you remember the couplet, Meera?"

She did. We want cloth to wear, cloth. Vote for Grandma, vote. The two demands made a couplet, he had said one day.

So what? Everything would be set right as soon as the gold came. There was the other way, but it would take ages. Maybe some day in the far future you would divide the land more fairly, a ceiling on all holdings. Maybe you would make the starveling earth more yieldful. Maybe you would give the people everything they needed. Maybe you would so touch their spirit that they would all work as one man for the common good. But it would take ages. Meanwhile the village would be dying slowly. The sick and hungry and helpless would not survive up to the time the battle against want was at last won. No, the village could not afford to wait until freedom gave it defenses.

Her eyes begged for understanding. "It is not for myself that I want all this gold. I—"

He nodded. "That's it. You will save the people with your gold. I remember your worry about the ten thousand rupees."

Joyously she cried, "Then you understand me?"

"Listen, Meera. With your gold you will save this village. You will save the Seven Villages. But there are eight hundred thousand others. Each has a Seth of its own. Each Seth waits to snatch the new power from the people. You cannot have gold enough to save all India!" He saw her face grow bewildered and went on, "It is the fight with the Seths that will save India, not a miracle, not armfuls of gold. You did have your share in the fight, a big share—"

All at once her heart felt sore. Had Grandpapa spoken in vain? She would hold her ground. She would face this challenge. Not with argument—she had no wit, no words, for the unequal combat. All she had was faith.

181

"My head spins!" A playful mood could be her escape. "Let me not hear about fights."

"But then, Meera——"

"Better let me hear about—about the Bedouin."

He cried in surprise, "Bedouin?"

"Away in the Arab desert."

Speechless, he gaped.

"Smart in your soldier's khaki coat-pantaloon, you must have caught the eye of some Bedouin beauty."

He made a gesture of impatience. "Meera——"

"They are wonderful to look at—so I have heard." Face averted, but the eyeballs swerving toward him in the way he knew.

"Listen, Meera."

"Tell me her name."

"Meera, let us ask Grandma——"

"About the Bedouin beauty?"

She saw the quick twist of hurt in his face. He rose abruptly and started to walk off. "Be in peace, Grandma," he called out to her, but Grandma on the veranda floor could not speak until the beads were completed. Her lips moved in silence, "Be in peace, my son."

"Wait," Meera called but he did not turn back, he strode away.

He would hate her from this moment—her throat felt dry, her alarmed eyes widened toward him. If only he would come back and sit again by her side. She would be silent, listening to his voice. Do not hate me, she begged of him in her heart. If only you had met Grandpapa. Then you would have known that Grandpapa could never speak the wrong word. Then you would share my feeling and my faith. You and Grandpapa would understand each other quickly....

Grandma, led by intuition, broke her ritual of silence. "Meera——"

In a moment she was on the veranda, her face buried in the aged bosom. Silence again—the last beads were not yet done. Grandma combed the girl's thick hair with her fingers, tender and protective, as if to say, "Do not be unhappy. All will be well." "He now hates me, Grandma——" in a barely audible whisper. Grandma in silence shook her head from side to side. No ... no ... no ... her fingers in the girl's hair fast and consoling. Meera grew quiet, the panic passing out of her, and said to herself, Grandma knows. Grandma understands.

A man came up the road, turned toward the fig tree and approached the veranda steps. "Meera's Grandma——"

Meera sat up. At sight of the beads the man gestured to Grandma amicably with his hand, bidding her continue, and sat in silence in one corner, but he did not have to wait long. The last bead done, Grandma said in greeting, "Ram-Ram, brother," and the man—it was the village barber—moved closer across the floor. "Ram-Ram, Grandma."

He talked of this and that while his listeners puzzled about the meaning of his unexpected visit. A quarter-hour went by before he disclosed his mind.

"Old Mother," his voice was low, "your Meera is destined to be happy."

"For sure," Grandma promptly agreed.

"Listen with care," the barber said. "Nature has so built a young maid that she must pine for a man. She cannot escape from herself. Even if she is a king's daughter, she is a woman. You are much too old, Meera's Grandma, to be able to recall the longings of your own far girlhood—"

Grandma bridled. "Do I not long for the minstrel?"

"It is Meera's great luck and yours, too, that she will live in Sona-mitti with her man. No tears of parting will have to be shed."

Grandma's eyes glistened with pleasure. "Why does he have to speak with a borrowed voice, ten tongues ever active in his own mouth? Even the phut-phutti does not make more talk. A bare half-hour is gone—" Her face turned beaming to Meera, as if saying, There! Now you must smile!

"All the world over it is the barber who has to fix up a marriage. I do not have to tell you."

"True. It was a barber who brought a proposal for me to my father who was one of the Five Elders of our village—" Grandma was ready for reminiscence.

"Halwai-ji cannot break the universal rule."

"Halwai-ji!" She was stupefied. The barber went on, "Mark my words, Meera's Grandma. A good mango tree hides its crop of fruit behind thick leaves. Halwai-ji is no mere sweetshop. Even the Seth links arms with him as a brother and equal."

Grandma was silent until she heard the barber say, "Your Meera will be the proud mother of two big girls, both married." Then she recovered herself. "Beti!" she cried with a grimace. "Such luck—to be Tuti-Kuti's proud mother." And Meera recalled the marriage proposal at the sweetshop. She had snubbed the man, calling him Old Uncle. Yet, here was his emissary.

"Wed to Halwai-ji," the barber resumed, "Meera will gain in caste status, remember. This is of great value—do I have to tell you? Even gold cannot give her this rise in caste status."

Grandma shook her head. "Our nothing-special Meera is unfit for such honor. Alas, brother, she is willful and flighty."

"Do not worry on that score. Halwai-ji will keep his household woman under his strong thumb."

But Grandma shook her head again. "I have a bride in mind. A better match for the lord of the sweetshop."

"No. He has set his fancy on—"

"One good look at the other and his fancy will wag like a dog's happy tail."

The barber was astonished. "Such a bride-to-be in this village? I have been eyeless then. Tell me her name."

"Buddhu's widowed mother."

"Who?"

"Barely forty, and lone ever since her man went into a panther's stomach. And remember, Halwai-ji will be the proud father of a son, a good little boy, a nice squint in one eye."

The barber gazed morosely at Grandma. "This proposal is no joke. Halwai-ji is a man of might. Beware! Pray consider what both of you will gain from this union. Maybe the touchstone will fail. Then the Seth will show his hand and you will need to be protected. Halwai-ji will tell the Seth, 'Dear brother, here is the money Meera's Grandma owes you; now drop her field from your ledger.'" He rolled his eyes toward his listeners, watching for effect. "Maybe," he continued, "the miracle will happen. Then the gold will have to be put to use. Halwai-ji has seen a big glass-paneled sweetshop on sale in town; this he will buy in the name of his spouse. One more word he said. I almost forgot. His spouse will be free to eat the best relishes, no payments to make, no questions to answer." He turned his face to the girl with a faint snigger.

Grandma was nodding to herself as she listened. "Our Halwai-brother's Buddhu has no lack of tongue for jilebi, laddoo, boondia, puri..."

The barber rose. "Think it over. We will meet again." Having gone a few paces he stopped for an instant to say, "Flouted, Halwai-ji will be a tiger. Keep that in mind, Meera's Grandma."

She was shaking with laughter. "Meera, beti, why did you have to turn that old one's head?"

The girl was quiet, sunk in thought. A young maid pines for a man —what if he hates her? She would be ready to die. But—if he approves her? That happiness, too, would be hard to bear!

Grandma, watching the absorbed face, spoke softly. "A matchmaker visits a house unasked—that is always an auspicious omen, even when he has come from the wrong door." Her expressive glance gave point to her words and Meera drew a quick breath and cried, "Grandma, stop!"

"After the matchmaker had come and spoken to my father, the village Elder, my ears heard nothing for many days but music, marriage music."

And Meera, as if she too was hearing some dream music, hung her head and remained silent.

22

The pice game had taken a sudden new turn.

"How shall I wear everyone's pice?" Meera had cried in protest. "Hundreds of pice—"

"Meera, beti, just one more coin will not be too much load. You know what it means to me—"

"Sister, dear, I take the dust of your feet. Do not break my heart."

"I will beat my head on the floor until the blood flows."

"Meera, I will lie down on your doorstep, night and day, with no food and water."

"We will all lie stretched at your housedoor, Meera. We will starve, turn into skeletons—and die."

Meera had wailed in despair, "I do not want to deny any of you. But what can I do? Why can't you understand?"

Moved by her misery the women had wakened to a sense of reality. The fact was that Meera must not only carry the coins but place them in contact with her body. How could she wear hundreds of coins under her sari and jacket? There would not be enough body area for the coins to touch!

The answer came out of the combined wisdom of all. Meera would wear fifty coins at a time, no more. Turned into gold, they would make a common pool and be divided equitably among all the households. The process would be repeated as the touchstone acted again and again and the pool was replenished. Fifty gold coins for all to share in each time the miracle happened.

Meera was ready to carry the fifty coins—that was the supreme bliss. Jai Meera Bai, Jai Sona Mai.

How long must one keep waiting? It was now so hard to have patience.

Let nothing be done to distract her from her quest. Even the Seth must be free from worry—it was only with his help that Meera could gain her objective. Before she signed the deed, the Seth gave her good

easons to show that she needed a business partner. Without that partner the touchstone could not be made to yield all its bounty.... Let
not the vote-mote processions upset the Seth's bile and delay the
coming of the miracle.

The Cowhouse women could not stop this tide of feeling—they were
swept aside. The banner ceased to be unfurled on Main Road.

The Five Elders met under the aged banyan in an emergency session.
This was one of the occasions when the neglected Devi on her mud
pedestal received a few flowers and scented leaves along with the
prayer that she keep a motherly eye on the deliberations, guiding them
to the path of wisdom. And today the path of wisdom had to run
through a sunless jungle where it could easily fade out of sight.

"The touchstone is a field ready to bear a golden crop. But, then,
you need plow-oxen to lay down the furrows, water to soften the earth
and good seeds to sow. Without them the field will be as a barren
womb. That is how I view it, brother."

"We do not understand the board-moard. Our Rajaram may get
his tail twisted by the wily ones from other villages. Or they may make
it up to him in such a way that he will eat out of their hands: when
he steps out of the board meeting, he will feel for his tail and lo! it is
gone."

"Leave my tail alone," said Rajaram. "I am not such a fool as you
reckon."

"There is a story about an old man returning from the market with
a goatling he had bought. A bunch of thieves decided to rid him of
his purchase. One of them met him on the road and said, 'Friend,
why do you carry the black puppy on your shoulder? Is it lame?' The
old man laughed. 'Fool, you cannot tell a goat from a dog!' He had
gone two hundred yards further when the second thief approached
him. 'Ho, will you sell me your dog for a rupee? I need it to guard
my guava trees at night.' The old man was now angry. 'Be off,
swindler.' But he gave a long look to his purchase. When he had gone
another two hundred yards the third thief was waiting for him. 'Little
black puppy, tchu . . . tchu—!' fondly, petting the animal on the head.
The old man was furious. Finally, when two more men had spoken,
his trust in his own eyes went altogether. He dropped the goatling on
the roadside and walked away quickly."

Rajaram said, "I have a wiser head than you people think."

"Even wise heads get muddled. There is the tale of a god turning

into a ghost. His fellow gods had decided in a merry mood to treat
him as a ghost. At first the god was amused, sharing the fun, then he
became annoyed. As the joke went on, he began to brood. It all ended
with his believing that he was a ghost, and he forsook his Devi and
took a *bhootni* for spouse."

"Wah! Wah!"

"In plain words, this is the lesson. Our Rajaram may go to the
board-moard and yet gain nothing for our village. Every benefit will
be grabbed by the other members who know the game. Sonamitti will
remain where it was. Years later, maybe, it will be a new tale. When
we have seen how freedom works, when we have more understanding—"

"This is only the beginning of the freedom road. There will be new
elections three years after. By that time we shall know what is what."

"Meanwhile the gold will have done great good to the village. We
will make a list of the things the village needs. That will help
Meera—"

An incongruous voice broke in. "The great good is not for the
village only. Our hands are ready to take whatever private benefits may
come to each of us."

His meaning was clear. The pice game!

"Everyone could do with a little gold," Rajaram admitted. "Even
we aged ones have a hunger in us, dear brother."

But the incongruous voice struck a harsher note. "Two Seths in
Sonamitti. Is not one bad enough?"

"Two Seths?" Heads shook in firm denial. "We know our daughter.
To think she will emulate Seth-ji! A parrot will not eat flesh even if
it gets a hawk's claws and beak."

"After all, we do not covet her gold. What is hers is hers. Now, let
us suppose the touchstone has come to one of us. It has come, say, to
Hanumanth. What will he do? Let us hear your voice, Hanumanth,
friend."

He answered with raillery. "I? I will give nothing to you fellows.
You will have to lick my toes before you get the smallest loan."

Loans, that was it. That would be the benefit. Meera would grant
loans at a fair rate of interest. Loans were a part of day-to-day living,
for evil times always came and even tidings of joy, the birth of a son
or grandson, drew cool cash. Loans by themselves did not hurt much.
They could be paid back when the harvest was sold. The trouble was

hat the crazy rate of interest made repayment hard or even impossible.

Here was Meera's God-given chance. She had every right to charge
interest, but not in the Seth's way, not with the aim to break the
debtor's back. Let her have a fair return on money employed, for that
was how things had always been done, but let her deals be tempered
with benevolence.

"Wise talk," several voices agreed, but the discordant note was not
silenced.

"There is one worry."

"No. Loans on easy terms will put an end to every worry."

"Pray listen. When you have money, much more than what you
need for food and clothes, you use it to buy property. Do you not?"

"True."

"Meera will have gold aplenty."

An Elder answered, "We do not grudge her the property she will
buy. A house like the Seth's, with a thousand fruit trees. Milch-kine—
ten, twenty, thirty. And all else that a woman asks for."

"Do not forget what a woman needs most," cried another Elder.
"A husband."

"Han! If only my Babua catches Grandma's fancy!"

"The old barber will earn good fees, bringing proposals for the rich
girl—from the Seven Villages and even from the city. He has a rival
though. The Kanhan matchmaker wags a more oily tongue. To engage
that sly fellow is as good as a marriage ceremony performed."

"Pray listen," the persistent voice came. "When you have a house
and cattle and heaps of money still lie unspent, there is one thing you
are sure to buy."

"What is it?"

"Land. Good plowland. Meera, a peasant's daughter, will see real
wealth in land alone. Land is power. Say 'No' if I speak wrongly."

The others burst into laughter. "Why, friend, for five breaths of time
we shared your terrible worry! Listen. Let our Meera buy all the land
she wants, let her have as much as the Seth's, or even more. We will
rejoice."

"Where will that land come from?" The voice was now sharper.
"The Seth's fields had once been ours. He took them from us piece
by piece. The only way for Meera to get land is to dispossess us, to
seize what is ours."

Silence fell.

"She will have the power."

Silence prevailed.

"Tell me if I speak like an ass and then every one of you may pull me by the two ears."

No answer.

"We are in a fix. We do not know if this thing is good or bad, thi touchstone. First, look at it from this side. Meera gets her gold. She gives the village all it needs, and much more than is expected from the district board. The benefits dropping on your lap like ripe fruit, why waste your breath and bile over the board-moard? And now, brothers you may look at it from the other side."

"Yes. Tell us."

"What do you see? There is Meera with her gold. She wears a hundred jewels on her person. She has a palanquin, eight shoulder sweating under its handlebars."

"No, the palanquins are gone. Meera will buy a motorbus, like the red ones on the highroad. She will ride in it all by herself, stretched full-length on a bench with a pillow under her head. And she will also—"

The gruff voice stopped this interruption.

"We do not grudge her the motorbus. We grudge her nothing. I will make us happy to see her live in the way of a king's daughter. Our only worry is the land. Riches have to turn into plowed earth. Vast tracts—you run across them, run hard and long until you drop on your haunches, out of breath, and all this while you have trodden no speck of dust that is not yours."

Awe-struck eyes saw that vision and tongues dried up as the unexpected menace took clear shape, but after a long minute a whispered comment came, "We hunger for the miracle, whatever else may follow, good or bad."

The voice now had an undertone of misery. "Even I who fear the miracle pray that it come to us soon. Maybe whatever plowland is left to us will be Meera's, one day. But then, our more urgent needs will have been met by her. Those needs cannot wait. We are like men ailing with a dread disease. We turn and twist in pain. There is a drug that can give us relief. Later, that drug will be our death. No matter. We reach out for the drug with both our hands. Nothing matters except the relief."

"So it is. So it is truly, brother."

"That is all I have to tell you. We have no choice except to wait for the miracle, but let us keep our eyes wide open. We must pray for the miracle, but let us do so with hearts undeceived."

The Elders walked back homeward with mixed feelings. The pice game had lost some of its bright promise; yet no one was prepared to give it up. *We have a hunger in us, dear brother.*

23

At the end of a futile fortnight the Seth's preoccupation yielded fruit.

He had been straining to get to the root of the problem—what is real kindness? The idea came at last that kindness had to be a natural impulse. Contrived, deliberate, it lost all value. Kindness could not be resolved into a business deal. It was a matter of the heart, as Meera, with remembrance of her dead cow, had said, even though that was not the whole truth. Feeling was not all. Neither purpose nor gesture could by itself avail. The act had to be done, the selfless, spontaneous act of real kindness.

Let Meera cease to think of making the touchstone work. Let her mind be free, as at the time her ring became transmuted. Easy to see now why the four hundred jilebis given to the poor were bound to fail. Memory of that episode brought a bitter taste to the Seth's mouth. How the Halwai must have laughed. No more jilebis to buy from him anyway. No more processions of schoolboys, the itch for sweets in their mouths; the election was as good as won. And now, let Meera do the act of real kindness, unawarely.

The trouble was that her expectations were afire. Her eyes saw nothing but gold. The strange turn in her fortune when she was facing disaster. Fifty per cent! Grateful and happy, she should have declined such a big share. Seth-ji, she should have said, what shall I do with so much gold? It will tempt thieves and robbers. Better keep my share in your safe custody. Yes, those were the right words for her to say. The disgrace that a simple peasant maid should think only of gold, gold, gold!

Spontaneity, the heart of real kindness. But—trouble again!—the uncontrived act might take months to come, or years, or it might not come at all.

The Seth bared his thigh and scratched it thoughtfully. He could not afford to wait.

Chances could be set up in such a way that Meera would be forced to act, not knowing what she did. Her natural impulse would carry her along—to success.

He reflected on this line a good while. The quill pen seldom left his ear and the ledgers lay forgotten. The clothshop door had been closed for the day. At last he was satisfied. The new plan was clear in every detail.

Meera had taken loans to help people in distress and those loans had pushed her into deep water. Every loan dated before the touchstone came to her, with one exception. Ten rupees, the last entry in her account. She gave the money to her aged neighbor who was almost a destitute. The court decree against him was ready to be served. That old rook could be the instrument of fate. His eviction would force Meera to act—act with one compulsive feeling and purpose.

The Seth felt laughter gathering in his belly. It was so easy!

One thing must be done, however. The copper Meera wore was not enough. She could surely carry twice as much. A new supply of ornaments must be procured from town before the new test. He himself would get them, selecting the heaviest pieces.

Two days later, the thunderbolt came crashing on Old Father's house. He had lived a long time in the shadow of peril and was not taken by surprise. When Meera came rushing to him and cried, "This cannot be, you cannot bow down to such tyranny," he shook his head sadly.

"Seth-ji owns everything we have. He has every right to take what is really his."

She was speechless for a minute. Then: "I will go to Seth-ji. He is sure to listen to me."

Old Father stared at her and under his glance Meera hung her head; today, for the first time, the shame struck her that she was so close to the Seth, she was his partner.

"Seth-ji needs my strips of earth. He needs them badly."

"Old Father—" she cried in grieving.

"All will be well with us, Meera. Do not worry."

Later in the day, when the plowshares and household goods had been sold off to Bulaki Rao, one of the scythes could not be found. Strangely, Old Father broke down under this petty loss as if it outweighed all his other misfortunes. "The scythe—" he moaned, looking about distractedly. His eyes were dim with the tears that he made no attempt to restrain. "The scythe.... Where has the scythe gone?"

Grandma's eyes poured blessing on the old man's kin, but looking at one face, she was startled. That face had no trace of sorrow, only anger. She gazed hard for a minute and nodded to herself.

When the night had deepened and it was time for sleep—the eviction was to take effect the next day—Grandma said, "Meera, I can see danger. We have to be wary."

"Danger?"

"The scythe."

"What about the scythe?"

"Roghuvir."

Their eyes met. Meera felt horror. "No, Grandma, it cannot be," she cried.

"All night we must keep watch," Grandma said.

"Shall I run to the Seth's house and give him a warning?"

"No. We may be wrong."

They sat on the veranda, eyes stuck to the neighbor's door twenty yards away. Somewhere in the front yard a frog half-swallowed by a snake croaked pathetically.

Time went by. When it was past midnight, the old man came out with his wife. They acted in a strange manner. The old man laid his hand on the outer wall and started to walk around with slow dragging steps, and behind him his wife did likewise. They circled the house, once, twice, thrice. They were like the blind feeling their way. Or— Meera had a curious fancy—were those two repeating the gesture she had made one night to her cow? Could it be that, like the cow, the mud wall needed solace?

"It hurts to cut your roots," Grandma said in a murmur. "How live with all your past becoming empty?" She looked up at the night sky preening its wealth of stars and saw one plunge into the void. "*They* don't care!" Her eyes glared at the million specks of light. "One more, one less—"

"Grandma, how stop Vir-brother with his scythe? What shall I tell him?"

"Your heart will guide you."

And time passed. The stricken house sank into exhausted sleep. All was quiet, save for a chorus of insect hum. Then, like a moving shadow, Roghuvir slipped out the door.

"Gran'ma!"

She was fast asleep, her head drooping to her breast, a weary catch in her breath. Her increasing years were telling on Grandma; awake one moment, asleep the next. Meera did not have the heart to shake her out of her rest. Vir was walking off and she must act quickly. She rose, hurried after him. She saw his steel blade catch the starlight.

As he whirled round, having heard the beat of feet, she lifted her hand: "Stop!" She drew close, then stood in silence, not knowing what to say. Seth-ji had destroyed the boy. How fight in defense of the tyrant?

"Go back, Meera."

Still she had nothing to tell him. She mumbled, "Listen, Vir—"

"It is as you think."

"Will you—"

"The village will rejoice."

"No. The village will never forgive you."

He stared at her. "Freed from the monster . . . all bonds cut to pieces . . . ." The resentful scythe jerked.

"Listen," she pleaded. If only she could tell him that she was trying to achieve the same end—release from the Seth's power—and there was no need for violence. No, she could not tell him that. Her approach had to be on a different line.

"The Seth suffers."

"The Seth?"

"He bears more misery than all of you."

The peasant lad smiled in disbelief. "You do not know what you say, Meera."

"He dwells in hell. They all do—people who make others suffer. Their peace of mind, their happiness is outward. Inside, they burn."

"It is not true," the lad cried hoarsely.

She drew closer. "Why must you end his suffering? Let him pay in full measure. Listen—"

"My folk, homeless beggars—" His voice broke.

She could not tell him about her decision that she would go to the Seth and beg for a favor. Do not evict them. When the gold comes, I will pay off their debts to you ten times over.

"You cannot betray Old Father," she thrust hard. "You cannot make his misery unbearable."

His face showed uncertainty and struggle.

195

"Go home, Vir-brother. Tomorrow, at dawn, when you walk your lone way, the gods will walk with you."

His eyes in starlight had a peculiar look, the depth of accusation clear behind the pain. She had lost contact with him for some time and in that brief space she had grown fast and now she was older than he! The common earth they had trodden since childhood was left far behind.

While she swayed between hope and fear, he turned round abruptly. He was walking away toward the house. He did not stop or even look back.

"Roghuvir," she whispered the name, tears welling to her eyes. She stood motionless a long while, weeping in silence.

She was restless all night and at daybreak she hurried off to the Seth's house. "Beti!" he beamed at sight of her. "You do not look well. Shall I send for the vaid? Let him give you a potion of bitter herbs."

"No no, Seth-ji. I have come to you with a begging bowl."

"For shame, beti. You do not have to beg, you must demand."

When she had revealed her mind, he was silent awhile.

"Beti." He scratched his chin with an unhappy finger. "This will mean a very big sacrifice."

"Seth-ji, you can well afford it."

"You do not understand. Whatever I have I simply hold it in trust; it is all Nago's patrimony. I have no right to squander a single pice."

She pleaded, "Nago has more than enough." Fear seized her lest he fail to relent.

He shook his head pensively. "Meera, there you are mistaken. I have slipped into errors for which poor Nago has to suffer. I have told you about Chamundi bridge—"

"Seth-ji, in due time this loss will be made up ten times over. I—"

He interrupted her. "There is a way. I can cut my personal expense. Each pice saved in that way will go to reduce the loss in question. Why, I will eat less, I will bid the Halwai rat send me six pieces of wheaten bread instead of eight—they are a half-anna apiece. In four or five years the big hole in Nago's patrimony will get filled up. Don't you think so?"

She was astonished. Did it really mean victory? "Seth-ji," her voice was low. "Such kindness—"

"Ho, beti, this is nothing. Can I ever forget who saved the life of that pig?" He lifted the lid of his cash box and picked up a pad of rupee-notes. "Give this to the old rook. Let him pay up. Then it will be my task to recover the big loss, pice by pice."

Grateful tears smarted in her eyes and she turned her head to hide her feeling. In a minute she was running homeward, breathless.

The doomed ones stood in the front yard, ready to depart. Old Father was mumbling a prayer with eyes closed. He stopped as Meera gasped out, "You do not have to go."

"Beti!"

"You will be rid of your debts. You will live in peace."

A chorus of surprised murmur. Old Father lifted his hand, commanding silence. "I do not understand. How can I pay back?"

She held out the rupee-notes, eyes ashine.

He had beetling brows, that Old Father, and in his rugged face the cheekbones stood out like ridges. His kith and kin were gazing at him, hanging on his response. He was calm-eyed, serene, with no trace of yesterday's sorrow.

"This is the Seth's money?" He pointed to the notes.

"The evil will be undone. You will be safe. Rejoice, Old Father."

The wheel had turned. The peril was gone. Overwhelmed by great relief, the women in the group started to moan softly. But Old Father said, "Beti, bid us farewell. It is not for you to settle our fate."

"Hai!" the women wailed aloud, sucked back into peril. Meera, struck dumb, gazed at the old man and saw him smile. Then anger came upon her. "You have to do this to your dear ones just for your pride."

"Happily would I accept help, my daughter. Happily would I take what our brethren give. But not one pice of the Seth's money, soaked in peasants' blood."

"Old Father—" He was wrapped in splendor, so far apart from the people who sat begging at her door.

His face grew stern. "Do not plead. Your Grandma would have acted the same way. There she stands. Ask her. Speak, Meera's Grandma. Would you accept the Seth's help?"

Grandma's silence was answer enough. Old Father turned back to the girl. "Homeless wretches, we still have our honor. Beti, do not grieve for us. Maybe we shall find work in town, in the cotton mill there. Maybe we shall pull rickshaws, my son and grandsons and I, while the women work at grindstones, pressing wheat. All will be well with us. Maybe we shall save money and buy land somewhere and be farmers again. Maybe I shall at last be able to make a pilgrimage to Holy Benares!" He ended in a muffled tone, "Beti, bid us farewell with an easy heart. May you always be happy."

The bent figure, stick in hand, passed from the veranda steps to the road, followed by his silent kith and kin.

Meera stood still, alone in the forsaken house, while Grandma walked along with Old Father, not to turn back until they were on the highroad. Thus had Grandma walked, every time men were made homeless. None else in the village had this privilege. "Bide well," she would tell the people in parting. "The gods walk with you. Bide well, neighbors."

Later, when the Seth came to know what had happened, his eyeballs grew stonelike. The old rook had scented a motive behind Meera's honest offer of help. He had to chop off his own nose so that Meera could be thwarted. The utter baseness. The monstrous malice. To think that such despicable creatures inhabited God's earth!

CHAPTER

24 Old Father and his kin were barely out of the village when the pice game took a sudden, reverse turn. It was again due to Subhadri, the young woman who had started the game. Meera, bemused on the veranda, was in her mind walking the highroad with the destitute people when Subhadri appeared at the foot of the steps. Her face was pinched, her eyelids swollen, as if she had cried.

"Let me have my pice back."

"Pice?"

"The copper coin I gave you. You do not have to wear it on your person."

Meera said, "Subhadri, why are you so upset? What has happened?"

Subhadri tried to restrain herself. "Nothing has happened. It is only that I do not want my pice to be turned to gold."

"Subhadri—"

"Yes," she answered. "I know what woes will befall my folk. Better far that we bear a hundred woes than use the accursed gold for our relief."

"Accursed gold, Subhadri?"

She seemed loth to explain. "All I ask is this, Meera Bai. Take a copper coin off your body and give it to me."

Meera grew angry. "It is as if I have stolen your treasure!" She unstrung her sari's waist knot under which the pice, fifty of them, lay against her skin, but as she fumbled, the displaced coins dropped to the floor, scattering down the steps. Subhadri picked up one.

"Maybe you know what your pice looks like," Meera made a dig at her.

"No matter. One pice is like all others. I have taken what I gave you." She stooped to help collect the coins but Meera cried, "Do not trouble yourself. My hands are good enough."

When Subhadri was gone Meera sat sunk in puzzlement. Subhadri needed the gold desperately. The look of prayer in her face when she

199

had offered the coin and the throb of hope in her voice: will the touchstone act soon? Yet today she dared say, accursed gold!

I will ask Gran'ma, Meera said to herself, Gran'ma is sure to know. But the question stayed back on her lips.. She felt humiliated. No, I cannot ask Gran'ma.

Subhadri seemed to have set a signal. In the next hour several other women came and took back their pice. Like Subhadri they were unwilling to answer questions. The grocer's third daughter-in-law, however, said, "In two or three days you will be rid of all the fifty pice. So much the better for you; no need to give away gold."

Meera felt a lump in her throat. In her unhappiness she yearned for her Cowhouse friends—she had hardly seen them in the past week. She recalled the silent, morose group at odds with the clamorous crowd under the fig tree.

Sohagi, I need you badly, Meera now thought and she thought of the wonder that had come upon her—not the touchstone but a greater wonder—and to whom could she speak about it if not to her dearest friend? Sohagi, will you understand my feeling—was that your feeling also, when your man came into your life?

Sohagi lived at the far end of the village. In the late afternoon Meera started to walk toward her friend's house. But, unexpectedly, the ox-cart was coming along Main Road, loaded with straw, and there was Sohagi atop the pile, as usual. The cart did not pull up, though.

"I am dead and gone and this is my ghost—is that what you think, Sohagi?"

"The Devi protects you, Meera Bai."

*Bai!* Meera *Bai!* And she stared hard. "Drop that nonsense, Sohagi. What have I done to you? Everyone has started to hate me as if I have become something evil."

Pause—and then, "Do you understand nothing, Meera? Have you changed so much that you cannot see a plain truth?"

Meera cried huskily, "Tell me what it is, Sohagi, I beg of you."

Sohagi hesitated again but forced herself to speak. The Seth with all his shrewdness could not keep a secret, especially when he was angry. He had unburdened his heart to Bulaki Rao as soon as Old Father was gone, and the story was soon handed round. It was now clear why the Old Father had to face eviction, prematurely.

Meera said, "It is I who have written Old Father's fate—that is what the people think?"

Sohagi was silent, looking down at the piled straw, breaking a piece between her fingers. But Meera would not give up her fight. "Maybe the miracle is a rainbow, a thing with no substance."

"Let the rainbow fade off and you will find us at your side. Until that hour—" She cut short, abruptly bidding the cartman, "Move along."

O Sohagi, Meera wanted to say, it is not the miracle of gold alone. There is the other miracle, and that anyhow you will understand. O Sohagi, you who said, "Who in Sonamitti is fit to wed our Meera? Her day will come. We will look into her eyes and see and know—and rejoice." Yet, now, you do not look into those eyes, you do not see the image, clear and ever-present.

"Sohagi—"

"May the Devi bless you, Meera, sister. May your inmost wish be fulfilled." The old warmth was in her voice. But the oxen had broken into a trot, the wheels churning dustily.

Meera felt the gold-washed metal weigh heavier on her limbs as she dragged herself down the road.

There was Munni still. She would understand.

When they met, ten minutes later, Munni, as of old, took her hand and squeezed it tightly. "Come to my kitchen, dear sister, and eat fishhead. It helped you once to defeat the Seth, remember?"

"Then you have not forsaken me?" wistfully.

"Why, Meera, it is you who have forsaken the Cowhouse."

"No. I have longed to be with you all. As in the good old days—"

Munni saddened and shook her head. "Not even a month is gone and it has to be 'the good old days.' Now that we have lost you, those days are best forgotten."

"No, Munni. Nothing has changed. If you could see into my mind!"

At that point Munni became a different person. She spoke with Sohagi's voice. The gold Meera hankered for was yet to come, but its evil was done in advance. Kindness was on sale. What an ugly form it had taken! Old Father's doom had been a question of time, but it was rushed for one reason: an act of kindness needed to be done.

Meera answered hotly in self-defense. She had tried to help Old Father with no secret motive. To mix her up with the Seth's tyranny was unjust.

But Munni was pursuing her own line of thought. "No one is safe from the threat of kindness, so people think. And they are afraid lest the new Seth grab whatever land is left to them—"

Meera made an imploring gesture for her to stop and Munni, looking at the pain-marred face, felt her eyes moisten. "Forgive me. I have spoken stupidly." She wiped her eyes with her fingers.

Meera walked homeward. In bewildered misery she asked herself, what shall I do?

Kindness was on sale—how true! In the days gone by, Grandma and she had given what they could with no second thought. "He starves and has no one to help him." . . . "She must buy a new goat; the only one she had is dead and she is grief-stricken." . . . "That boy cannot pay his school fee and Master-ji has no pity for the poor." . . . "They have to observe the naming of a newborn son; how will they pay the Brahmin for his services?" Feelings, not argument. Pleasure came out of the giving, even if it made one more red mark in the Seth's ledger. So it had been then—and now? She was simply unable to give. The taveez held her hand tied up! With cold appraisal she must ask: Is that the right act of kindness? The act that will produce gold?

Yet it was also true that the urge was strong in her to answer every prayer for help and to wipe every tear from every eye.

There, ahead of her on Main Road, was the slouching figure of the rag-woman, a shabby bundle under her arm. Three children dead and her husband eaten by a panther. No land to till, no one to come to her help. The struggle to feed herself and her Buddhu had added twenty years to her age.

"Listen, Buddhu's mother—"

The rag-woman turned round for a glance but she did not stop or even answer.

"One moment—" But the woman walked on, unheeding. With fast strides Meera caught up with her.

"You are not angry, Buddhu's mother?"

She stopped, watching the girl, eyes narrowed. "Now you have to fix on me, han?"

"Fix on you?"

"Use the rag-hag, get rich at her cost."

"I do not understand you."

"Plant a copper-worth, reap a gold harvest." Her voice was a croak. "No soil as good as this rag-hag."

Meera was dumfounded.

"This rag-hag is no goatling, my wily beauty! She will not make thee a Seth. No kindness, no gold. No chance for thine magic." She cleared her throat to rid it of strong feeling and spat thickly on the road and she spat three times. "Misery, our bone marrow, to bring thee riches?" She grimaced, showing her gums, three front teeth gone. "Like Old Father we all must hide our bone marrow from thine hunger, dear daughter." She turned, clasping her bundle against her body, and shuffled away.

25

It happened precisely as the grocer's third daughter-in-law had foretold. The pice entrusted to Meera steadily diminished in number until just five of them were left. The glint of angry accusation in every eye—she had written the fate not of Old Father alone but of all Sonamitti, leaving the people no option but to take their pice back lest they lose honor itself.

"The end of our miseries seemed near. The fairy-tale is over. She has played her cards well—truly, a king's daughter!"

The Cowhouse women had mixed feelings. Meera, they knew, did not deserve this indictment; she was not the maker of circumstance but its victim. The new situation had one blessing though. The vote-mote was round the corner and here was a chance to renew the fight! The Cowhouse took the heartening message around and a thin procession was again on the road, Sohagi holding the banner. "Vote for Rajaram-brother, vote!"

Rajaram was not happy, however. "The gold hunger, once wakened, will not be denied." And he added, scowling, "I heard a man speak the truth bluntly. 'We are split within us like ripe melon, each of us,' he said."

"Shall we never be whole again?" one listener asked.

The answering voice had a rough edge. "We need someone to slap us in the face, hard. A slap that will sting into our blood and bone. We need the thunder of a shame to pass from our toe nails to the bristles on our chin. Then we shall again be Rajaram or Harischandra or Chotalal."

There was a time when Meera, young as she was, could have given such a slap. Today she, more than any one else, needed it for herself. Her acts of "kindness" would continue to bring disaster on the head of this man or that, and there was no way to stop her.

On its second day, the new procession gained a strong impetus. Grandma came hobbling along Main Road and, "Hei-ee!" she called from a distance; "have you a place for an old hag?" The women stopped, amazed and happy, until Grandma drew abreast, and then Sohagi offered her the banner. "To have you with us, Grandma, what bliss! It is like the days when we flung our challenge at the Red Turbans and, laughing merrily, went to jail."

A swift cloud showed on the aged face. "Meera also went to jail with us—she was then only ten-eleven." But the brooding look slipped off as soon as she took her place in the line. "Forward!" But she would not accept the proffered banner. "No, Sohagi. It is yours. Old people must make way for the young, or else they will become a hindrance." Her heavy stick beat on the road in tune with the tramp of feet while the strain of dragging stiffened limbs made her gasp.

"Slower!" A hushed murmur ran over the column like a breath of breeze. Sensing the concern for her, Grandma smiled gratefully. "Look, we have not gone twenty paces and I have slowed you down. Old ones always do that—beware of them!"

"Call yourself old, Grandma?" the potter's wife countered. "You are younger than all of us. But why must we hurry? We are not flying from a tiger! Let the word go through the village, 'Grandma marches!' That will do us more good than a hundred processions without you."

Pleased, excited like a young girl, Grandma cried, "Let us shout in one big voice, 'Vote for Rajaram-brother!'"

The exertion grew until her breath came with a wheeze and her voice, crying the slogan, was low and empty. Yet she would not stop for a minute's rest. Struck with alarm, the women pleaded, "Grandma, let us sit awhile on the roadside." . . . "Let us have a drink of water from the well yonder." . . . "Ho, Grandma, a thorn has pricked into my foot. Will you stop, so I may pull it out?"

But she, heedless, went along. She could not help it. For, it was as though she had to be not just Grandma but Meera too!

The surprise came near Schoolhouse Lane. Meera stood there, waiting, watching. She had apparently taken the shorter path through the fields.

A hush fell on the procession and it came to a sudden halt. Sohagi, with a quick gesture, held out the banner toward the girl who stood rigid, and Grandma jerked her head toward the banner as if she also was offering it. And fifty women by gesture or look offered the banner to Meera. Their pulses quickened with expectation. "Meera-sister—"

they could have cried, the yearning hot in their breasts, but the hush continued.

She gave no response. She stared at the procession for what seemed a long time. Then she spun round and was walking away.

The women stood frozen for a minute. When they started again to walk, Grandma was hobbling slowly and painfully, all her strength gone. Sohagi took the stick from her hand and gave her an arm instead for support. Munni on the other side of Grandma gave her an arm. A thin voice from the rear cried, "Vote for Rajaram-brother!" and the others that followed were as thin and lifeless.

Meera, too, walking her lone way through the fields, had no strength left. She longed to sit down under a tree but pushed along.

"Meera—"

Startled, she saw him perched on top of a boulder, beckoning. She needed him at this moment, yet feared him—her defenses were gone. And as she came, he studied her face questioningly and read the answer. Yes, she had seen the procession. She had gone to Main Road to see it pass—under what inner compulsion? He recalled the other time when he had stood at the wayside waiting for her—she was returning from her first thwarted expectation of the miracle. Failure had not dimmed her hopes then, nor had she been torn within.

He gave her a hand, helped her up. The stone top was all gray-white with dried-up bird droppings; he was clearing a space for her but she stopped him, thumping down. Arms about her knees she cried, "Now speak. I am ready to listen."

"Speak what?"

Her lips quivered and stark misery came flooding upon her face. "It is my fate to wear the taveez for one purpose. To be scorned; to be despised; to be the scourge of Sonamitti. You do not have to tell me *that*."

The scourge of Sonamitti. He recalled what one of his companions, a peasant lad, had said the day before. "Let her become a Seth with plowland two *kos* on every side, let her land feed on the crushed bones of the dispossessed. For how long, I ask?"

The answer was not hard to find. The days of the Seths were numbered. Soon would the people, vested with their new power, fully waken and their thunderous wrath would make every tyrant whine for mercy. Meera was chasing a mere shadow, but hand in hand with the tyrant and polluted by the breath of his greed.

"Is it the end of the pice game that hurts you?"

That was too much for her. She burst into tears.

He sat quiet, letting her cry. She did have to cry for what she had brought upon herself. The hope she had kindled was quenched and she did have to suffer.

*It is my fate to be scorned, to be despised.* That was the stark truth. He understood the feeling of the people, for he too shared it. What would he not give to be rid of the revulsion within him, pushing him away from her inexorably? No, nothing could push him away from her. But the division in his heart. It would not do to worship her in one part of his heart and despise her in another.

Despise her? He felt the surge of an overwhelming tenderness. She was so young, so helpless. How can I stand above her, looking down with a superior frown, he asked himself, and with that thought he bent toward her, picked up a corner of her sari to wipe tear stains off her cheeks.

But new stains grew. She leaned her head against him and closed her eyes, yielding to his caress. Let not the tears stop, she prayed, or else the caress would stop, too. She would not be able to bear that—

The end of the pice game—that had pleased him vastly, she mused. How much more would it please him if it were the end of the touchstone! Why would she not pull the taveez off her arm and throw it away?

Grandma with her banner—no words could convey as much reproach as each hobbling step of hers on Main Road. And challenge—challenge to Grandpapa himself.

Could she let *him* down?

She felt the amulet press tight on her arm. *Beta, I have a wonderful gift for you. . . . In a world where gold has the last word. . . . Gold with which to do good. . . .*

Tears hurried back behind her eyelids. She lifted her head, sat erect. "Speak. I am ready to listen."

How could he sense her inmost feeling? "The taveez belongs to your heart, Meera, do I not understand?" And as she stared at his face, seeking mockery, he went on, "The miracle is just the means. The purpose is all that counts."

She was silent but her heart beat quicker.

"Do not blame the people if they see the taveez but not the feeling. All they have hoped for is the smallest share in your fortune. Seeking crumbs of charity from your hands they lost you, they assigned you to the Seth's world. If only they knew the truth!"

The rush of happiness made her breath quicken. Even though he had no faith in the touchstone, he understood her, he sympathized! There was nothing more to ask for. Grateful, she waited for him to continue. His face was thoughtful.

Where is true union between man and woman unless they accept each other as equals? he was asking himself. You cannot worship and yet despise. It is the conceit in you that makes you despise.

"The Seth's world?" she questioned.

"Yes, people see you in the Seth's world. Big tracts of plowland—"

She shook her head. "I do not need them. Our own fields are enough."

He longed to touch her again, caress her, but restrained himself.

"People see you in your big new house."

"What good is such a house?"

"Prestige."

"The hard work to keep it clean."

He smiled. "Three servants at your beck and call."

Her face showed horror. Then, relieved of tension, she too smiled. "Maybe people see the umbrella in my arm, one like Seth-ji's."

"They see you in your motorbus."

"Motorbus?"

"The rich lose face unless they make a show. You sit in the bus on a soft bench, all by yourself."

She gave him an arch glance. "Will the motorbus take me to Bombay?"

He was attuned to the light-heartedness he had created. "Leave that to the driver fellow. Let him decide."

"The driver fellow the motor bus company has sent me."

"What!" His face seemed to turn grim. "Let such fellows keep fifty miles away from this village." He shook a clenched fist at the invisible foe.

"Why, pray?" As if in all innocence.

For answer, he drew her arm upon his lap, to the clank of gilded metal. All the space of her arm was covered with the metal. He sighed for the blue glass bangles which had survived the first attack but were now gone—they had been part of herself. The new array of ornaments decorated her hair, neck, ankles. Many more lay under her clothes, he

208

knew, and all had to be next to her skin. The Seth himself had brought the new supply from town. He had given her as big a load as she could carry. And Meera was all too willing.

She saw the quick distaste on his face and something she was about to say died in her mouth. She withdrew her arm quickly and bangles and bracelets clanked again.

There was an awkward silence.

The sudden cry rang startlingly. "Vote for Rajaram-brother!" The procession was passing along the edge of the field, barely two hundred yards away.

Some fuel of bitterness within her seemed to ignite. "That Gran'ma! To tramp the streets like that. She should know better."

He was taken aback. "How can she help it?"

"Who forces her?"

"She has her spirit. Do I have to tell you that, Meera?"

The veiled rebuke stung her and she retorted, "*You* will not have to press her legs when they swell and ache after all the tramping."

"No matter."

"Let her keep on doing it and she will kill herself." Her tone was aggressive because of her lack of conviction.

"She has no choice."

Their lovely moments flickered like a spent flame.

"Sohagi can just as well carry the banner. The fifty voices can just as well cry, Vote for Rajaram-brother."

"So *you* think! If you could see your new image in some kind of mirror—" He stopped, aghast. Her eyes held the misty threat of tears. "No, Meera—" he pleaded, fumbling for a way to wipe off his harsh words, but she slipped down the boulder and was walking away.

"Meera—" And she started to run as if she dreaded pursuit and had to escape.

He sat dejected, aching with a renewed rush of tenderness. Stiff on his pedestal of pride, no longer could he stoop, reach down to take Meera's hand in his own. There could be no true union between them unless he stood with her on the same level.

It is my fate to be scorned, to be despised, to be the scourge of Sonamitti—the words returned to him with a new intensity. If only he too were scorned, despised. . . . If he could disgrace himself in his own eyes. . . . Pick a thorn off his heart with another thorn. . . .

The scourge of Sonamitti? The people must be told the plain truth. He would make them see that truth.

Later in the day, when he met his peasant companions, he spoke gravely.

"The pice game goes; the touchstone myth must follow."

"Han, brother." They were well aware of their city friend's unbelief and always seemed to agree with him while they thought differently; the pice game had nothing to do with the amulet's power. Sohanlal could have fought open opposition but against polite assent with mental reservations he was helpless. He had answered them before with a resigned shrug, but this time it had to be otherwise.

"Meera Bai," he said, "has one single aim in her heart of hearts."

"Land. Big tracts—"

"This you have to know," his voice sharpened. "The gold of which you are so sure will be for everyone to enjoy."

They did not doubt that. "Her charity will be generous, we know. She will give the village whatever the board could and much more."

"It isn't that. You do not understand her. There is no talk of charity. In her reckoning the touchstone belongs to everyone in Sonamitti."

"Everyone, indeed!"

"That was the minstrel's true purpose. She will carry out the purpose."

"It cannot be. The Seth's ally and partner—"

He made an impatient gesture. "Try to grasp this simple fact. She wants nothing for herself. I know her mind. She has less hunger for riches than everyone else in this village."

The peasant lads were struck dumb.

"That is why the minstrel gave her the touchstone. Do you trust my word? Meera Bai will bid everyone share in the riches, if they ever come."

The lads looked at each other in wonderment and there was still no answer.

"One thing, friend, you need badly. So badly, that it hurts you in the loins and guts and all the rest of you." Bulaki Rao, arms akimbo, peered down at the man beside the machine, polishing its body with dust-cloth and paste.

"What do I need so badly?" The voice lacked interest.

"A spouse."

"Indeed!"

Bulaki Rao resumed, "I have watched you, friend. I have seen you tend the phut-phutti until not one dust speck is left. The black engine limbs, the red bodywork, the silver hands made for display; you touch them up, over and again, even when the metal cannot take more polish. You do it at every hour of the day, even at night maybe."

"How true!"

"It is only a cover for you."

He looked up. "What evil have I done?"

"It is a cover for what good you have left undone."

He shrugged. "A riddle and a poor one at that."

"I may be a brother of a bug, as Seth-ji says," Bulaki Rao went on, "but there are things that a bug knows. This I can tell you: the phut-phutti is no substitute for a spouse."

"Maybe the bug can build a spouse with earth, air and cowdung?"

Bulaki Rao showed his teeth in a sharp grin. "Why, friend, there is the ready-made spouse. Several times I have told you about her and you have listened with half an ear, or no ear maybe." He took a step forward and blew the motor-horn playfully, once, twice, thrice, the sound enlivening him more and more. "Ho! A fellow like you wasting yourself on a machine and there sits the Bad Woman of Pipli in her lone abode, a lantern hung on the veranda, the door always ajar."

"How wonderful!"

"The Pipli beauty!" The voice was now thick. "This I repeat for your ears. She is a wheatstalk drooping with ripeness. She is—"

"A full-grown swan with luscious curves," Sohanlal supplied. "I remember that piece."

"Yes. And she is both a tigress and a sparrow—"

"Enough!" lifting an imploring hand.

"The spouse-of-all can make you gasp with laughter with stories out of her own life—so I have told you. Did I narrate the Brahmin's plight? No? Why, it is like a fable of the olden days."

"Brahmin? What name?"

Bulaki Rao closed one eye in a wink. "No name. The Bad Woman keeps every secret of hers locked up under her navel. A Brahmin of the Seven Villages. He visited the Pipli beauty one night."

"The swine!"

"Remember the One-tree Hill close to the highroad? It faces a pond at the left with lilies growing in plenty. Between hill and lily-pond is the house. No other house within a hundred cubits or more."

"What about the Brahmin?"

"The air in such a house defiles the apparel on one's body. A Brahmin has to be heedful. So our man took off his dhoti and vest and his sacred thread also. Only a strip of loincloth was left. He tied up his things in a bundle and left them at the foot of a guava tree before he walked into the house. You follow me?"

"Proceed." Like figures in a shadow-play he could see the naked man and the debased woman, the "spouse-of-all."

Bulaki Rao resumed: "At early dawn he was ready to leave. Returning to the pond, he immersed his Brahminic body in water while chanting the name, 'Vishnu . . . Vishnu!' so that he could be absolved of the unclean. On to the guava tree. The bundle? Gone! He rubbed his eyes, walked twenty yards from the guava tree on every side. The clothes were nowhere. He shouted to the Bad Woman, for it could be a trick of hers."

Bulaki Rao paused. "You are not listening, friend."

"Proceed." Along with the Seth and the Bug, the debased woman had to be there to complete the corruption.

"At this point the Brahmin heard a mockful huk-ka-hua-ah! So Brother Jackal had stolen his bundle and sat chuckling on One-tree Hill."

"Brother Jackal has a sense of fun."

"What could the Brahmin do?" Bulaki Rao shook his head sadly. "He was sweating with panic. Marooned in the Bad Woman's house with nothing on his body except his spectacles and loincloth."

"Alas!"

"The Bad Woman cried merrily, 'Why worry? You only have to live with me and never step out of doors.' That was too much. The poor fellow broke down. 'Take pity,' he begged. 'If I am seen without the sacred thread—I who have a wife and five children—' The vixen said giggling, 'Live in this house and no one will see you. Why do you want to go back to your wife? Look at me once more.' And she preened the best in her beauty. The Brahmin now lost his temper. 'What, woman! You forget my caste status?' Then the Bad Woman, a sparrow in bed and yet a tigress, pointed doorward with her finger. 'Go. Be off.'"

"What next? He walked out, naked?"

Bulaki Rao looked sad. "He bought a sari from the vixen; he had to pay even more than the 'black' rate."

"Shark eating shark!" Brahmin, steel spectacles, five children. Bulaki Rao had given himself away, maybe deliberately. "No one saw him walking in a woman's garb?"

"How do I know?"

"His wife? His children? When he returned at sunrise—"

"Let me repeat this, dear friend," Bulaki Rao changed the subject abruptly. "The Pipli pleasure will do you more good than your rubber-and-metal beauty." And he added reassuringly, "She is cheaper than city rates."

This Bug—Sohanlal mused—the irony that he and his kind would be the first in Sonamitti to use the rights that freedom would confer. The irony, too, that Meera had brought this about, she with her miracle.

And he himself had made the miracle tree break into blossoms of great hope! When, three days back, he had let Meera's real purpose be known, the reaction was even quicker than he had expected. The bitter tide receded overnight as if by magic! And the new expectation put into shade the humbler prayers made before—even the pice game now seemed to have been a child's play. The heart of the village beat in a frenzy of daily, hourly demand to see the great promise fulfilled. Jai Meera Bai! Jai Sona Mai!

"Sohanlal!" the Seth's voice called from the porch.

"Ji."

213

"Start the machine. I am ready to leave for town."

In two minutes the motorcycle sped out of the village. A seventy-mile stretch of road lay ahead. The Seth approved the slow pace—many drivers could not help rushing madly and imperiling their master's life and limb. The young rascal deserved a good word.

"Take every care of your charge, Sohanlal. One day it will be yours."

"Mine?"

"A gift. Remember that. Treat the machine as if it is your brother. Good for you in the long run."

"You will buy a car?"

"A car?"

"Since you will part with the motorcycle—"

"I have no use for a car," the Seth answered. "Do you think I am Henry Ford? I will retire from business and then there will be no need to run about."

"Retire from business? When?"

"After fifteen years, or maybe twenty. I will hand over the cloth stores to my Nago who will be a grown-up lad by that time, and I shall then fix all my thoughts and energy on the Hereafter. Nago, I feel sure, will buy a motorcar. That son of a pig with his expensive tastes. His mother has eaten his head."

"I see."

"Is it clear that in your own interest you should treat the machine as a dear brother?"

"Clear," he snapped. Here was the man who had debased the soul of a young girl. Two strange partners weaving kindness on a loom! Once he had spoken hard words about Meera to Grandma. "There is a dream in her," Grandma had said, answering his accusation; "she is all tight with the dream." "A disease, not a dream," he had blurted out. "So it is," Grandma had said placatingly and pleaded, "Give her time. She will need real kindness for herself. When the dream is lost it will hurt badly." "It may be too late then," he had said; "by that time the Seth will be on the board. Freedom will have died its first death at the polling booth of this village." Grandma had been silent for a minute, and then there was a sudden harshness in her voice as she spoke: "Why must you ask so much of Meera? She is such a child. She has seen nothing of life. She has not even gone out of this village —except once, to be sent to prison." Her face was tender again for the girl.

Yet, in an unguarded moment, he spoke cruel words to Meera and made her cry; and then felt deeply shamed.

No trace of accusation was left in him—that was the measure of her conquest. The yearning to be her equal—in ignominy. Let him be struck with some terrible dishonor so that he would be unfit to sit in judgment ever again.

Here was the placid creature by his side, totally unaware of what evil he had done. Sohanlal, with that thought, gripped the handlebar hard, the veins standing out on his knuckles. Was there to be no punishment for this creature?

*Treat the machine as a dear brother. It will be yours, after fifteen years, or twenty.*

A minute later the Seth was gazing in surprise at the instrument panel.

"Ho! Wings have sprouted from the wheels. Forty!"

The response came from the needle itself. Forty-five. The Seth straightened up.

"Enough of this trick, Sohanlal. Back to thirty. Do you hear?"

But the needle crept onward. The Seth's amazed glance moved to the driver's face. It had a queer look. The fellow must be dead drunk. He had gone to Pipli—

"Do you want to keep your job, Sohanlal?"

The answer came as a chuckle. There was something terrible in the man's face, the Seth noted. Madman! He was goading the engine as it were for more speed and yet more.

Past fifty!

The Seth felt an icy chill in his spine and his body became limp. It was as he had felt in the meadows one night, the bhootni at his heels, her skeleton fingers close to his throat. Ram-Ram! The name that scared off evil spirits was not reputed for its effect on a madman, yet the Seth spoke it under his breath. Ram-Ram!

Through the crashing roar of the full-throttled engine, he heard the driver's blood-curdling laugh.

A killer? He himself would share the doom. Both would lie under a twisted heap of metal, and the petrol on fire. Or catapulted upon tree trunk, skull smashed. That could happen in several ways. One of the wheels could hit a cobble. The madman might lose control. The Seth girded himself in his spirit to come to the fellow's aid. After all, he was not stark mad. Let his nerve be steady. Let his vision be sharp and sure. Steady, Sohanlal!

Would that the writ of destiny came after the touchstone had done its work, the gold acquired for Nago to inherit. The Seth felt the stab of a familiar regret on his son's account. That ever-luckless boy.

The engine was doing its best. One more glance at the needle and the Seth sat slumped, hardly daring to move a limb. His eyes alone lived in his inert body; they lay fastened on the sunlit road. An ox-cart loomed into view. The end was near. The Seth drew a deep breath and closed his eyes. He was drained of all emotion—and had one thought: let it be over quickly. Quickly.

He opened his eyes and looked ahead because of a change in the rhythm of speed. The ox-cart was not in sight. Something had happened to the machine; its thunder had dropped to a calm throb, a familiar volume of sound. He turned to the needle. Thirty-five. His chest bulged with relief. He looked at the madman who seemed cool, his usual self.

The outskirts of town. The welcome sight of fast traffic and the central part, Srinivas Street, lined with shops on either side. There— Gay Peacock with its bright-green door and behind the large panels of window glass a gleaming exhibit of the new stock of gold-thread fabric from Benares.

The Seth shuffled out of the side-car and standing on solid earth he felt a shudder of recaptured fear. He crossed the pavement and stopped, turning round.

"Sohanlal!"

"Ji?"

"Go back to the village. I'll come by bus later in the evening." He paused for a few moments before he added, "Take a month's notice to leave my service. The machine will be on sale after a month. Meanwhile you may carry the cloth."

"Ji." He drove off while the Seth on the doorstep stood watching, fascinatedly.

Twilight fell as he went along the highroad at a slow pace. Field mice scurried by—there seemed to be hundreds of them. A rabbit sat on its haunches, frozen by the light. The engine's din plunged across the vast stillness. Presently the moon rose and meadows lay white in the sheen. At every mile, a village showed its huddled shape.

The selfless image of a girl, pure gold, was gone and the new image was like the ornaments on it, gilded deceit. He, in his lofty pride, would never be able to reach her again with an outstretched arm. She would be lost to him forever—unless he destroyed his pride. Unless he found a way to demean himself to the level of the Seth or Bulaki Rao.

The motorcycle sped on. An hour passed, two hours. Possessed by his curious resolve, wondering how to carry it out, he hardly felt the passage of time. Sonamitti was close ahead. There, at his left, was One-tree Hill. Pipli.

Pipli? Beyond the thick screen of trees was the mud hut where the debased one lived. The Seth, the Bug, the Bad Woman of Pipli.

Struck by a thought he frowned hard. *There is the way.* His hold on the handlebar slackened and the speed dropped. *The way to be a Bulaki Rao.* He went at a crawling pace, veered sharply to the narrow track where it met the highroad. The trees made a dark mass and behind them was the pond with its white and pink lilies. He pressed the brake, switched off the ignition. Jumping down, he pushed the wheels along the track. In two minutes he stopped, fighting a tide of loathing, and clung to the machine in a kind of desperation. Then he whirled round and strode off. The leafless tree on the humplike hill stood as a sentinel, its outlines twisted and gnarled against moonlight. The revolt welled sourly to his throat, but he hurried on. Skirting the pond, he saw the lantern hung high at the veranda of a mud hut, beckoning invitation.

27 Meera heard the motorcycle story from the Seth's mouth and broke into a titter. That distressed the Seth almost as much as the incident itself. Meera was incapable of pity. Her heart was a lump of metal. Would that Lakshmi were here. Out of her rich feeling at his escape she would have sent a puja to the temple. He would write at once and ask her to come back home. She had been away long enough.

Meera followed up her titter with something worse. She said, her face turning very grave, "Pray do not try ever again to trick me into acts of kindness." Mockery rang in her voice. "Big sacrifice. Big hole in Nago's patrimony. *I will eat less.*"

The Seth did not lose his patience. Old Father's departure had upset her—she could not see how that wily rook had foiled her even at the cost of his own destitution. "I tried to stir the taveez into action," he pointed out; "we cannot wait and watch for endless time." "Why not?" she retorted; "if you want something big, the price you pay has to be big."

"True," he assented meekly, for he was now aware of his own miscalculation, he could see why the test could not but fail. Even though he had feigned reluctance before acceding to Meera's request, she had somehow seen through him, so that her offer of help to Old Father carried an echo of his own secret motive. So it could not be a selfless act. Kindness had to flow out of her like milk from a mother's breast. As the full breast yielded at the pull of the child's mouth, so must she yield at the pull of circumstance. He would know better next time and the test would be flawless. If only Meera had complete faith in her partner—

She was not without conceit! She had let it be known that all her gold was meant to be given to the people. She wished to be *parijat*, the tree in paradise bearing blooms of gold, and the blooms were for every hand to pluck. Let her bask in that wild fancy. When the gold came, when she felt it warm and bright on her limbs, it would be a new tale. Even ascetics were not free from the possessive lure of the wondrous metal!

The new idea came upon him sooner than he had expected. He was passing the well in the back yard of the clothshop and noticed that the parapet was badly in need of repair. His mind flew to another well and to the terrible accident that would have ended in disaster if fate had not willed otherwise. Then, of a sudden, he cried to himself, "What!" His face tensed. For it had occurred to him that the touch-stone could have acted retrospectively. The copper ring on Meera's finger had turned into gold by way of a deferred reward—that had happened as soon as the taveez was given.

"What!" he cried again under his breath. The more he reflected the more he felt sure that he had at last hit on the truth. The key to the mystery lay in his grasp.

His new line of action began to unwind itself like thread from the wheel of a kite. The act must be repeated. Meera would do it as spontaneously as before, without the least inkling that there was something else behind it. She would give herself body and soul to her terrific urge and be prepared even to face death. It had better be this cloth-shop well with its crumbling parapet. But, then, how expect the circumstance to repeat itself? How expect a little boy to stumble and fall into the well with Meera conveniently on the spot? Unless he lured ten or twelve little fellows with a gift of kites, to be flown from this yard behind the clothshop, with the well's parapet torn down for repair—

He leaned against a fat pillow and closed his eyes. To ease his body he stretched out his legs, wiggling his toes; relaxed, he could think better. In an hour the problem lay solved; every detail was in its place so that the picture was complete.

He would trick Meera again and trick destiny! Faced by the swift challenge, she would have no time for second thoughts. But an accomplice was required, one who would act in the dark, blindfolded. Bulaki Rao. There could be no better accessory to a murder!

When all the instructions had been given, Bulaki Rao stared at his master, eyeglasses and teeth glinting. "I understand." The Seth knew that look of plain greed. It meant a fee of fifty rupees. Be it so. Soon he would squash the bug between forefinger and thumb.

219

Two hours later, Meera came to the clothshop on an urgent summons. The Seth glanced at her face and tried to cheer her up. "Beti, keep this always in mind; failures are thorn-weed in a field of wheat, to be plucked, cast away. And now we must eat. I have a good curry for you, flavored with minced coconut." He busied himself, filling two brass platters out of his aluminum container, and poured out cool water from a jug.

"A girl of your age growing in body and beauty should have plenty of wholesome food. While you eat, I will dip into my yesterdays and regale you with a story. There was an earthen bridge at Chamundi—" Twice already he had regaled her with the story of the bridge.

"The hundred hands that hacked at the bridge hacked at my body itself. The precious earth they took with them was my ripped flesh." A dramatic pause. "When the bridge was all gone and I stood near the gap watching the tiny stream trickle by, I heard a voice and looked up. A very old man stood on the other side of the gap, supporting himself on a stick. 'The bridge?' he cried in alarm. 'Chamundi bridge?' He wiped his eyes with his palm lest they were deceiving him. 'Too late,' I shouted in answer. The man grew bewildered and said, 'There is a bridge, its earth working wonders. Three days, three nights I have walked to come and get a pinch of that kindly earth.' 'The earth is all gone,' I cried to the old man. 'You see the gap in front of you?' He blinked and shaded his eyes from the sun's glare. 'A pinch of earth for my ailing grandson,' he said in anguish, looking down at the gap and at the stream and looking at me. 'A pinch is all I need.' Then I knew that beyond the two man-lengths of gap in the road stood a creature even more denied and dismayed and wretched than myself."

At this point in the recital the strong impact of recaptured feeling silenced him for a minute, as usual. Now he would pass on to calculations, Meera knew, for it had been so twice before. Fifty thousand bottles could be filled with the magic earth; it meant just that number of rupees, the price kept low at a rupee a bottle. On the expense side, so much money to buy so many thousand bottles and cork stoppers, plus the cost of labels, a printed slip of instructions, gum to paste the labels on, not forgetting the labor charges involved at each stage. Add to all this the retail commission. The balance of profit stood out in five figures, and that was the amount of loss he had suffered, the extent of his heartbreak.

This time, however, he dropped the arithmetic. He ate quietly for some time, then resumed, his voice guttural with food: "There was the other episode, equally sad. A peasant boy in Orissa State—" he stopped, aware of her inattention.

"I heard a strange cry." She tilted her head slightly to one side, listening.

"It is the mangy dog, Tikri."

"There is another voice. Listen!"

"Beti, eat one more wheatcake while I tell you about the magic-making boy. It happened—" He cut short with a scowl. "Han! It is Bulaki Rao, howling like a jackal. He has gone mad?"

The cry was unmistakable. "Ho-oh! Buddhu has fallen into the well, little Buddhu!" The Seth rose to his feet. "What is this joke about little Buddhu?"

"Listen," Meera was intent. And then: "There is a well in the back yard?"

"Right at the end. The water is sweet and good for the stomach; you have it there in your bowl."

"The well has a parapet?" Her face was troubled.

"Of course. No, wait. The parapet has been pulled down; a new and better one is to be built. The mason must have started the work."

She jumped up. Bulaki Rao was at the door, his teeth exposed in a kind of snarl and his chest heaving like a blowpipe.

"Hai Ram!" he groaned and gasped.

"Speak, lobster!" The Seth flew into fury.

"He is all that the rag-woman has, for the others are dead and gone, and her husband sits in the tiger's stomach. Hai Ram! The light of her eye—"

"Buddhu? What about Buddhu? Use your precious tongue."

He stuttered until his tongue failed him altogether. He continued in pantomime, his hands sketching the well and the little boy with a kite. The boy walked backward, fast, and there was the well with its parapet torn apart. Down he went—"plop!" The precious tongue was released at last.

Meera started for the door and in an instant she was running hard across the back yard. The two men exchanged a quick nod before they followed her. She was soon peering down into the well, hands on the pulley-bar for support.

The Seth seemed to have grasped the situation at last. "Hai Ram!

The widow's sole offspring," he moaned. "The very breath of her nostrils. What evil fate that he came kite-flying to my shopyard."

Bulaki Rao picked up a thread-reel lying near the well. He turned his glance skyward. "The wonder that the kite stays high up in the air!"

"The woe that the frogling had to go into my well when there are four other wells in the village." The Seth's voice rose sharply. "The mason? Where is he? That son of a squirrel has failed to build a new parapet."

"The rascal has not turned up," Bulaki Rao explained. "Hai! The mother's only solace, the very pupil of her dim eye!"

"I will punish that scorpion. Hai, the mother's future support. I said to her only yesterday, 'Let your Buddhu-beta go to school. I will pay for everything—fees, books, slate, pencils. One day he will be your bread-giver.' She wept happily—"

Meera cried, "Stop! Do something. Each moment counts." She gazed into the well. Was it as deep as the one in the Seth's house?

"Bulaki Rao!"

"Seth-ji, I cannot swim. I shall sink like a boulder."

"There are fellows born of fish. Go—get a pair of such fellows. Rush. What! You simply stand, gaping at me! You want the little boy to die?" His eyes rolled. "I will charge you with murder, Bulaki Rao. I will see you hanged by the neck."

A hand to his imperiled neck, Bulaki Rao trotted off and the Seth now turned to Meera, hopefully. Here was the moment of moments he had created. With quick decision Meera had to win her battle. She could rock the world! Meera . . . Meera . . .

She was peering again into the well, one bare foot forward, the other on tiptoe, one buttock sunk in, the other bulging back for balance. Meera . . . Meera . . . let the feeling take hold of you, beti. Let it urge you on even to possible death. Meera . . .

He watched her with his enormous hunger while she, stooping over, saw another image of herself. Fingers clutching the pulley-rope, feet placed in the bucket. She felt the swing of descent and the water was at her knees and waist and at her breast and neck, and her head tilted back a moment, nostrils sucking the last air, all the air they could take, and she plunged on, cleaving the water column till the bucket stopped with a jerk. There in the slime she groped about. Her chest hurt as she gathered the little boy in her arms, her chest felt fire, and when at last her breath would have come out bursting in a blow she started to move up, and each moment was agony beyond endurance and so prolonged that it was timeless. When her head rose over the water and nostrils and mouth gulped with immense greed...

Looking into the well she gulped air with that once-felt greed—even before she had repeated her feat of courage. For, the ornaments weighed heavy on her body and spirit. They would hinder her at the well's bottom, adding to the strain of each movement. Maybe she would lose her foothold in the bucket. Maybe she would never return to the surface...

"Hai Ram!" The Seth's voice broke upon her panic. "The shame that I cannot swim. Or else I would have gone in and saved the little boy. Ho, my son—" He wailed out, beating his chest with both fists. "Ho, the only hope of a starving widow—" And his sharp eyes were prodding Meera. Make up your mind in a flash. Act, act. What! The poor cross-eyed waif lies at the well's bottom and you simply stand and peer. Feel, Meera, feel, and then act, as you did once before. What! As if you do not know dear little Buddhu! You who wiped his running nose with your sari—the Halwai saw you doing it. Meera, be true to yourself and feel—feel—

There she was, still impassive, gazing into the well. The disgrace of Sonamitti. To let a youngster stay buried in water. Cold-blooded murderess.

There was hope yet. Bulaki Rao was returning with the driver fellow and none else. No escape, Meera Bai!

"You could find none but that son of a city peacock?"

Sohanlal saw it all at a glance. Barely three breaths of time, and his shoes and shirt lay stripped. "Fix up the bucket," he commanded.

"What!" The Seth shouted with quick apprehension.

"Hold the rope, Bulaki Rao. Give him a hand, Seth-ji. You also, Meera Bai. I am no feather-weight."

"Keep away!" the Seth growled and his eyes were fierce.

Sohanlal glanced at him in surprise. "What is the trouble?"

The Seth raved. "Halfway down he will go, then shout, beg to be hauled up. Do I not know his kind, city nincompoops with bloodless liver?" This unexpected hitch, all his preparations imperiled. Meera... Meera beti...

She spoke. "I will descend." She was tucking her sari folds about her waist.

"No!" With quick strides Sohanlal grabbed the bucket. "Come now,

223

the three of you. Hold fast to the rope and let the bucket go slowly as soon as I ask you."

The Seth felt the ground under him rock. "Stop, Sohanlal," he bawled frantically. "And you, Meera, proceed. Do not get distracted. You saved my son's life!"

She turned to Sohanlal, speaking in a low murmur. "I have done it before. Do not stand in my way." But he seemed not to have heard her. "Seth-ji," his voice came snapping. "Bulaki Rao."

Her eyes met his then. "I beg of you." The dragging weight on her limbs was suddenly gone.

"This is man's work. You had to do it when there was no man on the spot." And the exciting thought came to his mind: This is the real Meera, she who reveals herself in every crisis.

Her breath was panting and short. She could not let him risk his life. She must hold him back. The Seth was coming to her rescue. "Sohanlal," he was pleading, "you are tall and hefty, too heavy for the three of us to bear your weight on the rope. One is a girl, one is a bug and I—" He left it unsaid, with a mere click of disparagement. "There is no time to get other helping hands. Each moment counts; in two more minutes Buddhu-beta will be dead. Let Meera have her way. With your help we can tackle the rope with Meera in the bucket. She has done this before. She is not the least bit afraid. Feeling holds her, resistless feeling—you can see it writ on her face. Now, beti, carry on. Go ahead."

Sohanlal's answer was brief. "This well is shallow, the water hardly neck-deep. I will stand straight, holding the boy above the water. Meanwhile, you can get other helping hands to pull us up."

"No!" Her voice was small, husky, yet full of authority. She moved up quickly to him, standing face to face, and with a sudden gesture she caught hold of his arm and cried again, "No!" Amazed, he looked at the hand upon his arm, the beringed fingers tight. His other hand rose, clasped hers upon his arm, his grip strengthening, until the girl's fingers were digging in his skin. He relaxed, pressed her hand once more and over again. And in that curious way they regained their union.

It lasted for barely five moments. Their hands withdrew while their eyes still clung for a little. Then he turned quickly and got busy fixing the rope to the cross-bar, and she made no protest. In trustful surrender she must see him do his man's work. She watched him descend by the

224

dangling stretch of rope. As he threw back his head, their eyes clung once more and now there was no fear in her heart, only pride.

"Perish!" the Seth yelled, his face twisted with anger and misery. It was as he had felt at Chamundi bridge, and a hundred times worse.

Meera, with one hand upon the cross-bar and the other pressed to her breast, leaned forward watching the ruffled water. In that instant her ears caught the words: "Bulaki Rao, produce the frogling."

Bulaki Rao shuffled off to the latrine at the yard's corner, a small structure with a roof of corrugated iron. "Out, frogling!" A boy pushed open the latrine door and came out with a leaf cup in hand, his mouth smeared with syrup. It was Buddhu!

"Bulaki Rao hid the frogling in the latrine with an anna-worth of sweetmeat to keep him content," the Seth explained blandly. "Now, Meera, if you had gone into the well under the urge of your natural impulse, the touchstone would have acted. The little monkey was not in the well..." His voice barked in anger: "That city mongoose had to upset everything."

In an instant she grew hysteric, running across the yard, screaming for help. The Seth spoke to her in a shout. "Stop! The mongoose is safe. Two divers sit and wait behind the latrine; I posted them lest you had to be rescued." He turned aside to Bulaki Rao. "Call that fish-born pair."

Five minutes later Sohanlal rode up the pit of the well, breathing heavily. "I scoured every inch of the bottom." He shook his head. He picked up his shirt from the ground and with it he wiped his mud-stained chest.

"There he is, the grandson of a bastard." The Seth pointed with a trembling finger.

Meera flared up. "You had to do it again. I begged of you—"

"Pray listen—"

She stopped him with her outburst. "I asked you not to work behind my back. Trying to think out acts of kindness, not even knowing what kindness means. You work out everything in your head, turn a feeling to figures in your ledger. You—" She cut short and while the Seth stood dumfounded, she walked away.

Seized by great exultation, Sohanlal hurried after her. This, again, was the real Meera! Falling in step with her, he said, "If only you knew what a conceited fool I have been!"

She gave him a questioning glance.

"If you knew how you saved me!" And as her face grew bewildered, he went on, "I reasoned all wrong. I thought evil could be mended by evil. Then, as I reached out for it, I heard you whisper in my ear, 'No!' I hesitated and you spoke again, 'No!' Then I had to turn back from evil."

He could see the lantern hung at the veranda of a mud hut, its light illumining a face, and heard the amused cry, "Why run away? You are not a laddoo that I can gobble up. Hei-ee, you will slip in the dark and break your ankle—"

"I—you—" Meera cried, and his next words bewildered her all the more. "I saw another Meera and thought it was *you*. Utter stupidity."

28     Lakshmi had a worried face when she returned to the village four days after the well episode. The Seth's letter bidding her come back contained a riddle. "You will be happy to know that your dear friend Meera has become our Sona Mai." Sona Mai—Gold Mother? Gold? It must be that the Seth had fallen headlong for the touchstone. And the fervent prayer filled her heart: Let him not suffer overmuch, O Mother of Mercy!"

Here she was at Sonamitti. As the train pulled in, her eager eyes surveyed the thirty-yard stretch of the station platform. Her wish was not to be fulfilled. *He* was not there; he had sent the cartman.

Nago greeted the cartman with, "Look! Push this button down— lights on! Push it up—lights off! Look again." While he worked with the switch the cartman greeted Lakshmi and picked up her green steel trunk and bedding roll.

"How is everyone?" They were walking to the exit, Nago running ahead.

"Everyone is sleepless."

"Sleepless?"

"Waiting for the gold."

"Touchstone?"

"Touchstone."

Lakshmi cried, "Do not walk so fast. Tell me. What has *everyone* to do with it?"

In silence he placed the baggage in the cart, waited for Lakshmi to climb up with her son, then prodded the oxen. "Run hard, gentlemen!"

"What mystery is this?" she demanded.

"How much do you know, Lakshmi Bai?"

"Nothing. Almost nothing."

He leaned toward the animals. "No city languor, gentlemen! Move your buttocks faster."

"Tell me."

"You will hear from Seth-ji. What do I know?"

"Pray tell me."

"Listen, then. Our Meera had a copper ring on her finger. Seth-ji saw the ring and he knew at once it was gold, not copper. He added two and two and deducted four and the answer came: the touchstone. The minstrel had given her a taveez, you remember?"

Yes, she remembered.

"Copper on her body has turned into gold. This will happen each time she does an act of kindness, with Seth-ji as her business partner." His voice thickened. "Meera will not keep her gold, she will give it away to the people, so the story has gone. But with each day lost, people get bone-sick, waiting and waiting."

Lakshmi struck her forehead with her palm. "Hai Ram! Hai Sita!" And after a brief silence, "All the people have gone mad? Even the Cowhouse?"

"Not the Cowhouse. They are for the vote-mote."

"That, at least, is good news."

The cartman went on, "Our Halwai fellow is out to make trouble. He is using little Buddhu's rescue—"

"The rag-woman's Buddhu? What happened to that boy?"

"Nothing happened to him, actually. But the Halwai knows how to build up bad feeling. He—" With a shake of his head, the cartman broke off.

Lakshmi felt a little dizzy. Things had gone too far. How would she bear the sight of Nago's father strutting in his fool's paradise?

He was not in the house—nothing short of a disaster could keep him away from the clothshop at this hour of the day. The house was all in disorder, cobweb at wall corners, dust in every nook. Even a sparrow would have kept the place more tidy! As she picked up a broom and worked, she sank more and more into dejection. Meera had escaped one peril, her debts, only to be drawn into another.

She felt her head ache and lay down in bed. After an hour she heard voices: "Hei-ee Lakshmi!" She hastened to the front door and there were the four of them—Sohagi, Bimla, Champa, Munni. Not Meera, however.

"The Devi's bliss that you are back, Lakshmi-sister."

When they were all seated on the balcony floor—no one felt inclined to go to the cowshed—Lakshmi left them for a minute and returned with a wicker basket on her arm. "*Burfi*," she said. "My birthplace is famed for this milk relish. You will like it."

"The goat of a Halwai we have!" said Sohagi, eating. "Twenty times he will have to be reborn in sweetshops before he can produce this kind of delight."

"Not even then," Munni chimed in. "A goat grows horns but does not become an antelope."

Then Lakshmi spoke in a sad murmur. "One mouth is denied."

A brief silence was followed by a retort. "This is no food for a king's daughter."

She studied the faces. It was not jealousy, no mean feeling. What was it?

"I want to understand you all," she said. "I want to feel as you do. Maybe Meera gives herself the airs of a king's daughter—or Sona Mai!"

"Must we talk of Meera? If you have no other theme, we'd better leave."

Lakshmi cried, "Do not make me wretched. I—" Words failed her. Moved by her anguished look, the women regretted their harshness. Sohagi said soothingly, "You have not taken good care of your hair, Lakshmi-sister. Let me do it up for you." And Bimla said, "Will you paint your finger nails red? That is the city fashion. The coloring is sold in small phials. A city hawker has come here with a boxful of his ware."

"Han!" said Lakshmi. "Let me paint my nails red and the Seth will paint my face black. He is not like the Ox-cart fellow who likes to see his wife neat as a picture."

"He?" Sohagi feigned to disagree, so that Lakshmi might feel comforted. "He grudges me even a tiny brass button for the nose. He says he likes my nostril bare. As if I cannot see his real motive. All men are alike."

"Only Meera is free to please herself," said Lakshmi. "The beauty mark she wears on her forehead. The red mark."

Cold silence.

Lakshmi changed her tactics. "You should be renamed Cowhouse Four. What do you think?"

Faces tensed. The answer came slowly.

"You cannot change your name with a snap of the fingers."

"I am Champa; supposing, one day, everyone begins to call me Sita, instead!"

"What if I, Munni, am called Bimla and Bimla is called Munni?"

"That will be terrible. The two husbands will not know which woman is his."

Lakshmi took heart. This was a good sign. She pressed her point:

"Why, we can get someone else in Meera's place and make up the five. That seems the best way. Do you agree?"

Silence.

"Sohagi?"

"No."

"Champa?"

"No."

The other two answered likewise. Lakshmi felt great relief.

"Listen," she said. "You remember how we once tried to sell the taveez to Seth-ji? He would have made a deal, but maybe he recalled the tricks we had played on him and was on his guard. It is a new tale this time. The Seth is mad about the touchstone. It should be great fun for us. What ails us then?"

"There is a difference. This time it is no trick. The touchstone is real."

"Who knows?" cried Lakshmi darkly.

"Sohanlal has spoken to you? Let him say how a copper ring can turn into gold."

Lakshmi said, "Maybe there is something hidden from our eyes. So many miracles are just that. There is the mango trick—"

"Lakshmi, the mango trick is no miracle, you know that well enough. Anyhow, that is not the point. Meera believes that she has a touchstone. She is resolved to get gold. This is no game for her, no fun. She has moved a world apart from us. It is better that we do not talk of her any more."

"Yes, Sohagi," agreed Lakshmi. She would have to bide her time.


"Now I understand something that happened to me." She nodded to herself.

"To you?"

"The very same day, the very same hour. I heard your voice, I heard you call, 'Lakshmi . . . Nago's Mother . . .' The voice was so sad that

230

tears came to my eyes. I was deep in misery until I received your letter."

He was staring at her. "There is a new fairness in your face. The air and water of your father's place suited you well."

"So it did." Her voice carried a challenge, but her eyes were soft. "Fairness!" she feigned to mock herself while eager for more compliments.

"I lost a tooth a week back." He pulled down his thick lower lip with a forefinger. "Can you see?"

Her tongue clicked sympathy while she swallowed her disappointment and tried to hide her feeling. "You are back home after the day's hard work and I do not give you even a sip of whey. I have brought burfi with me, the kind you like, with almond paste."

"Good! No rest for you until you have prepared twenty relishes."

"O-ho! They cost money, Seth-ji."

"Who cares?" He had a grandiose manner. "Money, choh! Are we paupers?"

She smiled. "We cannot let our son become a beggar boy due to our extravagance."

"Wait! You will see." And she knew what he meant. Gold.

Darkness fell. After a good meal, hand washed and mouth rinsed, the Seth clasped his wife's arm with his plump fingers. "Lakshmi!" His voice was hoarse.

She looked at him with bewilderment and a slight alarm.

"Come to bed, wifeling."

She turned away, a shy bride. "Nago watches me." She pulled her arm free with a playful jerk. "Have sense."

He turned to the boy. "Nago, son, time for you to sleep."

"Ma-ji will tell me a tiger-story," the boy answered gravely.

"Nago," the father pleaded, "an anna if you go at once to bed and sleep."

"No."

"Two annas."

"No."

His imploring eyes rested on his wife's face but she denied him help, smiling dimly to herself with an air of conquest.

"Colored marbles, Nago?" he turned to him again. "I will buy you a boxful. Go and sleep. You look tired, boy. Unless you have enough sleep, you will not grow tall."

And Nago still shook his head saying, "I want to hear a tiger-story."

231

"Balloons?" he coaxed.

"Big balloons?"

"Yes, yes." He drew a deep breath of relief. "Big ones painted with faces."

"No. Tiger-story." Nago stuck out his lip.

"Hai Ram!" The Seth felt crushed.

Lakshmi could not hold herself any more. The warmth in her heart was charging into the flow of her blood and rising to the pores of her skin in a balm of ecstasy. She turned to give her husband a deep glance. "I will put the boy to sleep." Her eyes darkened with meaning as she added in a whisper, "Go, lie down in bed. Give me a minute. Do not doze off, Nago's father!"

"A minute," the Seth agreed and walked off, humble and quiet, like a lamb.

**29**
Lakshmi felt a wrench within her as she saw the heavily adorned figure and the face with its fixed intensity. Not the intensity of old—brows drawn in musing, nostrils waiting to twitch—belied by a sudden smile or a self-mocking grimace. The set expectancy in that look was plain anguish. The dark under eyelids meant sleepless nights.

"Back home, Lakshmi?" Plying her *charkha* on the veranda floor in a patch of the morning sun, she looked up slowly, absently. In the days past, she would have jumped to her feet and clung to her sister.

Lakshmi held out a leaf-cup pinned with twigs.

"Burfi!" cried Meera.

"My village is renowned for this milk-sweet."

Meera seemed to relax, eating with enjoyment, her tongue picking a crumb off her lip. "Eat," Lakshmi urged softly. "Tomorrow I will bring you another portion."

"And deprive the little boy? The greedy goat's tongue I have?"

Lakshmi could have laughed. That boy owed each and every breath of his nostrils to the "greedy" one.

"I have worries buzzing in my head." The look of suspense was back in a minute.

"Worries?"

"The act of kindness. What is real kindness? Lakshmi, tell me."

"I? When you have the great man to help you! Maybe you know these lines:

'Even the crow's knowing failed,
And he, most knowing among beasts and birds,
The crow sat with beak tight, silent;
Then the tiny mosquito came humming and said:
Folks, friends, let me help you with my wit.' "

233

"You are no mosquito, Lakshmi, even if your Seth-ji is a most knowing crow." An amused smile lit up her face for an instant and she was the old Meera again.

Lakshmi said, "Sister, it is hard to believe that you are one in mind with the crow of false wisdom."

"One in mind? No. I—" She stopped, hung her head. Words were futile.

Lakshmi watched her. Over this young girl's head the people's fury of expectation hung. Trying to amuse her, Lakshmi said, "Look, Meera, I can give you a good chance for your act of kindness. I only have to be bitten by a snake!"

She clutched Lakshmi's arm. "Do not say that even in fun."

Lakshmi felt her eyes moisten. Things had gone too far. Yet it needed ten words to put an end to the miracle! Gazing at the young face, she saw the hunger that was almost spiritual. Meera was like one possessed. How could she bear the stark truth?

"Do not look so unhappy, Lakshmi," Meera smiled. "The act of kindness will come unawares, as before. Have you seen the gold ring? Seth-ji—"

Lakshmi cried, "I must see Grandma," and to conceal her feeling, she turned round with, "Are you in the kitchen, Grandma?" A response came from across the yard and she walked off into the house. "Come, sister," she called over her shoulder, but the *charkha* had started to hum again.

To speak the ten words would be far from easy.

The talk turned soon to Meera and Grandma's faded lips grimaced as she spoke, "It is an evil that holds her."

"The haunted look in her eyes," Lakshmi said. "Where is the girl always ready to laugh happily?"

"The Gold goddess has destroyed her," Grandma grieved. She saw Lakshmi press her lips together as if she was trying to control herself. "This is how it happened," Grandma went on to explain. "The Seth is gullible by nature, and Meera will have fun at his expense—so the minstrel figured it out. If only he knew Meera! She cannot connect her Grandpapa with any sort of deceit."

"That's it," Lakshmi agreed, tonelessly.

The thought came upon her that she could speak the ten words to her husband. No, she could not, for it would then be much harder for Meera. The Seth's thunderous wrath would fall on her unprepared head. Meera must be the first to know the truth; then she would have time to adjust her feelings. At first the truth would hurt her terribly. But the end result would be great relief. Meera would be herself again.

Her friends must not be so very sore about what they thought to be her betrayal of the cause. When the Cowhouse came to see her at noon, Lakshmi spoke with determination. "Mark my word, Champa, Munni, Bimla, Sohagi. Meera will always remain your sister, whatever happens."

The women sat in silence a long while, until Sohagi spoke in a quiet murmur.

"How can we change the past thousand years of our living? A river has flown between the rich and the poor. There is no boat to take the poor to the other bank. The rich cross the stream at their will. They put wary feet on the mud and from a distance they hail the poor and speak good words and feel pleased with themselves that they have been so kind. It is a game for the rich to play. But the river flows on and the rich return to their bank and wash mud off their feet. And the river flows on."

Lakshmi asked, "Where am I? On which bank?"

"You are the Seth's wife, Lakshmi, but you are also our sister."

"And Meera?"

"In all our talk must it be Meera, Meera, and Meera again?" Champa snapped.

For Lakshmi it always had to be Meera.

The Cowhouse Five had ceased to exist. Five faces of a crystal piece, the minstrel had said. One face was torn apart, as if the crystal had been trodden by an ironclad heel!

When Lakshmi met her again, Meera was lying on the floor, her head upon her joined palms. Lakshmi knew the reason—the girl suffered off and on from a painful headache. Squatting on the floor Lakshmi took the aching head on her lap, and pushed her fingers deep into the thick mass of hair to reach the scalp. Meera closed her eyes with a sigh. A black ant came sauntering and to flick it off, Lakshmi bent over, her breast upon the girl's face. Meera opened her eyes an instant and a smile came to her lips and lingered.

"To have a daughter like you!" said Lakshmi in a happy murmur.

"You are just twelve years older than me, Lakshmi."

"That is long enough."

"Will you not," Meera began and paused, "will you not ride on the phut-phutti to know what it feels like?" An unaccountable flush came to her face.

"Have you heard the story—how the phut-phutti went hurtling, racing the wind?"

Yes, Meera knew. Everyone knew.

"Pernam to the Devi that there was no accident. The Seth will never again ride on the machine. What devil took hold of Sohanlal, I wonder."

The head on Lakshmi's lap turned quickly. "It was a joke, nothing more."

"A joke? The phut-phutti could have gone off the road and dashed against a tree. It could have ended fatally—"

"No harm was meant, Lakshmi, believe me." The voice contained a pleading.

"There is a madness in Sohanlal."

"No, no. Do not say that."

Lakshmi in surprise looked down intently and saw more in the girl's face than protest. The flush deepened under Lakshmi's glance. Meera would have turned away again, but Lakshmi took her head firmly between her hands, watching. "Let me have a good view. Let me see clearly and understand."

And Meera, without reply, closed her eyes and lay still.

"What was it, if not madness?" said Lakshmi.

There was no answer.

"Was it *you*, then? You, Meera?"

No answer—only her breast heaved a little.

"What! You, Meera, had to do this to Sohanlal—make him so restless that he drives the machine as if he has gone crazy!"

She opened her eyes, a mist between the lids, and faced by the sudden revelation, Lakshmi in her turn fell silent. Her fingers, as they resumed the kneading, dug hard. "Ou-h!" cried Meera and Lakshmi, embarrassed, withdrew her hand. "Clumsy that I am!"

"No, no," bending her head toward those fingers, demanding them.

"Give me time to think," said Lakshmi. "O Meera—" And there was a mist in her eyes, too.

On her way back home she saw a knot of people in front of the sweetshop, listening as the Halwai spoke in a loud voice, and she caught the curious words, "This I will cry twenty times every day so that folks will at last hear and heed: we have been mere donkeys braying, 'Jai Meera Bai! Jai Sona Mai!'"

Lakshmi stopped at the edge of the crowd. She recalled what the cartman had vaguely hinted.

"Old Father had never harmed even an insect or bug," she heard the Halwai continue. "Our Meera Bai had to do an act of kindness and to suit her need, Old Father was evicted. Kindness—ho! Then it was the turn of an innocent little boy. He was expected to stumble and fall into a well so that there could be an act of kindness again."

A voice interrupted, "Why, little Buddhu simply stood in the latrine, eating jilebi!"

"No matter. Meera Bai wished to meet our Buddhu-beta at the well's bottom. A single thought holds her mind: let misfortune befall some man or woman or child. That is easy to understand—she will otherwise get no gold. Let a man be hit by a thunderbolt, so she may give aid to the bereaved and starving kin. Let there be a drought, and she will have a real windfall. Jai Meera Bai, Jai Sona Mai! She has to feed on tears of misery. When one prays hard for such tears to flow, they will surely flow. So, tomorrow, it will be your turn—" The palm-leaf fan in his hand darted toward a man and he shrank back. "The day after, your little boy, one like Buddhu-beta, will be the victim of kindness—" The fan darted toward a woman and she cried in terror, "Ram-Ram!" The Halwai paused briefly for breath and a renewal of energy. "You expect gold for yourselves—han! You make me laugh. If the gold comes, there will be nothing for the poor. Believing Sohanlal, you do not see the plain truth. The miracle has to happen again and again. Greed feeds greed. But when your woes cease, how can the touchstone continue to act? Tell me. If the springs for the deed of kindness get dried up—"

Lakshmi had heard enough. She started to walk homeward.

When Sohanlal came to the kitchen as usual for his midday meal, Lakshmi saw him in the light of their new relationship—he was her brother. But how unhappy he looked. Hair uncombed, chin covered with stubble. He was worried on Meera's account.

"I heard what the Halwai said," she spoke softly as she poured a ladleful of lentils on his banana-leaf plate.

He looked up for an instant, but was silent.

"About little Buddhu. The Halwai can turn broad daylight into darkness."

237

The words had swift effect. "That rascal," he responded. Maybe, at that moment, he realized that Lakshmi was the only friend left to Meera. "That rascal has been turning the people against Meera Bai with an evil motive."

"What motive?"

"Her effigy is to be burnt on Monday next."

Lakshmi was unmoved by the news. She had already heard about the effigy. "It is the goddess Gold," she told him. "That goddess has done enough mischief. Better that she now leave Meera alone."

"But then—"

"We burn the ten-headed demon king at a festival every year, do we not? This goddess is truly a demoness—"

His eyebrows drew together in a heavy scowl. "Everyone knows what the demon king looked like. Easy to make his effigy. But—Gold goddess? The effigy must have a face—"

"So what?"

"This effigy has the face of Meera Bai."

"No!"

"The likeness cannot be missed. The red mark on the forehead, especially—it is all too distinctive."

Lakshmi cried, "To think there could be such devilry! Who told you?"

"Bulaki Rao."

"Bulaki Rao!" she scoffed.

"He heard it from a good source—the Halwai. The man who is behind this mischief. All his wily talk against Meera Bai is meant to make the people approve the effigy-burning, even if tacitly. His purpose will be served if the people just stand aloof."

Horror came to her face. The feeling against Meera had reached such a stage! The girl whom everyone in the village had loved and admired was to be burnt in effigy form. What shall I do? she asked herself in alarmed grieving. She felt Sohanlal watch her, he who was now her brother, and all at once the words broke out of her lips, "It is I who deserve to be an effigy. I am behind all this trouble."

"Lakshmi Bai!"

The need to unburden her heart of its terrible secret could be resisted no longer.

"The miracle is a fake. It is I who slipped the gold ring on to her finger, having first removed the copper one she had. She was fast asleep

238

and felt nothing. I wanted her to wear gold and this was the only way to make her—"

His face was unsurprised. "It had to be something like that. The minstrel knew?"

"It was his wish that I give her the gold ring. I made the transfer the day before I went away."

He nodded. "I understand."

She sighed in great relief. Her ordeal was over. She would not have to break the truth to Meera.

The agony she had borne since her return had now gone to Sohanlal; it was stark in his voice as he cried, "How shall I stand by and watch her shame and pain when she has listened to the truth? What words have I with which to give solace?"

30   The menace of the effigy remained and drew closer, closer. Lakshmi saw her only hope in the Cowhouse women—they would not put up with such villainy, even if Meera was no longer their sister.

When she had spoken, Munni burst into fury. "It is Meera's effigy! Let them burn the effigy and other things will burn soon after. With my own hands I will set roofs afire. First, the sweetshop—"

Sohagi cried, "Lakshmi, you heard all this from Sohanlal? He cares, then?"

"Cares? He will happily help Munni to burn house roofs."

Sohagi, strangely, joined her hands and touched them to her forehead. Her friends noted the gesture, but asked no questions; a prayer in the heart must not be put into cold speech. Only Lakshmi could see what the gesture truly meant. Happy, she cried, "Sohagi, I love you!" and Sohagi, having betrayed herself, pulled a face.

All would be well again with the Cowhouse. But how solve the problem in hand, how stop the evil that was about to happen?

Not many were directly involved in the wicked plot. The people at large seemed not to care either way. A word of disapproval from them, a mere gesture, could tie up the hands of the few. But the Cowhouse knocked in vain against a wall of indifference.

"We have cried until our throats tore, Jai Meera Bai, jai Sona Mai!" the men answered. "What have we got in return?"

"It is not Meera's fault that there is no gold yet," Sohagi pointed out.

"Our Halwai-brother speaks rightly. Meera's purpose would have been better served if little Buddhu had actually fallen into the well."

"Meera believed he was in the well. Yet she stood back and let Sohanlal descend."

"That was because of his persistence. What could she do? She had no choice but to yield. She hopes for better luck next time."

As for the womenfolk, they did not even try to reason it out.

"Why bother us? We sniff the smoke of our own cooking pots and of none other."

"There was a time when many of you slept naked at night. Do you remember who helped you and how?"

"She also needed cloth."

"She earned it for herself. She went into the well. A small reward for a big deed."

That was true, the listeners agreed, and yet they added darkly, "She roused our hopes. She broke our hearts. We have nothing more to say."

The Cowhouse women were helpless. They had failed to discover the effigy and did not know where it would be burnt. They could do nothing except wait for the day and the hour. They had no word of comfort for Grandma—she with all her disbelief frozen with fear! One day at sunrise she would push open the veranda door as usual and there would be a heap of ash on the steps, effigy ash. Grandma burst into lamentation.

So the evil day came and the Cowhouse women, strung tight, met again.

"Woe to the creatures who try to do Meera harm." Sohagi glared at the invisible enemies.

"We will gouge their eyeballs out of the sockets." Munni made her fingers fierce, clawlike.

"It is the Halwai whom we must tackle. We must force him to give up the effigy."

That was the right answer. But there were serious difficulties.

"We cannot set our hands on a man."

"If we do, our own men will not see our faces ever again."

Sohagi shook her head. "You do not have to touch him. There is another way."

"Throw brickbats? Whirl bamboo staves? Pour boiling water on his pate?"

"No. You only have to eat his sweetmeat."

Lakshmi said, "Sohagi, talk sense."

"We will climb up on his counter and start eating whatever he has in his big brass trays," Sohagi explained; "each laddoo in our mouth will make him groan. We will not stop eating until he has given way."

"What if he demands payment from our husbands?"

"We will wear masks. There is a good stock in Munni's house—the festival masks."

"Maybe he will know us even if he cannot see our faces."

"How can we eat with masks on?"

Sohagi lifted her voice with impatience. "Cackle, cackle, like the fowl folk at dawn! I have shown one way. You may show a better way."

So the bold decision was taken. This was the hour of high noon and the Halwai would be asleep at the back of the counter. Wakened abruptly, he would be all the more weak in spirit. The surprise would be complete and effective. The rascal! Burning the effigy of a young girl. So crazy in his old age because he could not marry her. His dead spouse still in the house, as he claimed...

"If only we had words to shout in one big voice," Champa yearned.

"Down with the doll-burners!" yelled Munni promptly.

"Sh-sh!" breathed Bimla. "This is a secret mission. We do not want all Sonamitti to come and watch us."

So the Cowhouse with masks ready to be pulled on arrived at the sweetshop. Hands drummed on the door panel. A shuffle of feet in the room, and the masks flew to the faces. The great moment was at hand.

The door opened and a shaven head peered out—it was the servant-boy. He saw the masked visitors and broke into a scream. The women pushed him aside, stepping into the room. It was empty. The Halwai had foreseen his danger and fled.

The boy was now quiet, goggling in amazement. Sari-clad figures. Mere women! What game of fun was this? "Call your master," a high-pitched voice demanded out of a mask. "Let him show us what sweetmeat he has for sale."

The boy shook his head. "This shop is closed for the day." Why, dear uncle, that plump one with a horned buffalo mask is Munni Bai!

"The Halwai—where has he hidden himself?" A figure knelt down to look under the string bedstead.

Why, dear uncle, that big upturned mustachio is Champa Bai! And the black monkey-face...He paused in his speculation to say, "The Halwai has gone to his betel shop in Pipli village."

The masks turned to each other, not knowing what to do, then turned again to the boy. "The effigy? Where is it? Show us."

He knew nothing about the effigy. Munni Bai, Champa Bai, Sohagi Bai. Two more left . . .

Baffled, the women stepped off to the road but they did not remove their masks until a hundred yards away. That boy must not see their faces. He would have an excited tale for his master. Fierce robbers! Marauders!

What next? There was one hope: Sohanlal. Maybe he could do something.

Disappointment again. He was away on an errand to the Seth's clothshop at Nagpur. He would not be back before nightfall.

They would start a vigil as soon as the sky darkened. That was all they could do.

If only they could find out where the effigy would be burnt. The ceremony before the effigy was set aflame would take well over an hour. That was the right time for an attack.

The vigil, starting at sunset, yielded nothing. The sweetshop door remained closed. There were no people on the streets going about secretively, and no sign that great evil was in the air. Hearts shrank in defeat. Champa gave a pointed glance to Munni's hair; but Munni shook her head dejectedly. Her twigs had no power against effigy magic.

"Hardly a charm left," said Lakshmi, noting how bare of twigs was Munni's hairknot. She knew the reason. Munni had been prodigal with her charm on Meera's account.

At this point they heard the splutter of the motorcycle. But there was nothing that Sohanlal could do.

He saw the women on the road and pulled up. "The effigy!" he cried excitedly, twisting round on his seat.

"Where?" Five voices came as one.

He poured out the news. He had been passing through the meadow along the cart track. At some distance to his right he had seen lanterns swinging in the darkness. Strange! People kept away from that area at night because of the haunted neem tree. He had stopped the machine, gone walking toward the lights to see what they meant. When he was fifty yards from the neem tree the mystery became clear.

"You saw the effigy?"

"A big rag doll tied to the tree. I have come rushing to take you to the place. In pairs. One on the back seat, one in the car. Who will be the first load?"

In a flash Sohagi settled herself on the back seat. "The ox-cart fellow will twist my neck if he catches me in this position!"

Lakshmi was climbing into the side-car. "We are fools not to have thought of the neem tree," she said. "No better place for the evil ritual than the bhootni's haunt."

"No better place," Sohanlal agreed and turned to the women left standing on the road. In five minutes I will be back for the next load."

There had to be no third trip. Champa, running like a colt in spite of her ample hips, met the machine more than halfway in the meadow.

Stopping on the cart track some distance from the neem tree they planned what to do. They would walk up stealthily and seize the effigy. But Lakshmi had better keep out of it. Let her wait here with Sohanlal.

"Will there be a good fight?" Munni asked hopefully.

"Maybe. When four tigresses are robbed of their meat—"

"I will mark their faces with my handiwork!" Champa said.

"And I—" Munni began, her fingers fierce, but Sohagi interrupted her. "We have one regret. Meera will not see this fun."

The plan worked well. The evil women were engrossed in the ritual. When they woke up, Sohagi had already grabbed the effigy. Munni could not hold herself any longer. "Death to the doll-burners!" her mighty yell came. And those four were now on their feet. The two groups stood face to face, five yards apart, ready for battle.

"Corpses!" the evil women howled abusively.

"Fiends! Uncanny creatures!" the Cowhouse answered.

"Thrice we spit on thy faces," one set of voices flung. "Thoo thoo thoo!"

"Three kicks we give to thy arses," answered the other set. "Dhoom dhoom dhoom!"

"We will chop off thy noses and feed them to a vulture."

"We will gouge out thine eyeballs and cast them into filth."

"Areh-eh, come two steps forward and take thy medicine."

"Come even one step."

Then, abruptly, a woman broke away from the line and rushed back to the neem tree. Propped against the bark was a rag torch soaked in

244

linseed oil, and to this she applied a light. As the torch blazed, she held it aloft and sprang forward with a fierce cry, "Burn, effigy-stealers, burn!" Her face was spectral in the red glare.

Munni was the first to react. "Fly!" she screamed. "Fly for your life!" and she sprinted off, while the enemy, armed with the fearful weapon, went in pursuit.

"Help!" wailed Bimla as she stumbled and fell. "I have caught fire, I burn!"

The torch was still twenty yards away, but there was no option except to make a stand. Munni tried to revive her courage with her battle cry, "We will gouge out thine eyeballs," her voice ringing hollow. And the menace of the blazing torch tore through the darkness.

At this moment the unexpected happened. There was an advancing flood of light and behind it the motorcycle came spluttering up. "Stop!" Sohanlal barred the torch-bearer's path. The menace came to a halt, spurts of flame leaping in the wind.

"Women, have you no shame or fear? You have played at witch-craft. Will you add crime to crime?"

"Robber! It is no bellyache of yours that we burn the effigy."

He answered in a calm voice. "We know the truth. The effigy has the likeness of Meera Bai. There is a law against killing."

"Harken to the grandson of Law!" the women sniggered. "Where do you see the likeness, pray?"

"Do you deny it?"

"Why shall we say Yes or No? Who are you to question us?"

He shrugged. "Let that pass. But you have made a murderous assault. Let the Five Elders hear the facts. Let them give their verdict. Come with us, effigy and all." And he saw the women, frightened, turn round and beat a quick retreat.

"Monsters!" yelled Munni, shaking a clenched fist.

The rag doll, its neck adorned with a chain of cowdung cakes, lay reclined on Lakshmi's lap. Sohagi clasped it against her breast. "Meera!" She plucked the cowdung chain off its neck and threw it away.

"Where is the likeness?" Sohanlal asked with a twinkle. "This woman smells of linseed oil. Does Meera Bai, also?"

Three trips to Main Road, and the women stood together again. Lakshmi made a suggestion. "Let us go to Meera's house. We must tell

245

her the story." She looked prayerfully from face to face. Will not the Gold goddess be forgotten for one night?

The answer came from Sohagi. "No, Lakshmi."

"Sohagi—"

"Our greed for gold has prevailed at last, so she will think."

"Listen, sister. You know Meera well enough—"

But Sohagi shook her head, her eyes brooding on the rag doll. She cleared her throat of a lump. "Take that to Grandma. She will have peace."

Lakshmi waited for a minute, hoping against hope, then started to walk the dark road toward Meera's house. A night bird flew screeching overhead with a flap of heavy wings.

Grandma's reaction to the effigy took an unexpected turn.

She walked to the fields, next day, the rag doll in her arms, its head lolling over her shoulder. The peasants, startled, paused in their work to gaze at this apparition. As Grandma stopped, standing on a mound of earth, the people began to draw close. In two minutes there were scores of men and women gazing at the effigy with troubled eyes. The strained hush continued until Grandma spoke.

"This is Meera," she said and lifted the rag doll a little higher. "This is my granddaughter, Meera. Her father died before she was born and her mother, when she was a milk-infant. The Grandpapa whom she adored left home and became a wandering minstrel when she was a child of seven. Five years later she went to prison for a month with many of you. When she grew older, she joined you in fighting the village tyrant. The women gave her a place at the head of their marching column, though she was so young. That is her story. She is no witch, this Meera you see in my arms. Or, is she? Tell me if she is truly an evil creature, so I may know."

The silence lay heavy on the people until a meek voice cried, "Our faces are tarred with shame, Grandma." Then she resumed, as if there had been no interruption.

"This is Meera in my arms. She wears tatters of sacking drenched in linseed oil. A dung chain lay on her neck—one of the women threw it away. She stood strapped to the neem tree in the dark meadow, waiting for the fire, shuddering and helpless."

246

"Pray listen, Grandma, we beg of you. We touch your feet and beg—"

"She was condemned to be burnt alive, this Meera, my granddaughter. The ash of her body was to be strewn on my doorstep for me to collect. All the rest of my days I was to hold in my bosom the ash that had been Meera. I who have no kin to call my own except this girl, for the minstrel does not belong to our world—"

An agonized outburst came, "Stop, Grandma."

"What crime has she committed that she has to be put to death? She lives a dream. She wears a *taveez* on her arm and longs for a miracle to happen. That is no crime against man nor sin against the gods. You do not have to be wild at her. Pity her. Laugh at her. Take her to task. Why do you hate? Why must you kill?"

Out of the circle of peasants an old man came forward. "Listen, Meera's Grandma—" His hands were folded together in humility. "Pray listen—"

Grandma spoke on as though she could not stop herself.

"You forget what she is, a mere child. You try to make a savior out of her. You bid her fulfill an inmost wish of your heart. Your stern voice says, Do or die. She has no value for you apart from the gold she must be made to produce. Not for once has it occurred to you to ask yourselves: why must she?"

"Meera's Grandma—" the old man's voice rose to a higher pitch. "Those are terrible words that you speak. But you speak the truth. I, for one, know that our crazy expectations have deceived us. The wish for an easy end to our woes. Fools that we are! There can be no easy end." He grasped Grandma's arm. "You have given away all you owned to help the distressed—but it is now you who hate." His grip tightened. "Meera's Grandma, we cannot bear this heavy blow from you."

Her eyes blinked a little. "Understand this," the old man resumed quickly. "We never saw the evil in our hearts as we do now. Had we caught a glimpse of the effigy, the real thing and not a mere dark thought—" His voice broke off abruptly. The rag doll had dropped from Grandma's hands. It lay face down at her feet and she was unaware or uncaring, as if it had lost its meaning, as if it had ceased to matter. And the rigid expression in her face gave way to a quiver.

Stooping, the old man picked up the effigy and held it in his arms.

"Let not this straw and rag preen in the form of our daughter."

From Grandma as she stood with face lowered the sound of a snivel came, and her voice when she forced herself to speak was almost choked. "How save her from herself? How save her before it is too late?"

CHAPTER

31

The Seth had been losing heart. Two voices spoke in him. One, a new voice, said, "Let this pursuit of kindness stop. It hurts you more and more. It is not as if your life depends on the miracle. Your Nago may not become a prince, but he will never see the face of want."

The older, familiar voice answered, "Remember, you are a mere shrimp in the business world. Look at the three whales in the district town. Look further at the three hundred whales in Bombay. Your worth will be reckoned in material assets. There are other measures but they do not apply to you, brother. You, whose sole aim is to make money, must bear the label of money value only." And the voice went on, "Acquisition for its own sake, an end in itself. Piling the stuff simply to see the big grow bigger. That is the order of life, the purpose of existence. In its way it is a religion. You do not question, you simply believe. That idea came at life's beginning and will last for all time."

The new voice was hushed by such vigor of faith. The Seth cast his weariness aside and gave himself to his problem with refired confidence.

The fact remained that Meera, having lost her splendid chance at the well, had reproached him with bitter words as if it was all his fault, as if he had done it for fun. Reason was not the best point in a woman. Or else Lakshmi would not be so very upset about Meera's effigy. What stupid credulity! Were it possible to destroy your enemy by such a simple process, he himself would not hesitate to have the effigy of Mukhichand burnt; that rascal was set on ruining the cloth business in town by undercutting prices until no profit was left. Then, one or two other effigies might as well be assigned to fire....

Meera—no less an example of stupid credulity—bade her partner sit tight and smoke his hookah, for the miracle would come by itself, with no effort on anyone's part, dropping from the air like a sackload

249

of jewels. If only she could think, reason with herself. If only her mind was half as clear and perceptive as her partner's. Now that the effigy trouble had just ended (better that it had gone on until the election was won; then the village folk would have been fully occupied in that game), he was ready to break new ground. The minstrel had not said, or meant, that just one specific act of kindness would bring about the miracle. It had to be "real kindness"—that was all. To have limited the quest to Meera's experience—that was an obvious error. The broad human scene with its many areas of suffering had endless scope. Spontaneity? It had been overrated. There was no reason why an act of kindness could not be two-edged, with two different purposes. You helped people out of a true feeling and in that process did good to yourself. What really mattered was the impact of the deed, its strength, its effectiveness.

Dig for misery, then, in all the areas of dark lives, and dig hard. Rub off the outer dirt and scan the material.

Among the dark lives he could see, one seemed to hold out possibilities. A grown-up peasant maid possessed by a bhootni, maybe the same evil one who had pursued him in the meadow. The girl, no longer herself, would burst into pathetic sobs and in the next breath shriek with laughter. She was brazenly expose her body. The bhootni spoke dirty words with the girl's tongue, words that no decent maid could know. The ojha from Bhimtek had given the evil spirit hard beatings with his fist and it had screamed wildly. In vain. How to make the bhootni quit its chosen abode? The Brahmin in the temple had prescribed a puja—that was the only hope left—but the girl's father, poor as he was, could not meet the expense of the ritual.

"Seth-ji!" The veranda door swung open.

He frowned at the visitor, a tall gaunt man. "You again?"

The Drunk said, "Seth-ji, you are my mother and father."

He answered gravely, "Were I your father, lad, I would have whipped the life out of you. Were I your mother, I would have stuffed your mouth with salt as soon as you dropped from my womb."

"Beat me, sir. Kill me. But first of all—"

"Yes. The few clods of earth you still own." Those were good fields of maize. They would make a welcome addition to his estate. Pleased, he hurried to close the deal. The bond signed and money paid out, he threw a piece of advice. "Young bandicoot, you should marry again. You should have a home and a straight life."

The Drunk laughed pathetically. "As if any parent will want me for a son-in-law!"

The Seth tried to cheer him up. "There may be—" He groped for words and the Drunk helped him out. "There may be a woman who is my equal in repute. Then I can have a spouse."

When he was gone the Seth returned to the helpless peasant maid. She, also, could not be given in marriage—a hard problem for her parents. Unless the bhootni left its roost—

Meera, stirred to pity, could pay the cost of the ritual. There could be no better act of kindness. Why, this might well be the end of the search!

The Seth felt excited and happy, but only for a minute. For the dread thought came that the bhootni, expelled from its roost, might take possession of him by way of revenge. He could see his plight. Like the peasant girl he would shriek with wild laughter, shed tears, speak dirty words—he could foretell what words he would say. He might even take off his dhoti in public. Lakshmi, in despair, would send for the ojha and his associates. Fists and rods would be in swift action, thump, thump. Nago, seeing his father beaten, would wail in fear and sorrow and the men from Bhimtek would wag their heads and say, "The bhootni has to be hit hard. Only through Seth-ji's venerable body can it be reached. It is the bhootni who cries in pain, using Seth-ji's respected vocal chords, which are swollen and ready to snap. We will give that beauty a beating it will never forget in all its spectral existence. Now watch. Ah-reh-eh, bhootni!"

Caught in the agony of that vision, the Seth waved a hand before his eyes as if to break the web of fantasy.

Let the bhootni stay where it was. Trying to oust it was too risky. To think that Nago would have a ghost-possessed parent!

A man enslaved by drink and a maid haunted by an evil spirit. Both were good targets for kindness. But there was no means to give them help.

No means?

*There may be a woman who is my equal in repute. Then I can have a spouse!* Was not the ghost-ridden girl the Drunk's equal, in her own way? What if those two were united in wedlock? The wretch of a Drunk could not get a wife. The wretch of a peasant girl could not get a husband. What if their lives were joined?

No. Two miseries would not cancel each other, they would only add up to a greater misery.

The Drunk's equal in repute. There was another such person. She had no chance to get a husband. The Drunk of Sonamitti could marry the Bad Woman of Pipli! A chance for both to give up their evil ways and return to normal life. This, indeed, would be an instance of two misfortunes cancelling each other. And to bring this about would be an act of great kindness.

A matchmaker would have to be employed. Not the old barber with his loose tongue. Bulaki Rao? He would again demand fifty rupees, that greedy cockroach.

A quarter-hour later Bulaki Rao reacted to the proposal with, "No, Seth-ji. The Pipli woman will not have a cowlike existence. She cannot do without fun."

"Cowlike existence!" the Seth grunted. "That is your idea of married life, han?"

"What I mean is—"

"Fun. You also must have fun, so it seems."

"For shame! I, father of five children and one more soon to come—"

The Seth's face was like a thundercloud. "The Drunk will keep his spouse at her proper place. Fun—han!" He saw the cockroach cower and relented a little. "It is a delicate subject, Bulaki Rao. Meera Bai will have to be told all about the Bad Woman, she must know that such creatures exist, so that she may be moved to pity."

"Meera Bai knows all about the Pipli woman, for sure."

"What!"

"That woman is no secret. She lives just across the meadow."

"But, then, Meera Bai—"

"She is no breast-fed infant."

The point was settled. Bulaki Rao was willing to do more than his share—first as a go-between, then a priest solemnizing the marriage. For he was a Brahmin, though of a lower status than the caste-proud man at the temple who would surely refuse to join the hands of a pair so very disreputable.

Later in the day Bulaki Rao walked into the tin shed where the motorcycle was kept. "Petting the metal-and-rubber beauty, as usual? Why, friend, the Pipli pleasure is still there. Until her marriage—"

"Marriage?"

"Such a tale has not been heard in a hundred years. The Bad Woman of Pipli to wed the Drunk of Sonamitti. Seth-ji will not wait. Monday next has a good marriage hour, early in the night."

Sohanlal looked up. "What does this mean?"

Bulaki Rao turned his glance this way and that before he bent over, speaking in a thick whisper. "Do not breathe a word of this even to a goat or cow."

"I won't."

"And not to Meera Bai, especially."

He was astonished. "What has she got to do with it?"

"Kindness, dear friend!"

"Kindness?"

"Gold."

Sohanlal returned to his work. Gold, once more. Now that the Seth saw little good in the common human values, he would reach out toward the dead souls—with "kindness." And Meera would be his dupe again.

Bulaki Rao continued his patter. The Bad Woman had fought tooth and nail to get the best of inducements—compensation for herself in cash and the Drunk's land released from the bonds. Weak-minded as he was, the Drunk might regain his moral character under stern restraint. But his spouse? Bulaki Rao chuckled. Not she, the spouse-of-all!

He could not bear to see Meera make a miracle attempt again, Sohanlal brooded. This time it was going to be sheer madness. He sprang to his feet. He did not have to sit, defeated, polishing metal. The ten words were all that he needed to put the Gold goddess to instant flight. He had not spoken them, waiting for the right moment. That moment could not be pushed back any longer.


Meera was not in the house. Sohanlal felt both disappointment and relief. His task was to be left unfulfilled, but the strain of speaking the dread words was postponed. If only he could reveal the secret of the ring to Grandma and, through her, have it relayed to Meera. No, that would not do. Meera must hear the truth from his mouth. Her face would set in the lines of shock, then fill with dark dismay—and then the hot, overwhelming rush of shame. Was there ever such a comic figure anywhere on earth?

That would be the hour of his test. Could he pull her up from the depths of agony and make her share with him the joyous beginning of a new dawn? His very heart-beat was tied to the answer! If he failed —no, that could not happen. The first impact of shock easing off, Meera would simply laugh at herself. A good joke had gone too far, until it was a joke no longer, until it hurt badly. Meera would laugh, her mouth pressing down at the corners, eyes narrowed!

Grandma was watching his face. "You look so very worried. The Drunk marriage, I know."

"What is to be done?"

"The maker of all this mischief would come back hotfoot from Kushalpur if he knew."

"Kushalpur?"

"He is enjoying the big fair. Twenty-five elephants at the fair—think of that! The tuskers are priced—"

Sohanlal cried, "A letter from the minstrel? When has it come?"

"Yesterday." She rose to her feet, walked to the niche in the wall and returned with a crumpled postcard. "Here it is. Read."

Sohanlal spoke after a minute. "He has given an address. It is some Inn of Piety. He will stay on till Sunday after next, he says."

"That is his way—when he wants to have a word from us; a word to say all is well."

He was silent again, bemused over the letter, as if weighing every word. When he looked up and spoke, his voice had an excited ring.

"Tell him about that miracle."

"No!"

"But, Grandma—"

"He will be terribly unhappy, don't you understand?"

"In all fairness he should take over some of your burden on himself." Still she shook her head. "No."

"Pray listen, Grandma—" This was such a wonderful chance. What was hard for him was easy for the minstrel.

"He had not meant the taveez to go so very far."

"Having planted the seed, he must savor the bitter fruit."

"I will not let him be unhappy."

"Even if none but he can undo this evil?"

"Even so."

Sohanlal reflected for a minute, then tried a new tactic. "When he comes and sees what has happened, he will think of a way to discredit the touchstone. He holds Meera's mind in his fist, I do not have to tell you that. He means far more to her than ten touchstones. He will not let Meera be hurt—"

Grandma was silent.

"I beg of you, Grandma. Let me write a letter on your behalf. This is our only chance."

Still Grandma was silent.

"Say Yes, I beg of you."

Then she gave a slight nod and he, overjoyed, clasped her hand. "Han! How I envy Meera that she has such a Grandma!"

"Am I not yours, equally?"

"Equally. But she has had you for seventeen years. And I?"

She touched his chin with a caressing hand. "You can have me for the next fifty years."

"All to myself?"

"If you so wish—why not?"

"No. When I have a good thing, I like to go shares—with Meera." He shook his head as if ruefully. "If only your Meera had a like feeling!"

Grandma said, "Meera herself is all yours. Whatever she has must be yours, too."

He could not answer her because of the quick lump in his throat. *Meera herself is all yours.* The longing came heavily on him to hold the girl in his arms, her face pressed against his shoulder. He felt a queer tingling in his limbs and it was as though his blood was turning to water.

Grandma rose again, went to the niche in the wall and brought a fresh postcard. "Write. Have you a pencil?"

So the letter was written:

"The touchstone has acted. The copper ring on our beti's finger has turned into gold. We are waiting for the wonder to repeat itself, over and again. A bodyful of copper to make a king's wealth every time. . . . My faithless head bends humbly upon thy feet, hey Atmaram!"

32

The Seth had good reason to be pleased with himself. Meera had at first flared up at the Drunk marriage proposal. She had asked to be left alone. But he had pleaded with her and, finally, won.

With patience and tact he had met her strong resistance. He had explained what this marriage would do to mend two broken lives which would otherwise go to utter waste. Gold or no gold, such an act of kindness was worth while for its own sake. The redemption of the spiritually decrepit! Proud of his phrase, he had repeated it—"spiritually decrepit"—adding, "You are too young, Meera, to understand what such words mean. But the minstrel would be overjoyed when he hears of your great deed of mercy." After a pause to make sure that she was duly impressed—to invoke the minstrel was the best of arguments—he had gone on slowly, "Besides, it may be that we are only a stone's throw from our goal. We can run up to it at one breath, Meera, daughter."

So here she was, walking by his side, quiet, and the house of marriage looming close ahead under the shadow of the One-tree Hill. People might mock him for setting foot in an abode of sin. This, however, had better be kept in mind: Good and evil were twins dwelling side by side, one a foil for the other. Light needed darkness. Ugliness enhanced beauty. Riches were so welcome because of the all-pervasive poverty. What use was a healer in the absence of ailments? Where was the pleasure in giving, if no one would beg and receive?

The Bad Woman was a perfect foil; she was darkness itself. And so, almost, was the Drunk.

"None but the bad set in the village will go to this wedding," Lakshmi had given a warning. The people saw nothing good in this marriage. It was no deed of mercy, it would bring about no gold, only trouble. Trouble for Meera and even for the nuptial pair. The effigy Grandma had held up for the people to see was still fighting a battle on Meera's account. The Seth was blamed for everything that had happened to her. So Lakshmi said and she added with scorn, "Of course, you will be content to have the bad set alone, the fellows who will take you to the board-moard. Is that not right?"

"Enough of your wisdom, wifeling!" He had fondly pinched her cheek.

Yes, the bad fellows had turned up in full strength, along with their friends from other villages, drawn by the twin magnets, the Bad Woman and the Drunk. That rabble would have to be kept in good humor. The stage for the marriage stood ready, everything having been done in Meera's name. The Seth was her agent and worked at her bidding—a myth that could deceive none except destiny. The touchstone would act in the moments when Bulaki Rao chanted the *mantra*, the sacred words out of ancient times, invoking sky and wind and earth and fire to bear witness to the marriage. And now that the hour prescribed in the almanac was about to start, the suspense was hard to bear.

An acetylene lamp threw a circle of strong light for the groom and his party but they preferred to sit half visible at the edge of darkness. A voice from their midst came, "This is fun! The Drunk deserves his good title. Glory has come upon the pride of Pipli."

But the last jug of toddy was about to be emptied. What next? The party woke to the peril.

"Run to the toddy man."

"Grab all he has. Suck him dry."

"The money to pay with? Ho, Seth-ji, turn your eyes to us, dear uncle."

"Wait till the ceremony is over," he pleaded. "Then all of you may swim in toddy, like froglings in a pool."

"You will deny us on this night of nights? . . . Areh, Drunk, up on your feet. Move along. No toddy, no marriage. What does the Seth take us for? Let the Bad Woman wed a banana tree. Let the Seth have her for a second spouse."

"Ram-Ram!" The Seth clapped his hands to his ears to keep out the foul talk.

Drooping under his turban's ten-yard convolutions, the Drunk would have fallen asleep, but his companions had kept him awake by frequent nudges. He now straightened himself, rose to his feet and staggered up. "Seth-ji—" with a demanding hand.

"You have imbibed enough poison, more than enough."

"It is like your gold, dear uncle. The more you have of it, the more you want. Is that not true? Fellows?"

"The Drunk speaks wisdom," they agreed. "He has good sense in his guts."

The Seth had to be tactful. "Listen. The ceremony will start soon. Do not make a scene. Do not be laughed at."

"Dear uncle, what do we care? We are bad fellows, unashamed. They all know us. They spit at our shadow, thoo!"

"Thoo!" the chorus affirmed.

"Seth-ji—" The arm was still extended. Helpless, the Seth parted with a rupee. But twenty heads shook in glum disapproval.

"One rupee—choh! It will buy a single jugful. The drops will dry up in the throat; nothing will get to the seat of wisdom. Dear uncle—"

"This is a solemn hour," the Seth cried and provoked howls of laughter.

"So it is! The Bad Woman was never so busy in her life. Her night of nights, this, with roaring trade through the back door."

The Seth felt uneasy. Was that a joke? But there was no sign of Bulaki Rao. Han! The cockroach was at the back door, working a new kind of black market at the cost of his bread-giver.

"Who can blame her? Denying a Bad Woman her good work. Asking a tigress to eat fish."

"In my house the tigress will cry baa baa like a goat, baa baa!" The Drunk twisted his face in a comical expression.

"The Drunk is a lion. Beside him we are newborn kittens. Jai to the Drunk!"

The lion reached out a paw to the Seth, whining. "Our mother and father—"

"Take this. Take more." The exasperated Seth scattered money on the ground. "Drink my blood. Eat my guts. Go!"

"Jai to our mother and father!"

When the men were gone, the Seth sat slumped on a reed mat, trying to be calm. The Drunk now squatted beside him, exhausted by his brief bout of energy, and head propped on an upraised knee, he muttered vaguely.

The stillness gave way to the grave notes of a conch. The Seth grew alert. There was Bulaki Rao on the veranda, the conch to his mouth, cheeks puffed with breath, and behind him the Bad Woman dressed in purple, carrying trinkets on every visible limb.

"Meera? Where is she?" The Seth raised his voice in an anxious shout. "Beti—"

She had been sitting in the darkness on a pond step, ankles dipped in water. Hearing the Seth's call she rose and walked into the circle of light.

The Seth now turned to the Bad Woman. She was generously built, with an aggressive bust, her roundish face thickly decorated with sandalwood paste and her mouth betel-red. On her flat nose a gold button shone. She was perhaps thirty.

"Seth-ji, I bow to your feet, sir."

"Live long. Be the mother of many sons."

Her eyeballs danced merrily. "Take back your blessings."

He stuttered. "You, a proud wife—" but she cut him short with, "At last I stand before the great man of whom even the stars in the sky speak."

He shook his head. "What great man?" He was troubled, swallowing hard. The Bad Woman might use bold reckless words. She might even make a professional invitation. Up to the marriage hour she had plied her trade. The lamb of a Drunk would be content to eat grass at this hyena's bidding. Doubt struck the Seth's mind. Would the marriage fail? Was it no act of kindness?"

"I have a complaint, though."

"Indeed?" He clutched at this chance to steer the talk away from himself. "Bulaki Rao is in charge of everything. Has that bug made a mess? Tell me and I will twist his neck."

"My complaint is against you, sir."

His mouth hung open. The Bad Woman went on, "You have been gracious. You have found me a husband. I bow to your feet. Yet I say, you have made me lose face."

He felt uneasy. "Look," coaxingly. "The ceremony will start in five minutes and last for two hours. We will talk when the ritual is over and you have become the proud spouse of an honest young bandicoot."

She shook her head. "You have made me lose face. To agree to marry a Drunk—"

The Drunk burst into tears. "Hai!" he cried. "Hai!" His bride-to-be took three steps forward, her bangled arms rising to her hips in a

260

gesture of challenge. "Such indignity! Seth-ji, you must recompense for what you have done to me. Only then—"

The Seth shrank before her glance, wanton yet stern, but forced himself to speak.

"Look. Meera Bai has promised you a tidy sum and even paid part of it in advance, has she not? You will live happily with a good craftsman who only needs an iron hand to keep him yoked to his day's work. Yours—"

"Mine," her arm swung in assent, the array of metal agleam in the light. "But, first of all, I have to gain face. There is one way." Her cool eyes rested upon Meera, searchingly. "There will be enough gold for the two of us. Let me name my share. A pair of bangles; one armlet; the waist-chain. That is all. I am not greedy. Ask the people. Folks, tell Seth-ji."

The Seth turned to Meera in despair and saw her eyes flash strangely. He looked round for Bulaki Rao of whom there was yet no sign. Busy counting the money he had made, having sold the Bad Woman under his master's nose!

"Pray listen," he pleaded. "Let the ceremony start. Later we will have a hearty talk."

"Later, Seth-Ji?"

"Yes, yes." The Bad Woman was not immune to reason.

What was the commotion about? Trouble again?

It was a jumble of thick singing voices. The men were returning from the toddy shop. As they approached, slowly the words became clear.

> "Ho, the skin of our vixen!
> Ho, the skin of our vixen!
> Had our vixen's skin been gold,
> We'd peel it off her body; gold skin, gold hair, all!
> Gold skin, gold hair, all.
> Throat to toe!
> Throat to toe!"

The situation was getting out of hand and it was already the auspicious hour. In this crisis the Seth summoned his great strength. "Bulaki Rao!" he bellowed.

"Ji?" The man sprang out of the earth, just behind his master.

"Start the ritual. At once."

"There is a hitch," the Bad Woman spoke solemnly. "What if nothing happens to the copper? Once married, married for all time. Is that the right way to treat a helpless woman? She is made to lose face marrying a drunk and gets no gold, for there is no gold, and the marriage bonds tie her from throat to toe."

"Throat to toe," the grave chorus affirmed.

"Stop!" the Seth bellowed again. "Do not try your tricks on me, stupid people, for I have tricks of my own. Drunkards, you hear? With one word I can make the magistrate in town cancel the toddy shop licence. And you, woman, I bid you to be calm and get wed. Bulaki Rao, use your precious tongue." But as he followed the bug's amazed glance, his heart seemed to stop.

Meera was stripping the ornaments off her body. A madness seemed to have taken hold of her. "What is this?" the Seth demanded but she was too preoccupied to answer. The ornaments lay at her feet in a minute.

He felt his blood turn cold. "Meera—"

"Hai Ram!" wailed Bulaki Rao. "What if the touchstone is now ready to act and no metal on her person?"

A new voice rang out of the darkness, "That's it!" Sohanlal stepped forward, elated, hardly able to contain himself, and her eyes meeting his for an instant dropped, abashed.

"Come." His mouth widened in a boyish grin.

Then the Seth woke from his stupor. "Stop!" In vain. Meera was gone in the darkness.

He had no hope left. This was final—one more earthen bridge, one more teen-age healer, but a hundredfold worse. Would that he had accepted the offer of the bullion jackal in town. Six thousand rupees tossed off in scorn and here was retribution!

His eyes hung upon the gilded pile shining in gaslight and his face turned grim. He was now free to pick up a broken thread. The red scorpion in the ledger had not died! The stupid girl with her proud Grandma would walk out of the village as paupers, and not a soul to regret their departure.

But there was the driver fellow. He and Meera would be man and wife, even an owl could see that with eyes shut. They would make a crazy pair. Each would have enough to do urging the other on to the path of mischief. Sonamitti would be a better place without the peer-less pair.

He lowered his head in a spasm of grieving and yet with some vague relief. A bad dream had passed. It had tormented him day and night. Even the bhootni, making him her roost, could not have wreaked more havoc.

Obsessed by gold, he had let all his routine work slacken and stop. His second clothshop in town was still a plan on paper and his blue-print of a countrywide chain of stores, at least twenty, near-forgotten. And there was the district board, of course. So much remained to be done, and he was content to let his energy ooze down his fingertips. Time to set things right. Time for hard, honest donkey's work.

The copper, two hundred rupees' worth, could be sold off to a dealer at half the price. But—where was the waist-chain? Where was the nugget? Startled, he gazed hard and long at the discarded heap.

His fists clenched. Taveez—waist-chain—nugget ...

The married woman, far more than the frivolous maiden, would know the value of a life of security. The reckless fire-eater would yield to the compulsion of cool calculations.

She also had suffered. She also had known dark despair. No wonder she was at the end of her tether, defeated, despondent. No wonder she had acted on a quick impulse.

To make her gird up her loins. To bring her back into the fight. Take heart, beti. Onward to new acts of kindness! No gold ore was ever mined and processed in two months. Only cheap things were cheaply won.

She would get back her lost faith. There were paths yet to be ex-plored. Thought, the spur of action; belief, the core of energy; the gloom of despair, a setting for the bright final moment.

Have patience and grit, Nago's father. Have all patience and grit, son of a fathead!

Roused to quick action, he picked up his umbrella from the reed-mat and poked Bulaki Rao in the abdomen. "Call yourself a Brahmin?"

Bulaki Rao gaped in confusion while the Bad Woman clicked her tongue in pity and the Drunk muttered incoherently.

"You, a Brahmin, ready to marry off a hyena woman and a toddy barrel, with the fire god as witness. Your caste-honor is on sale for fifty rupees, greedy ape!"

Bulaki Rao cried in protest, "Seth-ji!"

"Rush back home," he growled and after one more prod with the umbrella, he turned, started to walk away. Having gone five paces he turned again, calling, his voice more gentle: "Let these two console each other. Hop off, Bulaki Rao. Follow my example."

33 The minstrel arrived at break of dawn, as before, but not heralding himself to the village, quiet until he was on his doorstep and then calling, "Beta!"

Meera was still asleep. Grandma was up and about, ears alert for a familiar melody. But he had sneaked up in silence—it was the measure of his caution. Grandma smiled with perverse pleasure and leaning against the kitchen wall, she closed her eyes for a minute. Here he was, back home and in trouble. He had brought trouble upon Meera, not thinking it might grow such sharp teeth, and now the teeth would hold him, too, in their bite. What would he do? Betray Atmaram? Debunk himself?

"Beta!"

Grandma greeted him at the door. "Here stands Atmaram, back home from the mountain top, lured by touchstone gold."

He clutched her arm. "Something has happened?"

"Come to the kitchen." Her eyes softened all too quickly.

He sat down on the floor, his bamboo staff by his side, while Grandma busied herself making tea. With hurried hand she dropped five pinches of tea dust in a clay pot filled with water and added sugar and milk. The clay pot placed on oven-fire, she was ready for talk. Turning to him as he sat in silence, arms drawn about his knees, she saw the patch of sunburnt baldness in his head grown larger than before, the mop of hair thin and awry, the eyebrows all white, and regret came sweeping back on her. He was old and tired, unfit for the task facing him, the hard task of breaking to pieces the Gold goddess he had made.

Could it be that he sensed her feeling? For he smiled and said reassuringly, "He who eats honey out of a hive does not fear being stung."

She prodded him with a question. "The gold ring?"

Firelight flickered on his face and his voice came muffled.

The Seth's all-swallowing greed had made him reflect. Could he, a mere minstrel, challenge the man of power? He had one asset, he was

Atmaram! The Seth was anxious to make use of Atmaram, he had begged for a taveez. So the plan took shape. A touchstone!

"The wicked plan," said Grandma. "Atmaram!" she hissed, closing one eye in a mockful wink. The minstrel ignored the gesture.

"Meera wore no other ornaments except a ring. It had to be turned into gold."

She wagged a stern finger in his face.

"A minstrel must not touch gold. The shame that you carried the gold ring in your kurta pocket."

He laughed. "I did not."

"Han! The ring came flying on to the finger of Meera Bai."

He would have laughed again, but the scowl on Grandma's face stopped him. "Listen," he began his story. "The Seth came to our house with Lakshmi, do you remember?"

She did.

"Lakshmi stayed on awhile after he had left. I walked with her up to her housedoor. On the way I asked her to give a gold ring to Meera, slip it on to her finger as she lay asleep. Lakshmi was overjoyed at my request; she had been longing to see Meera wear gold."

Grandma cried, "What! Lakshmi was your accomplice and I knew nothing!"

"I bade her not to divulge the secret, not even to you. I did not tell her what was in my mind. Maybe, later, when I had given the taveez, Lakshmi understood the gold ring."

Grandma beat her hand to her forehead. "The wonder that Lakshmi could sleep with such a big secret in her stomach!"

"The wonder," he agreed.

"She went away to her parents—maybe that was because she knew she could not otherwise keep the secret."

The minstrel said, "Tell me everything. The Seth has been duped, I can see that. It must be great fun!"

Grandma was now grave. Instead of fun, the touchstone became an acute hurt, she said. First, Meera gave up fighting the Seth, she allied herself with the tyrant. With the gold won, she thought, there would be no need of the district board. The village people watched her with contrary feelings—love, hate, expectation, anger—until it came to a point when hate and anger prevailed and her effigy was about to be burnt.

His face showed horror. "Meera's effigy?"

266

"Yes. Had not the Cowhouse Five with Sohanlal's help—"

"Sohanlal?"

He was a youth from town in the Seth's employ, Grandma explained. He would have no truck with the Gold goddess. He argued with Meera over and again, trying hard to make her see reason. But Meera was firm in her belief. Neither would yield ground. Both suffered equally.

"Both suffered?" His eyebrows lifted.

She ignored the question. "Three days back—or was it four?— Meera came home without her ornaments. How happy I was. The tale had ended. Our Meera was again the simple girl with her simple needs, a cool head on her shoulders. But—the taveez? It was gone, along with the gilded copper? At midnight, when she was asleep, I felt under her jacket. Alas, the taveez was still on her arm. I felt under her sari and, alas, the nugget was still there and the waist-chain also. The gold game was not over."

"Waist-chain worn against the skin, day and night?"

"She moans in her sleep." The voice was heavy with despair. "The chain grazes her skin and hurts it. Waking up she holds the chain loose with her fingers, drawing it off her body for relief. The misery. Why did you have to do this to our girl?"

"An earthworm has become a cobra," he said pensively. "I had hoped and calculated. Maybe, so I thought, the Seth would wait and watch and the village would have a spell of relief from his greed. And Meera, I had figured, would enjoy the touchstone—the Seth would keep her supplied with funds for acts of kindness. She would not take it too much to heart."

She shook her head. "You do not know Meera. When she sets her heart on something she goes all out for it. Everything else ceases to count."

"Even Sohanlal?"

She spoke slowly, meditatively. "Sohanlal is not clear to her yet. He is a beat of her pulse, she does not hear it. He is a flick of her eyelid, she does not feel it." Grandma smiled to herself and turned to the tea brewing on the fire. She poured the thick liquid into a brass bowl and then her voice came harshly. "An earthworm has become a cobra. Kill the cobra lest it kill our girl."

"Gran'ma!" It was Meera calling. He was about to answer "Beta!" but Grandma stopped him, a finger to her lip. "Let her first hear you sing," she said. "Otherwise your homecoming will not be quite real."

Barely had he sung a line when Meera came hurtling to the kitchen. "Grandpapa!"—as if she could not believe her eyes. "Days and days I have been thinking of you, wanting you, and you have come!"

He was startled by the fever in her eyes and the shadow of suffering in her face. Motionless for a time, he stood up and drew her close. "Beta!" He stroked her hair and his voice was a whisper in her ear, "You wanted me? What for?"

"Tell me, Grandpapa. What are acts of real kindness?"

"Meera," protested Grandma, "this old man had to sit up in a railway coach a full day and a night and you deny him five minutes' rest."

Her eyes, trustful, held mute prayer and his quick response came. "Beta, we will do what we can. We will put our heads together, you and I. Do not worry."

But it was Grandma who worried most. How would he undo the knot he had tied? He must have time to think. Meera must be diverted.

"Hei-ee," Grandma cried with sudden gaiety, "let the three of us forget our troubles. Let us laugh. Tell us, yellow-clad man, what you saw at Kushalpur." She lifted a finger by way of warning. "Only the truth."

He gave quick response and it was not long before Meera also shed her preoccupation and was in tune with the others. The lost merriment lived again in her and she clapped her hands in the old way. "O Grandpapa!"

He went on, "Now listen. There was a magician at the fair—he could put anybody to sleep and then make him act as bidden. One day he cast his spell on a policeman and made him say, 'I am a rascal. I am a son of filthy swine.' How the audience laughed!"

Meera and Grandma saw the policeman in his deep slumber and they also enjoyed his plight and laughed.


The stream, narrow yet full-bodied after the heavy rains, caught the midnight moon as a crystal pillar twisted and swayed in the whipped froth. Squat shrubs on the muddy bank made a patchwork of subdued dark relieved by lines of cowpaths. The minstrel felt his way with his stick and tapped lest there be snakes. Meera, a step behind, seemed rapt, moving in a heavy-lidded trance.

The miracle had happened, and much else had come in its wake!

The minstrel had built the illusion for her and it was no hard task, for she was pliable, ready for him, eager to believe. The act of real kindness was done, a king's wealth attained.

That was the starting point. The story grew real by the touch of art, its drama fast, time-space condensed. The minstrel could create vivid images, like life itself.

They had set out an hour before midnight, walking the sleep-laden roads and fields where a new world had arisen. There it lay before her in clear perspective.

See that house of brick? See that other brick house a hundred yards to the left? One was Munni's, one Champa's. Their mud huts had been pulled down, but the sites were not changed—those two women would not move off the ancestral earth. That earth, however, had spread out on every side swallowing a hundred hovels around. For Champa and Munni along with Bimla and Sohagi had been the first to share the touchstone's bliss. Those two paid fairly when they took over a hundred neighboring huts, let that be admitted, and the people, happy to get five times the price, moved off self-evicted—who could tell where they went?

Champa and Munni, simple-souled peasant wives, set their wits at work and as their tracts of new land were cleared of rubble, fenced, they engaged masons from town for the new construction. It had to be city-style houses, for Champa and Munni could well afford the expense with the abundant bliss they had received from their dear sister.

Champa's chief mason made floors of marble white as cow milk and mirror-bright. Munni watched and fell into thinking. The Devi be my witness, she vowed, I will have something to hit the eyeballs harder. She urged upon her masons and they suggested this and that, but the idea came in the end from Munni herself. She would have stone lions at her gates, a massive pair, like the couchant lions at the gates of palaces of old.

Han! said Champa, her face dark. She threatened her men with a wage-cut unless they used their heads and hands to better effect.

"It cannot be. They are friends and sisters, Munni and Champa. No, no, Grandpapa!"

All the same, there stand the two brick houses in moonlit splendor, clear to the eye. The houses of Champa and Munni.

So much wealth pouring on their lap and no knowledge of its right

269

use anywhere in their stomach. Hence the mind's corruption and the vying. One day Champa had something good to brag of, the next day it was Munni's turn. So angry, so unhappy. Hatred grew in their blood. No wonder their husbands were dragged into the quarrel. It went to such lengths that the two men, goaded by wrathful wives, fought fiercely yesterday. Munni's man lay felled by a blow from a thick bamboo stave and she, in fury, vowed to be avenged. She will set fire to Champa's house. She will do it later tonight, pouring kerosene to the front door and windows. Tongues of flame will lick the cool air. In the small hours when everyone lies asleep—

"No, no, Grandpapa. It cannot be."

Bimla and Sohagi, the other pair in the Five. They also have their full share of wealth. Sohagi's man has sold off his cart and oxen—they are no use to a man of riches—and he passes the day sleeping on a soft bed, making up for the drudgery of his lifelong toil. That is not the way of Bimla's husband, though; he refuses to be dependent of his spouse. He has stuck to his post of office peon at twenty-eight rupees a month. Ashamed of her man, Bimla has gone away to her parents and there is a move to get the marriage annulled. No dearth of rich suitors for Bimla!

"No, no, Grandpapa. Bimla is not such a goose."

But there she is, a woman of great wealth whose husband is a peon, clinging to his humble post, so that she is up to her chin in shame.

Sohagi, unlike the other, loves her fellow overmuch. She gave him rich food with ghee in abundance and she also ate well, but while he remained the thin reed he was, she became round as a barrel. The cartman disliked her new shape and his eyes became restless, roving about, seeking a neat figure and a comely face. He ate and slept and had no work to do, so he could let his eyes prowl freely. The barber brought him a proposal for a maid in Kanhan. He could well afford a second spouse, the first one fat and round as a barrel.

"Look, Grandpapa. The Ox-cart has no money of his own. Sohagi has to pay for everything."

True, but Sohagi, loving her man, could not tell him the money was hers alone. She was ready to be a doormat for him, lest in anger he left her. So she paid for his second marriage.

"Only to be kicked by the new woman?"

"She has no choice but to please them both. She has to be happy in self-sacrifice."

"Old-world talk, Grandpapa."

Sohagi is an old-world spouse. She only knows her husband and her baby boy. When the boy has grown up, she will be ready to leave her worthless man. Meanwhile, there is nothing for her but heartbreak.

"The Ox-cart is a good soul—"

The image stands clear. Having sold off the oxen, his partners in toil, the cartman ate and slept and let his lazy thoughts be possessed by comely faces.

The Cowhouse Five—the story started with them, but with time spinning on, the story covered the entire village. The gold grew into a stream which swelled to a flood and touched every housedoor. There lay the village, changed beyond recognition. The gold in its abundance was for all to share. Each and every peasant was a big man.

There, the proud brick houses with terraces washed by moonlight. The fields, the meadowland, all built over or fenced. Just as well, for Sonamitti did not have to grow food or pasture kine—food, fodder, could be bought in other markets. Every peasant who had sweated with his plow-pair, not heeding sun and rain and wind, now sat at ease on a flowered rug with fat pillows to lean on, wrapped in a bathgown like the Seth's and vaunting bright parasols and smoking hookah from flexible pipes two yards in length. Every peasant of yesterday had, at his beck and call, serving men hired from other villages.

It so happened that the rich began to hanker for the status of a landlord. Tenant unto master—that was something worth paying for. A word cast on the air was enough. Brokers came flocking. Money changed hands, big money. Twenty villages in the district listened to the gay music of silver. Many peasants sold their land willingly for a good price in cash. But there were stubborn mules who needed to be broken; their thumb-marked deeds to other money-lenders of the locality were bought up at a premium, then foreclosed. So it went on. Sonamitti's heavy shadow grew in length and depth across the countryside, east-west, south-north, mile on mile. The shadow of a new master. Ten thousand tillers gave up their title deeds and became day laborers on the soil they had owned.

Serfs selling labor for a daily pittance. But these men in loincloth combined against the Bathgowns and started a fight. *Leeches! Eaters of our blood!* The Bathgowns were perplexed, they could not tell what the trouble was about. The men in loincloth cried that the new freedom was for all to share. The Bathgowns laughed in honest disbelief.

Every tear would be wiped from every eye, the toilers cried, gazing ahead into the far blue horizon. The Bathgowns asked, eyes snapping in fun, Have you buckets enough to collect so many tears?

Peace-loving people like the Elder, Rajaram, had kept away from this trouble, happy to lend money and make entries in their ledgers. But the voices thundered against them as well, *Eaters of our blood!* Rajaram, disgusted, was ready to wash his hands of this business and quit the village with two good kicks at it, so he stated to the priest, who now had five assistants chanting to the Devi in her splendid new temple and to seven new Devis set up in smaller abodes. Rajaram said he would live in town and eat honey out of a hundred pots and then no tongue would dare complain that he ate blood. Other landlords wagged their heads wisely: Yes, they also were ready to quit the village with their hundred honey pots. One asked in doubt: What if the city folks wrinkle their noses at us and call us village donkeys? Seth-ji, himself a townsman, answered such doubts. Dear brothers, your gold will speak for you. City tongues will lick the soles of your shoes. Dear brothers, be easy. So he said, the Seth, who alone had not changed a whit in this new paradise, not parting with the least of his incalculable wealth, amassing it all for his dear son, Nago, to inherit.

Be that as it may, Sonamitti would remain a paradise on Earth, a sight for the gods and goddesses, and—let words of fire write the tale —all was due to one person who owned the touchstone and shared her great fortune with everyone. All glory to that large-hearted Devi. Jai to her, and jai to the Gold goddess, jai!

The minstrel's voice throbbed with feeling and the girl, as she gave him a deep look, shivered a little.

A cloud hid the moon while they walked in the reverie of their vivid vision, but sky and earth were bright again as they reached the riverside an hour later and sat down exhaustedly. The minstrel's voice flowed on, relentless in evocation. She, the builder of a new paradise, would have to be wed like any other girl, but the man must be her peer. Like unto like, the only key to happiness in marriage. Such a man was not hard to find—the war had created Seths by the score. Some followed queer trades. Take, for instance, the youth from Delhi who came to the fair at Kushalpur. With him came twenty-five elephants, all for sale. Twenty-five full-grown tuskers. A good business line apparently, for the huge beasts, the pride of the fair, were all sold off soon, eight thousand rupees apiece. That wealthy youth, people said, was not yet joined to a spouse. Many fathers of marriageable maids were sure to have noted the fact. A matchmaker of high repute could be found in the city and employed—he would travel to Delhi and speak to the elephant-merchant's folks. . . .

Like a coiled spring released of a heavy load she shot upright to her feet. The strong moonlight caught her body and illumined her face. Voiceless, hard-eyed, she stood gazing in front of her and her mouth hung open as she took deep breaths. With a sudden jerk of her hand she bared her right arm, pulled at the red string of her taveez until it snapped, and in the same movement she flung the taveez far into the river.

"Elephant-merchant!" she cried in a sharp hiss.

And the minstrel who had fought his battle with a strange weapon, watched the girl a silent minute, his eyes warm, and he nodded his head contentedly.

## 34

The news electrified the village. The sun had barely risen when the strange happening of the night was a theme for every tongue. The touchstone assigned to the river, the Gold goddess put to flight.

It was like a fable of old come to life. A peasant maid became a king's daughter. Glory and disgrace; glamor and ridicule. The seven weeks' wonder ended on the eve of freedom day. This was the day for which Sonamitti had fought and suffered and waited. Yet in the hour of fulfillment the touchstone, even if gone, was stealing a march on history; mere myth was usurping the emotion that belonged to an epochal reality. There was to be no procession, no public rejoicing. Sonamitti lay in a kind of daze.

Not all Sonamitti; not the Cowhouse Five. While Meera was still in bed after her sleepless night, her friends bustled in, their faces lit with happiness, and they pushed the girl awake. "Hei-ee, our own sister!" With loving fingers they touched her on arm and face and hair.

"Do you know, Meera? There are people who lament that the touchstone is gone. The loss is theirs! You have let them down!"

"We also have been mean toward our sister, be it admitted. But we have had one saving grace; we wanted nothing from her except that she be our own Meera again."

"Meera, how we missed you at the sweetshop! We went there wearing masks, like brigands. The servant-boy howled in terror. It is sure that in his sleep he sees our masked faces and whimpers."

Meera turned to Lakshmi and her voice was full of concern. "Sister, it is good that you are back home. The Seth will need you as never before."

"It is not as bad as you think." Lakshmi smiled. "The Seth is not the man who lies down in bed aching from a broken heart. He is deep in his plans. The vote-mote—two days ahead."

Sohagi gave a meaningful nod. Meera saddened. It was too late for her to help in that contest.

274

The talk turned to freedom day. Would it pass by like any other day of the year? No one could say what ought to be done. Grandpapa was silent, but maybe he had something in his mind. Champa had seen him emerge from an Elder's house with a preoccupied air. He had given her the new greeting, "Jai Hind, Victory to India!" and passed on. What did he wish to do?

Sohanlal had gone to town, five days back, just after the Pipli episode; he would take part in the great celebrations there. If only he knew that Meera was rid of her taveez. The two had walked back together from Pipli, and it was plain that they would be man and wife. Let that happen, O Devas and Devis, let those two unite, even though, with Meera gone, the village would be dark and the Cowhouse dead.

Grandma stepped into the room, freshly bathed, her white hair done in a neat bun. "Meera, will you stay in bed with so much about to happen?"

"What is about to happen?"

She smiled knowingly. "Get ready, girl. Why, the minstrel is here in the village!"

Meera coaxed, "Tell us, Gran'ma."

"First get up and put on the blue sari Lakshmi gave you, then we will talk."

The Cowhouse Five made a united demand. "Grandma, tell us." Champa and Munni took hold of her arms. Bimla and Sohagi knelt and clasped her ankles. Meera, springing out of bed, nestled her face to Grandma's bosom. With coercion and love they begged, "Tell us, Grandma dear."

"If only I knew!" she owned up with a bland smile, but added quickly, "The minstrel is up to something, I am sure. Maybe he will sing to the village about freedom."

That was it, the women agreed. The minstrel could not let this day of days pass uncelebrated.

"Meera, do you remember? In the cowshed, one day, you complained that the big struggle had come when you were too small. Do you still feel sore on that account?"

"Think of what is about to happen and the breath stops in each nostril, then blows fast—faster!"

"You remember how my respected father-in-law, constable-ji, warned us that day not to tickle the mighty British Lion? That was because he thought he might lose his job in the free country. Today he thinks otherwise. He says, 'Even in the house of freedom there will be thieves to catch. I have nothing to fear!'"

At this point all eyes turned to Munni. She had plucked a charm from her hair, the only one left, and was mumbling the mysterious words. She was warding off evil from the house of freedom, maybe!

Then Meera rose to her old leadership. "Friends, we must not let this day go to waste. Grandpapa must sing to the people. We will persuade him."

She went out for a wash. Behind her happiness was a hurt. *He* was away on this memorable day. Before he caught the early-morning bus he had come to see her for a few minutes. Not one word did he say about the touchstone. So it had been also the other night as they walked back from Pipli. To take her mind away from the ugliness of her experience, he had spoken eloquently of the new Republic that was about to write its name on history's page. However, at her house-door he had said, "Meera, it seems there will be real freedom for you too." Puzzled, she would have asked him to explain what he meant, but he had turned quickly and was gone. When he came again at daybreak she asked, "I step into freedom as soon as it comes to my country, do I not?" He answered, "That is one thing. The other is that each of us has to win the freedom to be free. It is a state of the mind, so Gandhi-ji tells us." Puzzled, she waited to hear more, but he smiled at her, took hurried leave and went away.

The taveez, he meant *that*, she told herself, while rubbing her teeth with wood ash. The taveez lay in the river—she had won the freedom to be free! He should have been the first to know, and rejoice. But he was away.

Ash and saliva spilled down her chin and she picked up a mug of water to rinse her mouth. How would she fit herself into her place beside her husband?

Her husband! She felt her blood throb. A rich man's whim had brought the stranger to this village. But for that whim. . . . To think of the time when he was nowhere in her world. . . .

"Meera, friend, hurry!"

If only he did not have to be away in town on this day, she sighed, as she came back to her friends.

Grandma was right—so it appeared when the women reached Main Road. The word was going round that the minstrel would sing in two hours' time; people must assemble around the old banyan tree at the meadow's edge. Happy, the women hurried away, each taking the word to her neighbors.

It was almost noon when the village sat under the hundred-branched banyan. Even the Seth turned up, wearing a new crimson bathgown, the best he had ever exhibited. His face showed no signs of what he had felt a few hours before. As news about the taveez reached him at dawn, he had sat stunned for a minute, as if out of his senses. Then the agony slashed him like ten knives. He could take a defeat, though. He had lost the battle for gold, but the battle for power could still be won. Since Meera's Grandma was not a contestant, he would give her fields back to her. That generous gesture would amaze the village and rally it in gratefulness to his side. And to get the minstrel's support, he would make a grand gesture—a half-year's remission of all debts. The shark of a bridge contractor would have to pay a fifteen per cent commission, not ten, by way of recompense.

"Jai Hind!" The minstrel greeted his audience as he stood under the flag he had unfurled. Would they let him say five words or ten before he sang? This day with its great gift for India's people—a touchstone! He paused, allowing the hum of astonished comments to stop. Freedom was the touchstone, he resumed, his voice stronger. It was a touchstone for everyone. To possess this touchstone was not enough, for it could wake to life and work its miracle only when acts of faith were done.

His words grew in power. "Brothers, now that we have freedom, we need acts of faith. Then only will there be a transmutation. Friends, then only will our lives turn into gold. Without acts of faith, freedom is a dead pebble tied to the arm with a bit of string, fit only to be cast into the river."

Silence prevailed until an Elder asked, "What acts of faith, minstrel? Are we to fumble for them in darkness?"

He could not say what the acts had to be. He was only a peasant with no learning or wisdom. But guidance was sure to come from other quarters. "Friends, the word will come at the right time. We must hold ourselves in readiness."

"So we must"—there was a burst of approval. "If it is as our minstrel-brother says—"

"It is up to us to attain miracles," he went on. "Miracles to make us strong, to make us worthy, to make us full-grown people."

The Elder cried, "Minstrel, you make our blood sing!"

277

"Remember, friends, all this cannot be cheaply won. The miracle will not drop upon us. It is we who have to create it with love and with sweat. Freedom is the means to that end."

"We understand. Nothing can be done without the means though. What good is a field if there is no plowshare, nor oxen, nor seeds?"

"You have spoken well, friend." His work done, he could begin his bhajan. He would sing in an abandon of great joy.

Half an hour later, as the audience sat bespelled and mute, Sohanlal appeared at the scene.

Overnight he had changed his plans. The voice of Jawaharlal Nehru had much to do with it. As the supreme moment drew near, all India waited breathless to hear that voice address the Constituent Assembly in session at the capital. People all over India crowded around radio sets and loudspeakers. Close to midnight the speech came.

"Long years ago we made a tryst with destiny and now the time has come when we shall redeem our pledge. At the stroke of midnight hour India will awake to life and freedom. A moment comes, which comes but rarely in history, when we step out from the old to the new, when an age ends, and when the soul of a nation, long suppressed, finds utterance."

Sohanlal had felt a thrill. "An age ends," he had said to himself. A tryst with destiny. That was it. But the words grew charged with a second meaning, a personal implication. He would not wait, he would fulfill that other tryst on this auspicious day.

He had caught the bus at daybreak and here he was in the village. To breathe its air again, to feel its earth under his feet! As he reached Main Road he heard the clear, singing voice and stopped, listening. The minstrel! The minstrel was back!

Happiness swept upon him and he ran toward the meadow. One thing he must know: the meaning of the touchstone. The elusive man whom Meera adored and whom the people trusted. . . . His brows knit. Why, here was the man who must take the people of this village to their tryst with destiny.

As he sat at the edge of the audience, a peasant lad hailed him, "Back in time!" "What goes on here?" he asked. The lad whispered out the news. The minstrel had brought about a miracle; the touchstone lay on the river bed among ten thousand pebbles! No regrets on that account. A new hope was born. A truer touchstone was at everyone's grasp.

278

Sohanlal drew a deep breath. A touchstone that was freedom's gift for the people. That was what Nehru also had meant, his language more direct. "India discovers herself again," he had said. "Are we brave enough to accept the challenge of the future?"

The songs flowed, one after the other. Patriots who had died for freedom lived again. The fight that had ended in total victory was refought in sharp images and vested with a spiritual content.

The minstrel stopped, but the audience still sat in utter silence. Then Sohanlal rose and made his way to the foot of the banyan. He turned round, facing the people. "Friends, I ask you—"

"Speak, son." The minstrel gave the stranger an encouraging nod and was then startled to hear him cry, "We will not let the wanderer go. We will make him stay with us. That will be his best gift to us, to the village."

A burst of approval. "You cannot leave us, minstrel-brother."

"That is not all we ask," Sohanlal continued. "He will have to use his wisdom for Sonamitti, and what is the best way to force his hand?"

"Tell us."

He answered in a big shout, "Vote for our minstrel-brother, vote!"

An astonished pause, and then the thunderous cry, "Vote for our minstrel-brother, vote!" The people felt shamed that they had not thought of it all this while. A city fellow and one so young had to point out to them what was so very obvious.

The minstrel was taken aback. "That is not right," a distressed murmur. He looked hard at the tall youth—where had he dropped from?

"You cannot deny us. This is the demand of one and all."

"No, no." His agitation grew visibly. "The board is no place for a minstrel. Am I to regale its members with bhajan song?"

The answer came:

"Brother, you will make those men share your faith in the future."

"You will release them from a past now dead and gone."

"You talk of a house to be built. Will you shirk the task of laying the first few bricks?"

And with hope and love and jubilation the people cried, "Vote for our minstrel-brother, vote!"

He folded his palms together, beseechingly. "Pray listen. It is not as simple as you make it—"

Grandma was stepping forward with Meera's arm for support. When she was close to the minstrel, she cried, "Why do you look so scared? You will not have to fight me for the vote-mote. Be easy!"

Amid the shouts of laughter, he cried, "Friends, I am a wandering man. You cannot tie me down. You must not." He shook his head vehemently.

Then Meera spoke.

"Grandpapa—" Her voice was husky. "Look at us, look at the village. What you seek in your lone wandering is here before you. Then why do you want to leave us again? The true touchstone is as much yours as ours." She turned her eyes to Sohanlal and the worship she saw in his face made her heart miss a beat. Her eyes moved on and as they reached Lakshmi she had an anxious thought. Lakshmi would suffer once again because of divided feelings. She would share her husband's unhappiness—the vote-mote was now finally decided. But she, brave one, nodded her head reassuringly as if to say, "This is wonderful, Meera, friend." Then Meera gave a quick glance to the Seth and many others were looking at him. He sat in calm splendor as if he had not the least reason to lose his self-possession. The trailing length of smoke-pipe climbed to his mouth and in the strained hush that fell, the hookah alone spoke, brrr . . . brrr . . .

"Pray, listen—" The minstrel tried yet again, but the conviction faltered within him as he spoke and the ring of his words was hollow.